GHOST KING

Valentyne

Robin Kaplan – Cover Design

Please support **Robin Kaplan - The Gorgonist**,

the profoundly skilled artist behind the cover of *Ghost King*.

The Gorgonist on Instagram, Etsy, Facebook, Twitter, and Tumblr.

Copyright © 2021 by Valentyne King

ISBN 9798583314614

This is a work of fiction. Names, characters, places, and incidents either are the product of the author's imagination or are used fictitiously, and any resemblance to actual persons, living or dead, businesses, companies, events, or locales is entirely coincidental.

Except the ghosts, the ghosts are real.

For my mother who claims she passed nothing good on to me,

but she gave me the gift of creativity.

The Boggle would also like to thank,

Jasper Jay

Kathie

Michelle Emmina

The Deschutes Historical Society

Chapter 1

ACCURATE REPRESENTATION

Was this the end, or only the beginning?

Choking as my head was submerged, sometimes it was hard to tell. Vision blurring as I was shoved back into the water, my world spun.

It had happened so fast, dying.

"Aren't you a Kloven?"

Pulling myself out of the pool, the insecurity was striking as my shirt and shorts clung to my skin. Shivering, I wrapped my arms around me, trying to hold everything in.

A series of splashes behind me sent ice through my veins as I quickened my pace.

"Your family is supposed to be cool," Russel called out, closing the distance between us with every word, "but you're just weird."

Looking for the teacher, they were never where they were supposed to be at times like this.

"Don't ignore me."

A pool noodle barely missed my head.

Watching it float in the kid's pool for a moment, I took a shaking breath and turned around. "I don't know what you want from me," trying to stand my ground, I knew it was useless, it always was. "I'm not like my family, I know. You don't have to tell me that."

Russel, ever charming, stood there, his posse of boys behind him as he towered over me. What I had done to earn such a prime seat in his attention, I'd never know.

Eyes on us, my classmates watched from the larger pool, unmoving.

A dark shadow jumped in my vision, startling me. Looking to the side, my eyes searched the area by the water fountain, but I saw nothing.

"What are you looking at?"

Another blur ran through my vision, making me step around. Facing the kid's pool, I could see a faint shadow at the bottom as bubbles came to the surface. Was it boiling?

"Don't turn your back on me."

The moment I went flying, feet slipping on the wet floor, lasted longer than any moment should. The anticipation of impact was overwhelming as the water grew near. Smacking into it, the first sensation that riddled me was the sting. It radiated over my entire front but was soon extinguished by the bitter cold. The shock raced through me but lingered on my ankle. The pool was only a couple feet deep, why was I still sinking? Struggling as pain shot up through my leg, what felt like claws dug into my skin, pulling me further. Eyes burning, I couldn't see anything except warped watery shapes.

When I hit my head, my ears rang louder than the air escaping my lungs. I wanted to fight it, to hold my breath as long as I could, but the aching need to breathe won and my body grew heavier, sinking further.

When we die, where do we go?

Hands yanked me up out of the water.

Blue.

The first thing I saw was bright electric blue as my eyes veered into focus. In the arms of a stranger as he knelt with me beside the pool, his long orange hair cascaded over his shoulder. Speaking to me, I couldn't hear him, the only sounds in my world were wobbly and wet. His concern was palpable as his glowing blue eyes searched mine as they struggled to stay open. Little white, blurry blobs floated around us, but my eyes failed to comprehend them. The only thing I saw was him, the only thing I felt was his arms as they held me. His touch, I couldn't tell if it was hot or cold. All I knew was that it burned.

"Kaspian," his voice was the first sound that met me as the ringing of my ears dulled into numbness, "not yet, it's too soon."

Being only thirteen, I hadn't the words to describe the way his voice made me feel. But as I stared up at him, his hair spilling over his shoulder, his furrowed brow, his glowing eyes, the reserved but caring tone, I did know something.

He was ever so slightly transparent.

People came rushing toward us but ran right by. Slowly moving my head to the side, Russel came into view as he screamed, tears bellowing. Adults jumped in the pool and water splashed, but it went right through me.

Pain shot up through my leg.

Yelling out at the sensation, I realized I had no water to cough up in my lungs. Eyes struggled to look down, all I saw was black as it crawled up my leg. The boy jumped when he saw it, taking one of his hands from my chest and moving it down to my ankle. A blue light grew from his palm and when it made contact with my leg, I tried not to let on how much it burned.

The water started to turn black and his eyes jumped up. A flicker of red flashed through them before he looked back to me. His voice was quiet, calm, though his eyes looked as if they held hell themselves in their blue swirls, "Until we meet again, Sire."

Standing from my side, he extended his hand. Materializing out of nowhere, a sword's form started to glow in the air until the full weight dropped into his hand. Stepping forward, my view of the commotion behind him was no longer obstructed. A crowd of people knelt by the pool, all surrounding something. Another person shifted over and only for a moment did I see it, my body laying there. After taking another step, the young man sprung into the air above the pool, plunging into it, sword first.

My world bleached white in an explosion of light.

Coughing, I was now face down, people yelling my name.

My lungs screamed.

I coughed so hard, I was nearly sick.

It happened so quickly, I hadn't even realized I was dead.

Head being ripped up and out of the water, a handful of my hair in Russel's grasp, nothing had really changed from back then.

"Where's your ghost now, Kasper?" He threw me to the bathroom floor, leaving me in puddles of toilet water as he laughed.

Hair disheveled and wet, dripping in my face, I didn't speak.

It had been five years since then and it didn't matter what I said, Russel was relentless.

Kicking me on the way out, Russel's laughter echoed as he left the bathroom to continue his endless reign of terror elsewhere.

Picking myself up from the floor, a sigh escaped me as I ran my fingers through my hair, pulling it out of my face. Clothing soaked, I was actually a little impressed as I walked up to the sink. Usually, Russel would just throw a few hits in, knock my books out of my hands and be on his merry way. He must have really been feeling inadequate in his manhood today. Though I couldn't blame him, I'd feel insignificant too if I were conceived on the back of a tractor.

A groan took me as I washed my face, desperately trying to salvage any dignity I had remaining. Staring at myself in the mirror, water droplets forming at the end of every clump of hair, I really hated high school.

Being shoved in the halls, people laughed as I passed. It really should have been an old joke by now, but my misery never stopped being funny. Rounding a corner, my eyes scanned down the line of lockers to snag on one. As I got closer, I tried to convince myself that it wasn't my locker that had some brown substance smeared on it. But as I stopped before it, my locker, I just stared.

I suppose this is what I got for being the way that I was.

Taking what I had on me and not bothering with my potential biohazard locker, I started up the stairs and down the hall. Slow, my left limp was noticeably bad today. My hand was so cold my fingers barely obeyed me enough to open the door handle of the unused storage space that was my club room. Closing it behind me, the light flickered to life above my head, flickering every few moments or so as I set my soggy books down on the table. As I pulled the chair out, my elbow knocked one of my notebooks to the floor. Bending over to pick it up, I paused.

Orange bled into blues, my drawing of the boy I saw was ruined by the water.

Picking it up, I set it open on the table, looking down to him. Fingers tracing the lines I had drawn so many times they were engraved into my soul. His transparent form, his glowing eyes and fiery hair, touch like ice so cold it burned, those fragments were all I had left of him in my mind. But there was one thing about him I knew to be undoubtedly true.

He was a ghost, he had to be.

Of course, when you're thirteen and you die but live to tell the tale, you're going to tell it. I quickly learned though, that that's not how one makes friends. No one believed in ghosts, and if they did, they believed they were bad.

Taking out the poster board from between the bookshelf and desk, I laid it over the table.

It was quiet up there, in my club of one. Phantasmal, Juniper High's own paranormal investigative team, or that's what the club brochure said anyway. Popping the cap off my pen, I stared down at my canvas. Ever since that day, my mind had been occupied with one thing. Drawing my message out in big bubble letters, my frustration with my hands grew. I knew ghosts were real, so why couldn't anyone prove it? Endless hours I had spent, researching, documenting, investigating and sifting through data.

But I was no closer to finding them than I was the day I started five years ago. Content with my sign, I nodded as I clicked the lid back onto my pen.

But I wasn't going to give up.

I knew ghosts were real, and it was up to me to prove that they were undoubtedly good.

"Boycott this movie!" I yelled, holding my sign in the air, "It misrepresents ghosts, they're not evil!"

People passing by fought to not look at me, some rolled their eyes, others laughed. The young man behind the ticket window shook his head at me. Yes, I was indeed protesting a horror movie. I stood out there, night after night, trying to fight for the rights of those who couldn't fight for themselves. I was a lot like those ghosts on the other side, though, so I couldn't really put up much of a fight. But I sure as hell was going to try.

"Come on, human rights are on the forefront and ghosts are people too."

"Give it a rest, Kasper," a classmate droned as they passed by, "go back to your cave or something."

"You're cruel," I followed him to the ticket window, "how can you support this?"

"Watch," he maintained intense eye contact as he bought a ticket for the movie I was protesting, "See, that was simple and normal." He started toward the door, "Not that you'd have any idea what normal was."

I glared at his back before returning to my spot. Determined to change their minds, I really did think I was fighting the good fight. I stood there late into the night, passionately protesting the wrongdoings of Hollywood. People did their best to ignore me, as if I was a panhandler or trying to get them to sign a petition. I could feel the sting of them pretending I wasn't there, making me invisible in their world. For all I knew, there could be a ghost standing next to me who felt the very same way.

"What, do you believe in aliens, too?"

"Of course not," I looked away from the person mocking me as they stood in the ticket line, "that's absurd."

"Oh yeah," he laughed, stepping forward, "you're right, my bad, *that* is absurd."

I think if he rolled his eyes any harder they would have popped right out of his skull.

"How about Bigfoot?" another person called.

"Or the Loch Ness Monster?"

I looked over the people before me, how could they be so callous? Holding my picket sign a little tighter, I stormed from the sidewalk. Their laughter behind me as I left made my back ache. The world was full of jaded people and to me, they were far scarier than any ghost could ever be.

I reached out for my car door handle but then it shocked me. Jumping back, I hissed through my teeth. Goddamn static electricity. I could barely touch anything without having the hell shocked out of me. Sometimes it even left a mark. Sitting down in my car, I placed my sign on the seat next to me. It had one phrase on it, the core of all my beliefs.

Ghosts Are Good.

I leaned my forehead onto my steering wheel with a deep breath. How long could I keep this up?

"If you're here, watching me, right now would be a good time to let me know."

I was met with silence.

As I drove home that night, my mind wandered. I knew they were there, so why had five years passed, and I still hadn't found a single hint of them? They had to be watching, they had to see how I felt about them. Did they not trust me? What could I do to earn that trust so that I could show the world that ghosts truly were good? Maybe then I could put a stop to the horror movies.

In the very back of my mind, a thought stirred that served to quicken the pace of my heart. If I could find a way to communicate with them, maybe I could meet him again. I didn't have a name, but I had a face and an infatuation to go off of. And while it wasn't much, it was enough to occupy my every waking moment, driving my obsession further. If I worked hard enough, put in the time, inevitably it had to lead to somewhere, right?

That's what I told myself, what I had to believe.

Because if that wasn't true, well, the alternative was far too heavy.

I pulled up to the front gate and it opened slowly before my car. Driving into the courtyard, I climbed out of my car and took my sign with me. Approaching from the darkness was our butler, Les.

"Good evening, Master Kasper. You're back later than usual."

I tossed him the keys, "I took the long way home."

He caught them and started toward the driver's side, "Young Master Hugo stayed up waiting for you, he's in your study."

Irritation pumped through my veins as I thanked him and stormed up the marble front steps. Struggling with the large mahogany door, I broke into a run through the front room. My shoes barely made a sound against the marble floor as I started up the grand staircase. Passing by maids and other house workers, I ran down the hallway. Busting through the library door, I went running to the back-right corner of the room. Stopping in front of the bookshelf, panting, I pulled a book out. The shelf moved forward from the wall then off to the side, showing my study. But that wasn't all, there on the Persian carpet sat my little brother, Hugo, holding one of my notebooks in his hands.

"What have I told you a million times?" I set my sign down as I walked up to him.

His big brown eyes wide, a giggle on his breath, he looked up to me, "To not come into your study and touch your stuff."

"Yes," I sat down on the carpet next to him, "Where are you?"

"Your study."

"And what are you touching?"

"Your stuff."

I sighed, ruffling up his spiky blond hair, "Well, at least you're aware," With a yawn, I leaned back on my hands and looked him over, "What is so interesting about my study?"

"Everything," He lit up, holding my notebook closely, "Have you found the ghosts yet?"

"No, not yet."

"Are they hiding from you?"

"I suppose they are," I slid the notebook from his small hands and stood.

He stood and followed me, "I was just getting to the good part."

"Oh?" I slid it back onto the shelf, "And what part would that be?"

"The part where you research Boggles."

"You like them?" I turned, leaning my back up against the bookshelf and crossing my arms.

"Yeah!" His youthful energy was exhausting to witness, but I wouldn't have wanted it any other way as the fire in his eyes brought a bit of warmth to me.

A smile found its way to my face, the only person in the entire world who took me seriously was my ten-year-old brother. Taking a book gently from the shelf, I knelt down and held it open. "But aren't Poltergeist more interesting?" He took the book from me and looked over my investigations into that type of ghost. "You know, some say they're actually the manifestation of the emotional energy generated from moody teenagers like me."

He giggled, handing the book back to me, "They're scary, but I don't think you've generated one, you're too happy."

I put the book back, "You think so?"

Nodding, I don't think he really understood what I had said as his eyes searched the spines of the books before us, "Tell me about Earthbound?"

I hesitated before pulling the next book out as a thought crashed into my mind, freezing my muscles. The more I told him, the more interested he became, the more likely he was to be cast aside like me. My gaze floated to him. He had our movie star father's face, our model mother's eyes, our millionaire grandfather's smile, and our corporate queen grandmother's spark. There was still hope for him. He wasn't like me.

"It's getting late and we have school in the morning," I retracted my hand from the bookshelf. "You've already stayed up late enough."

"But-"

I picked him up, "Until you're old enough to fight me off, I'm always going to win."

"You're stupid," he fell limp as I carried him out, over my shoulder.

"I know," I stopped outside my hidden study, "If you'd do the honors."

He pushed the book I had pulled, back in, triggering the door to slide closed. The gears groaned behind us, the click of the secret door closing as I put distance between us and my obsession. I carried him, a bounce in my step, around the library and he laughed the whole way. That mansion was far too big for the both of us, even for all the employees combined. Who needed a house that gargantuan, I had no idea. Especially when the owners were literally never home. I think we had seen dad more in movies than in person, seen mother smile more in pictures than ever at us. The outside saw an infallible mansion built on top of a legacy of wealth so towering that all who stood behind its doors must have been a god. But as the person standing on top, I saw nothing of the sort.

Dropping Hugo on his bed, he bounced, laughter unfading. Looking down to him, his spiky hair disheveled, his eyes unclouded, free of judgment, I couldn't help but smile a little. Hugo had so much promise, it was an honor and a curse to be his older brother. Staring out of the room, the creak of his bed followed me.

"Why are you never mad at me?"

Stopping, I looked over my shoulder to him, not turning fully, "You're just too little for me to justify taking revenge yet. Just you wait, though, I'll come after you someday."

"No you won't," he flopped back down on his bed, rolling over so that he was viewing me upside down, "you're too nice. I want to grow up to be like you."

My smile faded as I reached for the light, "No you don't, you want to actually have friends."

I turned down the light because I didn't want him to see my smile fade any more.

"You don't have friends?" The bed shifted as he moved, "Why?"

I started out of the room, hand on the doorknob, "Take a wild guess."

"But," he sat up, "aren't the ghosts your friends?"

Looking back at him, he was too precious, "Perhaps they are."

Walking down the hall that was grossly huge, hands in my pockets, I fought off the ache in my stomach. I had three goals in life, the first of which was to make sure that Hugo absolutely never grew up to be anything like me. After climbing an inordinate number of stairs, I walked into my room. It was always so cold. Taking off my black jacket, I tossed it onto my black chair next to my black desk. I changed out of my black clothing into my black pajamas and laid down on my black comforter covered bed. With a groan I ran my hands over my face, shoving my black bangs out of my eyes.

I really hate the color black.

As if my world was both destroyed and saved by that encounter, I wondered what my life would be like if I hadn't gone on that pool field trip. Would I have stood a chance in the normal world? Or was I simply destined to be the weird 'other kid' of the profoundly talented Kloven family? Actors, singers, artists, business tycoons, I was standing at the bottom of a line of horrendously successful people. But what did I amount to be? A ghost sympathizer protesting horror movies.

A knock came to my door, startling me.

"Master Kasper," Les' muffled voice came through my door, "the household heads have returned."

They were home? Both of them? At the same time? Standing, I panicked. Digging through my closet filled with, you guessed it, black clothing, I found the one suit I owned, hiding in the way back. Nearly choking myself, I struggled with my tie until I got it on correctly. My mind spun as I went racing down the stairs. If they had both returned, then there must have been a reason. And as I ran into the main hall, I feared that the reason was me.

Les looked me over, his tame green eyes falling to my tie. With a concealed chuckle, he walked up and fixed it, "You're a disgrace. Are you aware of this, Master Kasper?"

I sighed through clenched teeth, "Painfully."

He smiled after fixing my tie and stood off to my side, a few steps back. My heart dropped into the acid of my stomach when the door started to open. As if she had stepped off of the pages of a magazine, my mother swaggered into the room, followed by my father. Their presence was larger than life, making the air in the room drop.

Eyes hidden behind sunglasses; their gazes were unreadable as they approached. But despite that, I could feel their glares digging into my core. Stopping before me, the people who I knew better as their characters than my parents, they stood in apathetic silence.

"Kaspian." My mother began, "I see you look deathly ill, as always."

"Hello," I didn't look to her sunglasses.

"How are things at the academy?" My father wasn't bothered enough to look up from his phone as he texted.

"Good."

It was important to keep it short when you were lying, as to not garner unwarned suspicion with extraneous details. Not even I was too stupid to fear the hell that they would raise if they found out that I had been expelled from the academy years ago.

And as if I no longer existed, they walked past me. As far as they were concerned, I was the family dirt to be swept under the rug. They only lifted the rug on occasion to make sure I was still there. They needed to care about my existence just enough to keep the failure that I was hidden, but not care enough to actually care. It really shouldn't have hurt much anymore; it had been that way for a long while. But there was just something to the fading click of my mother's heels against the brittle tile that tugged at my insides.

I wasn't an accurate representation of the Kloven family legacy, and they made sure I knew it.

After standing there far too long, I started back up toward my room. Slowly, each step dragged me down a little more. The carpet rolled over the marble floors didn't soften its hardness, the windows, despite being needlessly large, didn't allow much moonlight in, and the stars were hard to see through the glass. I hated that mansion.

Falling onto my bed that was far too big for me, I stared at my vaulted ceiling. My room was so big and cold, it felt like it could erase me. I mustered the strength to shower away the dried toilet water and crawled into bed. After letting a sigh escape my lungs, I leaned over off of the side. Pulling a bin out from under my bed, I took a book from the inside. Opening the book as I sat up against the wall, I took my phone from my nightstand and activated the flashlight.

Earthbound, Boggle, Poltergeist, Demons, and Shadow People, they were my only friends. Flipping through the pages, my eyes drifted over the words I already knew by heart. There was a comfort in the unknown, something about the text on the page that felt more alive than the living. I knew they were there, I knew they were kind, and I was on their side.

So why couldn't I find them?

Falling over onto my pillow, I hoped I'd suffocate. Then I'd find them. When it became difficult to breathe, I groaned.

Rolling over, I held the book close as I stared upward into the darkness of my vaulted ceiling, an empty canvas for my eyes to paint anything upon.

Someday

Somehow

Someway

I'd find them,

I'd find him.

As my eyes closed, blue and orange collided behind them.

"Have a good day at school, Master Kasper."

"I mean, I'll do my best but," waving as I approached the front door, a yawn took me, "no promises."

"May I make a suggestion," He approached as I stopped at the door, placing his hand on my black sweatshirt, "maybe you'd be more accepted into society if you didn't go out of your way to appear unapproachable."

"Never," my voice strained as I struggled to push the door open, "for I am the night."

He just laughed at me as I bounced down the front steps. Walking out into the courtyard where Les had parked my car, I turned and took the last few steps backward. Looking over the mansion, I was humbled by its massive presence. It felt so cold, but it was a different cold than his eyes. This cold was dull, his cold was crystallizing.

The morning air felt different that day, a little livelier than it usually did. Electrified, building, something about it even felt a little exciting. Taking a deep breath as I paused at the door of my car, I looked into the sky. October was my favorite month, the time of year when everyone else was thinking about ghosts too.

Jumping back when my car door handle shocked me, I laughed.

The drive was nice, roads clear, green lights. It was almost enjoyable until the inevitable appearance of the rectangular box building polluted my view. Pulling into the parking lot, I left my car in one of the furthest spots. Eyes on the ground, I tried to not invoke anyone's attention. It never ended well for me when I did. I attended the last chance school, the place they put you when nowhere else wanted you. It went by the name Juniper High because just like the damn trees, the students were plentiful and unwanted. Sitting down in my classroom, I took out the library book and tried to lose myself in it.

"That movie was great," a boy a few rows over from me said so loud it was obvious bait, "what was your favorite part?"

knocked out of me. Standing there, staring up at Russel, every ounce of fight drained from me.

"Hey, Kasper."

"Good afternoon."

Russel leaned in, eyes hazy on mine, "I heard you were protesting a movie last night."

"I was, yes."

"That's something you should deny."

He threw me to the ground, ripping my backpack from me as I fell. Tearing it open, he dragged out a few notebooks of mine. Papers flew everywhere as my books hit the floor. Looking up to him, I watched his sick smile grow, twisting his tan face. His eyes hungry for more to exploit, they searched through the pages as he flipped them. I was always expanding my notes, building onto my knowledge, and giving him more to make fun of me for.

"Who is this?" He turned the notebook back around to show me my drawing.

I flew to my feet and yanked it back from him, holding it close to my chest as I stepped back. "They are none of your business."

He raised a brow, dropping my backpack and approaching, "Oh? Well this is new," he backed me up into the locker, "You're unusually protective of that drawing." Snatching the notebook from me, he quickly won the struggle and held it up over my head, "Are they important to you?" He let go of me and with his other hand, started to rip the drawing up, "It's too bad that no one could ever care about you."

After sprinkling the ripped-up paper over my head, he left me sitting there, among the ruins. Picking up my things, I swayed as I stood, eyes on the ground. Laughter followed me as I situated myself, bits of paper falling from my hair with every shaking breath. Eyes dropping down to the remains of my drawing, my heart slowed. It was the best one I had of him, the clearest image I was able to pull from my mind. I knelt and brushed the pieces up into my hand as to not litter the hallway. He had been rendered to nothing more than orange and blue bits.

Paper clenched in my fist, I stormed through the halls, head down as my jaw tightened.

Entering my one-man club, I flipped on the flickering light. Normally you needed five members to start a club, but the school board didn't care at all. We were but troublesome numbers in a collapsing system. Sneezing, the dust in the room was thick enough in the air to cut with a knife. While they did bend some rules to approve my club, they had definitely given me the worst room in the school. Apparently, a teacher shot themselves in it several years back.

I sat and slumped over onto my folded arms. Trying to breathe, the quiver in my shoulders took a bit to tame.

The lights flickered.

It was quiet in my club room, separated from the rest of the school, the rest of my life. I liked the quiet, but sometimes I wondered what it would be like to have someone knock on that door and ask to join.

Shivering even though it wasn't cold, I forced myself to stand. Taking my lunch out of my backpack, book in hand, I sat back down. Flipping to where I had left off, I jumped when the light flickered. Looking up, the fixture above me hummed and swayed. Trying to eat, it only made me feel sick. Why did nothing feel right? Adjusting my hoodie some, every sensation was too much. The weight of my clothing on my skin, the texture of food in my mouth, the effort it took to focus, I was never comfortable, never content. Shivering again, I rubbed my hands together.

"Are you making the room cold?" I said to no one in particular as I leaned back in my chair, staring at the light, "You know, as much as I appreciate it, could you perhaps haunt me in a less agitating way?"

The light flickered.

A sigh escaped me.

Taking a paper out, my markers spilled from the case on the table as I dug for a pencil. Bringing the graphite to the page, the moment it made contact it jogged the memory of my hand as lines started to form. The length of his legs, the shape of his torso, the elegance of his arms and the volume of his hair, they were all like second nature to me. With every mark, the ghost boy rose out of obscurity and became more concrete. Taking my markers out, there were two that I used far more than the rest. After lining his hair in black, I popped open the orange marker. With every stroke, the memory of his long hair regained its potency. Hovering over his face, blue in hand, I stared into his eyes. I could never do them justice, their depth, their glow, they haunted me.

Finishing the drawing, I admired his form.

This ghost boy, this nameless force, that's why I did it.

Looking around my club room, the humming light above, the dusty surfaces, it was all for him.

A light smile tugged on the side of my mouth, threatening to cheer me up a bit.

The final bell rang, making me jump. It was almost like that damn bell rang like fifteen times a day or something, one would think it wouldn't startle me any longer. Gathering my things, I wondered if the teachers even bothered marking me absent anymore. Something about being a truant felt empty, like I had let someone down. But as I pulled my backpack onto my back, I wondered who?

As I closed up the club room, I stood at the door for a few moments longer than usual.

Who was there to let down?

Staring at the darkened glass pang on the door, all I could see was my reflection.

Was there more to my character than this? More to me than a high school delinquent who didn't show up to class, a failed legacy, a lost cause? Being shoved around in the halls, I grit my teeth. I'd never prove myself to my parents, never be what they wanted me to be. Making it out of the building, it took me two steps before I bolted.

I'd never be who Hugo saw in me.

Reeling back when my car shocked me, I hissed through my teeth as I sat down. Hands to my face, leaning over against the steering wheel, I wondered if I had let him down. Part of me wished that ghosts weren't real, that way that boy could never see me like this.

The drive home that evening was unusually slow. Met by no one at the door, it was quiet. Hugo must have still been out. On my way to my room, I decided to stop by his. Without him in it, it was just a room, a still place. His light was enough to make any space more than a room, enough to make me feel like I was more than I was. Lingering there for a moment, I closed the door on my way out. After dropping my bag in my room, I started down the hallway. As several staff passed me, they bowed their heads.

I wasn't worthy of that.

Reaching the library, my steps were slow until I rounded the corner to see that my study was open.

"Hi!" Hugo looked up to me from a mess of machines on the ground.

I stood in the doorway, staring at him. As I sat down on the floor next to him, I wished that he wouldn't take me seriously, that he'd laugh at me like the others, because then he'd be accepted.

"What do these do?"

Looking over my machines, the tools of my obsession, each breath was harder than the last. "Nothing you'd be interested in," my eyes drifted out the door, "you really shouldn't hang around all this."

Picking up another device, he inspected it, probably only half listening to me, "Why?"

Jumping over to him, careful to not step on my devices, I pulled him close, tickling him, "You'll be cursed."

"No," he fought me, barely able to speak through his laugh, "but really?"

I didn't know how to explain it to him, that he and I were different. He was young enough to see the world without the tint that came with age. "You want to have friends someday, right Hugo?"

"Yes."

"Then you need to stay away from this sort of thing, it will bring you anything but friends."

"But," He looked up to me, sitting amount a mess of gadgets and notes, "if it'll bring me people like you, then it'll bring the right friends."

Staring down at him and his smile, he even made my study feel alive, "You're dooming yourself," I leaned forward, placing my elbow on my knee, "Are you sure you want to learn more?"

He nodded so hard I was afraid he was going to hurt himself. What he ever saw in me, I'll never know.

"Alright," I said with a sigh as I looked back to the gadgets, "but these are a little hard to explain," my gaze rolled back to him, "It would be a lot easier to just show you."

Hugo Kloven, what a little star in the night he was. Hopping to his feet, gathering gadgets and papers in his arms, he was rearing to go. I wanted to smile, to treasure his excitement, but the nagging in the back of my mind kept the line of my mouth flat. Loading a couple of cases of equipment into the back of my car, I helped Hugo with the heavier one.

"Someday I'll be stronger than you," Hugo huffed as he struggled to close the trunk.

Reaching up above him, I closed the trunk, "Undoubtedly, but for now, I'm still bigger than you."

After making sure he was buckled, I started my car. When was the last time we went for a drive together?

"Where are we going?" He looked out of the window at the slowly setting sun.

"I go to a few places to investigate regularly, but we're going to go to the cemetery and the historic district. Those are my most active spots."

His excitement was curious to me, so many people were afraid of ghosts, but he wasn't. Parking in the public lot in front of the library, I helped Hugo unbuckle- much to his dismay. Running around my car, he beat me to the back. Unlocking the truck, I was reaching for it when Hugo shoved me away. The trunk clicked and a moment later, sent Hugo stumbling back. Catching him, I laughed a bit as I reached for the briefcase sitting in the back. Closing the trunk, I handed him the keys to lock it. With a honk of my car horn, his satisfaction was palpable.

Tossing my keys at me, he laughed as he ran away and toward the grass. After catching them, I stood there, for but a moment, watching him. I had spent so long trying to deter his gaze from me, that I had missed so much.

When had he gotten that tall?

Joining him as he flopped over in the grass, I set the case down, opening it.

"Do you know what this is?" I held something up.

He pulled himself up from the grass, a bit of dried leaves in his hair, "A video camera?"

"Yeah," I turned it on and waited for the preview screen to load, "but this one is special," after pushing a button, the screen turned infrared. He gasped as I went on, "This makes it possible to film in the dark." I handed him the camera after turning it off then took the next thing out. "Do you know what this is?"

He shook his head.

"This is an Electromagnetic Field Detector, EMF for short. It will detect changes in electromagnetic fields on a level that it is believed ghosts emit." I looked down to the EMF, a gray rectangular box that had a line of lights that went from green to red. "But they also will pick up on things we have so," I took out my phone and turned both little hand-held devices on. The light gauge on the EMF went all the way up to red when I held it next to my phone, "we have to be mindful of where it is." After closing the case, I stood, "I've already been here and taken base measurements, but normally you'd have to see if there are any sources of electricity about so you don't accidentally document a false read." As I went on about other starting procedures, he watched as if every word was another great discovery. Being marveled at was quite a thing.

"Alright," I knelt and handed him the EMF, "I'll record, and you can walk around with this, make sure to show the camera if you get any fluctuations."

He accepted the EMF as if it were the Olympic torch and marched along. I followed close behind, my eyes drifting over the headstones. I had never tried to teach someone the things that I knew before. Is this what it would have been like, if someone came knocking on my club door? Would this make Hugo the first member of Phantasmal?

He stumbled about, jumping at every time the light went from its base of green to the next level of yellow. Those were simple, not uncommon, occurrences.

I couldn't help but wonder, as Hugo investigated, if someone had come knocking, would I have opened the door?

"Some people like to say a prayer before they start," I said, stepping over a headstone.

"Why?" He tripped over the headstone.

I picked him up by the back of his shirt, "Because they're afraid of the otherworldly."

He blinked at me as I held him, dangling there, "And you're not?"

Dropping him, I continued, "Not even a bit."

He nodded, humming happily, "Ghosts are good."

"Indeed they are." A thought struck me, and I stopped. "Hey, come here," I knelt and he hopped up to my side, holding the EMF proudly in view. Taking out my phone, I switched it to the front camera. Staring at our image on the screen, Hugo's smile that knew no inhibition made me smile too. Snapping the picture, it was sent into the memory of my phone as Hugo hopped away.

Straightening, I pulled it up on my phone. I wasn't fond of pictures of myself, but this was an exception.

After opening the settings, I set it to my lock screen.

Looking up, a smile took me. Hugo stepped around, EMF out, as he slowly approached a reading that grew stronger with every step. I could see it, the hesitation in his movements be overpowered by his stubborn will to prevail. Pocketing my phone, a rare burst of energy took me as I ran to his side. I hadn't felt this way in a long while, it was even hard to tag what it even was. It made me smile though, and that's all that mattered.

"Find something?"

Looking up to me, the red lights of the EMF reflecting in his eyes, he nodded.

Bringing my hand up to the headstone we stood before, it was old and worn, the name long gone, but I knew who it belonged to.

"It looks like someone may be here with us," I knelt next to Hugo, bringing my arm around him, "maybe you should say hello?"

Shaking his head, his eyes averted as his face lit up, sinking into his little red and white sweater.

"Alright." I ruffled his hair as I straightened, "Hello Graveyard Guardian. I brought my little brother with me tonight, he's a bit shy though. Would you like to show him that you're friendly?"

The air went cold, the EMF continued to jump between the orange to the red, the wind picked up around us. Hugo stepped closer to me, holding onto my coat as he watched. The leaves around rustled, the bushes shook, the temperature continued to drop.

The sun set.

Slowly, Hugo looked up to me, brows raised, eyes wide. Voice barely above a whisper, his eyes moved to the headstone, "Whoa."

Smiling, I looked to the headstone as well, "Thank you."

Of course there was the possibility that I was just talking to a rock while I stood on top of a rotting body, but I liked to think otherwise.

The world fell still around us, the energy in the air draining.

Quiet, Hugo followed closely at my side as we left the cemetery, the EMF no longer reading anything.

"Why do you thank them?" Hugo asked as we walked along the side of the road.

"Wouldn't you like to be thanked for your effort?"

He hummed, hopping over a pile of leaves on the sidewalk. "You really think there are ghosts here?"

"Yeah," I looked to the darkening sky, "somewhere. I think they're lonely, trapped even. The least I can do is give them the acknowledgment they deserve, even if I can't see them."

As cars zoomed by us, a brief silence settled in.

"Did mom and dad come to see you last night?"

He nodded, hopping about from one sidewalk segment to the next, "They woke me up to tell me they're switching me into a private school."

My grip tightened on the briefcase, "Oh?"

"They're also signing me up for football," he kicked some leaves, "I don't know how I feel about it."

"I'm sure you'll have fun there and with football," Shoving him a little, I smiled even though I didn't want to. If he saw how angry that made me, he'd ask why it upset me. And this sort of resentment was not something I wanted to introduce someone his age to.

loving me even though I didn't make it easy, about to suggest that we head home, but then the temperature plummeted.

Blue.

Looking up, I was faced with it, the color so important to me it was etched into my soul. The air went still, the EMF in my hand lighting up to the red. Passing before me and away, the light left a tail of electric blue behind it.

Stepping toward it, I let go of Hugo's hand.

Unable to breathe, I couldn't believe it.

That was it, the blue that changed my life, stained my heart.

That was the color of his eyes and I wasn't going to let it escape me.

Hugo reached out for me when I stepped into the street. I couldn't lose that blue, that captivating color that ruled my dreams. My heart raced in my ears; adrenaline tore through my veins. This was it, the moment I'd find them, I'd find him. Reaching toward it, the tips of my fingers became cold and tingly. A smile tore across my face, was this going to be the moment all my hard work paid off? The day I finally proved it, that ghosts were good?

The blue was suddenly drowned out by white, the pounding in my ears dulled by the honking of a horn.

I only saw the car for a moment.

Chapter 2

BOGGLE

It didn't even hurt.

That was the first thing that came to my mind as it reeled. Hugo.

Was the second.

Fingers digging into the pavement, that was the first sensation I got back. Eyes struggling to open, I started to feel the jaggedness of the ground on my cheek. The car horn echoed in my ears, the screaming of the breaks still staining my skin. With a shuttering breath, I willed my eyes open and saw so much of one color, it was overwhelming.

Red.

Tensing, my body fought against my every command. My arms shook as I pried myself up from the ground. I needed to find Hugo. Eyes blurring into focus, I saw bloodied asphalt under my ripped-up pants. Placing my hands on the ground to push myself to my feet, the blood on them caught in the headlights from a car stopped right in front of me.

Was I hit?

My spine seized, causing my entire body to lock up. Hissing through my teeth, I battled to stand. Turning around, I could see him.

"Hugo," stumbling forward, the only thing in my world was my little brother as he stood there, staring, "Hugo, are you okay?"

He didn't respond.

The streetlight above us flickered.

Tripping over my feet, I nearly fell but continued to drag myself forward, "Are you hurt?"

He stayed, unmoving, camera in his hand, blood splattered across his front. Reaching him, the hum of everything started to drum up in my bones. The blood dripping off of my wrist glistened in the headlights as people yelled behind me, but I didn't care about them, I just needed to get to Hugo. Extending my arms, they trembled as they reached out to him.

When my hands went through him, everything stopped.

Falling back, my hands crashed into the ground underneath me and landed in a lukewarm puddle. Breath struggling to come to me, my chest tightened as my eyes fought to focus.

"Hugo," when he didn't reply, my voice started to shake, "why can't you hear me?"

A hand landed on my shoulder, causing me to recoil away from them. Turning around, electric blue blinded me. Looming above, a figure came into focus. Long orange hair fell over his shoulder in a tight, thick braid, strands blowing about, framing his sharp face. Furrowed brow, concern shaded his glowing blue deep-set eyes as his mouth spoke words I couldn't hear over the screaming of adrenaline in my ears. Eyes jolting downward when I saw the flashing lights of an ambulance paint the world, the very fabric of that moment tore, leaving me in a rip as everything slid wayward.

Red.

Red and white and red and white, but mostly red.

Laying on the ground, in the same puddle of lukewarm blood, was me. But not me, but definitely me. Mangled, ripped, I laid, face down, eyes wide, gravel embedded into what was left of my skin, unmoving. A bystander flopped me over, my limp body nothing more than putty on the pavement. The hood ornament of the crunched up car sat, protruding from my ribs. Blood gushed from it, staining my shirt.

The streetlight went out.

Tears turned my world into a kaleidoscope of red and blue as I fought to stand up. The blood on my hands burned as I shoved the young man away from me. The blue of his eyes left a trail of light in my vision as I ran.

Where was I going?

I didn't know.

A car spread through me, causing me to yell out, stumbling to the side in an attempt to escape the collision. But as I sat on the concrete, staring into the headlights of another oncoming car, I couldn't move. Roaring through me, it took some of my mind with it as I was left, staring back at the gore.

The young man ran my way, calling out to me.

In a muddle of sloppy trembling movements, I was back on my feet and running again. The blue of his eyes haunted me, bringing back flashes of sensory, washing over my body as cars passed through me. Coughing, water, the numbness of suspension in that place after death but before anything else, I remembered that day at the pool clearly, too clearly.

Rounding a corner as I barreled down the sidewalk, I couldn't stop before I ran through a group of high schoolers. Some of them shuddered as I went stumbling away and into a building. Panting up against the wall, eyes so wide they felt like they were going to fall out of my skull, I watched as they moved on without a care.

Without seeing me.

Dizziness washed over me and a moment later, I went falling. Slamming into the ground, my head bounced against tile, sending my senses into a whirl. Eyes opening, my world jolted when I saw that half of my body had phased through the wall of the library. Dragging myself all the way through, I tried to douse the panic, tried to rationalize, but that was all shattered when the blue-eyed young man phased through the wall after me.

Before he could speak, I took off again.

No matter how far, how hard, I ran, I couldn't escape it.

A feeling was going inside me, a dread, a desolation. Gaining a gravity, it was growing like a dense rock in my stomach, weighing down my every step.

Phasing through bookshelves, they toppled one after another after I passed, the lights above us flickering, screaming echoing out around.

Where was I going?

Sitting day after day in the delinquent school.

What was I running from?

Never allowing Hugo to get too close to me.

Who was I scared of?

Running toward a mirror that lined the hall out of the library, I couldn't see my reflection.

Phasing out the other side of the wall, I was back on the street. Sirens surrounded me, the sound echoing in my head as my body burned, tingling in the way that your foot does when it falls asleep. Unable to move, I fell to my knees under the all-encompassing crushing stimulus.

Spinning, my everything was thrown into chaos.

Hands up to my head, my ears screamed, my skin crawled, everything begged for the end. The blood from my hands dripped down my wrists and into my hair, over my scalp, and down my jawline and mixed with my tears.

Everything halted, every nerve calmed, every sensation stilled, when I was met with an embrace. Closing my eyes as fatigue overpowered me, the last thing my blurring vision saw was the communion of blue and orange, the last thing my body felt was his strong arms, and the last thing my ears heard was the shaking of his breath, the cracking of his voice, as he said,

"Everything is going to be okay."

Submitting to the young man whose touch burned like a gin on my skin, the last thing I felt was comfort in his arms.

They say your life flashes before your eyes.

But what they don't tell you is that when it does, it will happen so fast. Fast enough for you to realize that no matter what one does in life, it lasts but a blink of an eye.

Blinking, I stared up at an unfamiliar ceiling.

My mind slowly coming back to me, I sat up. The satin of the sheets around me were far fancier than even my rich parents would care to have. The room surrounding me was reminiscent of a castle study, bookshelves lining several walls, a small bedside table with a fancy lamp, marble flooring, and vaulted ceilings. The curtains were drawn at my side, but from the ambient glow emoting through them, I assumed it was evening.

What a strange dream, being hit by a car.

I tried to shake the image of Hugo's shirt, the one I had given him for his birthday, covered in my blood from my mind as I stood and stretched. Something felt different, my body wasn't tired. Taking a deep breath, I tried to remember what I had done last, but my mind was foggy. I had gone to school, come home, played with Hugo. But after that? I couldn't remember.

Approaching the wooden door, I wondered if I had somehow wandered into the right wing. My parents never really allowed us over that way, so there were rooms in our house that I had never even seen. When my hand reached for the doorknob, I paused.

Red.

Blinking the image away, I was left staring at my hand as it rested on the doorknob.

Opening the door, it creaked a long show as it slowed to a stop. Cautiously stepping out the door, looking about, I came to the conclusion that I probably wasn't in my parents' house. The ceiling was far too high, the marble walls and storybook like architecture a stretch for even them.

But, if I wasn't home, then, where was I?

Starting down the hall, I tried to be as quiet as possible. Though that wasn't too hard, my shoes didn't make any sound at all against the marble flooring. Passing doors as tall as the ceiling, tapestries that held abstract arts, and podiums that housed vases and statues of nature, I started to wonder if this was another dream. Did Hugo and I come home after hanging out because it got late, and I just don't remember falling asleep? Chances where I was just at my desk, hunched over in that way I'd regret in the morning.

Laughing a little, I ran my hand through my hair.

Hushed voices snagged my attention as I passed by a set of slightly ajar doors. Creeping up to them, I glanced through the crack. Standing inside was a group of people, a bit too far away and obscured by the crack for me to see clearly, but I could hear them.

"Asleep? Ghosts don't sleep," a voice that was brighter than any light said, "what did you do to him?"

"I didn't do anything," that voice was so cold it made me shudder, "I didn't expect him to step out in front of the metal beast. I wasn't prepared and he panicked."

"Shock." A voice so dark it extinguished any light the first had put into the world rumbled on, "However, word has spread, they are beginning to ask questions. If he doesn't make an appearance soon, your faction's chances of being considered for the crown will dwindle."

"I know-" the chill of his words were cut off by those of another.

"Knight," this voice, panicked and warped, like a loud whisper, said as a white blur raced into the room, just, floating there, "he's gone."

"He's what?" Orange entered my vision as he stood from where he had been seated with the other two parties, "I told you to keep an eye on him."

"He's been asleep for like ever, I got bored."

An exasperated sigh escaped the orange party as he rushed toward the door and I couldn't step back quick enough as the door was sent, flying open. Thrown to the floor, everything spun out of focus. The marble sent a sting up my spine when I landed, causing me to double over, hand to my face.

"Sire," he sounded breathless, "are you alright?"

When I opened my eyes and everything rolled back into focus, I was left staring up at him. Exactly as he sat in my memory, the ghost boy from the day I died, had his hand extended toward me. Flashes of gold and black framed him from the room he had come from, leaving silence in their wake. Averting my eyes down, I couldn't even look at him and his jawline, his fiery hair and cool eyes, his formal clothing and long braid, wispy hairs and toned build.

The ground beneath us started to taint, turning black. He looked around and before the concern could fully take hold, we were dropped through the floor and into the black hole. My yell of surprise was choked out by the darkness. Jolted around, as if every bit of me was being ripped apart and put back together, my brain was scrambled. Like every system in my head was jammed with car exhaust, I found myself unable to grasp onto my thoughts. I should have been panicking in that free fall, but instead I was still.

Like a computer stuck on a loading screen, my everything was stalled.

My hearing veered back to me in an instant along with my balance. Feet finding the ground, colors washed back, and I was left, in a space large enough it could swallow me whole, surrounded. Countless eyes held me hostage in their gaze as I stood, center stage in what appeared to be the grand entryway of a castle. Creatures, they floated, bobbing up and down in silence. They were all looking at me, hundreds of them. They ranged in pale colors and had different shaped black eyes that matched the black of their small wings. They sat on the floor, hung from the walls, and hid behind each other. Some looked like animals, others were covered in sheets, none of them looked human, and absolutely every single one of them were translucent.

My stomach dropped.

Ghosts?

"Sire," the young man said from behind me, "welcome."

Spinning around, when my eyes met his, I was paralyzed. It was him, actually him. Well defined features, clearer than I could have ever recalled, he wasn't a figment of my memory, he was actually standing right there, eyes locked on me.

His voice was reserved yet bold, as if he held a certain pride in being humbled. "You are standing in castle Boggle."

"Castle Boggle?" After staring at him, I spun around, looking at the endless spirits that were watching me. "Boggle."

"Indeed, Sire."

I turned to face him again. "Why are you calling me that?"

"Well," He knelt down on one knee, bowing his head and putting his gloved hand over his heart, "You, Kaspian Kloven, have been chosen by our kind to be our next King Candidate." He slightly looked up to me, "We've been watching, Sire."

Suddenly everything in that room bowed to me. I stepped around looking to them as I felt the brunt of his words. This felt too real to be a dream, but too dreamy to be the real thing. Standing in the center, the weight of their bows was heavier than that of their eyes. One thought crashed into the next, the dominos of my mind colliding and collapsing.

"You're ghosts."

"Indeed, Sire," he said from the bow, not looking up to me.

"You're dead."

"Indeed, Sire."

"But…" I looked down to him and his obviously subtle growing annoyance, "why am I here?"

When he didn't reply, when nothing replied, when I was left standing, the center of attention, was when the last dot connected, effectively creating a picture in my mind too hazy to fully recall.

"I'm…dead?"

"Indeed, Sire."

I stood there, eyes on the complex marble floor that reminded me far too much of my mansion's. Each breath came quicker than the last, leaving me feel emptier as they left me.

"How?"

He slightly looked up from the bow that had lasted far to long, "Do you not recall?"

When all I could do was nod, trying to maintain my footing, he let out a quiet breath.

"That is, perhaps, for the best," slowly standing from the bow, his intimidating stature became quickly apparent as I took a step back, "I'm sure it will return with time, such things often do. Nevertheless, Sire, we have pressing matters to attend to." Refusing to make eye contact with me, his stiff posture caused the entire castle to cool down, "This isn't how I had planned it, and I do sincerely apologize, but it is paramount that you understand your position in this world."

"King Kasper!" A little sheet ghost came flying up to me, circling around like a hawk as I stepped about, looking up to them, "We watched you your whole life and now you're here! It's so exciting."

They bumped into my head, a light jingle taking the air as I stared up at them. "King?"

When they froze, I could feel the air drop around us, "Oops."

Flying away, they hid behind another bunch of ghostly creatures, watching us.

The ghost boy stared at the sheet ghost, entirely blank, as if he was tying to repress something as he bowed his head again. "Yes Sire, you will be competing against the other faction candidates, representing the Boggle, to earn the Almighty Throne of the Ghost King to rule over all the paranormal."

"A king?" Looking around, my surroundings and situation started to sink in, "If you watched me in life, you know I am the furthest from a king one can be."

"I disagree," for a moment the ghost boy may have smiled, I could hear it in his tone, "though it has been fated, there is no room for debate. You, Kaspian Kloven, are our new king." Bowing his head again, his braid spilled over his shoulder, "I am Oliver, your great knight and royal handler. It's an honor, to finally meet you."

A deep breath escaped me, long and deflating, as I stared at the top of his head. I didn't know what to say, was this a dream? If it was, it felt far too real. But this couldn't be real either, it felt too fantastical. They had been watching me? Endless nights played through my foggy mind, tinkering with devices, pawing through every book I could get my hands on, calling out into the night to get no reply, they had been there the whole time. I was right? I really wasn't alone that entire time.

My mind pulled an image of Hugo into focus but as quickly as it had been conjured, it was shattered by a wave of static, as if I had turned my TV to a restricted channel.

"I understand this is a lot to take in, and again, I apologize, however news of your arrival has traveled quickly and the Almighty King has called for a summoning and we have some business to address first."

"Oliver?" I laughed, "How stuffy. I think I'm going to give you a different name." I crossed my arms, smiling. "How about Oli?"

He gave me the same blank stare as the surrounding creatures cackled in a roar of different tones. I looked around at the Boggle, they varied so much, I was amazed. I had always thought Boggle were the least interesting ghost type, but as I stood, center of them all, I saw that I had been wrong. Oliver had said a lot of things to me, but my mind was able to pluck out the most important things, I think.

Ghost king, huh?

Competitions, factions, destiny, it was too much.

Pocketing my hands, I tried to hide their shaking.

Clearing his throat, he extended his hand to me, eyes slowly raising to lock on mine. He stood so rigid, as if he were at attention. "Sire, may I have your hand?"

Fist clenching in my pocket, my breath hitched as my heart jumped into my throat. Desperately, I tried to smother the feeling he had brought to rise in me. Those icy eyes of my memory, they made my heart race just like they did back then. No one had ever held my attention like he had, not really. That blue haunted the back of my mind, burning a hole in my skull. Now that it was in front of me, brighter than I could have ever imagined, I didn't know what to do with myself. Trying to calm my underlying tremor, I removed a hand from my pocket and took his. Even though I was dead, and so was he, I could feel his cool warmth. It was like his skin was cold, but underneath sat a radiant warmth. Staring at him, I was taken, captivated, unable to look away.

But when he slid a ring on my finger, that's when my eyes dropped. Some of the Boggle laughed at me and I could only find myself glaring at the little glowing cartoon-ish ghosts as I tried to tame the feelings coming to life. He took his time, sliding it down my finger, carefully, mindfully, it was like he wanted to savor the moment. When the ring was all the way on my finger, it shocked me. Jumping, taking my hand back, I muffled my yell of surprise with my other hand. Tears budding in the corners of my eyes, I looked down to my fist. When it started to glow, the pain faded and as I opened my fist, a light started to grow from the ring. The light rose, creating a ball in my hand, spinning around like fog encapsulated. It started to spin, the smoke inside creating a storm. As it sped it, the ball started to warp into a form.

In a puff of smoke, the ball popped and as the grey cleared from the air, I was left, staring, at a ghostly crown floating in front of me. It settled in its form as I admired its glow that reminded me of the one Oliver's eyes possessed. Floating higher, it hovered up and over me, slowly lowering to be a few inches above my head. When it settled, I felt a shift in the air, an unseen weight adding pressure to my shoulders. A gust of wind knocked some of the observing ghost friends over and I was left, standing there, something new depositing in my blood.

Though I had been alive for nearly twenty years, I had never felt more alive than I did in that moment.

The surrounding Boggle exploded into cheers; Oliver looked over me contently. He gave a curt nod then turned to face the others, extending his arms, he smiled boldly.

"Kingdom of Boggle, I give you your Candidate!"

The cheering swelled and as I looked around, I couldn't help but try to smile. What the hell had I gotten myself into?

He turned back to me, "Sire, they will be calling us any time so I should-"

"Hey Oli," I cut him off with a smile so he couldn't be mad at me, "please, call me Kasper."

"Kasper?" He repeated quietly, eyes studying me. "I was under the impression your name was Kaspian."

"It is, but Kasper was an unfortunately clever nickname that stuck and I ended up preferring it." My smile hurt less with every passing beat, "If I'm going to be stuck here, I want to be addressed properly. Sire is too formal," I shoved him a little, "don't you think?"

His eyes darted away from mine, "Due to our placement in the power structure, I shall continue to address you as Sire, Sire." He cleared his throat, "Now, I should really explain-"

The room went dark and the only one left in the endless black space with me was Oliver. He turned, sighing as he faced me. A brief crack in his composure, Oliver almost appeared human in that moment as he lowered his head, bringing his hand up to his face. Everything lit back up and we were in an entirely different room. It was a huge hallway, paintings of people who looked important lined its grand marble walls.

"Since I wasn't given the opportunity to thoroughly position you in your place here, it is in our best interest at this juncture if you do not speak unless directly addressed." Looking up to me as he started to walk, a new air had taken him, one a bit darker than before, "And keep if brief."

I followed Oliver, neither agreeing nor disagreeing with his command. Sliding my clammy hand into my pockets as we walked in strange quiet, my eyes drifted over the paintings on the wall as we passed. Going by a window, it was so dark outside that it was less of a window and more of a mirror. I stopped when my eyes caught on something, my reflection. Why had I looked deathlier when I was actually alive? Floating a few inches above my head in a slow rotation was the ghostly crown, emitting a slight light that left a faint sheen on my jet-black hair.

"Introducing the Boggle Candidate, Kasper."

I turned to see Oliver holding a door open further down the hall. Apparently, he hadn't noticed that I wasn't right behind him. As I quickly stumbled down the hall, he turned his head a tad to stare at me. Nearing the door, I was mentally preparing myself for what I was going to see through it. But then my transparent foot caught on my other transparent foot and I went smashing into the door. Sure, yeah, that made sense, a ghost running into a solid door.

Tumbling to the floor, hand up to my screaming head, I wanted to shrink away under the weight of the apathetic gazes I could sense digging into me. This was a familiar feeling, I got that look a lot when I was alive. When I removed my hand from my face, my eyes met with Oliver's. My gaze then saw the hand extended to me and I shakily took it, pain racing through my body still. When my hands met his and he pulled me to my feet, I felt something inside jump. It was soon smashed under the anxiety that came when I turned to face those on the other side of the doorway.

Sitting around a circular table were six beings. They stared back at me as I stood frozen in their glares. Olive walked past me, the door closing behind me, bumping into my back. Jumping forward, I quickly followed him. It sounded like the others at the table were trying to quiet laughter, but I couldn't muster the guts to look up at them as we sat down.

"The Boggle have a candidate this time?" A two-toned voice of death and darkness said off to my left.

I slightly looked up to its owner and felt my stomach twinge. Blood red eyes, rotting skin hanging from chard bones and exposed innards, they must have been a Demon. Above their held floated a crown like mine but it was red. They sort of resembled what was once a young man, but at this point I couldn't really be sure. The creature next to them appeared to be made of lava, their skin glowing and fading red through the flaky cracks. They didn't seem to have eyes, but they did have a horn atop their head.

"How adorable, they feel like they stand a chance." A woman directly across from me spoke. If I didn't know better, she would have probably made me think she was alive. Probably an Earthbound, she was really convincing. Clothing hailing from the Victorian era, she sat stiffly as her dull dirt brown eyes pried at mine relentlessly. Her crown was purple, definitely too pleasant of a color for her. At her side was a child who looked like he jumped out of selling newspapers on a street side in the forties.

I nearly flew from my seat when I happen to glance to my right. What sat there, hungry eyes sizing me up, was the most disturbing thing I had ever seen. They was like static if it were embodied in a glitching mass shaped like a person. Their body was jolting, like it scraped against the flow of time itself. Their eyes were two piercing pin holes that glowed green, the same color as their crown. Sitting next to them was a smaller version that was identical in all ways except the crown. I had always wondered what one would look like but now that I had laid eyes on it, I wished that I could unsee the Poltergeist.

As I looked around at the three, I was confused. Wasn't there one more major grouping of paranormal entities?

"Classless as always." Oliver looked over them. "Say what you will, but this time our candidate is different."

"A human Boggle is rare, yes," the Earthbound woman leaned forward, "but that speaks nothing to his ability to rule."

"Trust me," Oliver looked back to me, an unfounded boldness about him, "he's more of a King at heart than any ruler before."

"There's never been an Almighty Boggle King for a reason," the Earthbound said, "you should just stop now."

"No no," the Demon laughed, "it'll be fun to watch their struggle."

"Since they don't have the decency to introduce themselves, I shall." Oliver started as we approached the table, "Welcome to the company of The Demon King, Nolan, the Earthbound King, Ruth, and The Poltergeist King, Lyx. Like you, they rule over their respective factions."

"Boggle King," the demon laughed again, "what a useless position. Go back to the lower factions where you belong, you play with us and you're bound to get harmed."

Boggle, by loose definition, was a ghost type that simply wished to perplex and frighten, but never harm.

Sitting down at the table, I leaned back into my chair, studying the beings before me.

From my understanding, Demons fed off of the negativity and insecurities of people, draining and possessing them, parasites. Earthbound were people with unfinished business and lingering attachments, they watched over loved ones or were trapped by powerful resentments; but some chose to stay. Then Poltergeist, while neutral, were a form of mindless chaos so powerful and unsettling that I did my best to avoid them in my research.

I had spent years reading about them, searching for them, and now here they were, sitting at a table with me, it was unreal because they were. But a Ghost King, that was something that never came up in the books. And there was certainly nothing about a social system such as factions and King Candidates. Even though I had spent so long researching, it was quickly becoming apparent that I had so much more to learn.

"There's never been an Almighty Boggle King?" I crossed my arms, trying to be as confident as possible. I believed in ghosts for years, I could believe in myself for a matter of seconds. "Challenge accepted."

"You have no idea what you're going on about." Ruth's bluntness was truly something, a monument to apathy.

I smirked, uncrossing my arms and leaning my elbows on the table. "I didn't die yesterday, you know. I know exactly what I'm doing."

"Yeah," Nolan said, "you died today."

"This is true," I laughed, "but what I said wasn't untrue."

"Here we go again with the Boggle sense of humor." Nolan didn't seem amused with me.

"Just you watch," I sat back in my chair and I could just feel Oliver's glare of disapproval in my side, "I'm going to be a King unlike any other before."

The lights dimmed, the air went stale, the room became freezing. My dead heart stopped in my chest when I felt a suffocating presence appear behind me. The tone of banter and wit was executed in that moment, the air sliding sideways like a head dropping from a guillotine. A throaty chuckle accompanied the growing darkness as I turned around.

"A Boggle with bite, you will be intriguing. Welcome to my kingdom."

When my eyes met him, I felt myself die all over again. Gargantuan, he was a person of such stature that I would have thought him to be a giant. But he appeared human, so did that mean that the current King was of the Earthbound faction?

If he could become king, why couldn't I?

"Since my succession court has gathered, it will be time to start the process soon." His robes looked like they were made of noxious gas, his dead black eyes felt older than anything I had ever seen before, he was a timeless giant of deathly air. His booming gravely tone rocked the room, "I will summon you when it is time." His blunt gaze fell to me, making me jump, "Until then, I believe you have a lot to learn, Kasper."

As if a black hole had torn into the room, he was sucked away in a darkness so black my eyes couldn't see anything defining about it beyond its color. Like a vacuum, an airlock broken in deep space, the air was sucked out of the room making my hair whip around in my face. When it closed, it engulfed itself and took every sound away with it. Leaving a profound emptiness in its wake, the darkness was gone as I stared through my messy hair at where it had been.

The way he said my name made something deeply rooted stir. Oliver placed his hand on my shoulder startling me as I jumped to look at him. His eyes studied mine, but I had no idea what he was thinking. Quickly looking away, I fussed with my hair, pulling it back over my head and out of my eyes. As the others stood, Oliver and I joined.

"The Almighty simply called us here to tell us what we already knew," Nolan said as his body cracked with ever movement, "Typical." Turning, his rotting stench wafted my way, "Here's to another entertaining war."

"You can forfeit your claim to the Almighty Crown at any time," Ruth said as she patted out the wrinkles in her skirt, "don't forget that fact."

"Want to place bets on how long he'll last?" Nolan's laugh echoed into the hall as he left, his little handler by his side, "Loser has to host next year's New Year's party."

"That won't be necessary," Oliver started to herd me out of the room, "We may be a simple faction, but that doesn't mean you can underestimate our power."

"Like you have anything to say," Nolan started as he turned away from us and down a different hall, "traitor."

Oliver slammed the door behind him, separating us from the others as we stood in the hall, staring at Nolan as he faded away. We spent a moment in silence before he walked past me.

"Come along, Sire. I have much to tell you."

As I did my best to keep up, my mind wondered. A rigid faction system, a rare human boggle, the power dynamic, and apparent history, this place was gaining complexities faster than I could compute them. Eyes on Oliver's back, I wondered why he had so much faith in me? If he saw me in life, he would know I was anything but special, I was actually closer to the opposite. Weird, but not special.

His orange hair danced in the candlelight that illuminated the hall.

Traitor?

Shaken from my thoughts when shadows shot through the corner of my vision, I startled. By the time I had turned, they were gone. Staring at the ground, I stopped walking. Normally I'd think I was just seeing things, but now I knew better.

"The Shadow People," Oliver said quietly, "they stand on neutral ground, protectors of all."

We wound around hallways that seemed to fold around and over one another and I was left to assume that the rules of the world I used to live in didn't apply to this one. I made it to Oliver's side as we approached a door far larger than that of my mansion. He stopped, hand up against the door, as he looked over to me.

"This is a lot, I'm aware, but please bear with me." He pushed the door as if it were nothing and as I watched it creek open, the gravity of the unknown before me started to show itself.

My gaze dropped down to him as he walked outside. Each of his steps with purpose, his hair swinging with his movements, his controlled posture, Oliver was untouchable. Following him down the stairs, I looked around. We were in a circular courtyard that looked like it came straight from a video game that surrounded a grand castle. Turning around and walking backwards, I looked back at the castle. Humbled by its size, it towered above me and that's when my eyes rose to the sky. Dark swirling of deep purples and sparkling lights, it was as if the night sky I knew had come to life.

"This is the neutral area." Oliver started. "Each of these gates transport to the various Kingdoms." He gestured around to the four gates that stood before us, each unique. "This is the Demon gate," that one was black, sharp, the design was that of crushed metal which slowly became refined to the center where the door was. "Then the Poltergeist," that one was twisted and demented over itself, the metal looked as if it continually oozed a green slime, "Earthbound," That gate was simple, its modest metal working was nice. "And finally, the Boggle gate."

I stood there, staring at the last gate. It was simple, a little in disrepair, compared to the others it was so unassuming that I didn't even notice it until it was pointed out. He walked up to it and I followed, looking up and around at the dark dome that encapsulated the entire circular area, there was nothing beyond the gates other than the black swirls of the sky. It churned, ever moving, never still.

"Unless invited, those of other factions are not allowed through the gates of the others. Though, even if invited, do not enter one without me by your side. We are currently standing in the heart of Limbo, the Almighty Castle. It is the only true neutral place in this system of lands. This world is fragmented, sectioned off into five major realms, with several smaller factions." He started to reach up to the Boggle gate. "It's also timeless compared to where you came from, so the passage of time is far different than what you're used to. You'll get used to it, we all do eventually."

He stopped before the Boggle gate, looking back at me.

"It's time to meet your Kingdom, Sire."

Before I could say anything, he took my wrist and opened the gate with his other hand. In a glittery vortex of light blue light, we went tumbling as the color took over my world. It felt like a freefall, but with Oliver holding onto me, I couldn't get lost. Thrown out the other end, the glitter faded from my vision as I took a stumbling step. I fell to my knees, my world dizzy as I held my hand to my face. Oliver stood there, unfazed as he looked down at me, retracting his hand.

"You'll get used to that too."

I groaned, swaying as I stood. Before I could get my bearings, I was swarmed by little Boggle of all types. Lights whispered floated around me, they collided with each other as the floating Boggle bounced about. I looked around at them, surrounded by small cute ghosts. Oliver stood back as I didn't really know what to do. One Boggle in specific got pushed into me and after they noticed, they all jumped back a little. I bent over a little to be closer to the height the Boggle that bumped into me was floating at. It was the same one that had crashed into me earlier. How did I know? They looked just like the others like them. Though I knew, I just did.

"Hello." I said quietly, my heart jumping. I was talking to a little ghost, a friend. "It's nice to meet you, what's your name?"

Their large black eyes were endlessly dark, and they had no other facial features, a lot like a little ghost covered in a white sheet. After a moment of silence, they shivered as they whispered. "Boggle."

"Boggle?" I looked around to the rest and they all started floating around happily. "You're all named Boggle?" A chorus of whispers confirmed my question. "Aw, well, that won't do. Everyone needs a name." I looked back to the Boggle that bumped into me. "What do you think of Iris?"

Their little black wings jolted, and they went still before flying up and around me to land on my shoulder. When they landed there, they whispered. "Iris."

As I went on, giving names to the surrounding Boggle, Oliver just watched. It wasn't long before a massive crowd assembled around me. Ghost orbs, ghost house pets, shapeless clouds, little lights, small creatures that rolled around on the ground giggling, little bouncing balls of goo, there were many types of cute little Boggle. As I was kneeling and petting some of the dogs, I looked up to Oliver.

"What decides a ghost's faction?"

He pushed himself up from the wall he was leaning on and started toward me. "General temperament appears to be a factor."

"Appears?" I stood, stretching, "Do you not know?"

He shrugged, "There are a lot of mysteries around here that no one has been particularly interested in solving. Boggle are generally things of this nature, simple creatures of more docile intentions. Most people who don't move on properly become Earthbound, but Demons and Poltergeist are a little different. There are plenty of ghosts who don't get to become a part of a faction instantly. They are called Roamers. They're usually the ghosts of people, but if they can't resolve their lingering attachments on their own and move on that way or end up in Earthbound, they will become one of two things."

"Demons or Poltergeist?"

He nodded, "If they were rotten enough in life, they often find their way to the Demons."

Lowering my arms from the stretch, I pocketed my hands, "What about the Poltergeist?"

It was rare, a moment where his eyes weren't intently locked on mine. "I tend to keep my distance from them, I suggest you do the same." Shifting his weight away from me, he crossed his arms over his chest, closing himself off as his eyes remained averted, their glow dulling a bit, "They aren't people, just a culmination of miserable energy. A figment of the past, they aren't worth your time." When his eyes returned to mine, his tone lightened, "Eventually, most stagnate Roamer ghosts end up in a faction. Rarely is one able to stay pure enough to roam the world for all eternity, though they do exist."

"So, what about us?"

His eyes drifted over the Boggle around us. "Do you mean Boggle in general, or you and I specifically?"

Looking around as the little Boggle played together in the park outside Castle Boggle, I let out a breath I didn't know I was retaining, some tension leaving with it, "I wouldn't mind if you explained both."

"Well, Boggle, as you've probably noticed, are totally harmless." He bopped a little light as it floated about him, "Things like pets that couldn't move on properly come to us. But all these other things?" Plucking the light from the air gently, he held it, "I have no idea where they originate. They were never living, that's for sure."

"Ghosts that have always been ghosts?"

"That's the best explanation that I can come up with." He said as he let the light go, eyes following as it floated away, bobbing about as if it hadn't just been briefly kidnapped.

"So, what about us?"

He sighed, spectral eyes falling to the ground. "That Sire, is the greatest mystery of all. I'm here by choice, but you are not. You were instantly taken to us, placed here for a reason. But as you can see," He extended his arms, "we're the only humans."

"You chose to be here?" I walked through the Boggle crowd and they moved to the side, revealing a grey stone, single teared fountain before me, "Why?"

His eyes sat on mine before darting away again, the water from the fountain filling the quiet in the beat that passed. "I was convinced." He turned from me, "Although being a traitor is nasty business and I wouldn't suggest it."

As he walked toward the castle, I just watched. That person was the one I spent hours drawing and endless nights looking for. He said they were watching, but how much had they truly seen? He didn't act as if he was aware of my, for lack of a better word, infatuation. But now that he was in front of me, he was different than I had expected. There was something sitting in those mystical eyes of his that I didn't understand when he looked at me.

I ran up to his side. Had he just been roaming amongst the Boggle on his own? What would drive him to make such a choice? We walked into the castle and the large door closed behind me without anyone having to touch it.

Iris stayed on my shoulder as I followed Oliver up a central staircase in silence.

"This is your chamber." Oliver said, opening a door to show a large room. "Mine is next door, if you need me."

I stared in at the room, it was huge like the rest of the castle. Walking in, I was going to turn around ask him something but before I could, the door was closed. Silence sat in the air for a moment as I stared at the closed door but then Iris spoke softly.

"Don't mind him, he's just shy."

I didn't think Iris capable of complete sentences, so that startled me a little as they flew from my shoulder to float in front of me. "He is?"

They spun around, "Yup. He's spent so much time waiting for you that I don't think he knows what to do now that you're here."

"He was expecting me?"

"We all were, you've been chosen as our King from the day you were born. We've all taken turns, watching over you. And sometimes you noticed us with those machines of yours. Every ghost in this kingdom knows of your kindness, the hope you hold for us." Iris landed on my shoulder again. "Ghosts are good."

"Ghosts are good." I repeated quietly.

"And you were right, some of us are. But others aren't. And the King decides who gets to be the most powerful presence amongst the human world. The King hasn't changed in a very long time, but if the Demon or Poltergeist candidate win, then the world will fall into another dark age. That's why it's so important that you're here, Sire. If you win, then the paranormal will be at ease as long as your reign shall last."

I walked up to a desk and pulled out the chair before sitting down. Iris flew to the desk and sat on it, looking up at me with their black orbs as I tried to steady my shaking breath.

"This is a lot of information, a lot of," I looked up to their emotionless stare, "responsibility."

"It is, but," their tone became playful, "we believe in you."

Bringing my hands up, I ran them over my face, leaning my elbows on the desk, "Why?"

"Because you believed in us."

Staring down at the wood of the desk, I couldn't find my words.

"You could change everything, Kasper," Iris bounced about on the desk, "A King is the embodiment of all their Kingdom. Every Almighty has fallen, every king is one day destroyed by their greatest strength. For Demon Kings, they will eventually fall to the malice in their core. The Poltergeist King is destroyed by sadness, and the Earthbound King becomes weakened and defeated by deep rooted vulnerability. It appears as a blight and slowly devours them until they become nothing and then the next King takes over. But a Boggle may be different."

"What makes you so sure?"

Iris rolled around, "I don't know, I just know. Boggle aren't like the others, we just want to be spooky and laugh. Though, I think something is going on. We've fallen into complacency, but a major upset may be coming soon."

I just sort of stared at the outwardly harmless and adorable ghost as they rolled around. I felt bad for thinking them incapable of thought and speech as complex as this. "Why do you think that?"

"You're here." They floated up and bumped up into me, "The last time the Boggle had a candidate, things got nasty."

"That sounds like a story." I leaned forward on my elbow, the tension draining from my body again as I observed my new friend.

"It totally is, but it's not mine to tell." Iris floated up from me.

Standing, their wispy voice echoing in my mind, I saw my reflection in the window and was left to stare at the crown as it slowly spun over my head, "What will defeat an Almighty Boggle King?"

"We've never had one, so we don't know."

Ripping my gaze from the ground, I looked around the room when my eyes landed on the bed. Walking up to it, Iris followed. "Do ghosts need sleep?"

"Nope."

I stopped next to the bed, looking to Iris. "Then why?"

Iris flew above the bed then fell down to it, bouncing up then falling down again, "Everyone loves jumping on the bed."

I couldn't help but smile at that. "You remind me of my little brother." I turned away from the bed and continued about the room. "I still don't remember how I died, and really Iris, this doesn't feel real."

"That's normal," they floated around me, "or so I've heard anyway, I've always been dead."

Stopping at a bookshelf, my eyes scanned over the spines, "I'm never going to see him again, am I?" Those words felt hollow, like I didn't believe them as they came from me.

I knew that I was dead.

But I didn't know.

Not really.

Pulling a book from the shelf, its weight dropped into my hand as my mind took two steps too far and I wondered how I died, if I had finally…

"You can go back Flipside if you want." I stopped in my step, turning to look at Iris as they flew toward me and went on. "You, as a ghost, are not forbidden to, I mean. But you, as a King Candidate, are forbidden from showing yourself to the living."

I stared, my heart starting to race. "When I'm the Almighty King, can I?"

"When you're the Almighty King, you can do whatever you want."

If I was the Almighty King, I could entirely change the dynamic of ghosts and the living. I'd show them that I wasn't out of my mind, I'd watch over Hugo. And finally, I'd prove that ghosts are indeed, good.

A smile took me over as I resolved myself. As disjointed and rushed as this felt, I was going to take this by the reigns and own it. There had never been an Almighty Boggle King before, and to some that would be discouraging, but I wasn't afraid of a challenge. I fruitlessly fought to prove that ghosts were real even though no one had before. I didn't give up then and look at where I was now; I was in the running to be the Ghost King. Even though

His eyes drifted to Iris who then hid behind me. After a moment he looked back to me and almost looked like he wanted to protest but then he bowed slightly, his tone reserved and rigid like his shoulders. "Yes, Sire."

We started out of the castle, "You have a hint of an accent, Oli, where were you from?"

"My name is Oliver, Sire."

"I love those islands, great in the summer."

He looked to me, brow furrowed as I laughed.

"You're so serious, Oli, you need to chill."

"Chill?"

I followed him down one of the many winding stone paths through the park world. "Yes, chill. As in, relax."

"It's not in my job description to relax."

"Or your vocabulary, apparently."

Iris found me pretty funny. As I looked over to Oliver, his serious face home to those magical eyes and framed by his flippy orange hair, I set a goal for myself. I was going to make Oliver laugh. I wanted to know what he'd look like with a beaming smile;

I wanted to hear his laugh and know that I was the one who caused it.

"This is the portal to Flipside." Oliver started as we walked up to simple gate, old and worn, it held a faint yellow glow behind its metal doors. "But before we go through it, I need to explain some things first." He turned to me, "Time passes here differently than there. Sometimes a moment here is a moment there, other times a moment here is an hour there, and occasionally a moment there is a decade here."

"Alright…" I thought on what he said, my excitement slowing some, "So what are you getting at?"

He looked back to the portal then to me, "It's been over a week since you died, Flipside."

That took the air from my lungs. I had barely felt any time go by, but an entire week had passed Hugo? Clenching my teeth, keeping my smile, I nodded.

"I'm sure you've noticed it, but there are two planes of existence on the Flipside. There's the one visible to the living, and the one that is not. Most ghosts exist on the one invisible to the living eye, but sometimes they become strong enough to pass to the visible. Although you can influence things to the living eye from either plane. But I wouldn't suggest it."

"That's no fun." I folded my arms, inspecting the pulsing portal. "I had no idea being a ghost came with so many rules."

"And finally," He ignored me, "you, as the King Candidate, are not allowed to show yourself to the living eye."

"Why not?"

"It is imperative to keeping the secret of the Ghost King."

"It's a secret?"

Iris flew from my shoulder and around Oliver as they spoke, "Yup. If the living knew of such a force, they would try to influence, support, or take it down. You know how the living deal with power."

"They kill each other with it." Oliver went on. "They abuse it and destroy everything." He turned to the portal. "So, it is part of your responsibility to keep our King a secret, and now, you're a part of that secret. But as long as you understand that, then I don't mind going Flipside with you."

"Sounds good." I walked up to his side. "I just have to lay low and not scare anyone, shouldn't be too hard. But I do have to say that I am quite disappointed that I'm too important to be a lowly ghost who yells 'boo' at passing people."

"None of us say 'boo' I have no idea where that even started." Oliver sounded way too offended by that and I couldn't help but laugh.

Looking into the portal, I took a deep breath. I was about to go back a week after I died and see the fallout. What memories would be knocked loose? I didn't know, but I knew that it had to be done. I needed to know, to have every piece of my puzzle. Only then would I be able to heal.

Avoidance was a hell of a thing, but I knew that it wasn't the right thing.

I needed to be my best self so that I wouldn't squander this opportunity to shine. I was a Kloven, after all. We were destined to be stars. My stage just wasn't the same as the rest of my family.

As we stepped into the portal, I felt my balance get thrown. Spiraling into what felt like nothing, I really doubted what Oliver said. I was never going to get used to that.

Chapter 3

EULOGY

Iris laughed at me as I knelt on the ground, hand to my mouth as my world spun. Oliver extended his hand to me, not looking down. I took his hand and was again surprised by his cool warmth. That time he didn't briskly pull his hand from mine but allowed me to let go after I fully stood. I gently retracted my hand and put it in my pocket, looking away from him quickly.

My gaze drifted up to see that we were standing in downtown, not far from where I used to do research. Looking around, I asked, "How do we get back?"

"That's a little hard to explain, it's a power that you haven't even used yet."

I stood there, staring forward as I processed what he said. Jumping to the side, I looked to him, "Wait. I have powers?"

He slowly turned to face me, looking to Iris, "Oh, so you inform him of exclusively the least convenient information for me, but not something as fundamental as that?"

Iris just laughed as they floated around me.

With a deep groan, he looked back to me. "It's sort of a tradeoff, you lose your body, you gain the powers that it couldn't use when you were alive. Unfortunately, they are deeply emotionally rooted, so don't lose your temper. Other than that, it'll just take time for you to fully come into them. Generally, those who become a King Candidate have been dead for a while and had plenty of time to figure things out before they are amplified. But," He gestured to the crown above my head, "you don't have that luxury. The crown atop your head amplifies your preexisting paranormal powers. They are simple things like being able to invoke the portal or move things without touching them, though. You may have some others, possibly linked to the weather, but I'm not sure why. Don't get too excited, though, it's not like you're going to shoot fire from your eyes or anything."

"Aw darn." I laughed but then my breath snagged in my throat. Two girls who were walking by us and had stopped to stare at me.

I stared back at them; their eyes grew.

Oliver quickly reached out to my hand and pulled me close, making my heart stop. The girls looked to each other then ran off, leaving us standing there in silence.

"I told you not to show yourself to the living eye."

I stepped away from him, "I didn't know I was."

He considered something quietly for a few moments before letting go of me. "Fair enough, you are frighteningly new to this. I've been dead so long, I barely remember how much of a struggle it must be at first." He bowed his head, extending his hand. "I do apologize Sire, I meant no disrespect."

"It's alright dude," I said quietly, "but am I going to be struck down or something? They totally saw me."

He shook his head, still not raising it. "But we must be careful from here on. This is my fault, I shouldn't have brought you Flipside so soon. But since it was your request to visit, I won't revoke it now. Although, in order to continue this safely, you'll need to take my hand."

I looked from his extended hand to Iris, "What? Why?"

"He's ancient so he has pretty good control over his powers." Iris flew up to Oliver, "You're going to keep both of you out of sight, yeah?"

"Indeed. Now Sire," his voice actually faltered as he went on, as if he had to choke out his words, "please, take my hand."

I hesitated before taking his extended hand but eventually did. Eye contact was impossible as his fingers wrapped around my hand and he lifted his head.

Iris laughed more as they flew around us. "Don't blush too much Oli."

"I have no qualms about banishing you, Boggle."

Oliver was funny when embarrassed.

We walked along the side of the road as I looked around at all of the historic buildings. It was when I was looking at the second story of one of them that I stopped. There was a man pacing who I could see through the window. The thing that caught my eye wasn't that someone was up there, which was odd actually, but that the someone was transparent like us.

Without a word I took Oliver and dragged him behind me toward the building. A smile broke out on my face as I bolted toward the closed door. I had always wanted to do this. Oliver was going to say something, but I'd never hear it because I ran full speed, not through the door, but into the door. Falling backward into Oliver, he stayed unmoving.

"What in hell's name are you doing," his tone flattened again, "…Sire?"

I held my face, hissing through my teeth as I reeled from the pain. "I was expecting that to work."

Oliver sighed over Iris' cackles as he walked up to the door. Tightening his grip on my hand, he took a calm step forward and passed through the door, taking me with him. I could feel every organ in my body as I fazed through the door. A shiver tore through me once we were on the other side, my skin crawling with extreme discomfort. I could be mistaken, but I thought I saw Oliver's shoulders bounce slightly as he turned from me.

A smile took me over when I saw that, I had gotten a step closer to hearing his laugh. I then remembered what I was doing before gracefully blundering into the door. Starting up the stairs, I bolted past Oliver and started to drag him along with me in a mess of muddled steps. After taking a few turns and running down a hallway, I stopped. Pacing up and down the other side of it was a man dressed in old formal wear.

I started toward him. I could never get permission to investigate there so I could only speculate about the pioneer doctor who's office was on this floor. Rumor was that the second story of that building was haunted, but no one could get up there to investigate properly because of the attitudes of the owners. After looking into the place more, I found that the first pioneer doctor in the area had his office there. Of all the things that had been located in that building, something as horrific as a pioneer age doctor's office seemed like it would hail the most haunting.

"Hello." He stopped pacing and looked to us. "Are you here to see me?"

I was stunned, I had seen that man in pictures before, but this was unreal.

"Doctor James W. Thom?"

The man nodded, "Yes, that is me."

"What are you waiting for?"

He looked around then back to me, "My next patient. It's been ages and I used to have many regulars, but for some reason they've all stopped coming."

I looked over to Oliver, but he didn't react. My eyes slowly fell back to the doctor, my heartbeat slowing a little. "If I'm ever in need of medical help I will come to you, Dr. Thom."

He gave me a nod and as we started to leave, he began to pace again. Silence sat between us, my excitement slowing into something sadder. After we were out and Oliver had fazed me through the door again, I spoke.

"He's a Roamer?"

"Yes." Oliver followed as I pulled him down the sidewalk again, "A doctor unable to move on for their only life purpose was to help others."

"He's been there forever, why hasn't he been claimed by the Poltergeist or Demons?"

"I said it was rare, but there are those who harbor a light inside bright enough to ward the factions off, enabling them to roam for long amounts of time."

I steered him around a corner, weaving through an alley to get to the next place I wished to visit. Stopping in front of the old bakery, I jumped when I heard a loud banging. After walking around, I saw a transparent person kicking the black metal door, yelling at the top of their lungs about being locked out. My mind flew back to the interview I conducted there once. The workers at that bakery told me they heard yells and banging from the backside of the bakery, but they could never find the source.

"What's wrong?" I called out to them, a little too scared to get much closer.

They jumped, looking back at me. "I'm locked out and they're not far behind!"

"Who is-"

Before my question fully left my mouth, someone came rushing up to the man. Oliver kept me from running to his aid as the other person threw the first punch. A fight broke out, yells, the hollow thudding of bodies upon impact, a knife caught the light for a moment before the final screams rang in my ears. Looting the pockets of the victim, I couldn't do anything but watch, breathless. The baker's yells echoed in my ears as he fell limp, the darkly dressed man bloodied and smiling as he stood over the body. Suddenly the back door to the bakery flew open and the darkly dressed man fled. A living employee looked around, presumably saw nothing, then closed the door again. I was about to ask Oliver why he had held me back when he spoke instead.

"It's residual, there's nothing you can do."

I stopped struggling next to him and looked back to the man lying on the ground. It was widely believed that residual hauntings were simply events that replayed and didn't involve actual spirits. But that man spoke to me, he saw me, he was no recording. Were there still things that ghosts didn't even know about ghosts?

"Flipside isn't the most pleasant of places," Oliver said as we walked along, "I've only come back a handful of times."

"It's definitely different now…"

Dragging Oliver behind me, the reality I was living was starting to become a little more real than I was comfortable with. For some reason we traveled far faster than normal walking, as if we were slightly teleporting forward without my noticing. Before I even had time to think much we were standing before the old high school. I had never really gotten in there either, investigating on private property was tricky, especially when you looked like some high school punk out to cause trouble. Oliver fazed us inside and I had taken but three steps into the hallway when something ran into me.

Looking down, I saw a young boy on a tricycle. He was sopping wet, but his toothy smile gave the impression that he didn't mind. He looked me up and down, as if I was the coolest thing ever. Jumping from the bike he had hit me with, he ran to my front.

"Hi!"

I knelt down, accidentally taking my hand away from Oliver's. He quickly placed his hand atop my head, making my heart jump from my chest. Desperately trying to ignore the pleasant feel of his hand in my hair, I smiled at the little boy.

"Hey, what's up kid?"

He looked between Oliver and I, "I found this great place to ride my bike, but I don't normally have visitors." He extended his little hand boldly. "I'm Alexander."

I took his small dripping hand, "I'm Kasper."

"So that's your name," he giggled, taking his hand back, "I've seen you loitering outside a lot. But I didn't realize you were a ghost too."

That was surprising, the last two Roamers hadn't really recognized me or themselves as a ghost. "I wasn't, not yet anyway." I looked to his trike. "I like your bike."

"Thanks!" He hopped back on it. "Come visit me again, it gets lonely." And with that he rode off down the hall, leaving a trail of water behind him.

As I straightened, Oliver begrudgingly removed his hand from my hair and took my hand again. I could still feel the sensory of his fingers leaving my hair, causing me to shiver. Trying to hide that as I straightened, my eyes fell to the ground. Oliver was overwhelming, his presence, his touch, so bold. I was going to turn and leave when one of the doors down the hall opened and a worker walked out. I watched as he took a few steps but then slipped on the water trail the boy had left behind and fell hard to the ground. Laughing a little as the middle-aged man in a dirt color suit struggled to pick himself up, I couldn't help but be impressed with Alexander.

"Is the roof is leaking again?" He groaned as he sat up, "Yeah, let's put the offices in the school that's over a century old, that's a fantastic idea."

Still laughing as Oliver dragged me away, I wasn't paying a lot of attention when Oliver fazed us out and that time really got me, rendering me too nauseous to move forward for a few moments as we stood outside.

"How did he do that?" I asked, my voice muffled by my hand over my mouth.

"The water trail?"

I nodded.

"It must have had something to do with his death and he seems like a potent enough Roamer that occasionally things regarding him bleed through to the living eye. Children ghosts are often that way, since they were relatively innocent and youthful when they died. They are far harder for time to corrupt."

I straightened, taking a breath as we continued on. "He drowned in a pool that was in this building." I said as we passed the brick building next to the old high school then started across the street toward the museum. "These Roamers have no hope of being claimed by Earthbound? They will either roam forever or end up sucked into the other factions?"

"Under the current rule, yes. But if they were personally claimed by a King, then they could join another faction."

"I could change the current system?" we stopped in front of the museum. "Down with the man."

Staring at the front door, old, worn wood, I had opened it myself many times before. There was something about knowing that I'd never be able to open again that made me regret not appreciating it more the last time I had. Taking another breath, I held it as Oliver fazed us inside. The historical society and museum were an amazing resource for local history that I ended up at often during my research. Rumor had it that two ghosts roamed its halls.

Shoes landing on the wooden floor inside, we didn't make a sound. Looking up as my hand flew to my mouth, calm came to me easier in the still of the museum. Dust dotted the air like shooting stars through the beams of light as they streaked across the bottom story. Shuffling sounds from the other volunteers were muffled by the brick walls, the scene of decaying books in the air. Taking my first step, it felt weird to not be greeted by the sweet older lady who often sat at the front desk. Sleepy, warm, safe, this was my home away from home.

"I helped set up this exhibit," my eyes sat heavy on the case of old objects as we passed, "I volunteered here a lot."

As I dragged Oliver around the exhibits, I thought on the many days I spent there, and it made my core grow a little cold. I liked it there in life.

Turning a corner into an exhibit, I nearly fell over myself when I just about ran into someone. The man turned, his steps making no sound. Muted brown tweed vest, off-white balloon sleeves punctuated by pearl cufflinks, his black pants and worn mahogany shoes, I had seen them all in a photograph before. Looking him up and down as he turned to fully face me, my eyes landed on his and that's when I knew.

"George Brosterhous?"

Bushy brows raised, his wrinkled face lit up, "Kasper?"

We stared at each other.

Straightening, eyes wide, it was like meeting a celebrity as I tried to find words, "You know who I am?"

"Of course I do, you were here so much you were just about haunting the place too." He took a step closer, bending down a bit as his narrowing eyes studied me, "But it appears you really are haunting it now."

Trapped in his historical arura, I had so many questions. But when my eyes caught on what was in his hands, only one came out, "What are you doing?"

He looked to the book in his grasp, "Borrowing this."

"You know they blame you for making things disappear and move around, right?"

He sighed, his wide shoulders falling with his breath, "I am aware, and I really don't mean to cause issue. But by the time I'm done with what I borrowed I forget where it came from, so I just leave it somewhere."

"I'm sure Vanessa appreciates that."

He just shrugged and I was going to ask for the book so I could put it back where it belonged so Vanessa wouldn't have to spend an hour looking for it later, but then I heard a faint giggle. Looking back over my shoulder into the lobby, my eyes slowly widened with the realization. I took Oliver with me as I ran to the downstairs bathroom. Hesitating before going through the girl's bathroom door, I internally asked Vanessa for forgiveness. Stumbling through the door and immediately into the wall, I was discombobulated for a moment.

"Hello!"

I turned to see a little girl looking up to me, "Hi."

She hopped up to me in her jumper, smiling from ear to ear, "Are you a new friend?"

"He's the lonely kid I told you about, the one who was too embarrassed to come in here and investigate." I flew out of my skin when George spoke from behind me. He had just appeared out of thin air.

She looked like she came from around the same time George did, the early eighteenth century. She probably haunted the museum because it had exhibits that looked like classrooms for kids her age from that time. George was a construction worker who fell through the roof and died upon impact while building the structure. All of the employees and volunteers very much believed in the two ghosts standing in the room with me. It made me happy to know their faith wasn't misplaced.

"Oh you!" She stepped around me, "What happened? I thought you were alive?"

"I…was," looking down to her, I tried to keep my smile about me, "Please keep taking care of the people here, they cherish you both."

"Maybe that's why they've been so sad," George said as he reached for a soap container on the counter, "This last week has been a quiet one here."

My heart sunk and with that, I pulled Oliver out of the room and toward the stairs with me. Running up them, I was distracted and not really thinking about my footing. Missing a step, a moment later I went falling backwards into Oliver. We both went tumbling down the stairs and into the wall at the end. Each stair hit harder than the last, knocking the air out of me. Laying there, pain racing through me, I wondered what was fair about being able to still get hurt after death.

Oliver sat up with a groan, still holding onto me, "How did you not die sooner?"

"Arguably, dying at 18 is still pretty early."

We stood, George and Iris laughing at us as we did. Looking to George, I saw the soap dish in his hands. He looked down to it then back up to me and just smiled.

George was a terror.

This time I took care to walk up the stairs properly all the way to the flight break between the second and third stories. It was strange as we climbed the stairs, it was the first time they didn't creak under my weight. I was always horribly uncomfortable walking around in there because everyone could hear me. All you had to do was breathe and the old wooden floor would scream about it.

I stopped on the flight break, looking into the slightly open door. The office belonged to a wonderful woman named Vanessa who was the volunteer coordinator for the museum. She was one of the most knowledgeable people I knew, her vast internal database amazed me. She was also my senior when it came to the paranormal, she knew more about the local ghosts than I thought someone could. She sat at her desk and I was left standing there, stagnate. I wanted to tell her that she was right, George and the girl were here, but I couldn't.

Short hair and peppy smile, she was the heart of the museum, the firework that kept it all running. Taking a step in, my eyes met with her glow-in-the-dark skeleton hat she wore every year on the ghost tours we gave for Halloween.

"I'm sorry, the public isn't allowed on the third floor." She looked up my way and for a moment I was sure she saw me. She looked around, confused, as if she thought she saw someone, but no one was there.

George nonchalantly walked past me and into her office, holding that stupid soap dish.

"What are you doing?" I asked, my harsh tone hushed even though I was pretty sure Vanessa wouldn't hear me.

He just smirked at me as he approached her bookshelf. I yanked Oliver along with me as I reached out to stop George from taking one of Vanessa's books. I failed, though, and ended up causing him to drop it. We all jumped when it thudded against the ground, startling Vanessa also. She looked to the book then up to us and I totally felt like she could see us. But with a shake of her head, she got up and took the book into her hands. I dragged George out of her way as she put the book back.

"You really need to stop this. They work way too hard to have you messing up their research. It's annoying, I know, you messed with mine enough."

He just laughed, nonchalantly placing the soap dish on Vanessa's desk while she was occupied.

"We should get going soon." another museum employee, Shey, called from the third story as her each of her creaking steps brought her closer.

Vanessa looked away from her bookshelf to her desk, freezing when her gaze met the soap dish. After staring at it for a moment, her eyes rose to the woman coming down the stairs. "I think George is in here."

Shey smiled, her long silver hair cascading over her shoulder, clad in an olive-green sweater as she leaned in the doorway, "Hi George."

"Hi Shey." George nodded to her, though she didn't hear him.

Looking between the two ladies who treated me with kindness and acceptance when I felt as if I deserved anything but, I wanted to thank them. My grip loosened on Oliver, but then my wits returned to me, reminding me that I wasn't allowed to show myself. Dragging everyone out of the way, we evacuated Vanessa's office and I watched as they gathered their things.

"It's quiet here now," Shey said as they started down the creaking stairs.

"Yeah," Vanessa's tone was soft, almost too soft to be heard over the creaking, "It was nice to have a lively one around, kids are never too interested in what we do here."

I had never heard them sound so sad before, their smiles still there but their tones wavering. It was a strength that I admired in them. As we approached the door, I let them open it for us as to avoid another faze through. As I stepped through after them, taking one last look into the historical society, my gaze snagged on George as he reached his dumb hands out toward a cup of pens at the front desk.

He just laughed and waved at me as the door closed between us.

A little smile found its way to me.

Following the two ladies I had worked with down the brick path that led to the parking lot, I couldn't hear their quiet conversation as they approached a car. Watching as they got into the car, I felt the beginnings of a hole in my heart start to grow as they drove away. Standing there, holding hands with Oliver, Iris on my shoulder, the weight was starting to get heavier inside. There was somewhere else I wanted to visit, one more ghost I needed to know about. In order to distract myself from the reality that was starting to rear its ugly head, I thought on Oliver.

"How did you die?"

Oliver nearly tripped in his step, but didn't, because he's too cool for that. "I don't blame you for being unaware, but that's an insensitive question to ask."

"I suppose, but didn't you die a long time ago? I can't imagine it still being a sore topic."

"Have you ever wondered why you didn't have any friends?" Iris laughed.

"No," I rolled my eyes over to the Boggle floating at my side, "I knew why, because I believed in you guys." Stepping closer to Oliver, I continued to smile, "I'm just curious about you, I've wondered for a long time."

He made eye contact with me for a moment before breaking it. "1103."

"What?"

"That's the year I died. If you are capable of calculations, that should give you an idea."

I stood there, trapped in the swirls of his eyes. He had been dead for hundreds of years. He lived in a world different than mine in literally every single way and I had only barely noticed. If it was so easy to come Flipside, why had he gone so few times? Didn't the world changing interest him? That thought brought others whiling into my mind. I was going to be around forever. I was going to see wars, destruction, those I loved die, everything change. And as I stood there, looking over Oliver, I suddenly understood.

I started to walk again, tightening my grip on Oliver's hand a little. The desperation he must have gone through was probably enormous. My step hitched when I realized that I was tied to the same fate. Smiling, I tried to drive that thought from my mind.

"You really haven't come around here much?"

"Flipside?" His eyes floated over toward mine, "I haven't the need. I was here in life, the day you drown, the day you died in finality, and today."

"Then you really have no idea what's going on anymore."

My mind snagged on something and I dug my pocket with my free hand. Amazed, I took out my phone. I had so many questions about why that stayed with me in death but at the same time, I didn't want to question it too much. Oliver looked interested then tried to pretend that he wasn't, I could just tell by the way his eyes jumped away when mine met his.

"I wonder…" I stopped, yanking Oliver back next to me as Iris flew to my shoulder. Holding my phone up, I turned on the front facing camera. I saw us on the screen and I nearly dropped my phone. Again, I noticed just how healthy I looked. As if before when I was alive, I was a ghost of, well, my ghost. Pressing the button, I took a picture. Quickly I took it down and opened up the photo app to look at the picture. Staring at a picture of the sidewalk, none of the three of us showing up in it, I sighed.

"I don't know what I was expecting."

Oliver just about hung over my shoulder, looking at my phone, aghast.

I couldn't help but smile as I turned to him, but then our faces ended up quite close on accident and we both shuffled away. I held the phone out to him, unable to look him in the eye.

"You can take more, just not of us apparently."

Frozen, he stared at the phone, as if touching it would hurt. "But Sire," He started quietly, "what kind of witchcraft does that possess?"

"It's called Apple."

"Apple?" He slowly took the phone. "The definition of that word has vastly changed since the last time I heard it."

Forget being a Ghost King, I shouldn't be trusted with the amount of power this development had thrust upon me. "Yes, this apple hails from a country far away over the sea. Many people use their magics to mass create these."

"There are others like this?" He continued to inspect the phone.

"Their numbers are endless."

"How does the world not fall into chaos with such power at their fingertips?"

"Some would argue that it has, but that's just some boomer nonsense."

"Boomer?" the obvious depths of his horror grew, "Are there people who explode now?"

Blinking at him, I tried to contain my laugh, "No but sometimes I wish they would."

As we walked along, his hand a little more relaxed in mine, he took his sweet time looking over the phone. My mind wandered to something I slightly overheard in a health class somewhere along the lines about holding hands and how it helped maintain bonds. The let down from the picture not working stung. I was really hoping I'd finally have a picture of him that I didn't draw.

Was that why he seemed unknowing of my infatuation? He had only been Flipside a few times. But that just made me wonder, "You don't have to answer, but why were you Flipside the day I drown?"

Oliver nearly fell off of the sidewalk when he accidentally triggered the front facing flash on the camera. "Oh," his composure was visibly disrupted for a moment, "that day I was investigating the suspicious activities of the Demon faction." He dropped his hand with the phone to the side as to give me his full attention as we continued to walk. "For quite some time before then, the kingdom had been buzzing with rumors of a change in the wind, a potential switching of powers. It took me a while to track down the source of the rumors, but it was you. The next fated Boggle King had scared the Almighty Ghost King. I didn't know how or why, but he was deeply unsettled by you. I had sent more Boggle out to keep an eye on you upon acquiring that information. But something wasn't right that day and the Demon King was missing. Uncomfortable with this, I came Flipside to watch over you myself. I just happened to appear Flipside when you were pulled under."

My breath snagged in my throat. "Pulled?"

He looked to me as we approached a street, "Yes," His eyes fell to the bottom of my left pant leg, "now that you're a spirit, you should see the mark."

I stopped, kneeling down on the sidewalk, and pulled up my left black pant leg. Left staring, my vision blurred for a moment as my gaze rested on a black mark that almost looked like a poisonous magical burn. It was of a handprint, one that bore claws, grasping up my leg.

"That's where he made contact with you, the Demon King. The fear you struck into the Almighty Ghost King shook the entire Kingdom and the Demon King took it upon himself to eliminate you." I slowly stood as he went on. "But he wasn't expecting my presence so I managed to stop him before he banished you but, I couldn't keep him from blighting you. However, I was able to stop his blight before it tainted you further."

Hazy memories played behind my eyes of that day and how I did think I felt something grab me. I had never been out of my mind, everything had a reason, "What kept him from coming after me again?"

"I was somewhat," He paused, "holy, in life, so my blessing kept him at bay, like with the blight." He looked away from me, "Although don't think on the use of 'holy' there too much, that is a very relative term, depending on the context."

I didn't ask him about that, though I wanted to. Instead, I watched him take pictures of our surroundings. His surprise was so novel each time, it was endearing. That was a treasure to see in an apathetic technology dependent world. Things lost their wonder quickly, 'the next big thing' didn't mean much anymore. We could have landed on Mars one day and I would have just shrugged. But to Oliver, my phone was amazing and watching him made me smile.

I stepped out into the street after instinctively looking both ways. I was weary of that crosswalk because it had a blind corner on one side. I had crossed there safely countless times, despite that though. We were a few steps into the road when a car came racing up. I couldn't react in time as it barreled into the group. But as I stood, frozen in its headlights, it tore through us. I could feel it pass through my insides, shaking me up. A pain ripped through my ribs, exhaust clogging my breathing as my world spun. Another car roared through me, making me fall to my knees. I felt like I was rolling, but I knew I wasn't as my arms came around my chest, trying to hold myself together. Ears ringing with the horn of a car, my world barreled out of focus. The horn warped into something else as my senses fried themselves, a scream.

A hand landed on my back that turned into an arm wrapped around me that became the support that brought me to my feet. Electric blue dripped into my veins, passing through my entire being and calming me with each beat of my undead heart. Looking up, I only saw his concern for a moment before it erased itself from his features to be replaced with stone apathy.

"Sire…" Oliver's voice broke through the static screaming in my ears, "Are you alright?"

As my labored breathing began to calm, I was left there, staring at him as a whirl of thoughts stormed in my mind.

Alright?

Of course I wasn't alright.

I was dead.

"Yeah," a deep breath left me as I stepped out of his space, "that just startled me."

"Those were certainly not around in my time." Oliver looked up and down the road as we started to walk to the other side, his hand lingered near me cautiously. "What are they?"

"Cars," My eyes low, my tone lower, I dragged Oliver along with me, "they move people from place to place."

He stayed a step behind me, "There are people inside those? How are they not being digested?"

"Cars aren't living."

"But...how do they move?"

I smiled a little, despite the dread clawing its way up my throat, "Witchcraft."

"Witchcraft." He repeated pointedly, as if making a mental note.

We approached the grassy hills of a place I had spent many nights. Something felt different, though, as I stepped upon that hallowed ground, littered with headstones. Surprise ruled my mind as I looked around, not a ghost in sight as the sun began to drop in the sky. Of all the places I'd expect to be haunted, this was one.

We walked down the line of headstones, quickly approaching the one I wanted. I read the engraved names as we passed them, wondering what became of the people. Oliver did mention moving on properly, but I hadn't inquired about what that entailed. Though, since he was stuck here too, I doubted he had the answer.

"Kasper?"

I jumped when I heard my name. Looking up to the headstone I visited often, I saw a young man sitting atop it, his legs dangling over the side. He appeared similar to me in age and his attire would suggest he was more modern than not. Honey yellow sweater with a cute graphic on it, jean jacket with a couple cutesy enamel pins, he looked like a soft boy. Golden curly locks warm eyes and soft features, his dark brows were raised as he hopped off of the headstone. Studying me, he made me take a step back.

"But you-" He stopped, gasping. "No way. You're a ghost now too?" Oliver cleared his throat, making the guy go stiff. "And what are you doing out and about, Mr. Knight? I thought you resented Flipside…" He trailed off when his eyes fell to my hand that was in Oliver's.

"You're looking at a new King, show some respect." Oliver did not flinch under the guy's comments.

The young man before me nearly fell backwards when he looked up to my head. "Goodness." He then dropped to one knee, bowing his head, "My bad, Kasper. I didn't know, no one tells me anything out here." He slightly looked up to me from the bow through his small, thin golden framed circular glasses. "I'm Gaston, the Graveyard Guardian. It's nice to finally talk with you." His smile became pained, his brow furrowing, "But man, I'm sorry it had to be under these circumstances, dying sucks."

Looking down at the ray of sunshine below me, I could hardly believe it, "You were actually here."

"Always." He suavely stood, the setting sun a warm light reflecting off of his little heart enamel pin. "I've proudly protected this graveyard, keeping it a neutral zone for a decade or so now." He extended his arms. "This is my home, and you were one of my favorite regular guests. I can't believe you're dead now," His warm hazel eyes rolled over to Oliver, "And if that wasn't bad enough, you're tethered to this kill-joy."

"It's a pleasure to see you again, Guardian." Oliver's disinterest in the bright young man was palpable, "I trust that you're doing your job?"

"I am." He crossed his arms boldly, making his golden curls bounce slightly. "It's been pretty quiet around here, except for over there," he gestured to the left, "there's a funeral going on I guess. People just keep tromping through here as if they own the place. I wonder who's being laid to rest."

Just as he was asking the question we were all thinking, my eyes caught on a person approaching the far off tent.

Russel?

My entire body went numb.

Without a word, I started toward the tent. Oliver tightened his grip as he walked by my side, trying to slow me down but I wasn't going to be stopped. As the tent grew closer, my every step taking me that way sent pins through my legs. The corners of my vision faded away, my mind zeroing in on one thing.

"Sire," Oliver tried to pull me back, but when I yanked forward he relented.

My steps slowly quickened, running toward the tent as Russel entered. Gaston and Iris a few steps behind us as I turned the corner, I stopped dead in my tracks. The crack that destabilized my world left echoes in my mind as I stared at my family, classmates, and strangers. Their gazes were all ahead and as my eyes traced forward, my breathing stopped.

"Sire, we really shouldn't be here."

Gaston stepped up next to me, "It's bad karma to watch your own funeral."

Laying there in the casket, all dressed up, a bouquet of flowers folded in my hands on my chest, was my body.

"We are here this evening to mourn the passing of a wonderful young man, a beloved Kloven."

"Beloved?" My wide eyes rolled up toward the pastor who stood next to my body.

I was never one for anger, never one to hold onto resentment, never one to humor the darker emotions. Though I had also never heard such a blatant lie before.

As the pastor went on about death, about heaven and peaceful resting, I could feel a smirk claw its way to my face. What a fucking joke. Glancing around at the crowd of strangers, I wondered who they were. Sitting at the front were my parents, obstructed by my casket from my view. Tilting my head to get a better view, all I could do was scoff. I hated the suit they put me in, mostly because I hadn't owned it before. I suppose I shouldn't have been surprised, the Kloven's were all about appearance after all. When the pastor finally finished repeating the same shit, I'm sure he always said about dead kids, he stepped to the side.

Jaw tight, I watched as several of my classmates stood and took the stage.

Because that's all this was.

An act.

"Kasper was a good friend," some girl said as she conjured up the fakest tears of the century, "Just the other day I hung out with him after school."

As I tried to even recall her name, I realized she had been one of the kids harassing me in the parking lot. What was her sign again? Something about unicorns.

"He was always reading in class," the girl at her side said, not looking up from the ground, "I used to ask what he was reading about, he was such a sweet guy."

A chuckle took me, she was a bad liar.

Heavy footsteps caught my attention as they approached the stage as the girls left. Blood boiling in an instant, I watched as Russel, dressed in fucking camo, commanded attention at my corpse's side. "He was so quiet," Russell looked down to my body, shoulders shaking, "I was worried about him getting pushed around, I did my best to watch out for him but.." he devolved into tears.

"Bullshit," starting to see red, nothing in the world mattered more than the toxicity that had taken me. Taking a step forward, Oliver held me back. Turning to look at him, I was about to snap, to be far sharper than I would have ever truly intended, but then I heard her voice.

"My beloved son," whiling around, I saw my mother standing there, my father at her side, his arm wrapped around her. "My baby," My mother wept her photogenic tears, "I don't know what possessed you, but please know that you are loved."

Cameras flooded her in flashes as she sobbed.

The world grew darker.

My father pulled her close, "Our son was a talented young man, one we had high hopes for and loved with all our hearts." His movie star performance was Oscar-worthy. "I will always remember the last night I saw him. I said goodnight and wished him a good day at school. He smiled at me and that's the son I'll always remember. Loving, lively, talented. He's a treasure gone way too soon."

People clapped; scattered sobs accompanied the applause. This was a show, a farce, and everyone there knew it. But I guess no one could call out the lies, because then they'd expose themselves too. Light footsteps sent waves of hushing and silence over the crowd and that's when everything came crashing down around me, any semblance of handle I had was shattered. Breath hitched, blood frozen, everything stopped the second Hugo took the stage.

Eyes red, skin pale, smile gone, in a suit that made him look far too old, the look on Hugo's face told it all. This was not only my funeral, but his. The Hugo I knew had died, been tainted with something so dark, it managed to dim the undeniable light he once held.

"Kasper…" His little voice, the waver to his every word, the shake to his shoulders he tried to hide, Hugo was one step from falling apart, "You're here, aren't you? You're here and you're mad," he looked around, the furrowing of his brows breaking the tears loose from his eyes, "None of you cared about him, you're all lying." Turning to look at our parents, the bite to his words overcame the cracking of his voice, "Not even you." Turning back, he looked straight ahead and right through me, "If you're here Kasper, please," he started to fall apart, "please show me."

Laughter exploded at my funeral. It wasn't the type of nostalgic chuckle you used to hide the tears brought on by a sweet memory, no, this laughter was sharp and full of condescending mockery.

My heart snapped.

How dare they?

Surrounded by laughter, my world plunged into red. Thunder rolling above us, the tents started to shake in the whipping wind. Rushing forward, I was yanked to a stop.

Jerking around, I felt something inside spark when my eyes met Oliver's. "Let go."

His eyes lit up as he stood there, stunned as his grip went limp. Hand falling from mine he was left there staring as I bolted toward the stage. Hugo stood, sobbing, laughter echoing around him. Looking out over the smiling eyes, I could barely conceal my shaking. But I wasn't sad, no, I was seething.

"Liars," reaching up, I placed my hand on the casket door. Slamming it shut, everyone went silent, staring at the casket.

"Sire, you can't-" when Oliver tried to run my way, Gaston held him back.

Hand clenched at my side, I didn't even know where to start. Boiling, festering, my every muscle tense, my crown starting to spin faster, a smirk found its way to me. Eyes raising from the stage, they landed on the group of students who had spoken. Bringing my hand toward them, I could feel the electricity pulse through me with every pang of rage. "Now you're my friends?" A gust of wind knocked them from their feet. Bringing my other arm up, my glare snapped to Russel, "You looked out for me? Is that what you'd call that?" With a swing of my arm, Russel was sent flying through the tent, ripping a hole in it as lightening flashed in the distant darkening sky.

The smile that tore across my face hurt more than it helped.

Screams invoked satisfaction as I whirled around and knocked the stupid sunglasses off of my parents' faces. The world slowed as I stared into their eyes, and for the first time I saw through their act. Fear looked lovely on them.

"Now you love me?" I continued my pursuit as they backpedaled, knocking over vases and spilling flowers, "Now you're proud?" I could hear my own voice echoing around me, distorted and jolting.

Thunder rolled, shaking the ground.

My crown's glow intensified as clouds blocked out any warmth from the setting sun.

Anger, sadness, resentment, I felt them fueling something far darker and deeper than anything I had felt before. A gust of wind ripped the roof off of the tent, turning the space into a storm. Air whipping around, knocking chairs over, it muffled the screams as people fled. Lightning lit up the tent, casting long shadows across the stage as it grew closer. A struggling shadow caught my eye as lightning struck a tree nearby.

Turning around, I saw Russel picking himself up from the ground. Slowly approaching him, my every step echoed louder than the last. Bending down, I brought my hand to his collar as he sat there, sniveling. As my grip tightened on him, my hand started to glow like my crown. Lifting him from the ground with a strength I didn't realize I had before, I laughed. He choked, struggling against me as he tried to yell out. It felt amazing, being stronger than him. That sort of power was intoxicating, disgustingly so.

Oliver yelled something that I couldn't hear over the thunder.

"How's it feel?" The glow of my crown reflected in the tears taking his eyes.

I was going to go too far, was going to allow myself to submit to the resentment, to the bottled up emotions that exploded under the pressure of their theatrics, but then a familiar red light shone in the corner of my eye.

Dropping Russel, I watched him squirm and whine on the ground before I slowly turned to the side. As my gaze locked on the blazing red light of the EMF, I was paralyzed. Standing there, holding it in his shaking hand, was Hugo.

"Kasper..." His small voice rang out above the chaos I had caused. "I know you're hurting, but," He smiled through the tears, "Ghosts are good, remember?"

Every ounce of dark resentment washed from my core with the tears that overtook my vision.

"Hugo," I could only take a few steps running toward him before I fell to my knees, "Can you see me?" Crawling up to him, I sat on my knees before him, eye-level with him, "Please, Hugo, I'm right here."

He didn't react, tears falling from his eyes.

Lightning struck outside, the flash of light bleaching my vision. When it faded back, Hugo was still standing before me, but his shirt was covered in blood, his eyes wide.

Looking to the side I saw the blurry headlights of a car.

Unable to breathe as my world spun, I looked back to Hugo, camera in his little shaking hands, blood dripping down his cheeks. Lightning bleached my world again and when my vision returned, Hugo stood there in his suit, looking around. Reaching forward, I was about to pull him close, to hug him and never let go, but then everything stopped.

I'd probably go right through.

On my knees, my arms frozen out before me, the crown atop my head crackling, it hit me.

I was dead.

The screaming of breaks, tires squealing against the pavement, headlights bleached my vision as my ears were overtaken by the sirens of an ambulance.

"Oliver," Gaston's yell shook me from my memories.

Looking over, I could do nothing as Oliver collapsed.

I choked on my next breath.

Searing pain shot through my head, causing me to bring my hands up to my hair as I tried to muffle my yell. Like the floodgates had opened, everything rushed back to me. Every drop of sadness every bit of uncertainty, every shred of fear, it suffocated me.

King?

Doubled over, forehead on the floor, my yell won out and ripped through me, erased by the thunder as it shook everything. As the world roared, swelling into a crescendo of agony, a little laugh brought a moment of stillness.

Hugo smiled at me, not through me.

A bolt of lightning ripped the air, splitting everything in half as it struck me. In that moment I saw my reflection in Hugo's eyes. For some reason that reflection was different than the one I saw in the mirror. That reflection held something that my eyes wouldn't normally see, hope.

Desperately reaching out, I tried to pull Hugo close but the moment my arms went through, desolation ruled me.

Darkness washed over my world as the electricity faded, leaving nothing but numbness. Falling, snagging, tumbling, skidding, it was all so fast it felt like it was happening at once. Was this the power of a King? I was far too unstable of a person to be crowned with that. King of the underdogs, what was I thinking? I wasn't fit to rule anything when I couldn't even rule myself.

I crashed into the ground, eyes blurring out as I stared upward at an ever-churning twilight sky.

> Shaking, I brought my arms up over my chest, hugging myself as the tears fell.

Hugo, how long was it going to take before I forgot what it felt like to hug you?

My crown, despite floating over my head, suddenly became heavy.

Chapter 4

GRIEF

I pushed Russel's pencil off his desk.

He groaned as he bent over in his seat and snatched it off the ground with a vengeance. Standing I took a few leisurely steps to the front of the class. Stopping behind the teacher, I watched him as he just about lost it.

"Russel, if you keep purposefully dropping your pencil to disturb class, I'm going to have to send you out."

"I'm not dropping it," he looked around, "it just keeps, like, falling."

A smirk crawled to my face as I stood directly behind the teacher and took a bit of chalk into my hand. After scribbling something unsavory on the board, I walked around his desk and waited for him to step to the side. When he did, the class tried desperately to choke their laughter back but it was useless. He spun around, looking for the culprit but of course he couldn't see me. Laughing with the rest of the class, I wondered if any of them would be laughing if they knew the cause was me.

"Sire, I do hate to interrupt," Oliver gestured to the board, "*this*, but you have things to attend to at Castle Boggle."

I walked back into the students, ignoring Oliver. One of the girls who spoke at my funeral had turned around in her seat to say something to the girl behind her. I looked to her paper that sat on her desk, her pencil next to it. After I glanced to her, I bent over and took her pencil in hand and wrote in three wrong answers. When I straightened, I knocked over Russel's pencil again. The teacher spun around and glared death Russel's way but he just shrugged, exasperated.

"What can you possibly get out of this?"

I walked past Oliver, continuing to ignore him as I knocked over the trash bin.

"Sire," He started to approach me as I sat down in my old, empty desk. "please talk to me. We can't move forward if you resentfully sit in silence."

"I'm not resentful." I said, eyes lazily on the board and not him, "I just can't see you, you're a ghost."

"You're a ghost, too, Sire."

"No, I'm a student." I leaned back in my chair. "And you're hindering my education."

Oliver sighed, running his hand through his fiery long side swept bangs. "I understand that you are experiencing the backlash of death, and I apologize that I wasn't more sensitive to it, but what's done is done and we need to return to Castle Boggle."

"No."

"Sire…"

"Whatcha gonna do?" I rolled my eyes to him, "Make me?"

He looked shocked, and rightfully so; I was being anything but cooperative.

Spiky silence sat between us, the air stale with my bad attitude. Oliver was just trying to do his job, and I did feel bad for treating him so poorly over it. But I never asked to be a King Candidate. Oliver leaned up against the wall, crossing his arms and dropping his eyes to the ground. I couldn't help but wonder, did he ask to be a Handler? Or was he just as forced in this situation as me?

Denial coursed through my veins as I went about my business, going to each class that I used to. I tripped Russel in the hallways, closed every locker I passed, knocked over every trash can, and slammed every door. The reactions were priceless. Oliver followed in pensive silence, Iris laughed along with me. My dial had been set to self destruction but the button had already been pushed. I was dead, there was nothing left to destroy.

Lunch period was upon us and Oliver appeared quite started by the sudden flooding of the hallways. He stayed close by my side as we stood off in one of the door nooks. This was all new to him, he died so long ago. I could only wonder what he thought as we walked along after the students cleared out. I had managed to control my visibility, so no one could see me, but I still was not chill with walking through living people so I stayed out of their way. We walked up to a door and with grit teeth, I fazed through it.

"You'll get used to it." Oliver said as I stood there, hand to my eye as my world spun.

I silently disagreed with him as I walked up to the lone table. Looking around the untouched room, I wasn't surprised. It had been a month or so since I died Flipside, though less time than that had passed for me. Although exactly how much time was unknown to me. There was no day night cycle on the other side and the clocks were always spinning, so I had no idea how anyone knew what time anything was and at that point I was too afraid to ask. It was a good thing Oliver kept track of all that for me.

"What is this place?" Iris asked, flying around and bringing up dust.

"Phantasmal." I sat down at the desk, not fazing through the chair. "This was my one-man paranormal research and investigative team." I spun around in the chair, "This is where I spent countless hours trying to find you guys."

Iris landed on the table in front of me, bringing up more dust, "I heard from the others that you were alone."

"Thank you, Iris…" I sighed as the chair spun to a stop.

Oliver quietly looked over my collection of books there, his eyes snagging on one occasionally. My mind drifted to the day he saw my phone, the amazement in his eyes. But something about that also angered me. Although I don't think it had anything to do with Oliver. I was noticing random flairs of internal anger a lot since my funeral, though I never acted upon them.

I couldn't, not after…

Hugo's sad smile, the little EMF in his hand.

Closing my eyes, I tried to chase the image away.

Oliver shivered, looking over to me suddenly. I jumped at the eye contact but quickly looked away, pretending that I hadn't noticed. He didn't say anything, though, as he went back to looking at the books.

Standing, I started out of the room again. I hated fazing through things, but I hated staying in one spot more. I was restless, antsy, to the point where I'd rather pace about the hallways than stay in my precious club room. Oliver followed behind, Iris goofing off somewhere near us. Oliver and I had barely spoken, Iris normally filled the silence with their ramblings.

Maybe it was the fact that I didn't sleep anymore, or maybe it was not eating, or not going to school, or not seeing my brother, or just overall being dead, but something was not right. I didn't trust myself to open my mouth much until the storm passed. I logically knew it wasn't Oliver's fault, that I did step in front of that car, and that some sort of fate existed. So really it was fate's fault that I was dead now and having that issue. But fate was really hard to blame.

"Sire, where are you going?" Oliver chased after me when he realized I had left the school building.

"None of your business."

I raced through the parking lot and up to a car. With a smile that cut me more than it cheered me up, I raised my hand to the car in front of me. There were perks of being a King Candidate. On my mental command, blue lighting like lights shot from my hand

and into three of the car's tiers, making them pop. Russel was going to have a grand time. I remembered thinking many times that I'd haunt his ass if I ever got the chance, I intended to keep that vow.

"Sire," Oliver stopped next to me, "what do you gain from this?"

I started out of the parking lot. "I think the better question here is, what do I lose from this?" He tried to stay by my side as I went down the sidewalk, "It's not like I have anything left to lose, Oli."

Oliver stayed quiet, which struck me oddly, but I didn't think on it much. I had another place on my list to visit. Traveling places by foot took no time at all, as if we jumped from place to place in the blink of an eye. Approaching the elementary school play yard, I fazed through the fence. They were outside at this time, and I knew where to look.

Running up to the play set, I saw a familiar mess of blonde hair. I knelt down, my heart sinking with me as I sat on the ground. There Hugo was, alone, under the play structure, stacking bark chips. Oliver kept his distance, but Iris came flying right up to my brother. I wanted to reach out to him, but I didn't. I wouldn't recover from my hand fazing through him again.

"For some reason he came off as the type to be surrounded by friends." Iris bobbed around Hugo, careful to not interfere with the bark chip stack.

"He is." I looked around. "He has lots of friends. Or, I thought he did. There was one in specific," I leaned up against the pole behind me, "he never stopped talking about him. But it looks like even he's gone now too."

Iris landed on Hugo's head. "If he's not careful, he's going to end up like you."

I swatted Iris off of his head, "If you're not careful, I'm going to banish you."

Looking back to Hugo, I sighed. I wanted nothing but the best for him and now I had messed it up. He leaned back with a deep breath, closing his eyes. When he did, I lifted up a bark chip and added it to his pile. When he opened his eyes again, he noticed and stared at the bark chips for a while.

Smiling, my eyes threatened to glass over.

I was there, right next to him, but he had no idea.

"Hey Hugo!" A voice called out from across the playground.

He looked up to see a herd of boys. As I watched them approach, the one Hugo always talked about wasn't there. I couldn't remember his name, but I'd never forget the way Hugo lit up when he told me about him. Watching the leader of the group stop before us, I did recgnoize him, his name was Colin. Hugo didn't have a moment to speak before the boy kicked over the bark chip structure.

White anger made my heart jolt as I slowly stood. The sky started to darken as my gaze rolled up to the kids.

"Why you look so scared, Hugo? Don't you have a ghost brother to protect you?" Colin said, kicking more bark chips toward Hugo. "You're both crazy. Maybe you should go jump in front of a car too."

Lightning snapped in the clear sky, making them all jump.

"Crazy?" I approached them. "Sure, but after this," I knelt down to be close to his eye level, though he couldn't hear or see me. "No one is going to believe you."

As if the sun was being engulfed by the glow of my crown, the world around us took on a blue tint. The kids looked about, getting closer together, as Hugo slowly stood. The swings moved on their own, the monkey bars swayed, the metal chairs that spun started to creak into motion. Slowly as the blue tint took over the area, the entire empty playground came to life.

Thunder rolled as my jaw clenched. This sort of power was too much for me to handle for long. I didn't want to lose it like before. If they got too out of hand, my powers would turn on me again.

Oliver didn't look at me and Iris flew behind him. I turned the world the same shade of blue that had taken me over. Hugo looked up to the sky, then around to the playground. It hurt when his eyes passed over me. I made lightning strike behind the group of boys, causing them to scream and run away.

Hugo stood there, thinking, I could see his little cogs churn. His calm was staggering, in great contrast to me. A few moments passed that way before he started onto the blacktop. I followed, calming down more with each step. I couldn't let myself lose my grip, the last thing I wanted was to hurt anybody. He approached the tether-ball post, tapping the floating ball gently. It started to slowly rotate around the pole, floating above where the string would have held it. He watched it spin around a few times before it wrapped all the way around the pole. I stared at the ball as it stopped and slowly raised my hand to it. Glancing to Hugo, I pushed the ball back the other way. I couldn't show myself to him, and I wasn't sure if I wanted him to know that I was there or not, but I didn't know what to do. If I did things like this too much, he would catch on and fall down the same rabbit hole I did. He had potential, he had promise, he had everything I never did and I didn't want him to lose that.

But…

He looked around then back up at the sun, his eyes suddenly tearing up.

I couldn't leave him behind.

"Hi," He took the ball into his hand, "why are you hiding?"

"I'm not hiding…" I looked down, he couldn't hear me.

Oliver walked up to my side for the first time in a while.

"Please.. Don't hide."

My gaze jumped to Hugo, the tears streaming down his face shocked me. I took a step toward him, wanting to do exactly what he asked, but then a hand snagged mine. Teeth grit, I turned to look back at Oliver as he shook his head, taking my hand.

"I'm sorry Sire, I know this must be hard but you have to think of the Boggle."

Anger snapped in my core, this time definitely cased by Oliver, as electricity cracked around us. Think of the Boggle over my little brother? The same Boggle who watched me beg for them to show themselves for years and never did, leaving me to be crushed by loneliness? I was about to lose it on Oliver, about to be ruled by my emotions and do something I'd probably regret, but then Hugo spoke.

"Kasper…" Hugo's voice cracked, "I hate you."

He threw the tether-ball forward as he ran away. Watching him, frozen for a moment, I had never seen Hugo act that way. Yanking my hand from Oliver and becoming totally visible, I ran forward but Hugo already had his back turned. I was going to call out to him, I was going to keep running, but then the tether-ball hit me in the side of the head. Dropping to my knees, holding my face in my hand, I looked up to see Hugo's back to me.

This is how it needed to be. I knew it, but I didn't want to accept it. Oliver walked around me, his eyes apathetic, his expression unchanging, as he extended his hand to me.

I stood, going transparent again as I brushed past him. "Think of the Boggle? This must be hard?" He followed me as I left the school yard. "Why the hell would I think of the Boggle when they let me spend years looking for them? You guys could have shown yourself, you weren't King Candidates. I bet it was funny, watching me search endlessly even though I had no real reason to." Oliver tried to speak but I rudely cut him off, "And yeah, dying is fucking hard to deal with. Not like you'd know, you've been dead forever. So don't even pretend to understand because I know you can't." I stopped suddenly, startling him as we stood before my mansion. "And you're incredibly fake, do you know that? Everything you say is some scripted response, like you're just doing a job."

"But Sire," he stood, brows raised, definitely missing my point, "looking after you is my job."

All I could do was groan, exasperated as I turned from him. Leaving Oliver there, I fazed through the bars of the gate and Iris followed me.

"I think you're being needlessly mean." Iris flew to my side as we fazed through the large mansion door. "It is Oliver's only job, to look after you. You shouldn't carelessly toss it aside like that."

Taking my hand from my mouth after beating the disorientation of fazing, I started up the stairs. "Neither of you understand at all. You don't have family members you left behind; your entire world wasn't uprooted. How would you feel if one day you were the creep in the back of the class and the next, you're expected to be some King person?"

Iris didn't reply.

I tried my best to not look up, I didn't want to risk seeing a picture of my family. Starting into the mansion library, I noticed that Oliver had followed us. I didn't spare him more than a glance before going into my study. After fazing through the wall and getting my bearings again, I was startled by sudden alarms. Looking around, I saw my equipment taken from its boxes, set about and turned on. Hugo must have done that.

With a roll of my eyes, I looked about at my precious equipment. "Now you work…"

"It always worked." Iris flew around, making some other things beep too. "And I think you're forgetting something Kasper. A Boggle did show themselves to you."

"Oh yeah?" I knelt down and turned off one of the alarmed machines and stared putting it away. "Which one?"

"Oliver."

Hand paused, left hovering above a lit up EMF detector, I stared at it. Iris was right, Oliver did show himself to me. I would never forget the first time I saw him.

"And then you went and obsessed over him for years like a creep. No wonder we were all afraid to meet you."

"It wasn't…creepy…" I put a few more things away. "And I wasn't obsessed."

Iris swiftly flew past the back wall, knocking loose a few sketch books. They fell open upon the ground, showing many failed attempts at drawing Oliver.

"What were you saying?" Iris landed on my desk.

I quickly gathered up the papers and shoved the books back. "It's not like it matters now, he's not at all what I was expecting."

"And what were you expecting?" Iris sat there as their endless black eyes watched me go about cleaning up the rest of my equipment.

"I don't know," I zipped up a bag, "but not an apathetic reserved servant."

"Did you forget that he was just shy?"

I stood to put something back in its place, "But it's not even a personable shy. He's just cold, closed off. It makes me uncomfortable, sort of like he's a babysitter just humoring me and that's frustrating."

"You're sort of acting like someone who needs to be babysat."

I stopped, leaning forward on my desk to look at Iris. "Is that any way to talk to your King?"

"You can't just selectively play the King card like that."

With a huff, I stepped back away from the desk and continued putting things away.

"You don't have a choice, you are our King. The choice lies in whether or not you are going to represent us with dignity and win the Almighty Crown." Iris flew up and around me. "What happened to that confidence you had at the start?"

I sighed sharply, shoving something back into a box. "That was before I…" images of the collision flashed through my mind, the hood ornament imbedded in my side burned into my eyes, "before this all became real."

"It is real, but it's really cool," Iris flew around some more, just bouncing about, "If you become the Almighty Boggle King you'd be the first, known for all eternity."

I stayed silent for a while, finishing up.

"We believe you can become that king. That's why we chose you, and that's why Oliver devotes his time to serve you." Iris landed on my shoulder, "Please don't be so hard on him. What you say is true, he is jaded. But how do you suppose he got that way?"

What Iris said made sense, and they were right. But at that time it was like a veil had fallen over my mind. I didn't feel like myself, as if there was something tugging on me in my mind. I remembered how I felt at first, how I was confident. Now it was real, now it was my life, and now things were different. I thought on how Oliver's hand felt in mine, his fingers laced in my hair made me shiver, how his eyes made my core jump, but for some reason I was internally still.

It was as if that lightning had taken something away from me, leaving me broken and hollow.

I knelt down and picked one last thing up, my protest sign.

"Ghosts are good…" I took a deep breath, "And Oliver is a ghost." Holding the sign tightly, I tried to wrap my head around it all again but for some reason I couldn't. The fact that I was dead was very real, but the possibility of me becoming something more? Now that was still beyond me. And the fact that Iris, Oliver, and the others somehow saw something in me that I couldn't was even more out of my reach. How could anything see something in me?

My eyes lingered on the camera that I had just put back in its place. After walking up to it, I thought on how much Oliver liked my phone. Taking the camera out of its case, I looked it over before pocketing it. His obvious wonderment at something so trivial to me hung on in my mind. I wanted to feel the things I did before, admire his coldness, laugh at his reserved tone. I wanted to want to make him laugh but those thing all felt dull now. It was in

"No, I'm dead."

"Kasper?"

Jumping, I looked to Less. His gaze was unmoving.

"I thought I felt something off." He started to approach, slowly, as his eyes rose from mine to my crown. After he stared for a moment, his gaze rolled over to Oliver who, in a brief display of emotion, appeared shocked too. Les smiled at me, taking to one knee and bowing his head. "I always knew there was a King's heart beating in your chest, Master Kasper."

I looked to Oliver, Oliver looked to me. We stared at each other.

"You can see me?"

Les nodded, looking up to me, "I've always been able to, even when you weren't dead." He stood, "You remember that heart attack I had three years ago, yes?" His eyes grazed over to Iris, "Ever since then, I knew you were right." He looked back to me. "Young Master Hugo will be delighted to-"

"Do not tell him." Les stared at me, everyone stared at me, "Never tell him that I'm a ghost, never tell him that I was right. Because even if you know, even if he knows, the others won't believe him. He'll end up like me. Please guide him toward the things our parents have planned for him, that's his best chance in life."

Les looked heartbroken, "But Master Kasper, ending up like you isn't bad."

I didn't mean to laugh, "Really? Because the last time I checked, I stepped out in front of a car while looking for ghosts and died."

Les stood in silence.

"Please," a deep breath took me as I ran my hand through my hair, "I just want Hugo to be happy."

He looked away from me, "I will do as you wish, but I believe your self assessment is vastly incorrect." He forced his eyes back to mine. "I need to attend to the house before Young Master Hugo returns. But I must say," a smile took over his face, "you look stunning under a crown."

Scoffing as I started down the stairs, I didn't look back as I fazed through the door. Cursing under my breath as I stumbled to the side, I leaned up against the door with my hands to my face. Les had known, too, and didn't tell me? It must have been a game to everyone except me. I poured my heart into looking for proof, for finding the good ghosts I believed in. It must have been entertaining, that's the only reason I could fathom that I was kept in the dark.

It was only a matter of moments before we arrived at the movie theater. Iris giggled in the background as I stepped between the line of people waiting to buy a ticket. Sign thrown over my shoulder, I scanned the movie showings. Four theaters were showing ghost movies that night, horrible misrepresentations of an entire group of beings we had no understanding of. It was near Halloween, so those movies were rampant.

Fazing through the door, I held my hand to my mouth as I stormed down the theater hall. I was going to put an end to this.

"Oli?"

Oliver quickened his pace to end up at my side. "Yes Sire?"

"Can I like, curse things?"

"Curse?" A beat passed as he struggled to stay at my side, "As in what a witch would do?"

"Yes."

"Unless you're a witch, then I don't believe so. Though," another weird beat passed, "I have never tried."

Frustrated breath escaping through my clenched teeth, I stopped in front of the theater door. If I couldn't curse shit, then how was I going to get my point across? Looking up to the sign as the letters scrolled by, I handed my sign to Oliver.

"Wait," I started toward the door, fazing through it and walking down the darkened hall, "if I had to ask you that, that means that no living person knows if ghosts can curse things either." Shaking off the nausea, I entered the theater, "So, if they think I did, will they really risk defying it?"

"Don't underestimate the folly of man, Sire." Oliver followed me up the stairs past the movie audience.

A stupid ghost movie was playing, loud and obnoxious, on the screen. Making it to the top of the stairs, I was left facing the wall that led to the projector room as a blood curdling scream took over the theater. Turning, I saw Oliver standing there, hand up to his mouth, eyes were locked to the movie. I guess a movie would be amazing to someone like him.

With a deep breath, I fazed through the wall. Falling to my knees, dizzy, on the other side, I stayed there for a few moments. Doors or bars were one thing, but entire walls were terribly hard. Looking up, I saw the camera and computer it was plugged into. Standing, I walked up to it and looked it over. I would just have to fry the camera to stop the movie, but that wouldn't send a message. I couldn't show myself, but Oliver said nothing about typing.

Probably because he didn't know it was a thing, but I was willing to exploit that.

Taking mouse in hand, I clicked around until I stopped the movie. The screen went white as I opened up a writing document. With each letter I typed, I felt the electricity in the computer interacting with my fingertips, shocking me a little. It made the screen jump, static out, as I typed on, watching the words project through the little window. My message was simple, my curse, final.

Dear Blazing Star,

Go ahead, play another stupid ghost movie here.

I dare you.

-Kasper.

I let that message sit on the glitching screen for a few moments, long enough for people to take pictures. Then, with a wave of my hand, I fried the projector. My current went through the cord, into the outlet, then through the entire theater blowing up every light, destroying every projector, and taking out power to the entire area.

Screams echoed from the theater as I fazed through the wall again. I was able to enjoy that for all of two seconds before dizziness took me to my knees. Looking up, I ignored Oliver's extend hand as I stood from the ground and walked out of the theater. Silence sat heavy between all of us as I stormed down the hall and toward the front door. Fazing through the glass door, I could hear the whispers of everyone in line as they looked up at the fried display screens.

    Taking my sign back from Oliver, I perhaps ripped it away with too much force. Walking up to where I used to protest, I set my sign down. Standing there, I was faced with the motto of my life. Ghosts are good. I was a ghost, so maybe it wasn't as true as I wanted it to be. Raising my other hand to the sky, the world began to darken. Clouds swirling about, the wind whipped my hair as a rumble grew in the sky. Bringing my hand down, lighting snapped from above, striking the sign. Screams exploded from behind me as the people waiting in line fell away from the sparks. When the light faded, my sign was left, standing there for all to see. Reaching back out to it, I jumped back when it shocked me. Shaking my hand, I was content. No one would be able to remove it, keeping my message there forever.

    Looking over the people, I smiled a bit at their wonder as I walked away. Oliver and Iris said nothing as we continued on. That was my final message to the town that made me feel so insignificant. I didn't really think on where I was going, I just ended up at the cemetery again.

Gaston stood from atop the headstone he always sat on and waved, jumping off. "Hey!" He bowed to me as I approached. "I saw your storm brewing a couple times. Causing issue are we, Sire?"

"I don't believe that's your place to ask, Guardian." Oliver spoke before I could.

Standing there, eyes down on the tear soaked grass, I wasn't sure what had compelled me to come here. It was where I gravitated toward when things were hard, someone to talk to. But now, that person could do more than just listen.

"Hey, Mr. Knight." Gaston said, each step of his causing the grass to glisten under his shoes, his eyes unmoving from me. "How about you go be useful somewhere else for a while. I want to talk with Kasper."

"I don't feel comfortable leaving him alo-" Oliver was cut off by Iris flying into his face.

"I'm going to cause problems!" Iris laughed, flying away. "Better come stop me!"

With a long sigh, Oliver turned away from us and chased after Iris. Gaston smiled at me, a light about him that I hadn't noticed before. He reminded me of something, but I couldn't quite place my finger on it.

He hopped up onto his headstone that he perched on and tapped the area next to him. I walked up and leaned against it, not sitting on it. I didn't feel as if I possessed the balance required for that and I had no idea how he did it.

"Rough go so far?"

I nodded.

"It gets easier. And I know that's easy for me to tell you and hard for you to take, but it's true. Grief will run its course, though, and you'll come out on top."

"Grief?" I looked over to him. "Why would that-"

"The dead grieve, too."

I stared at him, as if the world stopped for a moment. In that second of pause, I could have sworn I saw something glint above his head. But when I brought up my eyes to look, nothing was there.

"Not only did everyone who loved you, lose you. You, in a way, have lost them too. You lost the life you had, the routine you lived in, all very unexpectedly. I know you, Kasper, you've spent many nights here with me. And I know the person you are right now isn't him. But that's to be expected, grief does that to people. And it'll be okay, it really will be. Not now, not even tomorrow, but I promise you, it will be. And you know what will help that process? Not shutting everything out." He looked up into the distance where Oliver was expressively arguing with Iris out of earshot. "Mr. Knight is a good guy, he's just dense."

He was right. Bringing my hand up to my chest, the ache was there, but it was empty. Grief, that thought had never even crossed my mind. That's why nothing meant anything, why things felt dull, why my personality was wiped. I had seen tons of movies and shows about people after they die and there was something they rarely covered. How hard it was to die. Having him acknowledge it, having him notice and address it so boldly yet kindly, calmed me.

"Why do you call him Mr. Knight?" I was embarrassed at how soft my voice had become.

"Well, he did earn the title. Might as well use it." He smiled when I looked to him. "We all have a story, Kasper. Why do you think you two are stuck here? You're not Earthbound, you didn't choose this afterlife." He looked back to the sky a few moments later, "It's hard to get along with a stranger, sometimes it's even hard to get along with an acquaintance. The only people you won't get along with are those you don't know well enough. And if you've tried to get to know them and still don't like them, then you haven't tried hard enough."

I had to do my best to not be captivated by him, something about his light was too much. "You're an angel."

He laughed quietly, "Oh, am I?"

A beat passed.

"So do you know what you need to do, Kasper?" His gaze drifted back to Oliver. "You're hurting right now, but you're not going to get through this alone. I know that you and Mr. Knight don't get along very well right now, but what reason do you have to get along? I doubt you know anything substantial about him, the same goes the other way. No matter how you feel about it now, you're going to be stuck with him for a *very* long time, so I suggest you start to get to know each other." He leaned forward a little, a smile on his face. "I also know you find him very attractive, so bonus points."

I pushed myself up from the headstone with a huff, "No wonder you're chained to this place. If they let you loose, you'd preach everyone's ears off."

"This is true." Gaston laughed, effortlessly standing atop the headstone, as if he weighed nothing. "But there are other reasons that I'm here. You just don't know them because you don't know me well enough yet, either." He leaned down, becoming eye level with me as he impossibly balanced on the headstone. "Now go on, Sire. You're stuck in the middle of a deep and dark lake, but," He gently put his hand on my shoulder, turning me to the side slightly so that my gaze was right on Oliver. "your paddle is in sight. Now go get yourself out of the water so that you can get used to standing on land again. Only then will you be able to do that crown of yours justice."

He pushed me forward and begrudgingly, I continued on. I didn't look back at Gaston, though I felt like if I did, I'd see him smiling at me. My eyes refused to leave the ground as I approached Oliver and Iris, both of which had fallen silent. I stopped a few steps away from them before forcing myself to look up.

"Hey…"

"Hello Sire, are you alright?"

I stared at Oliver in slight disbelief. Who even spoke like that? Averting my eyes, I saw Gaston smirking at me in the background. Annoyance pumped through me as I looked back at Oliver. "Want to go for a walk?"

Iris, without a word, bobbed along through the air toward Gaston, leaving just Oliver and I. For a brief moment, it appeared that Oliver wanted to protest Iris leaving but stopped himself. His eyes jumped back at me for a pause before he replied.

"Of course, whatever is your desire, Sire."

That sent a shiver of discomfort through my spine. I think I found the one sentence in the entire universe that I hated most. The way the rhyme sounded in the rumble of his voice was enough to make my skin crawl. "I really don't like being called Sire."

He put his hands in his pockets as we walked into the park that was next to the cemetery. "But it is the proper thing to call someone of your status in our society."

"It makes you feel so distant. My name is Kasper."

"I know your name…"

Oliver fell quiet as we walked along and the silence cut, making it hard to breathe. I couldn't do this, interacting with him was too hard. I felt like I was in a box made of his reserved air, the hollow respect, the empty tones. He was too formal, too stiff, and it scared me.

I nearly jumped when he sighed, it startled me so badly.

"I'm sorry. I'm not good at this whole casual thing."

I stopped walking, eyes wide on him as he stopped too.

He didn't look up to me as he spoke on. "Where I came from, titles are highly revered and hold a lot of weight."

My heart started to quicken, eyes locked on him. It was the first time he'd broken character and as I stood there, I wanted to see what was underneath.

"Gaston said that you were a Knight?"

He looked up to me, over to the direction of the cemetery, then back at me. "I was, yes." His eyes fell away from mine, "Was being the key word, there." He paused. "I have failed as your usher into the land of the dead, I'm sorry. I spent so much time preparing for this and still fell short. I feel as if full disclosure is needed. I haven't given you a single reason to like or trust me, of course you'd be angered by me."

"You don't..." I looked away, "anger me. You just...scare me." He was silent as I started to walk again and he followed, "This all scares me. Being dead, when time passes weirdly, this crown above my head, the powers I now have, the fact that I was right. It feels like too much, like it's all swarming me at once and I'm the only one. This is normal to you now, you knew this was coming, you were preparing, but this is all new to me. And when you treat me so," I forced myself to look at him, "coldly, it just makes me feel more alone in this."

Stopping, far out of the view of Gaston's perch, I leaned up against a tree. Something was starting to slip inside, and I wasn't sure what I'd fall into once it lost its grip. I felt pathetic, angry, sad and scared and I didn't know what to do. It was like there was a dissonance in my mind. I wanted to have the confidence I started out with, I wanted to be the person I thought I could be, but the dark haze in my mind wouldn't let me see the light.

"I don't mean to be cold. I just don't know how to not be." I was surprised by the emotion in his voice. It was something I had never heard before, "I thought we were getting along but then suddenly everything I did was wrong and I'm sorry." He bowed his head, "I've never been a good servant, though I have tried all my life." He took a deep breath, unable to look up to me. "Hold onto those emotions, no matter how unpleasant they are, because after a while, it's going to become hard to feel anything anymore."

For the first time in what felt like days, I felt my heart jump. There he stood before me, more human than I had seen him before. Was that what unsettled me about him, that he was numb?

"Once, a long time ago, when I was alive." He started, turning his back to me, "I was a Holy Knight, the top of my kingdom. The personal choice of protection of the royal family, we were in war time and the kingdom was torn. I had a family, but I left them to lead the army and well," His shoulders dropped, "I highly overestimated my abilities. But before I was slain, my hands were not without blood. So many men fell to me, I've never been able to count them all. Because of that, I was assigned to the

Demon Faction. A place for rotten humans, people so evil that the only place for them is hell."

I stood, my heart chilled to the point of stopping, "What did you say your full name was again?"

He turned slightly, looking at me with glassy eyes, "I don't believe I ever gave it to you." He turned to face me fully, dropping to a knee and bringing his hand to his heart, "Knight Oliver Vestile, The Great, at your service, Sire."

My world shuttered as he knelt before me. History lessons flashed behind my eyes as his name rang through my ears. I did know about him, he left a gouge in history so large he was often thought to be a legend. A Knight of such dark power and heartlessness, he and his army pillaged across all of Europe. He was depicted as a man of huge stature, not a slender young man with fiery hair and ghostly eyes. To this day, it was unknown what force was strong enough to kill him. My first reaction was to step away from him, to put distance between us, but I didn't. Because, even though his reputation proceeded him, he did not seem like the monster of legend any longer.

"Why…"

"Why what, Sire?" He looked down to the ground, remaining on his knee.

"Why did you leave? You must have been a big deal to the Demons, you could have even been king. But to join the Boggle? They must have nothing to offer you. I know you said you were convinced, but by what?"

He slowly stood, his eyes staying on the ground. "The last Boggle King." He looked to me. "The Boggle King before you changed my ways and brought me to their side. They gave me one job upon their defeat, and that was to look after the next and help them become the Almighty Ghost King. That way maybe we could bring a little more whimsical mystery to the world instead of sadness and taint." He turned from me again, "And so far I've done a fantastic job at failing both of you."

I had been reading him wrong. Why had I been reading him wrong? I started to feel the haze of bitterness in my mind raise, allowing me to step back from my mental storm. He was cold because he never knew warmth, he was rigid because he's lived on high alert, he came from a different time and place and now we were clashing because of that. And for me, it would be far easier to understand him because I had the power of looking backwards. For him, it would be far harder. I lived in a world of inconceivable magics and views comparatively.

Suddenly the off kilter air around us hit the ground with my heart. I couldn't bare the thought of those magically blue eyes covered in tears. Clenching my jaw as something new tore through me, an internal tension broke. I didn't have the will to fight the tears that wished to take me over. I was such a mess, there was no way I could become a King. Sliding down the tree I was leaning on, I sat on the ground and buried my face in my hands.

"Sire-"

I tried to hide that I was losing it but there was no stopping it. With every sharp breath, every quiver of my shoulders, I felt my mind's clutter clear. Oliver sat down next to me after a moment and that was startling, but what made my breath hitch was when he gently laced his arm around me. Looking up to him, I was frozen by those eyes. The fact that they made my heart jolt again was enough to convince me of something.

If I was able to see them for all eternity, then living forever wasn't that bad.

"They told me that someday the next Boggle King would rise. They said that when they did, it was my job to protect them. So I've trained, thought of every possible issue, and came up with a battle strategy to assure their victory. But I never once thought that I'd have to protect them from themselves." His grip tightened on me, "The others told me about you. About your bold front, your charismatic smile, your undying loyalty and faith in us. I'd eagerly wait for their return so they'd tell me more. So I apologize if I expected something a little different at first when you finally joined us."

I could barely speak but managed to say, "I'm sorry I wasn't what you wanted."

"No," He shook his head, "you're better." His soft smile made my core melt. "You're exactly what the others aren't. You so vastly different than expectation that you may just be a force great enough to change this. We're playing a broken game in a rusty system, and after observing it as long as I have, I think it's time for a change. So when I say that you're not what we were expecting, Kasper, I mean that you are exactly what we need."

The way he said my name made the world stop. I actually felt the rotation of the planet still, the warmth in his voice was otherworldly. Every moment my eyes were locked on his, I felt my world start to come back into focus. It had been blurry, tainted by a grief ridden haze that aimed to drown me in the middle of the lake. But here I was, paddle at my side. And I knew that not everything was fine and it was still going to be hard, but the strength in his grip made me feel like the day that it would be okay was actually in sight.

"Thank you." I leaned back into the tree, looking forward. "But that sort of faith scares me, too. How can you be so sure that I'll live up to that? That I can actually change anything? You're saying that I'm all these great things and I don't see your proof." I gathered myself some, "I mean, if the previous Boggle King who sounds so wise and kind, was defeated, what chance do I stand?"

"They weren't defeated," He leaned his head back into the tree, too, "they gave up." After a moment of pause he rolled his head to the side to look at me, "And that's something you don't do."

Our faces were very close but I didn't care, I was too busy being trapped in his eyes. I wondered what he'd think of me if he knew the way his eyes made my heart race. From the time he was from, those sort of feeling would get you killed. That thought slowed my heart.

"How do you know I won't give up?"

"You haven't yet."

"Yeah, well…" I smiled a little, "Don't underestimate the folly of man, Oliver."

I will never forget the first time I heard Oliver laugh.

The sky around us became painted in deep reds and light yellows as the sun set.

I wanted to force myself to look away, to rip my eyes from his, but I couldn't. I was trapped, defeated by his smile. His laugh was so kind, soft, shy, it was the sweetest thing I had ever heard. That was a good word to describe what I had observed about Oliver, he was very sweet. Though his cold exterior would aim to show otherwise. He was just from an entirely different culture than me, one where someone like him wasn't allowed to show what was underneath.

I still didn't know much about Oliver, but Gaston was right. I simply didn't know him well enough. Looking away, I couldn't tame my smile. The smile felt so good, like it brought my spirits up with it. I shifted my weight a little and took the camera out of my pocket.

"This is for you," I handed it to Oliver and he took it with the hand that wasn't wrapped around me, "It's better than the other camera you were using. This one even works in little light so you can take pictures of things like the sunset."

He stared at it, "Witchcraft."

I smiled as I turned it on for him. His eyes lit up as the welcome screen appeared and he sat there, frozen, as I chose a few options to make it work in the low light that we were in.

"Alright, it should work now."

He looked between me and the camera, "This is advanced witchcraft."

"It is," I shoved him up and followed as I stood, "now go on, the sunset isn't going to last forever."

He seemed rather surprised then utterly confused as he stared at the camera.

I laughed a little as I stood up behind him, moving his hand up to the button on the top. "You're going to press here, but first," I moved his arms to situate the camera's view on the sunset, "there." I stood there, my hand on his, my heart beating a little faster than I'd like to admit, as I helped him press down the button. I stepped away when I realized I was very comfortable that close to him.

He looked at the camera in his hands then slowly turned it around it look at the front. A few moments later, he stepped back next to me and held it up. After a slight struggle, he pressed the capture button. He turned the camera back around and after testing out a few buttons, he managed to pull up the picture he just took.

"I don't know what you were expecting." I said with a laugh when I saw that there was just a tree in the picture and we didn't show up.

"When you look at this next, you'll remember this moment, correct?" I nodded as he took another picture of the sunset. "Then that's all that matters."

I watched him snap a few more pictures, totally beside myself. He was such a sweetie, I couldn't even imagine him slaughtering thousands.

He took a few more pictures before turning and taking one of me, that I wouldn't appear in, but it was the thought that counted. "Thank you for this, Sire, I truly do find it astounding. Are there other forms of witchcraft that I was absent during the birth of?"

It took me a moment to realize what he had asked. I wondered if I'd ever get used to the odd way he worded things. "There's endless forms of witchcraft now, and I wouldn't mind showing you them. I could even make those pictures you took appear on paper to be hung in the castle."

"Like a painting?"

I smiled, "Yeah, but instant."

He looked to the camera, whispering to himself. "Witchcraft." After a few moments, he put the camera into his pocket and looked back to me. "I feel as if we got off to a rushed and clumsy start." He got down on one knee again, bringing his hand to his heart and bowing his head. "King Kasper, allow me to serve you and aid you in your rise to the Almighty Throne of Ghost King."

I looked down at him, a little startled at how easy it was for him to bow to me when I felt as if I didn't deserve it. With a smile, I bent over and took his hand in mine. Yanking him to his feet, I didn't let go of his hand. "If I'm going to do this, I can't do it alone. But I can't do it with a servant, or even a Handler, either. If I'm going to become what the Boggle think I can be, I'm going to need a friend." I ruffled his hair with my other hand, "And friends don't bow to each other, they stand on even ground."

The sun set.

Oliver stared at me, eyes wide and glowing, hair slightly messed up, hand in mine. And in that moment of pause, I could only wonder what was going on in his mind. It was like I broke him.

"A…friend?"

I nodded.

"I've never…" He looked away, his voice shaking as if I had sent him off balance. "had one before."

"Well then I'll be honored to be your first."

"You? Honored?" He looked back to me, "No Sire, it is I that holds the honor."

He stared at me when I laughed.

Talking became easier with each step as we walked along.

"You've never had a hamburger before?" I asked as we walked back toward the cemetery.

"I don't even know what that is."

Looking over to him as the night sky framed his colorful features, I couldn't look away, "Dude, I have so much to show you."

"What does the word dude mean? Are you addressing me by it?" He took a picture of a passing car as we stood on the side of the street.

"Don't worry about it." We crossed the street and I couldn't wipe the smile from my face.

We walked into the cemetery and saw that Iris and Gaston were chatting it up, but as we got closer I could overhear their conversation.

"I give it a week."

Gaston gasped, "That quickly? I think it'll take longer than that."

"They are hotblooded young men, how long do you think they're willing to wait? And I can assure you that Kasper has never seen any action and if Oliver ever did, it was hundreds of years ago. I bet they're both-"

I hit Iris out of the air. Oliver and Gaston stared at me, Gaston far more amused than Oliver who was probably confused. I was very happy that Oliver was so old he probably wouldn't understand what they were talking about.

"Oh hey, where did you two come from-" I cut Gaston off by shoving him from the headstone he was perching on. I wanted the satisfaction of seeing him hit the ground but he floated back up to his place.

"...Sire?" Oliver asked slowly, looking between the three of us.

Gaston's grin made me roll my eyes away, trying not to smile too.

Iris giggled, flying around us. "Remember when you asked about why there was a bed in your room? There are plenty of other things one can do in a bed," they landed on my shoulder, "than sleep."

I shoved them off of me and back into the air. After a moment of quelling my annoyance, I looked back to Gaston. "Alright, I think I got my paddle and I'm on my way out of the lake. What next?"

Gaston jumped gracefully from his perch and stood before me with a classy smile, his thin glasses shimmering, "Now Sire, you conquer." He lifted his hand up to my crown and when he tapped it, it jingled and lit up. As if light entered my blood stream, I felt like my pain was being lifted away. "Normally we are a faction of a neutral standing, just like our counterparts, but I think it's time for a change." Oliver gaped as Gaston eloquently bowed to me, a white light glowing from my crown. "With the blessing bestowed upon you by I, the King of the Angel faction, go forth King Kasper. Show the world that ghosts truly are," he looked up to me, "good."

A bright light flashed and the world around me went white for a moment. Standing before me was Gaston, straightening from the bow. In that bleached second I saw them, glorious white wings and a sparkling golden halo. When the moment passed, I was left staring. He simply winked at me with a smile. Taking my crown from my head, I was awestruck by the new gem. A feather sat inside, golden, surrounded by the white gem. Though the inside looked anything but solid as the light churned around, making the feather slowly dance. Oliver leaned over and looked at the gem too, the light reflecting off of his glowing eyes. Letting go of my crown, it floated up, returning to its place over my head.

With a renewed strength in my core, I turned to Oliver. "We have one last stop before we go back to Castle Boggle." I took him by the hand and started dragging him behind me. With a wave to Gaston, we ran off.

"I thought you were ready to return, Sire." Oliver did his best to keep up and not stumble, his coat tails flailing out behind him.

"I am but I just need to grab a printer."

"What is a printer?"

I laughed, rounding a corner, Gaston waving back in the distance. "Witchcraft!"

Chapter 5

EARTHBOUND

"Sire..." Oliver's whine caught my ear from the other room, "I think I slayed it."

With a smile, I stood from my desk where I was reading an ancient ghost text and walked next door to Oliver's room. "Slayed what?"

He looked up to me over the laptop I had brought from my house. "This."

I walked around his desk to his side to see that it had gone to sleep due to inactivity. With a tap on the track pad, it flashed to life.

Oliver jumped, looking back to me with a smile. "You have the magic touch, as always."

"You give me too much credit." I smiled as I straightened and leaned against the wall. "Learn anything yet?"

He turned back to the computer, "I discovered that if you press this," he touched the brightness button, "it changes the time of day." I watched him make the screen brighter and then darker again.

He turned back to me, a look of pride on his face until I couldn't hold it back anymore and lost it laughing.

"You know Sire…" He stood, his tone flat as he crossed his arms and approached me, "Methinks you're playing a sadistic game here."

I could barely speak through my laughter, "What would make you think that?"

"Oh nothing." He leaned a little closer. "Just you wait, we'll be out of your element soon enough."

"Is that a threat?" I caught my breath, raising a brow to him.

"And if it is?"

"Then I'd say you're a brave soul, having the audacity to challenge your King."

He turned away from me but I saw the smile he flashed before he did, "You are my King, yes, but you're also my friend," He turned to look at me slightly, "Kasper."

My heart jumped.

I was going to reply but then Iris flew into the room. "Is it official yet?"

"Is what-"

I cut Oliver off. "Stop shipping us, Iris."

"Shipping?" Oliver asked.

"Just," I sighed, smiling at him, "don't worry about it." My eyes rolled back to Iris. "What?"

After a few giggles, Iris landed on my shoulder. "The Earthbound have sent a formal invitation to their ball."

Oliver went stiff, "When?"

"Today."

His eyes jumped to me quickly. "Follow me, Sire." And with that, he walked out of the room.

Startled, I quickly followed. "What's so bad about this? I don't understand."

"It wouldn't be so bad if you had any social skills or tact whatsoever, Sire."

"You can't just add 'Sire' to the end of an insult like that and make it okay."

He turned a corner and I struggled to keep up with him as he went on, "The Earthbound are all about manners and class. This sort of event is important."

"Why though? Can't I just stand in the back and-"

"No." He stopped in front of a door and I almost ran into him. He opened the door that I had never seen before and walked inside. I followed him and was amazed to see a huge closet brimming with formal clothing. I wanted to turn and run in that moment but Iris flew from my shoulder and closed the door.

"There's no getting out of this, Sire."

Oliver shifted through some suits, "The Boggle is right for once." he pulled a couple out. "You can't just hide, this is them sizing you up." he held a suit up to me, "Think about it, if you win the Almighty Crown, you're going to need all the factions to like you to avoid uprising." He shook his head, holding up the other suit.

I wasn't sure how I felt about him looking at me so intently, I was scared he'd notice my face going red. "But if I'm the King, won't they have no choice but to follow me?"

He pulled out another suit after putting those two back. "You may be able to shoot some lightning and blow people's hair around, but do you really want to face an insubordinate Poltergeist?"

That thought sent a visible shiver through me.

"Exactly." He held up another suit. "Before the King trials even begin, you're going to have to present correctly to the other factions so that they will take comfort in you. Of course they will still root for their own candidate, but you want them to be at least somewhat satisfied with you if you win. The last thing you need is to send the Kingdom into turmoil upon your victory."

He dug around for another suit after hanging those up.

"Sadly you're at a disadvantage, being one of us." Iris said as they continued to guard the door. "So you're going to have to be on your best behavior."

"When am I not?"

Oliver and Iris paused, staring at me.

I just smiled at them.

Oliver continued his search. "I mean it, Sire. You mess this up, you can expect an uprising later." He smiled when he held up another suit then shoved it toward me. "There's a changing area over there, I'll wait here with the Boggle."

Holding the suit close, I muddled my way to the changing area. This was my castle and I didn't even know my way around. Although I really did hate the castle, or any castle. They reminded me of home.

How long had I been dead? It must have been a couple months or so Flipside. But since the passage of time here was different, I couldn't really tell how much time had passed me. It didn't feel like very long but at the same time, it could have been. The endless hours were spent making food that we didn't need to eat so that I could show Oliver modern wonders of cooking, exploring the castle's massive library and learning more about the history and structure of the ghost realm, watching Oliver struggle to fathom the technologies I brought back from Flipside, and slowly but surely admiring his eyes a little more every time I saw them.

Iris knew, Gaston knew, but they didn't even know the half of it. Oliver was nothing like I excepted, but he did have one commonality with the ghost boy I obsessed over. He was undoubtedly kind. It showed itself in funny ways, though. Behind every scold was a worried warning, under every 'Sire' was a

'Kasper', and his stare was my favorite. I had only managed to earn that stare a few times, as if his mind had disconnected for a moment because I had startled him so greatly. It was when he was at a loss that I saw the churning in his eyes, as if he was trying to figure me out. But the reason it was my favorite was because without fail, when his expression changed, it turned to soft laughter.

I looked at myself in the mirror of the changing area as I took off my shirt. The crown atop my head now had the golden white wispy gem in it, representing the Angel's allegiance to me. I hadn't interacted with any other factions since then, so none of them knew that I had earned a previously neutral faction's loyalty.

I hadn't seen Hugo since he ran away from me at the school. Every time my mind wanted to dwell on it, I felt my heart shutter. But I knew it was for the best, it had to be. Les would steer him the right way, he would make sure Hugo would reach his potential. No matter what, Hugo had to be different than me, he just had to be.

Struggling with the suit, I did not want to admit defeat.

"Sire," Oliver drawled, "having issues?"

"No." I called back through clenched teeth as I fought with a button. I had no idea how Oliver did that, but he somehow always was right on the mark when it came to what I was feeling, as if he could feel it too.

"Oh? Then you won't mind my coming back there then?" I could hear his voice growing closer with each word.

Embarrassment flushed through my system when Oliver rounded the corner, a smile on his face. He looked me up and down as he approached, making my pulse skyrocket as I stepped back. Iris flew up behind him as he stopped in front of me.

"Has my King been defeated by buttons?"

I looked down to my poorly buttoned dress shirt, annoyed. I only ever owned one button down shirt and it belonged with that suit I wore all of two times, both of which I was able to pull my coat over to hide my crappy buttoning skills. It was way harder than it looked. The buttons were so small and I had like no dexterity and if I messed one up, they were all out of line, and it was just…frustrating.

Oliver chuckled as I averted my eyes. "You know, Sire," He started to unbutton my shirt, "you are far too old to be lacking in the dressing yourself department."

I could not look at him as he unbuttoned my shirt, one button at a time, without a single issue.

Iris giggled as they flew away, "Well I'll give you two some space…"

I wanted to yell at them, to tell them to get back here and to stop insinuating weird things, but they were long gone before the thought even processed in my mind. Holding my breath, the silence between us grew heavy. Oliver was a presence like no other, so refined yet innocent, knowledgeable but clueless. He knew the ins and outs of the society we lived in but the moment Iris said something dirty, he had no idea what was going on. It was precious, really, and I felt very inconsiderate being so attracted to him. But how could I not be? My eyes slowly drifted to his. Who wouldn't be attracted to eyes whose churning told a story of their own. His glowing blue iris' were enough to keep me captivated for an eternity.

It was funny, the more time I spent in that realm, the more solid everyone looked. Before we were all slightly translucent but now just about everything looked as normal as the living. Oliver stood at nearly six foot, just a little taller than me, and that made moments like that one very hard.

"Is something the matter?"

I shook my head, looking away from his eyes.

He smiled a little as he spoke softly, "I understand if you're nervous. But I believe in you. And I won't leave your side so you really don't have anything to worry about."

He was totally right, I should be nervous for the upcoming crucial social event. But there I was, the biggest issue in my world was the lack of physical distance between us. I had shitty priories.

Every thought jolted from my mind when his hand brushed up against my bare chest.

I grit my teeth, keeping myself still. His touch burned with cold but was warm at the same time and I had no idea how. I wanted to think that he did that on purpose and was meanly teasing me to get back at me for something, but he wasn't intimately advanced enough to be that sadistic. He was just going about his business, doing his job, taking care of an incompetent King Candidate. To him that's all this was, there was no way he could have known it was far more to me.

He reached the top button and paused before buttoning it. His eyes jumped to mine, startling me. He stared into my eyes, as if looking for some sort of answer, before turning away from me. I stood there, paralyzed. What was that about? I could feel my heartbeats bleed into one continuous one as I tried to take a breath. This was getting bad, really bad. I had never experienced attraction before, and it was a potent thing to recon with.

He quickly returned with a tie and held it up. "This matches your eyes nicely."

"My eyes?" I was quiet as he popped my collar.

"Yes, the color." He put my collar down and pulled the tie down my front.

I stood there, eyes on the wall, thinking hard. The color of my eyes? I glanced down to the tie to see that it was silver. That couldn't be right. Leaning back a little as Oliver tied my tie, I looked at myself in the mirror. I was so startled that I lost my footing momentarily and went backwards into the wall. What the hell? Since when were my eyes grey? It was like shredded silver had been placed in my iris', catching the light and trapping the shadows. I couldn't even remember my eye color, but it was safe to assume that it was brown like Hugo's. What happened?

Oliver fell over with me and a moment later, he was basically pinning me to the wall, hand on my tie. I stared at him, barely able to focus on his eyes he was so close.

"Get spooked by your own reflection, Sire?"

His voice was so soft yet overflowing with mockery. I wanted to hate that tone, but unfortunately I felt the exact opposite. Gently pushing myself up from the wall, he stepped back also.

"My eyes haven't always looked like that, right?"

He shook his head, straightening my tie again. "No, but now you've been blessed by an Angel." He looked to my eyes that were partly covered by my black, shaggy bangs. He brought his hand up and softly brushed my bangs to the side, his eye contact unwavering. "It's quite a gift to be bestowed with."

It was like he was trying to make my heart explode.

He stepped away from me, fixing one of his cufflinks. I stared at him, his long orange hair in a braid trailing almost half way down his back. Wouldn't hair that long be problematic in battle? His entire body just seemed incapable for the type of fighting he would have had to have been skilled in to kill as many as he did. He was young, too. But I guess people had shorter lifespans then so he actually wasn't that young, comparatively.

After situating some of my clothing begrudgingly, I followed him out of the room and back down the hallway. Falling into step with him, I looked over to see that he was smiling.

"So, I'm going to take a shot in the dark and say that you don't know how to formally dance."

I nearly tripped in my step, "That's an advanced idiom for someone as old as you."

He seemed proud, "Modern speech is so strange, but I like it and the books you've given me." He cleared his throat. "I figured if I could learn about the world you came from more, I will be of more use to you. So," He sighed, his smile unmoving from his face. "that's a yes then? Since you tried to change the subject."

I didn't get a chance to reply because as we walked back into my room, Iris laughed. "Wow, that was quick." they flew closer to us, "But I guess that is to be expected, it has been a long time for-" I hit Iris out of the air and onto my bed with a book I snatched up from my desk.

For the record, Iris didn't feel pain and Boggle bounce.

The little bother of a ghost flew out of the room, laughter on their breath. Oliver just stared at me, raising a brow. It was only a matter of time before he started to catch onto the things that Iris and Gaston said, and I didn't even want to think about what would happen then.

"So," Oliver took a step from me, "if it's an Earthbound ball that means that dancing will definitely be an issue. But," He cleared his throat, "as you can see, there is quite the lack of humans here so unfortunately Sire, you only have one option as a teacher."

It took me a moment to catch on, "You?"

He turned back to me, bowing slightly, "My sincerest apologies. If you are uncomfortable with such nonsense I may be able to-"

"Nonsense?" I asked without even thinking, my heart a step ahead of my mind.

He looked up to me from the bow, "It is quite improper for two men to dance together."

I want to say that didn't sting a little but that would be a lie. "Maybe from when you came from, but during the time and in the country I came from, it wasn't improper. I mean, a lot still thought so, but enough out there realized that people should do what makes them happy so they-"

Iris cut me off with their laughter from the hallway.

"Oh," Oliver started, paying no mind to Iris, "so customs have changed then? I was unaware."

"A lot has changed."

He took a step back toward me, extending his hand. "Time does that, I suppose."

I took his hand, trying to keep mine steady. His touch hurt a little, but I liked it. He pulled me close, making my heart jump into my throat. I averted my eyes as he took my other hand. I was expecting him to take me forward in a step or something but he didn't, he just froze up.

"So Sire..." He looked away from me, "Did you happen to ever read anything about me in your historical texts?"

"Just that you were a genocidal monster."

He hummed, "That is accurate, yes, but they forgot to include something."

Iris flew around us, making Oliver go tense, "Oli can't dance, Oli can't dance, Oli can't dance."

We stared at each other as Iris bounced about. Oliver did his best to hide his embarrassment but I could see it in the furrow of his brow.

With a smile, I pulled him to the side in a step. "That's okay, you guys are too uptight here anyway." We stumbled about and I could just laugh, "You said it was time for a change, right?"

"But...But Sire," Oliver struggled to keep balance as I clumsily danced us around the room, "dancing like this will do nothing but harm your reputation."

"Or maybe," I tried to spin him out but failed and ended up knocking us both to the floor, "it'll send a message." I laughed, sitting on the marble floor looking at Oliver at my side.

"A message?" He looked over me as he sat up. A few moments later he smiled and straightened my tie. "It'll definitely say something about you, that's for sure."

"Something good?" I asked as I stood, this time extending my hand to him.

He looked at my hand then up to me before taking it. "I do hope so."

I decided that I couldn't be the King they wanted me to be, but I was going to be the King that I could. And if that meant going through all their traditions and old fashioned views with a sledgehammer, I'd do it. It was the weird in me that Hugo liked and I wasn't planning on losing it to a crown.

"You have to be personable." Oliver started as we left the castle, "You can't go yelling at people or starting fights."

"What? Me? Starting needless fights? Whatever are you talking about?"

Oliver sighed, "I mean it Sire. This is important."

"I know," I ruffled up his hair as we approached the gate to the King's Castle. "but you're just so stressed about this, I'm trying to get you to chill."

"Chill..." He repeated distastefully under his breath.

Oliver didn't care for my modern slang.

We started into the gate but it lit up and someone came hurling out of it, knocking us to the ground. I immediately reached out to Oliver to make sure he was okay. He sat up, nodding at me as if he already knew what I was going to ask. I stared at him for a moment but then I remembered what had just happened. Turning around, I looked behind me to see Gaston, laying in the dirt. He stiffly sat up, rubbing his head.

"Guardian." Oliver groaned, standing up and taking my hand in the process. He pulled me to my feet before I even realized he had taken my hand. "Don't you have a graveyard to watch over."

"I do," he stood with a deep breath, "but I also have a ball to attend. Could I borrow your lead Boggle buddy to watch over things in my stead for the night?"

"Iris?"

He nodded.

I looked to Oliver and he just shrugged.

"Alright," a moment later Iris came flying out of the castle and toward us. "could you go watch Gaston's graveyard while he attends the ball?"

"What do I do?" Iris floated around Gaston.

"Don't blow anything up and you should be fine."

"Okay, I'll try not to, but no promises." Iris landed on his head, "Have fun. Make sure to tell me how horribly those two fail."

"Fail?" He looked over us.

"You'll see." Iris laughed, flying away and toward the Flipside portal.

Gaston looked at me then smirked with a shrug. "Let's go guys!" He ran between us, taking us by our arms and yanked us into the gate with him.

We went tumbling into the gate portal and around until we were spat out the other end. That was anything but graceful. As Oliver and I picked ourselves up from the ground, we saw Gaston standing there boldly, already on his feet as if he had landed that way.

"This aught to be fun." He turned to look at us a little, "Come on guys, get it together."

Oliver hissed something under his breath as he helped me up. "Alright," Oliver started, "once we walk through that gate, we are in Earthbound territory. Our powers are nullified there so we are just about as useless as the rest of the Boggle. So even if you lose your temper there, nothing will happen, so don't count on it. If you get separated from me-" He paused, looking between my eyes, "well, just don't get separated from me." He straightened my tie, almost nervously fiddling with it, "Your only goal there is to get on the Earthbound's good side, pay no mind to the Demons or Poltergeist. They'll have their events, too, and you don't want to risk spreading your attention too thin."

I was a little startled, he seemed frazzled, almost seriously worried. I mellowed out my tone, making sure to not come off playful in any way, "I'm not going to purposefully disobey your guidelines here, so don't worry so much Oli. I understand, it's serious." I messed up his hair, "I may rarely be serious, but I know when the time and place is to put on my best Boggle King face."

He didn't look like he believed me as he begrudgingly fixed his hair. "Do not leave my side, Sire." he turned to face the Earthbound gate, "Though foul play is frowned upon, it is not forbidden and none of them are above it."

I didn't expect him to take my hand after Gaston walked through the gate portal. But what was most shocking about that moment was just how strong his grip was. That didn't make me feel too eager to step through that portal. If what stood on the other side was a situation so dangerous, it managed to strike fear into a legendary genocidal knight, then it was a situation I wanted no part in.

I always hated the way portal travel felt, but that time was different. I could actually feel the lightning inside my core grow still. When we came stumbling out the other end, Oliver let go of my hand and I nearly lost my footing. I felt so empty, it actually hurt. Had I somehow gotten used to the electricity that sat under my skin? Looking up to Oliver, my world stopped.

His eyes had lost their glow. Now they were a cold blue, a sad blue, a sharp blue. They were stilled, no longer churning with the spectral haze they once held. He just about refused to make eye contact with me as we walked toward another castle. I didn't pay it much mind. As we walked up the steps, I looked up. A towering white castle, it was lovely against the pale blue sky. It was always a sort of pleasant twilight in the Boggle realm, there it was like a sweet summer afternoon.

The Earthbound castle was quite a contrast to that of the Boggle. It was certainly from a different time or location, but I wasn't versed enough in history to accurately tell. The doors opened for us, Gaston walking in before Oliver and I. As we stepped inside, I saw hundreds of eyes on me. Gaston elegantly stepped off to the side and followed behind, looking around quickly.

Standing atop a staircase above a ballroom, I froze.

"Introducing Kasper, The Boggle King." A disembodied voice from the ceiling boomed around me.

Reserved clapping was sprinkled through the pretentious aired crowd before me as they looked at me with their beady judgmental eyes. I could feel them ripping into me, trying to take me apart bit by bit as Oliver and I descended the stairs. As we reached the bottom, Gaston caught up with us after his introduction. He then gasped out of nowhere, startling me.

"Favio!"

I watched, confused, as Gaston went bolting into the shadows. He jumped into the darkness, and when he was in the air he snagged on something, or something, I couldn't see. With a horrendous thud, he and another person went crashing onto the marble floor. Oliver stepped closer to my side, startling me, as Gaston sat up. Underneath him, trapped in his arms, was another young man. This one was Gaston's exact opposite. The whites of his eyes were black, the iris gray. His hair was black except for three white braids that sat up against his scalp on the right side of his head. His voluminous black hair draped over the right side of his face and the tips of each clump of hair were white. His attire was totally black except for his tie, vest, and gloves, all of which were white.

"Hello Angel." His deep, gravely voice was startling. "Get off of me."

"But Favio," Gaston whined, not letting go of the guy as they sat up more, "it's been forever."

"It has been less a month," his voice strained as he tried to shove Gaston off of him, "I would hardly call that forever considering that we live forever."

His gaze then trialled up until it landed on me. He paused, staring at me, then with great force he shoved Gaston away. He boldly stood, towering over me in height. Without missing a beat, he gracefully bowed to me and brought his hand to his heart. Gaston sat, deflated on the marble floor and watched.

"Do pardon my insolence, Sire. Allow me to introduce myself. I am Favio, the neutral Shadow King." He slightly looked up to me from the bow but then went stiff when his eyes met mine. He then whiled around to look at Gaston. "What is the meaning of-"

Gaston stood. "Relax, your high strung Highness." He stopped next to Favio, slinging an arm over his shoulders. "It's exactly what it looks like, my faction has decided to support the Boggle King." Favio seemed like he wanted to protest but Gaston spoke again, "The broken game has gotten pretty old. I recon it's time to toss a few new cards into the mix."

Favio looked from Gaston back to me, "You must be something special to earn the holy loyalty of the Angels." He bowed his head briefly, "It is truly an honor to meet you."

"I bet you thought Oliver was uptight," Gaston chuckled, yanking Favio around, "He's nothing compared to this eight day clock."

"I would appreciate it if you'd allow me to continue to do my job." Favio ducked out from under Gaston's arm and started away from us, "Go have a good time."

Gaston followed Favio toward the shadow, speaking under his breath, "Oh, I will."

Favio stepped into the shadow and like that, disappeared into it. Gaston looked back at us with a wink then he too jumped into the shadow and became one with it. I stared at the shadow, half tempted to try to jump into it too to see where it led. So that's what a Shadow Person looked like when they weren't a shadow?

"Are there more neutral factions which don't participate in the candidacy?" My voice was low as Oliver and I wove our way through some of the ball attendees.

"Just those two and one other. We'd normally fall into that too, but this time we have you."

"Is having Gaston on our side something special?"

"Generally the Angel faction is present in the background as guides, not as leaders. So to see Gaston take an offensive action is quite special indeed. When those who normally are content in complacency feel driven to act, then something is not right in the normalcy."

"They're guides?"

Oliver kept me from running into someone, "Yes, they help bring clarity to the storm that death is for most. Many who move on are ushered to the beyond by Angels. And like the Angles, the Shadow People are also neutral forces in the background. They protect and quietly keep order among the factions. But don't mistake their neutrality for weakness, they could far overpower the Earthbound and probably the Demons if they wished."

I thought for a few moments, my eyes drifting over the room of people who looked as if they came from all over history. "So when the living see Shadow People, what are they doing?"

"Protecting."

I smiled a little, "Ghosts are good."

Oliver gave me a small nod but then stopped walking and startled me. Looking to him, I noticed his gaze was locked on someone. I turned to look forward and to my surprise, there was a short young man standing before us that I hadn't even noticed. He was rather normal looking, at least compared to Favio. He had unmemorable shaggy strawberry blond hair, normal build for his height, a simple suit and tie on. But there was one thing that stuck out about him, his pupils. They resembled the complex green eyes of a cat.

His eyes lazily grazed from Oliver to I. After staring at me blankly for a moment, he sighed, long and drawn out. "Hello new King, welcome to limbo." He spoke so flatly it could have crushed everyone in the room. "You don't really fit in here." He yawned, "That's good. Everything around here is too formal anyway." He started to walk off, a sway in every step as if he was drunk or something. "See you around."

I watched as he walked away, silent, confused, and a little uncomfortable. But that was until I saw that the back of his suit coat held a long tapered hood, the type that I had only seen on one type of being.

Quickly I looked back to Oliver, a smile on my face and my tone hushed, "Was he the Grim Reaper?"

Oliver was far less excited, "*A* Grim Reaper, yes. That was Nirvana, he's very close to retiring. He's always been that apathetic and dull, though. He's the King of the last neutral faction, the Reapers."

"He didn't seem that bad, why were you so startled by him?"

Oliver didn't make eye contact as he continued on through the crowed, "It's always a little jarring to see the first person I saw when I died."

Sometimes I forgot that Oliver died, too. I didn't like to think about it, because it reminded me of my own death and the emotions that came with it. Just the thought that Oliver once suffered through that too made my stomach twinge. He claimed that it has been so long, he no longer remembered the pain and how to deal with it. But that didn't mean that he once didn't suffer like I did.

I wanted to ask about how Reapers worked and if there were more, but I figured I'd save that for later. But that was a hard choice to make because I really wanted to know where Reapers retired to. Did they go to Hawaii or what?

Whispers followed us and I only caught bits of what was being said. People were nitpicking at my posture, my age, my Handler. They were commenting on my eyes and my crown, going on about how I should just give up. But I ignored them as I kept my gaze locked on Oliver. I didn't care what the others said, as long as I had my knight there with me.

We finally came to a stop and when I stepped around Oliver, I saw why. Standing there was the Earthbound King, Ruth. She looked over me as if I was a piece of trash in the wind before taking a sip of her tea.

Oliver bowed his head slightly, but not to the degree that he bowed to me. "Thank you for inviting us to this lovely ball, Earthbound King."

"It was out of pure obligation, I assure you." She reminded me of my mother. "I see you haven't cracked yet, young man. It will happen, it always does to human Boggles."

"What do you-"

Oliver stepped on my foot, silencing me. I slowly looked over to him, eyes wide. Was there something he was hiding from me?

"You have no proof for that claim. So with all due respect, don't say such baseless things needlessly."

Ruth lightly rolled her eyes with another sip. "Nothing but ruin can come of a powerless faction trying to fight."

When her eyes drifted back to mine, she actually looked at me for the first time. Her gaze locked on mine, staring into my eyes intently. Her eyes then rose to my crown and that's when they went wide. She stood in pensive silence for a moment, looking my entirety over.

"You're with the Angels?"

"No," I smiled, "the Angles are with me."

Oliver curtly nodded in agreement which was quite affirming. I opened my mouth and didn't make things worse.

She hummed sharply, quickly covering whatever shock I had invoked with my confidence. "Two neutral lower factions banding together is nothing. Don't go thinking yourself important because you won over the bleeding hearts."

I decided that continuing on that banter train would only cause issue and make Oliver disappointed in me, so I simply looked over to my friend. "I feel that this is an important occasion to remember. Oli, would you do the honors?"

It took him a moment to catch on but when he did, he dug out the camera with a small smile. The Earthbound King was interested but did a good job at trying to hide it as Oliver held up the camera and turned it around.

"Dairy product." Oliver said before hitting the button and taking a picture. He looked at the camera in his hands as I nearly died laughing. "Why do you always find that so funny, Sire?"

I think I said it once before, that I shouldn't be allowed to have that sort of power over someone.

"Isn't that what you said that one says before capturing a moment in time?"

I nodded, suffocating on my laughter.

The piercing glares of all around me didn't bother me much because there was one pair of eyes on me that made it all worth it. I loved it when Oliver smiled so innocently, his eyes held a certain light I didn't see anywhere else. Straightening, I looked to the camera to see the picture we had taken. A simple table sat in the background, none of us showing up in the picture. I glanced over to the table behind the Earthbound King. It was rather curious, that the ghost world and objects showed up on camera, but not the ghosts.

"What was that?" Ruth asked, looking over Oliver and I.

Oliver turned to her, holding up the camera, "It's modern witchcraft. An object able to capture a moment of time and transfer it upon paper to be displayed for all time, like a painting almost."

Her eyes narrowed on the camera, "That is similar to something from my time, but it wasn't witchcraft it was-"

I pulled Oliver to my side, not allowing Ruth to ruin my witchcraft fun as the music continued to play in the background. I had no idea where the music was coming from, but it wasn't anything digital.

"It was nice conversing with you, Earthbound King, but I'm a busy dude with things to do." She gawked at me as I pulled Oliver close and I went on, "Like dancing."

Without a care in the world, I yanked Oliver around with me. He clumsily tried to get a grip on me and not trip over his feet. "Sire," he started quietly, glancing around, "you're going to make a show of yourself if you do this."

I pulled him around, dancing to our own beat with the others simply in the backdrop. "There's something people from my time say to express a sense of social freedom, no longer chained by the weight of the opinions of others. It's a simple phrase, so please do remember it." I spun him out, smiling, "fuck it."

He chuckled as I pulled him back. My heart raced uncontrollably, everything about that moment was perfect. If I was going to be stuck in this limbo with them, the other ghosts were going to have to accept me and the oddity that I was. Only then would they be able to look past that and see me. I wasn't going to get anywhere pretending that I was anything other than me.

Oliver was tense at first, but eventually loosened up. And that meant the world to me. In the time he lived, something like this was suicidal. But the fact that he trusted me and my odd judgment enough to not only go along with it, but enjoy it, was amazing. While it is true that Oliver was nothing like I was expecting, I wouldn't want him any other way.

I nearly tripped over myself and stumbled into him. My world exploded into color the moment he laughed. He then took the lead and took me around, following in utter awe. We were being hardcore judged from the surrounding eyes, I was well aware, but when I saw Oliver smile like that, I did not care. I feared that these feelings were dangerous, they held such a power over me. I had never had my heart taken by anyone but him. I never knew love before he pulled me out of that pool, and ever since he was the only one I pined for. And even though I knew nothing about him, I just knew. Now that I was there, dancing around in his arms, I knew why.

I was destined to die and meet him.

Loving quietly was an eternity I was alright with, if that meant I'd get to be by his side. It was absurd to think my feelings would ever be returned, especially considering when and where he came from. And I was alright with that. I didn't need reciprocation if I could watch him take pictures of the sunset for the rest of time.

But sometimes it was hard to not lean forward and close the space between us. Especially when we were so close, his grip so tight on me, that smile on his face. I knew that wouldn't end well, so I refrained as we danced about. I tried to not let that slow the pace of my heart, but it did. I didn't know Oliver well enough to say for certain, but I had a feeling that these feelings were only going to grow stronger, the more I learned about him.

I saw Nirvana standing near the back of the crowd mouth agape as he looked at Oliver. Actually, all eyes were on Oliver and his smile. Were the others captivated by it like me? No, there had to be some other reason. I couldn't be bothered, though, because he was having such a good time.

"Hey, Kasper?"

My breath hitched upon hearing him say my name. "Yes?"

"I want you to tell me more about how the world has changed, later."

I looked away from his eyes that, despite being normal now, were just as entrancing as before. "Why is that?"

"I want to know all I can about a world that would make someone like you. Someone so unafraid to be themselves. It's irksome, really. Because I used to pride myself on being firm in stance, unable to be moved by another. Yet, here you are," He looked around, "having convinced me that I can make a fool of myself and it's okay."

His grip tightened as he pulled me a little closer so that I wouldn't run into someone. His touch stung my hands with pleasant cold, his smile sent stardust through my veins, everything about the anomaly before me rocked my world. He made me smile so much, I could feel my eyes start to tear up. I could never remember being this happy before.

The lights went out.

I was yanked from Oliver's wonderful grip.

The last thing I heard as sharp static took over my ears was Oliver yelling my name. Not Sire, but Kasper. Even the racing of my heart became nullified under the static. I sat in emptiness for a moment, a second in time where nothing mattered. But then my wits were knocked back into me when I slammed into the ground somewhere. Sitting up, I was surrounded by darkness. My ears rang, but through the haze I heard whispers. They were heavily accented, full of haste. And even though I could barely understand them, I knew nothing good was going to come of this.

Oliver warned me not to do one thing: get separated from him.

And look at where I was: separated from him.

Shakily, I brought myself to my feet. "Hello there, I don't believe we've met." The whispers stopped as I went on, my crown the only faint light in the darkness. "I'm Kasper, the Boggle King, it's nice to meet you." I stretched to dull the aching pain in my back from the impact with the floor, "Now, who might you guys be?"

A few moments of silence passed before they started to whisper amongst themselves again, ignoring me. I couldn't see anything in the room, but I could feel that it wasn't very big.

"Come on guys," I approached the whispers, "I can't work with you here if you won't talk to me." I stopped after I walked into a box or something. "I don't want any trouble-"

I heard something move. My heart dropped, my blood spiked, I froze. I wasn't afraid, I couldn't be afraid. Ghosts were good, I had to believe it. Keeping a smile on my face, I stayed standing tall in the darkness.

"Have I done something to anger you? Let's work this out peacefully-"

My voice was cut off when something latched their hand around my throat. My crown faintly illuminated the face of a large doll, its light reflecting off of the doll's porcelain skin and glass eyes. Its touch burned like acid, as if it were rotting my skin under its grip. I yelled out, the sensory ripping through me, making me weak. When I made contact with it, my hands burned too. It tightened its grip, choking my yell away. I knew this pain, I had felt it once before. It was why there was a blight on my ankle, it was the poisonous grip of a demon.

That made no sense, though. If my powers were turned off upon entering Earthbound territory, why wasn't the Demon's? But then I realized, demons could posses things. I was being attacked by a simple doll, the demon possessing it could be far away somewhere else.

My already black world shook with dark taint, as if the longer the doll touched me, the less life I had inside. My eyes flashed to a time in the past, one where Russel had me up against a wall, hand around my throat. I remembered the fear I felt then, the desperation and panic, but most of all I remembered wondering why? Why would Russel do such a thing to me? And that's the question that sat in my mind as I faded in that dark room. Why would they attack me here, now? Why would they go through the trouble of possessing something in another faction's castle to destroy me when it would just be easier to wait for me to come to them?

Why me, the harmless Boggle King?

One last pang of tainted pain tore through me before I collapsed.

What kind of King was I? Defeated by a damn doll. When I came to, I could barely breathe. Every breath felt like the air was laced with needles, like my throat was coated with poison. But I had to persevere, that's what a King would do. My arms shook violently, my weight felt as if it had quadrupled, but I pushed myself to my feet. The world spun around me and my hearing barely worked, but I could hear enough to hear the whispers stop. Spinning around, I swayed as my eyes locked on the doll. With all the might I could muster, I stepped forward and lunged for the doll. It couldn't run in time and I latched onto its arm. With a step to the side, I pulled it back and with grit teeth, I swung it over me and into the ground, shattering it.

Running in the darkness, angry whispers flooded around me. Red eyes flashed in the shadows, claws scraped against the floor. I was surrounded but I had to get out, I had to warn them, I had to get back to Oliver. Running into things I couldn't identify, creatures crawled around my feet, trying to trip me. I don't know what guided me in the darkness, but I felt a pull inside that told me where to go. It was like every step took me closer to the source of that internal connection.

I went barreling into a door and to my surprise, it opened. Falling to the ground outside of it, I laid on the marble floor for a moment as my eyes adjusted to the light. When I opened my eyes, I saw demons come pouring out of the dark room. They crawled toward me, trying to hold me down as I struggled to get up. They piled onto me but I managed to get to my feet, throwing them from me.

Ghosts were good, they had to be. They must have had their reasons, rarely were things evil for evil's sake. But like they were the protagonist of their stories, I was the protagonist of mine and I couldn't fall to them. They scratched at my ankles, making the blight there sting. Every muscle started to fail me, my breaths became more labored, my eyes blurred, but I had to keep running. Stumbling around corners in the empty marble halls, I knew that I was being led somewhere. I just had to make it there. The others would see the wave of Demons chasing me and fill in the rest. Oliver would know what to do, Oliver always knew what to do.

I didn't expect the next turn I took to lead right into a staircase and as I went tumbling down them, my world went out again. When it laggardly came back into focus, my entire body hurt. The Demons leaning over me whispered of a sacrifice, but I was too out of it to catch much more. It was almost pointless, my trying to shove them off of me, but I didn't stop. I was so weak, even my wrists were failing me. An opening appeared and I pushed myself up. Tripping more than running, I started toward the large door. It must have led to the ballroom, it looked just like the one we entered through.

I crashed into it, slowly causing it it open. Falling through the small opening, I landed on my knees. Looking up, I saw every set of eyes in the ballroom on me; including Oliver's. I shakily stood and bolted toward Oliver but as my feet carried me, I heard the Demon's whispering behind me. They had a new target, The Earthbound King. As much as my deepest desire and internal pull wanted me to run to Oliver, I altered my course. I was already covered in their blight, I couldn't let them harm Ruth, too. She was a King standing before her people, I couldn't allow her to fall. Because just as I was the star of the Boggle's world, she was the crowning jewel of the Earthbound.

Ruth's eyes caught on the demon's behind me as she took a step back. No one had time to react when I stopped in front of her, arms extended and eyes on the massive wave of Demons racing toward me. Really, I had no idea if what I was doing would actually help, but it was the best that my pained hazy mind could come up with. There I stood, face to face with a wall of Demon's quickly closing in. In the moment before contact, I wondered what it was going to feel like, being banished by a Demon blight.

A shadow darker than the Demon's overtook the room, making everything nothing but white outlines for a moment before it imploded. The Demons were gone and standing behind where they once were was Favio and Gaston. Favio panted, looking over me as he and Gaston stood, visibly concerned. He quickly straightened, all eyes on him in the silence, as he fixed his tie and clothing.

Thunder exploded into the ballroom, shaking the air. A bitter noxious haze took over the air as a dark figure appeared before me. Emerging from the haze was none other than The Almighty Ghost King himself. I stood, paralyzed by his presence, my world falling in and out of focus.

"Favio." His voice shook the entire realm.

Favio quickly came to the Ghost King's side with a nod.

"What is going on here?"

"It appears that the Demon faction has infiltrated Earthbound territory and made an attempt on the lives of the Boggle and Earthbound Kings."

The Ghost King looked at me as I struggled to stay standing. "Until this matter is fully investigated and resolved, it is forbidden to enter the territory of another faction. I hereby decree it law. It shall stay in place as long as candidacy shall last, in order to ensure the safety of the candidates and the validity of the election. If anyone should break it, you shall be considered a suspect in this investigation and held indefinitely. And if a candidate breaks it, it shall be taken as formal a resignation from the candidacy."

He lifted his staff into the air and with a grimace, he summoned a cluster of small black holes. They flew down to people standing in the crowd. One approached Oliver and I as he ran to my side. I stared into it for a moment before looking around. Why were all the Earthbound staring at me? Before I could think on it any longer, the black hole engulfed us and we were sent tumbling. When we were spat back out we were in my room in Castle Boggle.

I couldn't stand any longer as I started to fall to the side but something stopped me.

"Sire." Oliver held me steady, looking over me. It was when his eyes caught on my neck that he went rigid. As he gently helped me to my bed, he grew more concerned. "This won't be easy to purify."

I leaned over, elbows on my knees as my legs dangled over the side of the large bed. Oliver had done it before the last time I had contact with a Demon, so why did he sound so unsure of himself now? I tried to look up to him but before I could, his hand was on the side of my face. He trailed his finger down to my chin, lifting up my face. I was trapped in his glowing eyes as he spoke quietly to me.

"That was very Kingly of you, Kasper, but please don't go jumping in front of a sea of Demons again." Before I could even say anything, he leaned forward and kissed me.

My entire world was put on pause. I didn't even notice the pain fading as I closed my eyes. The contact made me smile, the cold pleasant sting of his lips against mine stopped my heart. He brought his other hand up to the back of my head, lacing his fingers through my hair softly as he pulled me closer. I had no idea what was going on and was so overwhelmed that I couldn't even kiss him back. All I knew was that in that moment, I was happy.

When he pulled away, my stomach flipped and my world turned into a dizzy mess. I tried to not lose my balance as I sat there, but I ended up falling forward and into his embrace. He stood there, holding me close for a moment before laying me down on the bed.

I could barely see him as he sat down next to me. "That should take care of the worst of it, but you're not in the clear yet." He took my hand, "I have to stay in contact with you for my ability to purify the rest, so I do apologize for any discomfort this may cause you."

I wasn't thinking straight, in a couple different ways, so maybe that's why I trusted myself to speak. "I've never been more comfortable."

Oliver's eyes drifted over to me, a brow slightly raised. "Oh?"

I laughed, covering my face with the hand he wasn't holding. "I died without having my first kiss."

Oliver simply stared at me for long enough that even I, in my dazed state, found it jarring. "You never loved anyone?"

I closed my eyes because my world started to spin again. "No, I did. But I only ever loved one person like that."

The bed shifted, he must have laid down next to me. I bet using those powers was draining on him, too. His kind voice came from my side, his grip on my hand unwavering. "Did you leave them behind in death, too?"

"No, actually I finally found them."

I must have totally zoned off after that because I don't remember much beyond those words. I knew that ghosts couldn't sleep, but I suppose under the right circumstances their mind could just shut off. The brief break into the mentally unaware was welcomed. But I wasn't entirely out of touch, I could feel Oliver's grip on my hand stay strong the whole time.

Coming from the individualistic, driven, go-getter, control obsessed culture that I did, it was a little hard for me to resign to the idea of destiny. The notion that things were fated, no matter what I did. But once I let go of the fear of losing control and accepted that some things were simply meant to be, it was a lot easier to not be so hard on myself. I flailed through life, never feeling like enough. So when the Boggle crowned me their King, I was beside myself. How could anything value me like that if I saw no value in myself? But if I was born to be a King, then I was going to be a King. No matter how much of a loser I was in life, I was going to follow the path fate had placed before me and own that crown above my head.

When I was finally able to will my eyes open again, I was immediately met with Oliver's. He jumped away from me, still laying at my side. Was he just…staring at me?

"Are you alright, Sire?"

I was speechless for a moment before nodding and slowly sitting up, my hand still intertwined with his. "Thank you."

He shook his head, sitting up next to me. "No need to thank me." When he let go of my hand, I felt like I had lost a bit of me. "I'll do anything to keep you safe." He turned and smiled at me a little, "It's my job as your friend, right?"

I watched as he left the room, stunned. He was my holy genocidal knight, my Handler, my best friend. They sometimes say that your first love is your most potent, and since I had never had a second, I couldn't tell you if that was correct. But as I sat there, bringing my hand up to my lips as a smile spread across them, I was sure of one thing.

Someday I'd fall hopelessly in love with Knight Oliver Vestile, The Great.

Chapter 6
TRIAL OF LEADERSHIP

"Wait, so, the world isn't flat?"

I shouldn't have laughed but it was just the way he said it, it was so damn adorable.

"Yes Oli, the world is indeed round."

"So you can't just…fall off the edge?" He turned from me as he hung up another one of our 'selfies' on the wall. We had amassed quite a few of them, all pictures of some background since we never showed up. But it was the memory that mattered, not something as vein as our appearances in the pictures.

"No, but we've flown off of it." I reached my hand up, leaning up against the wall. "Way off into the sky then landed on the moon."

Oliver stared at me, eyes so wide I feared they'd fall out. "The moon? Really?"

I nodded, smiling way too much. "Science has made great bounds since you left the world."

"Science," He turned to straighten one of the photos, "you mean witchcraft?"

"Sure," I chuckled, pushing myself up from the wall. "anything else you want to know?"

He turned back to me, putting his hands in his pockets as he thought for a moment. "How about your family?"

My heart snagged a little. "What about them?"

He took a few steps back, looking over all the pictures. "If you don't wish to answer, that's alright. But you seem too apt to tell me about the world you hailed from, not your world." He glanced over to me, "If that makes any sense, Sire."

I couldn't blame him for asking, I had gone beyond out of my way to avoid the topic. I had no idea how much time had passed me by, but I knew it had been nearly half a year Flipside. But that was only because time was in a disproportionate spin, the moments on Flipside were flying by comparatively and none of us knew why. Not nearly that much time had passed in Castle Boggle, perhaps a few weeks maybe. Oliver suspected it had something to do with the Ghost King's apprehension about the upcoming trials. He was slowing things down for us, so a moment here was several hours Flipside. Every moment I lived in was hundreds of moments for Hugo.

"Well," I started slowly, "I had a mother, father, and brother. You saw them at the funeral, but I don't expect you to remember. My mother was a model and my father an actor. My brother is little but is destined to be something great. My whole family up until me were famous and wildly successful in one way or another, so I was a let down."

After a moment of pause, Oliver said, "Well now you're a King." I was surprised by Oliver's smile as he slightly bowed to me, "You're my King." He looked up to me from the bow, "And soon you'll be everyone's King."

"Yeah, well," I laughed, a little more flattered than I probably should have been, "we can only hope at this point."

"No," He stood from the bow, his glowing eyes locked on mine. "I know you will be."

I had to turn away from him, that sort of confidence in me made my blood spike. "Anything else you want to know?" I wanted to change the topic because if he went on like that much longer he was just going to make me more embarrassed.

"Yes, I had one other question off the top of my head." I kept my back to him as he went on. "Has the definition of love changed at all?"

My hand paused as I reached to straighten a book on the shelf, "What makes you ask that?"

"Well, when you said that dancing customs had changed, it made me wonder."

Taking a deep breath, I turned to face him again. He had scared me for a moment there, but that reasoning totally made sense. "A lot, actually." It was hard to make eye contact as I spoke on, "Like I said before, there are still people who hold other views. But a fair amount of people believe that we should be able to love anyone we want."

"So peasants can marry into royalty now?" he was flat out amazed, gaping at me.

I stared at him, "Uh, yeah, that actually happened in England I think. But that's not entirely what I meant." I paused and in that moment, I wondered if I should even tell him since the thought had obviously never crossed his mind. But he was just standing there, waiting on my every word, and I couldn't bring myself to omit things from him. "Now people can love out of their class, sure, but they can also love people of any race, gender, or religion." Was the most eloquent, inclusive way, I could figure out how to put that so that he'd understand.

"Two people of the same gender are now allowed to love one another?"

I nodded, averting my eyes.

He just stood there for a while staring at me, as if his mind had snagged. "That is certainly different. It's, how do you say it," he thought for a moment, looking down before he lit up again, "awesome."

My gaze jumped to him. Caution still lacing my blood, "Wasn't something like that horrible back then?"

He nodded gently, "It was indeed considered sinful, you'd get burned to death for it in some places. But, as much as they tried to hide it, there was a lot of that behavior in the church I served. Although I'm amazed that people don't kill each over it anymore."

"People do still kill others because of the hate around it. But it's not like it was in your time." I stepped back, putting a bit of space between us, "You're very accepting of that, having been a Holy Knight yourself."

"When I cut them down, everyone was the same. The blood that stained my blade was always red, so I don't see why something like that should matter in the slightest." He raised his arms a little, laughing, "May God strike me down for speaking such sinful words." He smiled, looking back to me. "If there's a person up there, they probably have far bigger things to worry about. Like you guys escaping the planet. Do people live on the moon?"

I had never been so pleasantly surprised before. "No," I walked up next to him, looking out the window, pointing up, "but there are people who live in a ship in the sky. You can see it pass by at night sometimes."

Oliver was nothing like I expected and he was perfect.

I went on about the modern movements of science and the amazing things it had done since he tuned out. It was hard for him to understand, but that didn't crush his interest. I wondered what Oliver would have been like if he grew up when I did. I felt like he'd become some scientist, pioneering great discoveries with his soft spoken confidence. That made my mind drag behind a little, tugging my smile down. What would have become of me someday? I tried to not think on that much.

"Sire!" Iris came bouncing into the room, floating up to be eye level with me. "You've been summoned to the King's Castle."

I went stiff when Oliver glared at me. I looked back to him, laughing a little. "I don't think I did anything."

Iris flew around me in circles, "The Shadow King, Favio, has summoned you and the other Kings to help in his investigation."

"Oh, alright." Oliver's glare lessened on me as I went on. "I have no idea how you guys tell time here, so just tell me when we need to leave."

"Now would be preferable considering time changes from realm to realm."

I didn't even ask what Iris meant by that because I didn't want to know. It was already confusing enough, trying to fathom how differently time ran between me and Hugo. I didn't need another layer of nonsensical paranormal crap confusing me more.

I followed Iris out of the castle, glaring back at it as we approached the gate. It was way too big, too cold. The only thing that made living there tolerable was Oliver. My mind wandered, wondering if I could ever live somewhere other than that castle. We stepped through the gate and my world was thrown into a spin before I fell to my knees on the other side. Oliver knelt down, smiling at me as he extended his hand. I took it without a second thought, I loved the way his touch felt like gin on my skin. But my racing heart stopped when I was on my feet and I saw the way he was looking at me. I couldn't tag what it was that unsettled me so badly, but it was just something in the churning of his eyes.

He continued forward toward the King Castle as if nothing had happened, leaving me a few steps behind in confusion. I put my hand in my pocket, trying to forget the feel of his hand on mine. Had I done something to anger him and he didn't want to bring it up? My mind flew back to the time I had spent with him and I had no idea what I did. My stomach dropped when I realized that the fact that I had no idea was far worse than the initial thought. If I couldn't sense an issue between the person closest to me, how was I to correctly lead a kingdom?

We walked into the main hall, led by darkly dressed ladies I assumed were of the Shadow People faction, until we stopped in a side study type room. Sitting on an old style fancy couch was Favio. His dark suit looked as if it swallowed up the light that met it, erasing any folds or seams as he stood and bowed as I entered the room. Nodding his way, I studied the room as I walked over toward the couch across the small coffee table from where he had been seated. Oliver followed closely, his guard obviously up as we sat down.

"Hello, Boggle King." Favio sat, too. "Knight." He sat back, crossing one leg over the other as he looked over us, "Thank you for cooperating with the investigation." I nodded and he went on, "As I'm sure you're aware, but I'm required to restate, members of the Demon Faction bypassed the power barrier into Earthbound territory through the rare skill of inanimate possession.

Their motives are unclear to us, though we suspect you may know something, Sire. You were their target, after all. And it is my understanding that this isn't the first time a Demon has attacked you. Would you mind sharing what you know so we can resolve this as quickly as possible?"

I sat there for a moment, he was very thorough and serious, it was rather scary. But I suppose that was a good thing, considering he was the King of the security faction. "I don't remember it too clearly, I was in a lot of pain at the time. But they were saying something about a sacrifice."

Favio's eyes widened, ever so slightly.

"But that's all I heard, most of it didn't sound like words to me. They used a porcelain doll as a vessel to choke me out. I don't know why they didn't just do away with me then, maybe I woke before they could. It was a fight, but I managed to destroy the doll before fleeing through the castle. When I saw their path alter from me to the Earthbound King, I couldn't just let them attack her too so I tried to stop them but…" It was really hard to maintain eye contact since he was such a fierce presence but I forced myself to, he deserved the respect. "Thank you for saving me."

"How did you find your way back to the ballroom?" He asked, unmoving and seemingly ignoring my gratitude.

I was a little unsettled by that but I figured it was just his nature. "I'm not entirely sure, I just felt a pull. Something that told me where to go."

He looked between Oliver and I for a moment, "Interesting. And why would a King such as yourself, one who has an entire faction to look after, do something as stupidly noble as jump in front of an attack aimed to a rival King? Surely your path to the Almighty Throne would have been a little more clear with the Earthbound King out of the way."

I must have been visibly shocked by his question because his eyes narrowed on me. "That didn't even cross my mind, I just didn't want the Earthbound King to get hurt, too. I know the pain of a Demon blight and wouldn't wish it on anyone."

Favio looked away from me and in that moment I saw anger flash over his features. "Keep up that act, Boggle King. But nothing good will come to a lower faction trying to earn the Almighty Crown. Your fake kindness and hollow heart will only get you so far. You will fall like the last one to wear that crown." His demeanor returned to stiff professionalism when his eyes drifted back, "That's all I needed from you, thank you for coming here today."

His words left me so cold I had to fight the shiver crawling under my skin. Standing, my body became numb as my feet carried me away. I couldn't look up to Favio as we left, the heavy door closing behind us. Following Oliver down the hall, my eyes rested on the intricate carpet.

"I didn't put my foot in my mouth or something just now, did I?"

Oliver slowly looked over to me, brow furrowed. "I don't believe you put your foot in your mouth. I think I would have noticed that, Sire."

Sighing, I remembered who I was talking to, "It's a figure of speech, Oli."

"Oh? I haven't come across that one yet. Enlighten me?"

"It means to say something wrong that causes issues without intending to."

He nodded pensively before replying, "I can see why you'd feel that way. However, you haven't done anything wrong. Favio's job is to be suspicious." He looked over to me as we entered the main hall. "And a person in power with genuine intentions is, well, uncommon."

"Decency is truly a rare trait, it's a shame that it invokes suspicion." Oliver and I stopped when Ruth stepped around a hallway corner before us. As she approached, I was disarmed by her smile, "I do believe an apology is in order." Slightly bowing, she stopped before us. "It was wrong of my faction and I to belittle you on such arbitrary grounds. Thank you for your kindness and bravery." She lifted her head, "Your faction is blessed to have a King as golden as you."

I was speechless for a moment before I found my voice, "I'm just happy everyone came out of that alright."

She studied me for a moment before she walked past us and toward the hall we had just exited. "I wouldn't have saved you. We are competitors. Just know that, Boggle King." She stopped, looking back to us over her padded shoulder, "Your actions have not gone unnoticed by my faction, either. You have earned my respect as a true rival. I look forward to facing you in the trials."

As she walked away, the click of her heels ruling the air, I must have stared at her back far too long because Oliver nudged me toward the door. Was that her saying that I got on the Earthbound's good side? A smile fell upon my face, I wasn't doing too shabby at this whole King thing so far.

Eyes catching on a tapestry on the wall, I saw that it had been greatly damaged. From what I could see as we passed, it looked like it depicted some sort of war. A large army on the ground was partially visible and made up of Poltergeist, their front ranks had been destroyed by a scorch mark on the tapestry. Above it all was a great man, and as my eyes lingered, I realized that it was the Almighty Ghost King. He had ruled for so long, there must have been an epic tale of his history. I wondered what that story was, but knew that it was not my place to ask. Asking those sort of questions would surely cause trouble.

As we left the King Castle, we crossed paths with another upon the front stairs.

"Yo Boggle." My blood solidified upon hearing the Demon King's voice. I looked up from the stairs to see the rotten mess that he was, gazing at me with those horrid eyes. "Already get interrogated? I heard it was quite a ruckus over in the Earthbound Castle."

"Oh I'm sure you only heard about the mess." I probably should have ignored him but he had startled me so badly, I just spoke.

"My my, how accusatory." He said, slowly holding his hand out in front of him, looking to his claw boasting fingers as he moved them around, "Now why would I ever send a Demon after you?" With a laugh, he walked past us and into the castle.

Oliver and I continued down the stairs and onto the path back to the Boggle gate.

Oliver laughed quietly, "Now I believe that would be considered putting your foot in your mouth, Sire."

"Whatever…"

I followed Oliver into the gate and as he disappeared into it, I wondered what was going on with him. He seemed just fine now, as if he hadn't looked at me like I offended his entire bloodline not long ago. When I fell through the gate, landing on my knees, I didn't take his hand to stand. I retired to my room without talking much and just laid on my bed in silence. It was moments like that one that I truly felt the brunt of the size of that castle. It was just so big, too big. I rolled over onto my side, smothering my face in the pillow. I really wished that ghosts could sleep.

Thoughts raced about, things I didn't want to think about. Did I really come off as fake? Was that why Oliver acted that way, did he think this was all an act? It was the first time in my life I could really just be me, and I get accused of putting on a show.

Groaning into my pillow, I laced my fingers in my hair.

"Sire," Iris came floating into my room, "It's time."

Rolling over, I glared up at them from under my disheveled bangs, "For what?"

Landing on the bed next to me, they bounced about, "The first trial."

Blood dropping from my head, everything went cold as I flew up, "What? We just got back."

"What do you mean?" They floated up and bobbed around my head, "It's been a day since you returned."

Time was an illusion, but that was particularly true in Limbo.

Oliver stepped into the doorway and when his eyes met mine, I knew.

The first trial was upon us and I wasn't prepared.

It was all a nervous blur, getting my best kingly suit on, Oliver fussing with my tie, leaving Castle Boggle as my subjects cheered, stepping into the portal, falling out the other end. Oliver offered his hand to me but I didn't take it, picking myself up from the ground and starting back toward the King Castle. It sat, a monolith against the sky, towering over me. Each step back up the steps I felt like I had descended a matter of minutes before, my world fell wayward. Stopping before the door, I took a deep breath. Reaching forward for the handle, before my hand could make contact, they began to creek open. Stepping back, I bumped into Oliver.

Without a word, we exchanged looks and in that moment I felt it, the brunt of the nerves.

Walking in, the halls were empty, so much larger than they had just been. Following Oliver, he seemed to know the way like it was second nature as he brought us to another large set of doors. Pausing before opening them, he turned to look at me.

"You're going to do great," straightening my tie, he smiled, "Kasper."

I tried to smile.

When the doors opened, I was blinded by the light and when it drained away, I was left standing on a stage. Staring forward at an insurmountable crowd staring back at me, I had to swallow the shock. Looking around, I saw every other major King standing on the stage with me, devoid of confusion, their handlers near by. How did I get up here? Glancing over to him, Oliver appeared unfazed as well. A shuddering breath left me as I buried my hands in my pockets, trying to conceal the tremble that was taking me over.

With Oliver by my side, I should have been confident, but I wasn't. I was too distracted by the ache in my core to feel anything but apprehension for the upcoming event. I was to stand before my Kingdom, as their King, and I had no idea how I was going to do it. The last thing I wanted to do was misrepresent them by coming off as fake.

"Welcome Kings, Handlers, and members of my Kingdom." The Ghost King's booming voice vibrated the stone floor of the castle as it came from everywhere and nowhere at once. "Today is the first of three trials. The trials are not to decide who will succeed me, that is up to me in the end. These trials serve another purpose. To show me, and all the paranormal, what sort of ruler you'll be." Cheers roared from the crowd, taking the air from my lungs, "This trial will test your ability to strengthen your Kingdom in numbers. You shall travel Flipside and win over all the Roamers that you can. Their numbers have been growing at a worrying speed and once King, you will have to deal with that problem." A dark cloud started to form in the air above us, "You may use whatever method you see fit and you have an undisclosed amount of limited time. When the trial is over, you will be brought back here with your new subjects. There we shall see which of you has a talent in getting those to follow you, who is a leader. That is an important trait for a King to have." A shadow emerged from the cloud and from it came the Almighty Ghost King. His noxious presence, his overbearing height, it was too much as he landed on the stage, causing a seismic event with each boot, "Is all I said understood?"

We each gave a nod, not daring to look the Almighty King in the eyes.

"May the fates smile upon you, Kings."

Suddenly a black orb appeared before each of us and like that, we were engulfed by it. I was tossed around in nothingness, a familiar but unwelcome disorientation, before being thrown to the ground. Laying there, looking into the blue sky I didn't realize I'd miss so much, I was really getting tired of this teleportation bullshit.

Oliver sat up next to me, looking around as he stood. I didn't stand, I didn't even move. We were in the park that sat near the river. It was a pleasant peaceful place, one I often walked in on my own many times. The air was clear, cool, not stuffy and one dimensional like that of limbo. The grass felt nice under my back, the light breeze in my hair, it reminded me of a time when life was simpler.

"Are you alright, Sire?" Oliver extended his hand.

I looked from his hand to his eyes before laggardly standing. My muscles were tired, not wanting to move or work with me. Swaying once I reached my feet, I ran my hands over my face. Teleporting really took it out of me, but the weird passage of time was the worst. With a painfully deep breath, I started down the path that went along the river.

Oliver walked quickly for a few steps to end up at my side, "Is something troubling you, Sire?"

"It's just…" clenching my jaw, eyes drifting to the river, I wanted to jump into it and drown my agitation, "nothing."

Oliver hummed as he fell into step with me. "Methinks you're lying."

"Methinks you should stop prying."

I wasn't paying attention to where I was walking until I just about walked through a couple of people. Yanking Oliver to the side and out of the way, I watched the two young men walk past. One of them had the weirdest hair. It was auburn, like red and not orange. The color sort of startled me, but for no reason in particular. He was walking with another young man, one with black hair and glasses. They were in uniforms from that special private school I was expelled from. It was then that I recognized the one in glasses as the Student Council President of that school. It was shocking, though, because he was smiling. I didn't think that guy could smile. But what shocked me most of all was when they started up the stone stairs that led to a higher part of the park, they started holding hands.

I didn't get to stand in awe of that very long because something crossed my vision. My gaze jerked over to see a ghost squirrel running around. I stared at them for a moment before I realized what that meant.

Kneeling down, I extended my hand, "Hey there friend, want to come join us? We're a lot of fun. You'll get to spend eternity in a nice park like this one, but there aren't any cars zooming by."

"You're talking to a squirrel, Sire. I do hope you realize this."

I slowly turned to glare Oliver's way as I knelt there, "What do you suggest I do to win them over, then?"

He didn't reply, just continued to stare at me, brow furrowed.

Looking back to the squirrel, I reached for them, "Come with me, it'll be great."

The squirrel didn't seem afraid of me as I got closer to them. Sniffing my hand, they made me smile as they reached out their little rodent fingers my way. I will never forget the moment they decided to end my life. Leaping forward, they knocked me back into the ground. Clawing, biting, scratching, that little dude was determined to fuck me up.

I managed to get a grip on them, holding them up off of me as they squirmed and squeaked in protest. Sighing, I looked up at the little creature. "It's okay, I won't hurt you," petting them with my free hand, they began to relax in my grip, "You're probably scared, but I promise," my expression softened as I looked them over, "It'll be alright."

As I pet them, the friend stopped struggling. When they fell still, they glowed a little more, making their transparency hold a blue tint. When they blinked, their eyes changed to a similar blue glow as Oliver's. Sitting up, I loosened my grip on them. With a couple of chirping sounds, they ran up my arm and onto my shoulder. Making a risky jump to my head, they thrashed around in my hair before managing to leap up into my crown. After struggling for a moment, they stilled, content as they spun around with my crown.

I stood, smiling a little, "I'll name you Gus."

Oliver stared at the squirrel as they spun around in my floating crown. "You're still talking to a squirrel, Sire."

"Yeah," I shoved him a little, "and it worked."

"Indeed it did." He smiled, walking closer to me as he looked over my face. "But Sire, you can't allow yourself to get injured so easily. It'll look bad."

He lifted his hand to the side of my face, making my heart stop. I stood there, stiff, as I felt his powers healing the cuts on my face. His eyes locked on mine, his smile unmoving, I couldn't help but be trapped in that moment. For a second I forgot about the way he looked at me and just stood, captivated by his mystical glowing eyes.

"Please do be careful." He smiled, making my elated heart race even more.

Turning away from him, I tried to tame my smile. I couldn't let him get to me, there was too much storming around inside for it not to taint every moment I wanted to cherish. Walking a few steps ahead of him, I tried to not let my heart ache. Was I overrating?

"Sire."

I was going to turn to look at Oliver but then I noticed what made him speak. Hiding behind a tree, looking around at us sheepishly, was a little girl. Unfortunately, she was transparent. After exchanging a silent glance with Oliver, I slowly walked up to her, kneeling down to be her level.

"Hey."

She backed behind the tree a little but not all the way, "Hi."

"My name is Kasper, what's yours?"

She looked me over, stepping out from the tree a little more, "Lilith."

Her little jumper, her white blond braids, brown eyes and pink shoes made my heart drop, she was so young, "It's nice to meet you, are you lost?"

She shook her head, averting her eyes and lowering her voice, "No, I'm running away."

"Running?" I tried to cover my concern with a smile, "From who?"

She looked around, stepping fully out from the tree, "The bad man. He stole me, but I got away." Her smile started to fade, "I'm trying to find my way home but I can't get out of the park."

My breath hitched when the dots connected, "I'll keep you safe from him." Extending my hand, I watched as she started to reach for it but then my mind snagged, causing me to take it back, "Hey Oli, if she touches me, will she join us?"

"No Sire, she has to choose to."

I opened my hand again and looked back to her, "Sorry Lilith, ignore that."

She seemed confused but also like she couldn't be bothered enough to really care as she took my hand. She was so cold, different than Oli.

"Do you know where the others spawned?"

Oliver stepped to my side, "The other Kings?" I nodded and he went on, "I have no way of telling, but you should be able to sense their crowns." He waked around to my front and lifted his hand up to my face. Gently running it down my skin, he softly closed my eyes. "Do you remember what color they are?" I weakly nodded, it was all I could do with him so close. "Just think on that, you should be able to locate them."

After a moment, faint colors appeared in the darkness and when Oliver removed his hand and I opened my eyes, they stayed in my vision. But I didn't immediately take notice of them, I was too busy staring at Oliver. His hand was so careful, controlled and kind. I wanted nothing more than to enjoy that contact but every spike of warmth from his touch was followed with a suffocating pang of unsettled tension. His eyes searched mine until I turned away from him and toward the Earthbound's light.

"I know someone who will take care of you," I said to Lilith as she walked at my side, "she's sort of frigid but I have a feeling that she has a heart in there."

"But Sire," Oliver followed, "that would be helping the Earthbound in the trial."

"This isn't about the trial, this is about her eternity. Do you really think she'd be happy with a couple of teenage guys and a squirrel?"

Oliver didn't respond. The silence that sat in the air cut but it didn't hurt as much as the razors jumbling around in my stomach. As the light grew in my vision, I knew we were getting closer. As Oliver fell a few step behind, I felt something pull me back but I ignored it.

"Hey! Earthbound King!" I waved to her as we walked up. She had a few ghost standing around her, along with her Handler kid.

"Hello there Boggle." She sounded less than pleased with my appearance.

"I'll get out of your hair, don't worry. But I brought someone for you." Ruth watched me as I knelt down to Lilith's level. "I know you were trying to find it home, but I think they can explain why you can't go back there, better than me. They're good people and they'll take care of you." I let go of her hand, "And I promise that if I find that man I will take your revenge. So please, go have a lovely eternity with the Earthbound."

Ruth slowly walked up, silence in the air as she stopped next to Lilith. The little girl looked between Ruth and I, nearly shaking. It must have been so confusing for her. But when I nodded, a smile on my face, she weakly nodded back.

Looking up to Ruth with all her might, Lilith smiled. "Hi."

Ruth blinked at her. "Hello…"

"My name is Lilith, what's yours?"

Ruth grew more awkward by the moment, "Ruth."

"It's nice to meet you."

Ruth looked from the girl to me and after a moment of staring at me, she put her hand on Lilith's head. "It's nice to meet you too."

Lilith's transparency started to glow with the tint of Earthbound and with that, Oliver and I left, waving back to them. As Lilith happily waved to me, I laughed a little when Ruth waved a bit too before sharply retracting her arm to her side. Turning back around, the whole park before me, I tried to breathe and calm the unease. Walking in painful quiet, side-by-side, Oliver and I continued through the park. Ruth had four people, including Lilith. I was behind already.

My entire world stopped when Oliver took my hand in his. I nearly flew from my skin, looking over to him. I couldn't even speak to ask what he was doing. He just studied me, looking between my eyes as if he would find an answer. My heart crashed into my ribcage as his grip tightened and I tore my gaze from his.

I had almost caught my breath enough to speak to him when I heard a loud bark. Looking up, I barely had time to see the huge dog before it pounced on me. Knocking me to the ground and my grip from Oliver's, the golden retriever seemed quite proud. They licked me, pinning me there and I couldn't help but smile a little. Ruffling up their hair as I softly pushed them off of me, I looked to the dog. Sadly transparent, they didn't seem to know they were dead. They had a collar on, the tag holding an address and phone number along with a name.

"Albert?" I looked back to their eyes. "Who names a dog Albert?"

Albert snuggled up against me and as I pet him, he started to glow with the blue of my crown.

"Welcome to Kingdom Boggle, Albert."

His big brown eyes jumped up to my crown and a growl took him. The squirrel chirped back and I laughed as I stood. Continuing along, Albert stayed at my side obediently. I never was allowed to have a dog, though I always wanted one. Walking in silence, my mind raced. Tightening my fist in my pocket, my skin remembered the feeling of Oliver's. Why did he take my hand like that, it wasn't like I was blighted or harmed.

Oliver walked on the opposite side from Albert, tense, as if Albert made him uncomfortable. I sort of hoped he was uncomfortable after what he did to me just then. There was no way that he could know, though. He just barely grasped the concept, why would he be making moves on it?

A bird swooped by and startle me, but then I noticed it was transparent also. Looking up as the bird circled us, I wondered if I was attracting them.

"Is there some reason this trial starts in the park?"

Oliver nodded, looking up at the bird, squinting in the sun, "Just as the living gather in this area, so do the dead. If they don't have a specific haunt, that is."

Reaching my hand up, I only flinched a little when the bird swooped down and landed on it. Bringing my hand down, I studied the blue bird as I pet them with my other hand. Their blue glow intensified as they chirped, rubbing into my hand.

"Why does this get easier every time?"

He looked to the little ghost animals around me, "One is more inclined to follow a King who has already earned the loyalty of others."

I looked to the bird and they hopped onto my shoulder. "You'll be named Jeff," looking back over to Oliver, I didn't want to have to keep relying on him but I hadn't any idea how this worked, "Am I stuck at the park, or can I go other places?"

"You are free to go wherever you see fit. Just remember, we are acting under a time limit."

With that I started out of the park. Luckily the other places I wanted to go were all in the same downtown area. With how fast we walked, it was only a matter of moments before we were at the school district building. Oliver seemed like he was going to speak but I started up the stairs and fazed through the door before he could speak Standing on the other side of the door, dizzy, I took that moment of brief separation to breathe. Starting forward, the animals followed me happily down the hallway. Looking up and down the locker lined walls, there wasn't anyone in sight. He had to be here somewhere. When my foot slipped a little, I looked down to see water on the floor.

"Hey kiddo!" I followed the water, running next to it, my silent footsteps accompanied by the jingling of Alber's tags.

A squeaks came from the corner behind me and as I turned, the little boy rode up on his trike.   He rode into my leg, causing me to stumble away as he jumped up and hugged Albert, "You have a dog now?"

Smiling, I kneeled down to him, "Didn't you say you were lonely here? I can help you go somewhere where everyone will see you, and you can bring your bike."

His eyes lit up, Albert snuggling up next to him, "Is there such a place?"

Petting Albert too, I smiled, "It's called the Earthbound Kingdom, I know who can take you there."

He beamed, nodding as if he hadn't ever made an easier decision. Peddling his bike along side us as we started toward the exit, he hummed. Fazing through the door appeared to be no issue for him while I was left standing there, bracing myself on the railing atop the stairs. Oliver didn't say anything as I picked up the trike and carried it down the stairs, little ghost boy in tow.

The only sound in the air was the faint squeaking of his bike as he pedaled next to us, along the street for the short distance it took to reach my next destination. Oliver tensed when he saw where we were, looking over to me. Pretending to not notice, I kept my eyes ahead.

The ghost of the baker locked out back banged on the door before us.

I wasn't going to let him relive his death ever again.

Starting forward, I was suddenly stopped, "Sire, it's residual, it can't be helped."

"I disagree," turning back to look at him when he didn't move, I became more annoyed than I had intended, "Let go."

His eyes flashed a little brighter for a moment and he looked genuinely startled as he revoked his hand. As he looked to the ground I instantly felt bad for being short with him but the time limit hanging over my head grew heavy as I turned back around.

"Hey, do you work here?"

The man jumped, turning to look at me as if he hadn't noticed my presence before. "Yes sir."

"Great," I crossed my arms with a smile as I stopped near him, "I've been looking for you. I hail from a land not far away where a King is in need of a baker of your caliber." I bowed slightly to him, "I would be honored to escort you to her."

Slowly turning from the door, his weathered tired features frowned at me, "Why should I believe you?"

I looked up from the bow and around, "You're running from someone, right? They won't ever find you in the Earthbound Kingdom."

He stared at me then looked around, too. After a few moments of consideration, his eyes drifted back to me and he nodded. "Alright, they will just have to mange without me here," with one last bang on the door, he started our way, "will teach them to lock me out."

When he reached my side, he pet Albert and slowly came to notice the squirrel and bird.

I wondered if the silence was as awkward for everyone else as the unspoken tension between Oliver and I grew. Following the glow of Earthbound in my vision, I wasn't paint to utmost attention to my surroundings until a faint sound caught me. Stopping, the others seemed confused as they continued on for a couple more steps before noticing. After hearing the little sound again, I ran into the alley we were passing. Stepping over rainbow puddles and trash, I investigated about. Brushing past a couple of garbage bags, I found them.

Seven sets of transparent little eyes looked up at me as quiet mews and purring filled the air. A saddened sigh escaped me as I knelt down to them. Reaching out my hand to the mother, my eyes drifted over the babies surrounding her. Little tabbies, they didn't deserve this. The mother was skittish but when I stayed still, she walked up and rubbed her head on my hand. The kittens soon followed and it wasn't long before they all let me pet them. Soon they all glowed blue, like my crown.

"Hey, Oli, come here?"

Oliver started toward me so quickly that he tripped over a hunk of trash and all but fell over as he tried to regain his composure, "Yes, Sire?"

"Here."

He didn't seem to know what to do with himself as he was handed several kittens. Picking up the last couple myself, we started out of the alley, the mother keeping close to my feet as she meowed and purred. The kiddo begged to carry a kitten and Oliver handed one to the Baker as we went along.

"What should we name them?" I looked over the kittens in my arms as they squirmed about.

"Nichole!" The boy said as he set the kitten down on the seat of his trike, pushing it along from the back, "That was my mom's name."

"That's a great name," I looked to the baker, "Do you have any suggestions?"

The baker thought for a moment as he pet his kitten, "Pie."

I tried not laugh, he seemed very proud of the name.

"Tola," Oliver was so quiet I almost hadn't heard him as his eyes sat, heavy on the kitten in his arms.

Studying him, he didn't look up to me though I'm sure he could tell.

"That's three so," the kid counted on his fingers, "we have four more to go."

Jumping when one of the kittens bit me, I laughed a little, "I'll name you Russel."

Getting closer to the park, my attention returned to closing in on the Earthbound's light.

"Hey!"

Startled from my attention, I looked over to see that we were passing the cemetery.

"Sire, Mr. Knight!" Gaston came blundering toward us, jumping over headstones with reckless abandon. Panting as he slammed up into the fence, he beamed, "Is the trail over yet?"

When I shook my head, he lit up.

"Great," turning around, he turned back to face us with a little ghost orb in hand, "I think your team is missing a Boggle staple."

He let go of it and it floated toward me, bobbing, slowly. Carefully, I reached up to touch it and when the pad of my finger made contact, it turned blue. Taking my hand back, the sensation lingered. It sort of felt like smoke, but a little more solid than that.

"Hello," I started quietly, "would you like to join us? There are more like you, where I'm from."

When it bobbed up and down, quicker this time, I nodded. Studying it, letters strung together in my mind, "What do you think of the name Emily?"

It flew around me in a circle, making me smile.

Gaston whistled, crossing his arms with a huge smile. "You're a natural, Sire." He then looked to Oliver and jumped when he saw the kittens. "I love cats." He reached out and pet a few.

"We're trying to name them, have any ideas?"

"Name one Furvio." He looked to me, his smiling growing, "Please."

I couldn't help but laugh. "Sure. But don't you think the Shadow King will come after you for that?"

He shrugged, laughing a little but trying to conceal it. "He never does." He cleared his throat. "And who are your human subjects?"

"Oh they're not mine." I looked around to them. "I'm delivering them to the Earthbound King."

"Now why would you do a thing like that?" Gaston asked, but his smile didn't fade.

"That's what I keep asking." Oliver said through his teeth at my side, obviously annoyed with the bunch of squirming kittens in his arms.

"Not everyone chooses to take company with squirrels and ghost orbs, Oli." Sighing, I looked back to the guardian, "Thank you for the addition, Gaston. I'd stay, but I have somewhere else to visit before returning to the park."

Gaston waved, calling out wishes of luck as we continued on.

I listened to the boy tell the baker all about his trike and I wondered if they'd be happy in the Earthbound Kingdom. The Earthbound couldn't be full of just high class uppity old time people, there had to be more modern ones there too.

We walked up to the Historical Society and with a breath, I fazed through the door. Almost instantly after entering the building, I saw George.

He jumped, looking at my little army as he held onto a coffee cup that definitely wasn't his, "Hello there."

I nodded, hand to my mouth as I tried to gather my bearings. The little girl came running from the bathroom to meet us, squalid upon seeing the kittens.

"Do you guys want to come with me? I'll take you to a Kingdom I think you'll like."

George smiled at me, putting his hand on the little girl's head. "We're happy here," He looked up the stairs, "we have some people to look after."

"I figured," the smile that came to me was warm, that was the answer I was hoping for, "Want to name a kitten? We have two left."

Oliver knelt down so the little girl could look over the kittens and she pet every one.

"Tiffany," she kissed one atop their little head.

"And Ed," George's full-body laugh shook the pictures on the walls, "that was my brother's name."

"Good luck," the little girl bounced and waved as we left.

After fazing through the door, I tried to chase the dizziness away so we could keep going. Forcing my eyes open, I saw the Earthbound glow once again as I took a few wobbling steps. When I blinked, we were no longer in front of the Historical Society, but back in the park, standing in the shade of the trees above.

An aggressive sigh startled me as my view dropped down to see Ruth standing there, dull eyes digging into me.

"I know, I know, I'm sorry," I laughed as I picked up the kittens from the bike and the baker, "but I have a couple more for you."

"You're sabotaging yourself." Ruth turned to face us.

"Am I?" Waving to the boy as he pushed his trike up to Ruth's side, my eyes drifted over her crowd. "If I'm counting correctly, you have six and I have eleven." Stepping around, I stooped right before her, "I have Gus, Albert, Jeff, Nichole, Tola, Pie, Furvio, Russel, Tiffany, Ed, and Emily." Crossing my arms and shifting my weight, I looked her dead in the eye. "I bet you don't know the names of all your members." I turned from her, still smiling, as Oliver and I walked away, "Step it up, Earthbound King. You wouldn't want to be defeated by a simple Boggle, now would you?"

She said something under her breath and I was going to turn and ask her to repeat herself but the look on Oliver's face stopped me. He looked terrified for a moment before correcting himself and going back to looking over the kittens in his arms in irritation when one bit him. As we walked along, I gathered three more birds of different kinds, a puppy, a deer, a snake, a bunny, and a very upset hamster.

But that's when we saw…it. Stopping dead in our tracks, Oliver, the animals, and I starred into the pond. It was a large area of the river that opened up and often had silt issues. But this time instead of silt sitting in its waters, there was a humongous something. It almost looked like a...

"Is that a dinosaur?"

"A what?" Oliver stepped back, shifting all the kittens into one arm. "It looks like a dragon."

I looked over to him, a little confused. "Had they not discovered dinosaurs yet in your time?" I paused, "Wait, what? A dragon-"

I didn't get to finish my sentence because something started to materialize in his hand. A long knightly sword whose blade glowed with the tint of my crown appeared, the sunlight being eaten by the blade. I had always wondered how he'd try to protect me, if the situation arose. But as I looked back to the dinosaur, Hugo's words playing in my mind, I didn't think fighting it was a good idea.

I gently pushed the sword back down as he raised it, "I don't think you'll win, Oli."

Handing Oliver my kittens, he struggled to hold them all and I almost felt bad, but it was adorable. Starting toward the fence that separated the brick pathway from the pond, I sized the great beast up. The gargantuan creature looked down at me, moving slowly. It reminded me of the Loch Ness Monster with a long neck, round body, short fins, and stubby tail.

"Hello!" I called to it, just barely earning its attention. "You're a Futabasaurus, aren't you?" It started to move toward me and I wondered what the hell I was thinking. That was a dinosaur and I could be eaten in like, two bites. "You've been a Roamer for a very long time," I tried to not look away as it continued to get closer, "My little brother really likes dinosaurs and he talked about you a lot. You look just like what they thought you would, but you're a long way from home, aren't you?" Pointing to the side, I smiled, "Japan is that way."

Glancing back at Oliver, I could just hear what he wanted to say.

Yes, I know, I was talking to a dinosaur.

When I felt a gust of lukewarm air, it startled me. Turning, my breath caught in my throat. Eye level with me, the dinosaur looked into my soul. Trying to stay still and calm, I wondered if they could smell fear. Bringing my hand up, I tried to stop its shaking as I rested it atop the large head. It only took one touch to send a blue tint racing over it, claiming it for the Boggle. It was so large that its glow radiated around the whole area, making the trees and grass blue, too. Staring at it as it floated up and out of the water, I wished Hugo was there to see it.

"What should I name you?" I started back toward Oliver and the others who seemed horribly unsettled by my new friend. "How about," I stopped, looking at the huge floating creature as it eclipsed the sun, "Domino?" Shifting my weight, I pet them. "Domino the dinosaur."

Albert hid behind Oliver as his sword vanished and the cats hissed but I could just smile.

We continued on, the army one more strong. I had done a good job at filling the silence with aimlessly talking to the animals who couldn't understand me, desperately trying to not talk to the person who would. I suppose Oliver got tired of it because he stopped walking. Stopping too, my gut dropped as I stood under the weight of his gaze. Gently he set the kittens down and watched as they flocked to their mother. Walking slowly, he got closer to me. I stepped backward and into a tree, paralyzed by the intent in his eyes. He was set on doing something, and I didn't know what.

He just about pinned me to the tree, one of his legs between mine as he looked into my eyes so deeply I was afraid my insides would freeze over. I was going to ask what he was doing, but he brought his hand softly up to the side of my face. Going stiff, my heart raced into one hum of embarrassed confusion.

His touch felt so good despite me not wanting it to.

"Kasper," His voice was sad but I couldn't look at him, he was far too close to me. "what's wrong?"

"What's-" I turned to look at him but saw that his face was very close to mine, making my heart jump into my throat.

I could visibly see the sadness on his features, "Why…" He stepped back, allowing me to breathe. "What have I done to make you feel such horrible things?"

The animals went still, watching as I stood there, eyes frozen forward. Slowly looking to Oliver, my world came to a halt, "What do you mean?"

The way he was talking, it made it sound like he knew more about me than I did.

"There's something I might have forgotten to explain, Sire." He took off his coat, dropping it to the ground as he stepped toward me again. "I'm sorry it's taken this long to come up." As he slowly unbuttoned his shirt, my eyes flew away. "This is the King Connection."

I cautiously looked back but felt as if I was violating him when my eyes landed on the tattoo on his chest. A glowing blue crown that looked like mine sat on his skin over his heart. Its faint light pulsated with every beat of my heart.

"This connection is one between King and Handler. It's meant to help gauge the King's stability and relays their feelings to the Handler. It also makes sure you can always find me, if you happen to be separated from my side. At first you didn't feel poorly toward me, then you did, but then it got better, but over time it's gotten worse again and I don't know what to do to help you." He got close to me again, speaking softly, "Like right now, you're unsettled, on edge. Something about me being close to you causes it. Have I done something wrong?" He dropped his hand to mine, gently taking it in his, "When you saw those two people holding hands earlier, it made you happy. But when I do it, well, I can't understand the feeling it causes but it certainly isn't joy." He dropped his eyes when he let go of my hand and started to put his shirt back on. "I don't know what I did to cause this reaction in you, Sire, but I'm deeply sorry."

He had been toying with me to gauge my reaction? He knew how I had been feeling this entire time and I had no idea? I felt like his hand was inside my chest, squeezing my heart. As if he could open me up and see everything inside without my permission. I felt violated, like every emotion I had felt since dying was being sent to his mind. But what irked me most of all was that he had no idea what I was feeling, despite having the ability to know my feelings. The fact that he thought he made me feel awful, that he thought he had done something wrong, that he couldn't recognize the emotion taking me over for what it was, tore my core. I felt like a science experiment that his analytical eyes were struggling to quantify when what he really needed to be doing was to look for qualitative hints.

"What emotions do you sense in me?" I asked through clenched teeth, eyes on the ground.

He finished putting his coat on as he spoke. "Embarrassment, tension, heightened self awareness, anxiety. Your heart is racing and your mind is fuzzy. It happens every time I get close, sometimes when I make eye contact or say a certain thing. It always seems to come back to me, which has led me to believe that I am guilty of a wrongdoing toward you that I am somehow unaware of."

He said it so coolly, through a technical lens that made it feel inhuman. "Maybe if you had asked me instead conducting tests and being a fucking creep, I would have told you." My eyes jumped to his. "The emotion you're describing is love."

The way his eyes widened, the wave of understanding that crashed into him, it was a sight that would haunt me.

A black orb appeared between us and a moment later we were dropped into a free fall. The world blurred out when I was thrown out and right into the ground. Shakily pushing myself up from the floor, I looked over to Oliver. Heartbreak, it painted him as he struggled and failed to pick himself up, hand to his head as pain took over his features.

I wanted to tell him I wasn't angry with him, that I knew he didn't mean anything by it, that he just wanted to navigate it the right way and was in a weird position, that my mouth ran before my mind in the midst of my vulnerability, but my thoughts were shattered by roaring cheers.

"Welcome back, Kings." The Ghost King's voice boomed out around us.

Looking up, I was crushed under the gaze of the entire kingdom. Scrambling over, I helped Oliver stand as a spotlight flashed to life over us. To our side stood the other kings and their handlers, behind us was a large black curtain. Not letting go of Oliver's arm, the tension from the moments before still under my skin, I wasn't about to let him fall over.

"Let us see who is truly a leader at heart, one worthy of a Kingdom as great as this!"

All of the curtains fell at once and the crowd before us went silent. I looked to the side to see that the Demon's had two people, the Poltergeist had seven, Earthbound had eight. Turning fully around to look at my small army of cute things, and a dinosaur, I counted twenty.

Gus the squirrel came running toward me, climbing up my leg and onto my shoulder before jumping to sit in my crown once again.

"Very surprising outcome," The Ghost King said from his cloud floating above us all. "It appears the Kingdom wasn't expecting you to be triumphant, Boggle King." I turned back around and looked out over all the eyes on me as he went on, "You are proving to be a real competitor." I could feel the evil in their glares, hardly anyone in that room wanted me to be standing before them. The Ghost King laughed, "Or perhaps it's dumb luck."

The room exploded into laughter.

The Earthbound King cleared her throat sharply and some of the laughter stopped when her faction members fell silent. But I was still overwhelmed by the roar of laughter that echoed out from the Demon, the Shadow People, and the Reapers. Oliver slowly looked over to me, probably aware of the ruin that laughter wreaked inside. It reminded me of other laughter, the kind my classmates and family threw at me and my entire being, belittling my existence until there was little left.

The laughter Hugo faced at my funeral.

He reached out for my hand and I jumped away from him.

We stared at each other.

"Congratulations, Kasper." The Ghost King said, starting to fade away into his smoke. "Until the next trial, Kings."

Several black orbs were expelled from his cloud and as they hurled toward us, I couldn't bring myself to look at Oliver. He had done nothing wrong, this was on me. As the orb turned my world black, sending me into another free fall, I didn't struggle. Thrown out the other end, I crashed into something before falling to the floor. Books fell from the shelf in my room in Castle Boggle, landing around me on the floor. Staring up at the ceiling that was too high, I didn't want to move.

Iris came floating into my doorway but I lifted my hand and used my powers to slam it shut, locking them out. Hissing through my teeth as I stood, hand up to my face, I fell back into the bookshelf and stayed there. Watching through my fingers as Oliver struggled to stand, his pained eyes locked on mine. Taking a few slow, cautious steps forward, I could see the care in his every movement.

He was about to say something, something that probably would have calmed me down, something that would have made things better, something that would have turned into a productive conversation and not the emotionally charged words jumbled in my skull. I didn't trust myself to speak again, I didn't want to say something hurtful to my knight. He had done absolutely nothing wrong. But the backlash of the surprise, the fallout of my heart shaking, the knowledge that he could feel what I did, all those things tugged at each other in my head until something came out.

Something I regretted before I even said it. "Get lost, Oliver."

It was an order, a statement undeniably bold. His eyes flashed as he reached out toward me. He looked like he was struggling with himself as he tried to continue to reach out to me, but his eyes glowed brighter. I had no idea what was going on as he stood there, paralyzed. I hadn't seen his eyes glass over quite like that before, the glow of them reflecting in the budding tears.

Without a word he turned from me and left the room. The sound that door made when it closed reminded me of how big and empty and hollow and cold that castle was. I fell to my knees, arms wrapped around myself as I let out a harsh breath. That was way more dramatic than it needed to be. That could have been handled so much more maturely, in a way that neither of us would be hurt. I knew this, so why did my mind decide to rock the boat, causing Oliver and I to fall out?

With every step he took away, I felt the tug inside grow stronger.

As I fell apart, alone, kneeling on that hard ground, I desperately hoped that Oliver knew I didn't mean those words, that I wanted him to come back, that I needed him there, that I didn't want to hurt him. And most of all, I wished to my very core that Oliver could feel how much I cared for him and to know that I wasn't lashing out at him, but at myself.

I didn't deserve to be his King.

Chapter 7

WHAT SHADOWS KNOW

Time was such a terrible thing.

How long had it been?

My spine jolted, making my entire body seize.

Quickly muffling my yell, I stood from my knees.

The Royal Connection between Oliver and I bound us with that tug, helping me always find him if we were to be separated. Though I had felt it before, I didn't understand fully what that meant beyond the simple explanation Oliver gave me; I just knew what was hurting. Oliver was too far away from me and it didn't like that.

I had to find him, I had to apologize, I had to fix this.

My spine stung as I went stumbling out of the room and barreling down the hall.

Iris flew to my side as I ran, "What's wrong, Sire?"

"I'm stupid."

Iris hesitated for a moment, "What's new, Sire?"

"Where is Oliver?"

Landing on my shoulder, their playful tone faded, "He left through the Flipside portal."

I nearly tripped, "What why?" Worry deposited inside as every step left me feeling stagnate, like I wasn't getting any closer or any farther. He must have been moving still, so the space between us wasn't closing. But why would he go Flipside? He knew nothing of the world that was on the other side of that portal. He would end up lost for all eternity if he was left to his own devices there.

Wait.

He'd…get lost?

I ran into the goddamn door.

Laying on the marble floor, Iris floating around above me, I groaned. "It was a figure of speech, dammit." Picking myself up, I yanked the door open and bolted down the stairs and onto the path. "You stay here. Send someone to tell me if Oliver comes back, alright?"

Iris slowed down. "Yes Sire." Their whisper grew louder as I approached the portal. "Remember Sire, he's just shy."

I ran into the portal. The discombobulating spin it threw me into was nothing compared to the churning in my core. Oliver was shy, Oliver was kind, Oliver was loyal, Oliver was my knight, and Oliver was lost. Did he even understand what I said? Did that count as a confession? Or was it lost on him, a needless omission?

Stumbling into a tree as I was thrown out of the portal, I leaned into it, face against the bark.

What even was love?

My parents at my funeral flashed through my mind as I ran along the sidewalk Flipside. Their sunglasses, their act, the way they laughed at Hugo with the rest at my funeral, they didn't know what love was. But then my mind drifted to Les. Did he love Hugo and I? He took care of us, looked after us, smiled at and supported us. Or was he just doing his job? Was Oliver just doing his job, too?

I clenched my teeth, rounding a corner toward the cemetery. Why was I so terrible at communicating? Why couldn't I just say what I meant in a calm manner without hurting the only person who was close to me? I guess I didn't have a lot of practice, getting along with people. Only a handful of people looked at me like anything more than dirt under the rug. I was too old for this shit, but too young to know how to do it better.

Barreling into the graveyard, I was about to call out to Gaston when I heard someone speak from somewhere I couldn't see.

"But the Ghost Hunters, they're just-" Favio's sentence was cut off.

A few long moments later, Gaston spoke. "Like I said, I'm loyal to King Kasper now." He paused for a few more moments before picking back up again. "So if you want my help, you're going to have to take it up with him."

There was another pause and I just couldn't seem to find them, despite hearing them close by. Their pauses were strange, far too long for a normal beat, but too short to be a long silence.

"They're here because of him." Favio said before another pause, "They're trying to investigate the tantrum he threw at the cinema."

Gaston spoke after yet another strange pause, "Why can't you handle this one on your own?"

I stopped walking and just looked around when they paused again. Where the hell were they?

"Normally I could take care of it," Favio paused and that's when I realized his voice was coming from behind Gaston's normal perch stone, "but they're attracting too much attention from the demons and I worry it won't end well. I'm only so powerful, being a lower king."

Starting toward the headstone, I tried to think about what I was going to say.

"I'm sure Kasper will allow me to help," Gaston paused, "you just have to ask."

"No, I will never ask him for his-" Favio's word was cut short, muffled.

Walking around the headstone, what I saw made me stop mid-step. Sitting there was Favio, his back up against the headstone, Gaston straddling his lap. They were locked in a passionate kiss and hadn't even noticed me, Favio's arms wrapped around Gaston, up under his coat. Standing there feeling like a creep, I looked away. They acted like they didn't get along, but it must have been just an act because they were really getting along now.

I cleared my throat.

They jumped then absolutely flew away from each other when they saw me. Sitting on the ground, eyes wide as they were locked on mine, they both looked as if they were grappling to somehow explain that situation.

I continued to look away, "Have you seen Oliver?"

As if nothing had happened, Gaston sprung to his feet, floating for a moment before his shoes made contact with the ground, "No, why? Get lost?"

"No…" I still didn't look at him, "I said some awful things and he left. But I need to find him and do my best to apologize."

"A king should never apologize to his servant." Favio's dark tone tainted the air as he stood, slowly as his lanky limbs straightened to showcase his threatening height.

My eyes snapped up from the ground, anger sparking inside, "What a callous way to be, I'm lucky to not be in your faction." I took a step closer, "And Oliver is not a servant, he is my friend."

Favio looked like he wanted to roll his eyes but that would be too much effort. "You are not a king I shall acknowledge. Go back to the potato fields, it's where your kind belongs."

"Hey now," Gaston slung his arm around Favio, mischief on his breath, "I'd be nice to him if I were you. He totally has blackmail now. He saw us."

Favio went stiff.

I scoffed, starting to walk away, "I couldn't care less."

My skin crawled when Favio's hand landed on my shoulder, stopping me. "No, you have to care. You're playing a political game. Everyone thinks you're so kind, but I know you're acting."

I clenched my jaw, the sky above us darkening in that moment. "Oh do you now?" As I turned to look at him, he let go, "If you're so sure I can't just be nice with no ulterior motive, help me out and we'll call it even." I tried to calm myself, I didn't want to disappoint Oliver by losing it. "I need to find Oliver."

"How did you even manage to lose someone you're connected to? Can you not feel his presence?" Gaston asked as he let go of Favio, inspecting me.

"I can sort of feel it, but I don't have a lot of practice with it so I can't seem to actually locate him. He hasn't stopped moving,

I've been running forever with no luck." I looked up to Gaston, "And I know you can't leave this place normally, otherwise I'd ask you instead, I far prefer your company."

"Aw, I'm flattered Sire," he bowed his head slightly, "but give Favio here a chance, he's not all bad."

"Alright," Favio's slow words dripped like molasses into my ears, "I'll help you find your servant. That way we will be even and if you break your end, your reputation is cracked and not mine." Favio walked from Gaston and closer to me. "Do you have a general direction? Or should I use my subjects to search the area?"

"You can do that?" I nonchalantly took a step to the side as to keep distance between Favio and I.

He simply sighed. Raising his hand from his side, the shadows of all the objects around us came to life. They spun around us on the ground before dispersing, crawling over the ground quickly.

"It shouldn't take them too long to locate him." Favio started to leave the cemetery. "In the meantime, I feel like I need to explain something to you."

Could he get any more pretentious? I begrudgingly followed him, waving to Gaston as I left. "What wisdom do you wish to bestow upon me, Shadow King?"

He scoffed, tossing his gaze my way. "Do you have no respect?"

"Do you?"

He stared at me, very obviously not amused.

"Really, Shadow King, why should I respect you if you give me no reason to? Last I checked, I hadn't personally wronged you, so I have no idea what I did to earn this treatment." Stopping, I extended a hand his way, doing my best to be cordial and smile, "Though I'm new, I'm just as much of a King as you are."

He looked up to me from my hand as he brushed past me, ignoring my gesture. "I owe you no respect." I tried to stay in step with him, but his legs were longer than mine.

It was hard to try to find something to talk with him about. I could barely look him in the eyes because they were so creepy. His dark presence was sharp, his voice shook my bones, and his glare made my blood spike. Everything was telling me that he was no good, that I needed to stay away from him, even Favio himself. But I felt that I was reading him wrong. Like if I looked a little harder, I might see the King inside him.

I jumped when a little shadow came racing back to us. It got to Favio's feet then when it made contact, it filled out into the full shadow of a man.

The shadow then spoke, "Sire, we have located the Ghost Hunters. They are again attracting Demon attention. How should we proceed?"

Favio groaned, holding his face in his hand for a moment. "We'll take care of it, continue your search for the Knight."

"Yes Sire." The shadow saluted him then broke off, crawling away on the ground.

Favio dropped his hand and looked over at me, "This is your fault, you know."

"I didn't mean to attract people, really didn't think anyone would take it seriously. I was the only one around here for years that did, so I have no idea where they came from."

He immediately turned and started in another direction. "Follow me." I did my best to but he just walked so quickly. "Because of your irresponsibility, you've become somewhat of an urban legend already since your death. It has brought television show ghost hunters from all over the country and we've been able to ward all of them off except this one group. They're daft and so incessant that they won't leave no matter what we do and because of that, they're getting the demon's attention too. It'll be a whole lot more paperwork and effort for me if they end up possessed or something so you're going to help me scare them off once and for all."

I couldn't really argue with that, I was smiling way too much. Me? An urban legend? I had become one with the ghost stories I loved so much. I felt as if my legacy was completed and that, regardless if I won the Almighty Crown or not, I would have still accomplished something. As we rounded the corner to the theater, I could just hope that they had cameras because I was about to put on one hell of a show. And maybe if I was lucky, Oliver would see the storm and come scold me.

"Hey guys, look at this," A young lady said, holding up her EMF detector as it lit up to the red.

Another lady and a man leaned over and smiled at each other when they saw it fluctuating. They were standing next to my sign, which I was happy to see that no one was able to remove. It was now roped off with the things they used to section off waiting lines inside the theater. A little sign hung from the rope in front of it. It read:

Kasper's Curse

Do Not Touch

I liked the sound of that. Walking up to it, I made the hunter's equipment beep and hum. They looked up and around, whispering to each other excitedly. I knew who they were, they were a group just starting out with a show on the internet. No big television network had picked them up, but that didn't stop them. They were from the other coast, far away from my Central Oregon city. They traveled a long way to look for me, so I was going to return the favor. Hopefully they were recording because my show was about to get them theirs.

Lifting my hand, I summoned my storm clouds, making the air rumble with thunder. They jumped and I even managed to startle some of the people waiting in line for their tickets. They had been glaring at the ghost hunters the same way they looked at me once. I wasn't going to let them get away with that.

My crown sped up above my head, snapping with electricity. I wasn't allowed to show myself, but they never said anything about trying to talk to people. "Hello."

The fact that they nearly flew from their skin told me that they heard me. Favio looked like he was about to snap at me but then a wave of small demons came rushing at the hunters and he jumped into action to stop them.

I walked up to the hunters, reaching out to touch their equipment. The man had a camera that he recorded the sensors with as he quietly narrated what was happening. I couldn't stop smiling as I walked around them to stand behind them. Looking over their shoulders, I saw they had the calibration wrong on one of their machines. I reached forward, focusing for a moment to be able to dial it to the correct number but not be seen.

"It's totally him," One of the ladies whispered.

"Well, what do we say?" The other whispered back.

I walked around to be in front of them, crossing my arms with a smile as the concentrated storm above us grew.

"Uh," One of the ladies started, "Kasper, is it you?"

I nodded and a mild bolt of lightning struck my roped off protest sign.

They jumped back.

"Did that mean yes?" The guy asked and the others didn't have any reply, "Okay," the guy went on, "if you're not Kasper, do that again but twice."

I did nothing and they exploded into hushed excitement.

"My turn," the other lady looked up from the sensor in her hand, "Kasper, did you curse this theater?"

I nodded and lightning struck the sign.

They looked to each other then back toward the sign.

"Are you trapped here?" The first lady asked.

I shook my head and lightning struck the sign twice.

"Then why are you here?" The other lady asked.

"You have to stick to yes or no questions." the guy said.

"Oh, uh, yes, I'm sorry." She thought for a moment. "Are you here to see us specifically?"

I nodded and lightning struck the sign once as the storm continued to grow. I was simply humoring them until I had enough power above me to give them the greatest paranormal experience of their lives. Favio fought off the occasional demons, returning them to the demon realm with his shadow powers. That kept him busy enough that he couldn't interfere with me. I could feel Oliver's tug getting further away with each moment which worried me, but I had to keep calm. I was starting to get better control over those powers and I didn't want to lose that grip there and accidentally hurt someone.

"Are you happy as a ghost?" the guy asked.

I nodded, lightning striking the sign once.

"Are you ever going to move on and stop haunting this town?" one of the ladies asked.

With a smile, I shook my head. Lighting struck the sign twice and with that, I was ready.

Raising my hands slowly, the wind speeds in the area around us started to pick up. The lights on the theater's sigh flickered, the people waiting in line began to step further away. I had a plan and it was going to make paranormal history. The sky rumbled, the ground vibrated, lighting danced in the air. The ghost hunters were not fazed, I liked them.

The demons attacking exponentially grew in numbers and they were starting to make it through Favio's defenses.

Lightning started to hit the ground around the hunters but they didn't move. The clouds began to lower, filling the surrounding air with fog. I obstructed my view of Favio with the fog as I approached the hunters. With a snap of my fingers, lightning rained down around us, constantly striking the ground in a circle around the hunters and I. They still didn't seem scared, and at that point I started to wonder if they were just stupid, not brave.

Once we were fully surrounded by fog and lightning, I summoned one last bolt of lighting to strike me. When it did, I became visible to them. I knew it was against the rules, but I was confident in my ability to get away with it.

They all jumped, their eyes huge, when I appeared.

Oh, so a barrage of unnatural lightning wasn't scary but I was?

With a sigh, I started, "Hello there." Looking from their camera back to them, a smile took me. "I'm flattered that you came all this way to find me, but I have to ask you to leave. It's not safe here right now, things are in unrest in the paranormal. But I'll come find you again and give you another show someday, I promise. But for now, please do get far away from here." I stepped closer, "Do you understand?"

They stared as they smiled and nodded.

"Alright, good," I bowed slightly. "Until next time."

I snapped again and the lighting surrounding us exploded outward, taking out all of the demons, rocking the ground, and knocking everyone off of their feet. There I stood, no longer visible to the living, with a chorus of car alarms in the background. I looked around to see everyone picking themselves up. The ghost hunters went running and I waved at them as they left. Favio sat on the ground, looking up to me with a frozen glare. I walked up to him, extending my hand with a smile. He stared at me for a few moments more then stood on his own.

"A Boggle shouldn't possess that much power." He took a step closer to me but I didn't budge, "What are you?"

After a moment of unbroken eye contact, I stepped around him to his side, "I'm just me."

He stormed past me, anger obvious in the tension in his jaw.

"Did I earn any respect with that?"

He shook his head.

"Aw, come on," I hurried to his side, "That's not fair. I was cool back there."

"Why should I respect a kitten who foolishly believes himself to be a lion? You should get back in your place before you follow the last Boggle King into shameful obscurity."

I had heard mention of the King before me, that she was important to Oliver and a wise soul, but beyond that I knew nothing of what happened. And since Favio mentioned it, I did have an opportunity. "Who was the last Boggle King?"

"Have they not told you?" He didn't look at me as we walked along the side of the empty road. "I suppose I can understand why, they don't want to plant predictions of failure in your mind. Although it is inevitable either way, so I shall be the bearer of bad news." He paused, the air growing heavy around us. "Her name was Tola Vestile."

My breath hitched. I knew both of those names, and they both connected to Oliver.

"She was the younger sister of your servant. Upon his death, Oliver was claimed by the Demon faction due to his rotten humanity in life, but Tola was different. She was the first, and previously only, human Boggle. She, like you, became apart of the King Trials, and she, like you shall, failed disastrously."

"How does one fail at a King Trial?" I didn't want to ask what I wanted to ask. Oliver had a sister who was claimed by the Boggle? He said that she convinced him to join the Boggle, and that she wasn't defeated. He said she gave up. There was a story there that was already heartbreaking and I didn't even know it.

"She let her heart lead the way and was conquered by it. She allowed a demon to get close, and that demon inflicted a blight so potent that she was banished from this world."

"But Oliver can heal blights," I grasped for straws that I feared had already hit the floor, "why didn't he-"

"One can not heal a blight they inflicted."

I stopped walking.

"I see you know very little of the person closest at your side." He stopped a few steps in front of me. "Your ignorance is sickening." He raised his hand and shadows came racing back to us. Spinning around on the ground, they jumped into the air and created a circular wall of shadow around me. "You must know the past, Kasper. That's the only way you can make sure to repeat it."

The shadows closed in on me, making my world dark.

"Not every demon starts off that way." Favio's deep voice came from all around me as a scene faded to color in the darkness.

Before me was a throne room, an audience, a king, a kneeling knight. I watched as Oliver was knighted, his eyes full of bold determination as they sat on the ground beneath the king's feet. When he stood, he stood proudly, his chin held high, his gaze strong. I was stuck in his presence; it was so vivid it made my heart stumble over to the side. I ran up to him, reaching out, but then I went through him. Turning around, I saw the shadow reforming into him. This was nothing more than an illusion.

"Some humans start out with good intentions, like you."

The scene around me changed to a homey cottage. Oliver entered through the door and was immediately met by a young lady, not much younger than him. She crashed into him with a hug and he held her close. I had never seen that sort of smile on his face before. She had long wispy orange hair like his, and eyes that held a similar coldness, but with a spark of something Oliver's didn't posses.

Oliver and Tola disappeared from the scene.

"But they will always fall to the same thing."

The house was suddenly engulfed in flames. I turned around to see Tola, collapsed on the floor behind me. I lunged toward her, trying to help her out but my hand went right through the shadow. Running out of the house, I saw a flag stuck in the ground. When my eyes drifted from the flag to the crowd of people watching, I saw Oliver. He fought with all his might against the men holding him back from running into the house. He was annihilated, yelling things I couldn't hear. But I didn't have to hear him to know what he was saying.

He fell to his knees as the house collapsed in on itself and when he looked back up, his eyes were on the flag next to me. He slowly stood and approached the flag. In the moment he took it, I saw something so dark in those eyes of his I don't think I'll ever forget it.

The world turned to shadow around me until suddenly I was surrounded by death. An army led by Oliver relentlessly cut down every member of the opposing one, the army that bore the flag that was left before Oliver's burning home. It was unlike anything I had ever seen, the surrounding buildings on fire, the ground littered in gore. The fighting happened all around me, constantly bodies were falling from both armies. I wondered if it would ever end as I spun around, looking for Oliver. When I blinked, every man had fallen except one.

I ran to Oliver as he stood atop the bodies of both sides, blood covered his clothing and dripped down his face. The darkness in his eyes had left, replaced by the tears streaming from them. I reached out to him, the shadows starting to dull out around us, but my hands just went through.

This wasn't what the history books said happened. They painted him as a monster, someone so evil they deserved the title of a demon. But that's not what Oliver was at all. He was a flawed, terrified, angry, heartbroken human like the rest of us. How dare they teach us otherwise?

He took his sword in hand, looking around at his revenge. I couldn't stop him, but I did try, as he turned his sword around. A pause took him as he looked around, the fire reflecting in his tears. Tightening his grip, he impaled himself. He fell through my arms when I tried to catch him and I was left, kneeling on the ground at his side. His hands fell limp from the handle of his sword as his eyes closed, tears still pouring from them. I saw the life leave him and I wanted nothing more than to pull him up into my arms, but I couldn't.

History had no idea what ended up killing Knight Oliver Vestile, The Great, but I did. The only force strong enough to end his life was his broken heart.

The world plunged into cold so suddenly it shocked my system, making my hair stand on end. Turning around, I saw Nirvana. I didn't even notice his presence before. He strolled up to Oliver's body as if it was just another day. He looked over him then lifted up his arm. A bit of the clouds above swirled down and formed a scythe in his hand and a moment later, he sent it plummeting into Oliver's chest. I fell back, startled as I stared up at Nirvana. He yawned then a light flashed. When it faded from my eyes, Oliver's ghost was standing next to his body, looking around until his gaze landed on Nirvana. He slowly looked down to see his body and panic only had a moment to run through his features before the ground beneath us turned into a black hole and we all fell through it.

The discombobulating darkness threw us around reminding me of what it felt like to die, until we were dropped in the middle of somewhere I didn't recognize. Standing from my knees, I looked around at the castle that appeared as if it was constructed of embers. Standing in a group around us were endless demons. We must have been in Castle Demon. I was startled when Nolan approached, but even more so when he bowed to Oliver. When he stood from the bow, he produced a ring in his hand and my world came to a screeching halt when he put it on Oliver's finger. In the same way that mine did, a crown materialized in Oliver's hand then floated above his head.

Knight Oliver Vestile, The Great, was the Demon King.

He looked around when the other Demons bowed and my heart hurt when I saw how confused he looked. But then the Demons rose from their bows and started cheering, rushing up to him. He was surrounded by rowdy demons, creatures that seemed to accept him. And I saw it, the moment he decided that wasn't a bad thing because he felt like one of them. I just knew it, the way the sheen on his eyes changed and his smile tugged. That was the reckless look of someone who had no self value.

The scenery changed to the King Castle hall, the one I followed Oliver down to meet the other Kings. I was alone, though, so with no other thought I went to the room where the meeting had been held. Walking through the door, I saw several beings sitting the table. But three caught my eye. Sitting the furthest away was the Earthbound King, the man who would go on to be the current Ghost King. Next to the Earthbound was Tola and Iris. There was a couple Poltergeist there, too, though they all looked the same to me. But where was Oliver?

The door flew open, startling everyone in the room. I turned around to see Oliver and Nolan smirking as they entered.

That was not the Oliver I knew. His eyes were glowing red and with them his smile was toxic. He sat down rudely, Nolan just as obnoxious at his side. They were truly Demons. How much time had passed since Oliver died? How long had he spent in the company of hell? How did he become like that?

He was laughing with Nolan until he scanned the others in the room. When his eyes met with Tola's, he went rigid. Suddenly in a large flash of light, someone else appeared in the room. It was the Ghost King of that time, a Demon. They were not much more than rotting flesh clinging to bone, a zombie if I had ever seen one. And as I stood there, desperately trying to yank my eyes away from them, I was thankful that this was but an illusion and that I couldn't smell him. Eyes finally falling down, they were trapped staring at Oliver as he stared at Tola. As if I could see his world falling down around him, I wanted to do anything to stop it. But I knew I couldn't.

"Your servant fit right in with the demons. He gave into his hatred and acted upon revenge, earning himself the demonic crown. A person like that doesn't simply change." Favio said, his voice booming through the illusion.

The scene changed to somewhat of a montage surrounding me, as if days passed me by in the matter of a few blinks. I don't know all of what I saw, but it must have been the trials. They passed by so quickly, as if Favio didn't want me to see them. But I did catch a glimpse of something; Tola's beaming smile. I hadn't even heard her say anything and had only seen her a handful of times, but I already knew she was something different. Her presence was so soulful and loving that I could feel it through the illusion.

Everything around me came to a stop.

Looking around, I was now in what appeared to be an arena, the entire Kingdom watching. I turned around and was faced with Tola. Stumbling backwards, I went right through someone else. When I got my balance, I looked back up to see Oliver's back. They were facing off against each other in an arena. Why? Before I could think on that more, they drew their swords and like that, they were fighting. Was this a trial? Why would two Kings have to fight each other? I looked around to see the Demon Ghost King sitting up on a throne, a smile torn across their rotting face. It must have been their doing.

Oliver's crown glowed brightly, as if the red of it grew with every beat of his heart. His eyes followed that trend to the point that they were entirely red. He looked like hell itself sat in his core, driving his actions. Tola fought gently, never landing a blow on him even though she could have. I could see her mouth moving, as if she was speaking to him quietly. His fighting was sloppy, a true disgrace to the accurate slashes and blows I observed him make when he was alive. It was like he was power drunk and mentally absent.

The crowd roared, chanting many different things when Tola tripped. Oliver stepped over her, a chuckle on his breath as he held out his hand. I ran up, trying to push him away but I went right through him and fell to the ground next to Tola. I looked up to Oliver and my blood solidified. The look on his face, the smile, the red of his eyes, it was the scariest thing I had ever seen. But when I looked over to Tola, I just saw that she was smiling.

A red glow emitted from Oliver's palm and a moment later, it blasted at Tola, drowning the world in tainted red light. When it faded, the Kingdom exploded into cheers. Tola lay, motionless on the ground, her skin covered in a dark, massive blight that nearly engulfed her completely. Oliver stood, frozen, eyes on Tola. When he dropped his sword, it never hit the ground; it turned into smoke before it could. His face was flat, not wearing a smile or a frown. He just stood there, staring.

The Ghost King came down and was starting to approach Oliver when Iris came racing down, too. Oliver took back his hand and slowly looked around at the surrounding Kingdom. The red light in his eyes fading a little. I jumped when Tola started to move, the Kingdom went still and silent.

Oliver looked back to her as she shakily stood. She started to flicker, as if she was fading in and out of existence as she fell onto Oliver, wrapping her arms around him. She said something to him and that's when the red in his eyes snapped away, leaving the naturally cold blue that they were when he was alive.

He stood, paralyzed for a few moments before tightly hugging her. He said things back, obviously panicked. She shook her head, burring it into his shoulder as she spoke on and with each passing moment, Oliver's eyes glasses over more. He shook his head, saying things in protest as he held her tighter. I saw his hands emit a different glow, one that was a soft golden color, but nothing happened. She started to fade more as his grip tightened. I could physically feel the desperation washing over him as she stepped back.

She brought her blighted hand up to his face and said one more thing to him before she faded away.

I have never seen a heart destroyed so violently before. Oliver reached forward, trying to pull her back but she was no longer there. The arena around him roared, cheers and yells alike took over the air. He stood, looking around as tears welled up in his eyes. As the Ghost King approached him, Oliver's breaths became jagged. He quickly looked down to his hand and without a moment of hesitation, he tried to rip the ring off. He yelled out, the air around him jolting with a ripping red aura. The crowd fell quiet again as the Ghost King broke into a run toward Oliver. Oliver fought with the ring, as if it was the most painful thing he had ever done. The air shook when he got it off and a moment later, he threw it to the ground and it shattered. The red crown above Oliver's head imploded, bleaching the world in red.

I sat on the ground, horrified, as the world faded back. The Ghost King stormed up to Oliver, picking him up by the collar and yelling something at him. But Oliver was silent, still, eyes wide and tear stained. He shook Oliver but he didn't react. Obviously frustrated, the Ghost King threw Oliver to the ground. Iris flew up to him as the Kingdom broke out into chaos. Oliver weakly looked to Iris, slowly bring up his hand. The moment he made contact with Iris the world was covered in a blue light and with it, we went tumbling through nothingness again.

When I sat up from the ground, I saw that we were in front of Castle Boggle. Before me was Oliver, hunched over hands in his hair, forehead nearly touching the ground, as sadness so potent tore through him I could understand why he'd be numb after that. Boggle slowly gathered around him, offering silent support as they glowed with the Boggle blue tint. When he looked up to them, his eyes started to glow, too, as tears still streamed down from them.

I sat and watched Oliver absolutely fall apart, the only human in the entirely of Boggle, as Favio spoke.

"The last Boggle King tried to reach for a power too great for a Boggle and suffered the consequences. And Oliver fell to it too, ruining his future as the Almighty Ghost King. Just because his allegiance changed, don't assume that monster doesn't still live inside. A human has to be of an exceptionally high caliber of evil to be considered for Demon citizenship, and of an ungodly level to become their King."

I stood as the scene faded from around me, leaving me surrounded by a shadow. "How do you know all of this?"

Favio stepped out of the darkness to face me, hands in his pockets. "The shadows see everything."

"That's funny, because you missed something very important."

"You think so?" His tone was sharper than before.

"Yeah," I smiled despite having my chest tightening with every beat of my heart. "you missed the part where Oliver changed."

"You'll regret your faith in him, Boggle. And because of it, you'll fall to the same fate."

Crossing my arms and shifting my weight, I looked away. "Thanks for the warning, but I don't understand why you're giving it to me; since you want me to fail."

"Oliver's actions then caused a huge state of unrest in the entire Kingdom. I'm simply trying to keep the peace, it's my job."

I looked around the never ending shadow, "Hey, do you believe in fate, Shadow King?"

"No, I do not."

I turned back around to look at him, "Well that's a shame, because I do. And I have a feeling that this all happened to lead up to right now. I'm going to change things, Favio," I looked him right in the eye, "and it's up to you which side of history you wish to stand on." Starting toward him with each step I felt my fear fade, "I get it, your thing is darkness and shit. But maybe if you were to lighten up a little bit," I poked him in the forehead, "you'd see the people and not just the shadows they cast."

Favio's eyes were so wide, I almost expected to see white. But no, the whites of his eyes were just totally black. "What the hell are you?"

I stepped back with a bounce, "I answered that already, I'm me."

The shadow around us disappeared when I blinked, showing that we were in the far end of the park the first trial was held in. A few steps behind Favio my eyes caught on Oliver as he walked away.

"Oli!" Breaking out into a sprint, I ran past Favio. I ran around Oliver when he didn't react and when I stopped, I was shocked. He didn't look up, he didn't stop, he didn't even notice me. "Oli?" I stepped out of his way as he continued to walk past me. "Hello?" I waked by his side. "I'm sorry I'm such an asshole, Oliver. And if you're too angry to talk right now, I understand. But…" I looked away from him and to the path in front of us. "I have something I want to talk to you about as soon as possible."

My mind was made up, I wasn't going to let me put my foot in my mouth any longer. I would say what I felt and if there was bad fallout, then I'd have to deal with it. I'd rather that than spend eternity wondering, 'what if'.

"Boggle." Favio called out. "What are you doing?"

I turned to look at him as he jogged to catch up with Oliver and I. "Well I'd like to apologize, but Oliver obviously doesn't want to talk to me."

Favio stopped in front of us, grabbing Oliver by the back of his coat and causing him to stop walking. "Do you really have no idea what is going on here?" When I just stared at him, he sighed. "Shit, they just threw you into this didn't they?" He looked to Oliver who acted as if he was utterly mentally absent, staring at the ground with his eyes that were glowing brighter than normal. "You have a gift, as a King, called Royal Command. When you order one of your subjects to do something, they must. If they fight it too much, they'll be brought to unconsciousness through excruciating pain. It's not something to use lightly." He rolled his eyes over to mine. "So what did you last say to him, exactly?"

I could barely breathe, that power horrified me. It took everything I could muster to not be brought to tears as I looked back to Oliver. "Get lost…"

He groaned. "Yes. That would do it. You must be more careful with your wording, if you don't want to misuse that power." he shoved Oliver toward me, "And you're the only one who can break its hold on him."

Oliver stumbled into me and as I held his arm in my hand, I just stared. I had playfully ordered things in the past that he would simply banter back at me over. When I thought back on the night I lost it at my funeral, something sort of like this happened. I told him to let go, and he did, but he collapsed afterward. Was that what happened? He tried to defy my order so strongly that it took him down?

I pulled him into a hug, speaking softly. "I'm sorry Oliver. I didn't mean to do this to you. You did a good job, you got lost." I hugged him tighter. "But you're not lost any more because I found you."

A moment passed.

Oliver jumped, "Sire?"

I smiled, tightening my grip. "I'm so sorry, I didn't mean what I said. I don't know why I said it, but it wasn't what I wanted to say." My voice cracked, "I'm so bad at expressing things and I'm sorry you felt the brunt of my personal flaw."

My heart spun when he brought his arms up around me. "Sire, why are you so sad?"

I couldn't even answer him as I fell apart in his embrace. I had just watched a part of his life he had kept from me, probably on purpose. I didn't want to make Oliver uncomfortable by telling him that I knew, but at the same time seeing him so destroyed tore me up.

Oliver rested his head on my shoulder, a smile in his tone. "'Get lost' is an expression, isn't it?"

I jumped back, glaring at him through the tears. "Yes. Yes it is."

When he laughed, I couldn't help but join him. Favio stared at us as we laughed, his eyes particularly heavy on Oliver. Now I knew why people looked at him like that. If he was once a monster of a person and a hell of a demon, of course they'd be surprised to see that he had changed. He spent a long time alone in the Boggle realm, and he had changed. I couldn't wait to show them all that.

Turning to Favio, I wiped my eyes and smiled. "Thank you for helping me find him. We're even now, your secret is safe with me."

Favio simply nodded and turned away from us, starting to walk the opposite way down the path. He stopped before turning back to look at us. "I'll ask you this one more time, Boggle King. What are you?"

Before I could answer with my cop-out again, Oliver replied with boundless confidence. "Exactly what we need."

Favio froze. Looking over to Oliver slowly, he just smiled at me, his eyes churning with certainty. I didn't even notice that Favio had started back my way until he was right in front of me. I stepped back, a little startled when my eyes met his.

"I still don't know what to think of your kindness, Kasper. You are either too stupid to fear the system, or too confident to be defeated by it." He paused, his eyes scanning mine. "But, if you're able to invoke that level of loyalty in Knight, then I would be a fool to not follow you."

He brought his hand up and lightly tapped my crown. A dark flash of light took over my world for a moment and when it faded I was left, staring at him. Favio looked from my crown to me as he took a step back. Shock raced through me as he took to one knee, bringing his hand to his heart.

"If you ever happen to be separated from your Knight, call upon me. There are shadows everywhere." He looked up to me from the bow. "Now that you know the history that you're mirroring, you can do one of two things." He stood. "Have the audacity to try to do everything differently, or have the bravery to follow the same path, but do it right." He turned and started to walk away with a wave. "I trust that you can decide which is best, Sire." Stepping into the shadow of a tree, he disappeared.

I had managed to win over the Shadow King too? I ran over to the railing that separated us from the river pond. Looking at my reflection, I saw my crown as it spun above my head. Next to the Angel's gem sat a new one. It was black and churning as if a shadow itself was encased inside. So that meant that I was now actually three factions strong?

"Something like this has never happened before." Oliver said quietly, walking to my side. "You are something special, Sire, to win over the hearts of those who would normally be your rivals for power."

I watched my crown spin around and when the new gem appeared in my reflection again, I smiled a little. I really was changing things. Favio was right, I did have two options. As I stepped away from the railing and looked to the shadow Favio stepped into, I decided that I was going to be audacious.

Oliver and I stood in silence for a moment but then my heart hit the ground. I was resolved to tell him something, but I didn't know if I had the guts to. He could sense my feelings, but without the thought context they were in, he'd never be able to understand what I was experiencing.

"So…Oli?"

He looked over to me, making my heart jump back into my chest. "Yes, Sire?"

"Want to…uhm." I was choking on my own words this early on? There was no way I was going to get out what I wanted to say. "Go for a walk?"

He looked around, "Well, considering that appears to be what I was doing already, sure."

I couldn't bring myself to laugh at that, I was too busy drowning myself in nervousness.

"A secret?" Oliver asked with a smile as we started to walk. "What do you know about the Shadow King that I do not?"

"I promised not to tell. But it's a fantastic, adorable, secret."

We walked along for a few moments before he spoke again, "Are you alright Sire? You're extremely nervous."

I groaned through my teeth, "That's so violating…"

"I'm sorry Sire, but it's not really up to me."

"I know." I sighed as we walked along the river, the light wind blowing the trees around but not touching us. "It's just unfair. I have to guess what's up with you like normal, but you just know what's going on with me."

"Actually Sire there is one-"

I had barely heard what he said as I stopped. It was now or never. "Oli."

He stopped, staring at me in surprise, "Sire?"

"I have something very important to tell you. I'm going to say this now, if anything I say makes you uncomfortable then I can stop. But I want this out in the air instead of locked up in my head. If I don't explain myself, then even with your ability to sense what I'm feeling, you're still just getting half of the picture."

Oliver looked a little too serious for comfort, "Alright, I understand."

I took a deep breath, so deep it made me cough and look like an idiot. Oliver stood there, brow raised as he watched me grapple to regain my composure. I straightened, face red, embarrassment coursing sharply through my veins as I looked back at him.

"As I'm sure you've noticed, I'm not the best with words. I'm not really sure how to articulate things correctly sometimes and I don't have much practice with intense feelings so…" I started to run out of breath, totally not sure what I was trying to say. "What I mean is, I'm not trying to make an excuse for how I treated you earlier, because I was entirely in the wrong and you were being totally reasonable. I overacted because I didn't know how to handle the information and I shouldn't have said anything at all. But I did and I'm sorry…"

I took a nearly gasping breath.

Oliver was looking at me, a small warm smile on his face. He was patiently listening, kindly watching me, and I could only wonder what was going through his mind.

"But that's not all that I wanted to say. I'm not entirely sure, because I don't even know if what I'm feeling is worthy of the title, but-" I stopped myself when I felt my heart beat so hard I was sure it exploded. Looking to him, nervous, scared, worried, I didn't feel worthy of the words I was about to say. But something about the way his smile was slowly growing made my heart beat steady. It was still smashing against my ribcage, but now it felt like it wasn't racing out of control.

I stood a few steps closer to him, "I had a feeling that this would happen from the moment I met you at the pool. I didn't know anything about you back then, so it was naive to think I had any right to think anything about you back then. But now that I've officially met you, been with you, and gotten to know the person behind those amazing glowing eyes, I think I know how to articulate my feelings into words." I forced myself to look up from the ground to the eyes I was captivated by. "Oliver, I love you."

A duck landed in the water next to us.

Oliver's eyes churned as they sat, locked on mine. Why wasn't he saying anything? Had I worded it wrong? Was he disgusted? I plummeted into internal turmoil. He smiled a little more, a small laugh on his breath as he brought his hands up to his shirt. Confused as he started to unbutton it, I stepped back and away from him.

"Oliver, what are you doing?"

He didn't reply as he unbuttoned the top few buttons on his shirt. I stepped back into the railing that separated us from the calm river pond. He stopped in front of me, the glow of his eyes softer than before. Dropping his hand, he took mine gently. His touch felt so wonderful as he brought my hand up with his. He paused, looking at my hand for a moment before looking back to my eyes. Softly, he took my hand and brought it under his open shirt. I didn't have the breath to ask but it didn't matter. The moment my hand made contact with his tattoo, I heard my heart pound. As if electricity flowed between us, I was suddenly flooded with emotions that weren't mine, but mirrored them.

My eyes jumped to his, was that what he was feeling too? Did that mean that he felt the same?

He just smiled softly at me with a light nod of his head.

I found my voice as his grip tightened on my hand, "Are you sure? I mean, I totally understand if you don't... I mean, it's such a foreign concept to you and-"

He smirked, his voice soft, "I remember when you were dragged in that pool. I had just managed to find you as you were cornered by some other boys. I was going to step in but you ran away. I wasn't fast enough and you died, I know you died, but by some witchcraft, they brought you back to life. I remember holding you there, you were just a kid. But you were the only person who made my heart jump– do you have any idea how horrible that made me feel?" He cleared his throat, his smile not fading. "I couldn't handle being Flipside much, but I wanted to know everything I could about you. And it was naive of me to feel anything for you at that point, I hadn't really met you. But that didn't stop me. I asked the Boggle who watched over you all sorts of questions, slowing building up an image of you so I'd feel more justified in my feelings. Then you joined me here and threw me through a loop. I guess somewhere along the way I forgot that you hadn't known what I did. You are nothing like I expected, Kasper." He moved forward, leaning his forehead on mine. "You are so much better."

I was awestruck. I had been so nervous, so unsettled, and scared, but after hearing that, all I could do was smile. I could feel his heartbeat under my hand and it was just as fast as mine.

"I wasn't sure if I'd ever be able to say it but," he got a little closer, "I love you too, Kasper."

When he kissed me, thunder rolled through the sky. He let go of my hand and wrapped his arms around me. His emotions exploded like mine as he pushed me back into the railing. It became very obvious very quickly that he knew how to kiss and I did not, but he just smiled and kissed me anyway. I had never felt so absolutely amazing before. Every moment was electrifying, exhilarating, as if I could actually see the sparks fly. His body pressed up to mine, he deepened the kiss and surprised me in the best of ways. We went falling backward, fazing through the railing and into the water. Though we didn't get wet, we just sort of floated, suspended under the surface as we lost ourselves to the kiss. The water flashed blue and a moment later, we were in my room in Castle Boggle.

He pressed me against the wall, not relenting and I loved it. I had never felt intimacy before, and it made every inch of me that he touched burn with perfect cold. I could feel the adrenaline making me tremble, speeding up my heart as his hand held the back of my neck and pulled me in closer. I wanted that to last forever, I could have been caught up in that for the rest of eternity.

He pulled back from the kiss, panting slightly as he brushed my bangs from my eyes. "I'm sorry, I thought I'd be able to hold back better than that."

I just stood there, staring, before shaking my head. "No, it's…uh," I looked away, "alright. I'm sorry I suck at this."

He laughed a little too hard at that.

My eyes drifted away from him and to the open door. Floating there, black eyes larger than normal, was Iris.

They jumped when they noticed my glare, "Oh my."

I stormed around Oliver and toward the stunned Boggle. "There? Are you happy now?" I shooed them out, "Now stop teasing me." I slammed the door, staring at it.

I heard Oliver approach. "I have been wondering what Iris goes on about from time to time. So it was that then?"

I couldn't even turn to face him, I was so mortified. There was no way that just happened, he couldn't have felt the same way this whole time. A soft but strong hand landed on my shoulder, turning me to face him. Standing there, eyes on Oliver, back against the door, I was trapped in that moment. Could it be possible that I was facing eternity with the only person I've ever loved like this? How could I get that lucky?

I laughed a little, looking away. "Iris said that you're shy. But now you're being rather," I looked to him, "straightforward."

He shrugged, looking away as his face went a little red. "If you're going to put in so much effort to try to work through the things that hinder you, the least I can do is try to do the same. And if you've taught me anything," He looked back, "it's that being comfortable in complacency is, um," his brow furrowed as he searched my eyes for the word he was looking for, "stupid."

"Indeed it is. Although," I looked away, "I think I'm a pretty bad choice. You have poor taste."

He looked down with a shake of his head and a smile before looking back to me and bringing his hand up to the back of my head, lacing his fingers in my hair. "Don't underestimate the folly of man," he tightened his grip in my hair "Kasper."

Pressed against the door in another kiss, I wrapped my arms around him tighter than I had ever hugged another person.

This was dangerous. As he smiled in the kiss, I knew this was a game over.

I had speculated on it before, but now it had happened. I had fallen hopelessly in love with Knight Oliver Vestile, The Great.

Chapter 8

IN THE EYES OF A DRAGON

"Have you made use of that bed yet?"

I raised my hand and shot Iris out of the air with a small bolt of lightning. They laughed at me as I chased them around the main room of Castle Boggle, yelling at them to shut up or I was going to banish them. Oliver stood in the background, leaning up against the wall with a smile, watching as Iris and I blundered about. This was life at Castle Boggle and it was perfect.

"Sire," Oliver drawled, pushing himself up from the wall and walking toward us, "You're going to accidentally banish Iris one day. Do you have any idea how lonely you'll be when that happens?"

I ran past him. "I don't care."

"You don't mean that." Oliver watched as I chased Iris back toward him again. As I passed that time, he reached out and grabbed my tie, causing me to stop running and choke. He smiled, pulling me closer. "Now don't we have a trial to prepare for? They'll be summoning us any moment now."

I clawed at my collar, glaring at him and his smile. But I couldn't keep my face flat for long, his smile was contagious. "Yes, yes." I stepped away from him but he didn't let go of my tie. Stopping, I looked back to him, "What?"

He just looked at me a moment longer before letting go of my tie and allowing it to slowly slide from his fingers. "Nothing." He turned from me and started down the hall. "Are you ready?"

I stood there, staring at his back, his long orange hair shifting with each of his steps. I could feel the flush of my face as I started after him. What was he looking at me like that for? "As ready as I'll ever be, I guess."

How long had it been since I told Oliver that I loved him? Since time passed so oddly, I didn't have any clue. But that didn't matter because I enjoyed every moment of it. Though we tried to hide it, the entire Kingdom of Boggle knew. But it was forbidden, a King and their Handler to be in a relationship together, so the Kingdom swore to keep that information inside of the Boggle gate. Those little dudes really had my back and I was so thankful for my amazing subjects.

We walked into Oliver's room. He didn't spend much time in there anymore though, so it was more of just a room. It was a lot like mine, with books lining the walls, a bed, and a desk, but it somehow felt colder. I never cared for that room much.

"The Almighty King really is taking his time with this one." I said, leaning on the wall next to the window.

Oliver pulled out a book and flipped through it, "He's fading fast, the entire Kingdom knows it, but he's in denial."

A paused passed.

"Hey Oli?"

He looked up to me from the book, "Yes, Sire?"

"Will I fade out someday, too, if I earn the Almighty Crown?"

Oliver was silent as he closed the book and slid it back on the shelf. Walking up to me, he spoke softly, "Well since we've never had an Almighty Boggle King before, we can't know for sure what will be the cause of your downfall. But I have speculations."

I could barely breathe. "And?"

He trailed his eyes up to mine, "I firmly believe that only one thing has the power to make a Boggle King fade," He raised his hand up to his chest, "their heart." He then took that hand and brought it to the side of my face, "But that's alright. You'll be able to rule forever," He got closer, "as long as I don't break it."

Stardust ran through my veins as he pulled me into a kiss. If Oliver was right, could I be the King forever? Would whimsy and mischief rule the paranormal for all time? Bringing an end to the fear and pain it had brought upon the living in the past? In that world, ghosts truly would be good.

We jumped when something tapped on the window. His eyes flew behind me as he stepped away and I turned around.

My heart raced, terror spiking in my veins, until I saw what it was. With a deep breath, I smiled, "Hello Domino."

The dinosaur tapped on the window again with their long snout. I opened the window and a moment later, Domino sent their head in. Snatching the back of my coat in their mouth, they dragged me outside. I tried not to yell out in surprise as they held me high above the ground, dangling from their mouth. Grabbing onto my coat so I wouldn't slip out of it, I looked around. Nearly, if not, all of the Boggle Kingdom sat on the ground, looking up at me.

Iris flew up to be level with me, "We wanted to show you something." The Boggle started to rise.

"You miss the stars, right?" Oliver asked, leaning in the open window. I looked back to him, he was totally in on this.

"As a thank you, we wanted to show you them again." Iris floated up with the rest. As they entered the sky, they just kept going up. The sky started to grow darker, as if some were blocking out the setting sun's light. And when things became darker, their lights started to shine. A few moments later the darkened sky was full of little lights, little stars. Domino set me on the ground then put their head down. It took me a moment to realize it, but they wanted me to stand on their head. After I carefully did so, they rose back up. It was hard to keep my balance but once we were all the way up, I was stunned. It was like the night sky, but better.

I caught a glimpse of Oliver smiling at me from the window. Looking up and around at all my Kingdom, I knew that even if I didn't earn the Almighty Crown, I already had the greatest followers. I just wished that the others could see them as more than stupid little Boggle.

"You've given the Boggle a hope that they've never had before, so from all of us to you," Oliver smiled, "thank you."

I adored how Oliver had absolutely no qualms about being a Boggle, he wore the name with pride.

Nodding to him then looking back up, I spoke with a smile and slightly glassy eyes. "You guys are the best Kingdom I could have ever possibly asked for. I know many of you watched over me in life, so I do hope you see how happy you've made me."

Whispers flooded the air, saying that they loved me and that I was the perfect King. Hearing that was amazing. Oliver was probably right, at the core of every Boggle was a heart so powerful, it was the only thing able to end them. I looked over to my knight. That would make sense for him, too. Favio said that her heart was Tola's flaw in the end, but I think it was her strength. Had she destroyed Oliver in that fight and rose to the Almighty Crown, she would no longer hold the core trait of her Kingdom.

The next trial was upon us and this time, I was ready for it. This time my head was in the right place, my heart was beating strong, my Kingdom was behind me, and I now had the allegiance of the shadows. I was ready to conquer, I could only hope that the others were prepared for the defeat. Because if they couldn't suck up their pride and bow down, they were going to be stepped on by a Boggle with a crown.

When the black orb of the Almighty came barreling toward me from the sky, I greeted it with a smile.

"Welcome Kings!" The Almighty Ghost King's voice boomed out around us as we stood upon the stage, bowing before him. "You are here to partake in the second trial. Today you shall travel Flipside once again, but to an island. There you will have a set amount of time to reach the den of the only being higher than I. The Great Ghost Dragon."

I looked to Oliver at my side, eyes nearly popping from my head. He looked back at me, obviously confused with my surprise. I slowly looked back to the Almighty Ghost King, beside myself. A Great Ghost Dragon, that's something I wasn't prepared for. I stood there, listening as the Ghost King went on. What exactly was fiction again? I didn't even want to open that can of worms. I could see that going *real* well. Next thing I'd know I'd be face to face with Santa or some shit.

"Your time limit is four Earth hours, that should be ample time to locate the Great Dragon from anywhere upon the island. The journey is not the trial, the real test will be what the Great Dragon sees inside you. If you don't meet his standards, you will no longer be eligible for the Almighty Crown. Is that understood?"

We all bowed our heads in response. Looking over to the Earthbound King and her Handler, I wondered if their new subjects were doing well. As we lifted our heads, I looked to Nolan, the

Demon King. I wondered how he became the next King after Oliver. My eyes drifted to the Poltergeist at their side. They were the combined hatred and evils of man, but did they have specific personalities and memories? How would the Great Dragon judge something like that?

I noticed the Almighty King's gaze locked on my crown. Perhaps he was surprised that I had won Favio over, too? I slightly nodded to him with a smile and he looked away to the Kingdom audience behind me.

"Let the trial, begin!"

And with that, black orbs approached us and within moments, Oliver and I were tossed to the ground somewhere else. Picking myself up, I guess I was more surprised than I should have been. Looking around, we were on a tropical island. Straightening my clothing, I looked up and down the beautiful beach we were on. I helped Oliver up and together we stood in what appeared to be paradise. Looking out over the horizon, I saw hundreds of ships docked along it. Large ships, freight ships, smaller boats, but there was something sort of odd about all of them. They looked quite old.

"Where are the others?" I looked to Oliver as we started to walk from the beach to a stone path that wove through the lush green area.

"They were dropped at different points around the edges of the island. It's to discourage sabotage."

As I followed him along the path, I looked around more. It was truly beautiful, warm, and overall pleasant. It almost felt unreal, and I know that's strange to hear from a ghost, but it did. It was otherworldly, like the ghost realms. But that didn't make any sense, The Ghost King said this was Flipside.

"Where are we?"

"Somewhere in the North Atlantic Ocean."

I ducked under a low branch, "Does the island have a name?"

He slightly looked back to me from the branch as he ducked, "Not that I know of."

So we were on a nameless island in the North Atlantic Ocean somewhere, very informative, thank you Oliver. Sighing, I tried to not trip on something at the same time. I bet this place was full of spiders and snakes and all sorts of things that would eat you, given the chance.

I was surprised when I heard laughter near by. Looking up as we approached, I saw a restaurant of sorts. It was like a patio tiki-bar. Small lanterns strung up from one palm tree to the next, the ground covered in colorful stones, grassy tables and bar stools sat around. Sitting and standing about were tens of people and as I looked over them, I was very confused. They looked like old time pilots and sailors, military men and explores. Their clothing, their tones of voice, the way they spoke, it was like I fell into World War 2 era or something. They were barely transparent, but I could tell they were all ghosts.

They stopped their hardy laughter and bold conversation to stare at me. A moment later I was surrounded by wide grinned men who had alcohol in hand, and camaraderie in the air.

"Hey stranger," One man said as he shoved into me, "welcome, I haven't seen you around."

Oliver seemed irked by the rambunctious men, stiffly standing there as he spoke, "Show some respect."

They all looked over me and when enough of them noticed my crown, they jumped. Apologies flooded around me and I just shook my head, smiling.

"Don't mind him," looking around, the lively atmosphere was a welcomed surprise, "you guys having a party?"

I was met with cheers of agreement.

"It's always a party here in the Bermuda Triangle."

I don't think I could have deflated faster, "The...of course."

"This is an island right in the middle," someone yelled as they raised their sloshing pint into the air, "a living thing has never set foot on it."

"Yeah, that's because they can't seem to find it."

They all exploded into laughter.

All those scientists working hard to figure out the secrets of the Bermuda Triangle were doomed, the truth was ghosts. Looking to the sky, it was perfectly calm. A ghost island, maybe this is where the Reapers retired to.

"Well we are on a time limit," Oliver said, his coldness still about him, as he shoved me along.

"What are you up to?" One of the men asked as he stepped from our path.

"I'm going to visit The Great Ghost Dragon."

The silence hit heavy as the party came to a pause.

It wasn't until we were nearly out of earshot that one of the men called out to me, "Good luck kid! He's a real ass!"

"He sunk my massive ship!"

"He knocked my plane from the sky!"

"Be careful!"

That's exactly what I needed to hear.

I followed Oliver around a corner on the path, eyes low. So it wasn't storms, weird gas deposits breaking free, shallow waters, massive waves, or aliens that caused the issues in the ocean around here. It was a moody Ghost Dragon, and a moody Ghost Dragon that I needed to like me. The Almighty King said something that worried me, he made it sound as if the Ghost Dragon would be able to see inside me, to know what I was under my skin. That was unsettling, because even though I was more confident now, I was still a flawed teenager. Would he see that and deem me unworthy? But was I even worthy to start with, if I was just a flawed teenager?

As much as I felt compelled to earn the Almighty Crown, it was more important to me that the right person earned it. And if the right person wasn't me, then that was alright. As long as they were what was best for the entire Kingdom. But for some reason, I didn't think any of my competitors were what was right for the Kingdom. They all had something in common that unsettled me. To me, we were rivals, to them, we were enemies.

A Kingdom divided like that from the start was bound to fall.

I walked into a spider web and stumbled to the side.

Oliver caught me before I fell and just laughed as he helped me stand. "Graceful as always, Sire."

I shivered as I wiped the web away, "I was a shut-in before, I'm trying."

He brushed some of it from my hair then looked into my eyes for a moment. My heart jumped but I couldn't look away, his churning eyes were too perfect. He leaned forward and gently kissed me before taking me by the hand and continuing forth.

"Have you met this Dragon before?" I asked though I felt like I already knew the answer. Had Oliver once competed in the trials, he too would have had to earn the approval of the Dragon.

"I have, and the undesirables were correct, he is indeed nasty tempered."

I debated my next question but ended up asking it anyway, "Why have you met him before?"

I still hadn't told Oliver all that I knew about him, I didn't know how. I was just sort of really hoping I could get him to tell me that way it wouldn't ever matter and I wouldn't have to think of a way to explain. I know I like, just went on about communicating my feelings and not running from conversations, but, y'know, the folly of man…and stuff.

Oliver was quiet, probably thinking over his words, "This isn't my first time being involved in the King trials. The second trial is always the same, facing this Dragon, but the first and last are up to the Almighty King."

I felt bad for asking these things, I knew that it must have hurt to think back on, "Were you a Handler then too?"

He made that small sound that meant he was smiling, "No. I will tell you, if you wish to know. However, I don't I feel as if right now is the best time."

"That's all good," I shoved into him a little, closing the space between us, "So, do you happen to know where we're going?"

He chuckled as we started up a slight hill in the dense greenery, "I'm flattered it took you this long to ask." Pulling a branch out of our way, he ducked under it, "Yes, of course I know where we're going, Sire.

"Great, you always know what you're doing," when he tightened his grip on my hand, my heart slowed a bit, "Are you sure this is alright?" Pulling up our intertwined hands, I looked from them to him. "I mean, I'm not complaining. But if someone sees us, that won't be good."

"The likelihood of any of the other Faction members being anywhere near is very low. It's set up that way so we can't kill or assist each other. All roads lead to the Dragon eventuall,y so there's no need to put us near intersecting ones."

Desperately trying to believe him and relax, a deep breath took me. I didn't want my own personal affairs to interfere with the good of the Kingdom. Not even Oliver knew what they'd do if they found out, the situation had never come up in his memory.

A few beats passed as I looked around at the scenery. It was beautiful, like something out of a movie. Although I could only see out on occasion because the plants were so dense most of the time. I saw things like little animals and birds pass us, they were ghosts too. But the plants were actual living plants, so to those who couldn't see us that island would be rather confusing. They'd look over the whole place and find that it looked like people lived here but wouldn't be able to find any of them. They probably wouldn't be able to explore for long, though, because a moody dragon would swoop down and kill them. That must have been the scariest thing ever, to be sailing or flying along then suddenly be assaulted by a fucking dragon.

A shiver ran over me.

I didn't even have to meet this dragon to be afraid of him.

"Are you alright Sire?"

Nodding, we started to enter a denser area, "I'm just nervous. I didn't even know dragons existed."

He stopped walking, staring at me with brows raised. "What?"

I let go of his hand, stepping away, "No one thinks they were ever real."

"No," His shoulders dropped, "they've faded into obscurity?"

"They are pure fantasy nowadays."

He didn't seem to know what to do with himself as he looked down in a slight existential crises. "That is unfathomable. When I was alive they plagued the entire world and killed many."

"How have we never found the bones?" I was just as lost as he was, "We found dinosaurs, but not dragons?"

"Do you not know?" He blinked at me. "Of course you don't know. When a dragon dies, they turn to a dust of sorts."

After a moment I sighed and continued on, "How convenient."

Oliver caught up with me, his boots hollowly thudding against the stone path. "What is the biggest threat to mankind now, if it isn't dragons?"

"Themselves." I didn't even have to think about that one. "It may be hard for you to fathom, but there are some people who have access to a button that if they were to press it, they would end the world." I put my hands in my pockets, momentarily losing out to the inner cynic. "The world is a horrible jaded place where no one trusts each other and no one is as they seem. Everyone seems to have an agenda, a plan, a use for you, and it's never in your best interest. They preach about being open minded and turn around to pass judgment on you. It's nothing like it was when you were there, and it has gotten vastly better, just worse in different ways."

A whistle came from off of the path, startling Oliver and I, "Somebody was an edgy teenager in life."

Oliver and I stopped and looked to the side, unable to see the source of the voice. But we both knew who it belonged to, the unique flatness of it was a voice I had only heard once before but I'd never forget.

"Nirvana?" I asked, still looking around. "What are you doing here?"

"Just hanging about."

It was then that I realized his voice was coming from above. Looking up, I saw him tangled in a mess of vines, dangling from the trees above. He lazily waved with a yawn.

"How did you get stuck up there?" Stepping back, I looked around for a way to climb up to him.

"I'm supposed to be monitoring this trial, after the weirdness that went down at Castle Earthbound. But while jumping in the tree tops, my foot slipped and I haven't cared enough to get myself out."

"Good job at doing your job." Oliver joined in, trying to climb up a tree.

"My job is to take people like you to the afterlife. Not to play babysitter."

After struggling to get up the trees on either side of the path, Oliver and I made it up to Nirvana. I had only seen it a couple times before, but I had never asked about the sword Oliver could materialize out of nowhere. I watched in awe as it appeared in his hand and he cut the vines. Nirvana fell to the path with a thud. Staring at his motionless body, I would have been concerned but then Oliver caught my attention by jumping from the tree and landing without a hitch. Feeling my hands start to slip, I wondered if landing was easy or he was skilled. My life would have flashed before my eyes when I slipped, had I not been already dead. Picking myself up from the ground, Oliver's concerned face was the first thing I saw. A laugh taking me, I nodded when he asked if I was okay as he helped me up. Turning, my eyes landed on the

Reaper. Walking up to Nirvana, I extended my hand. He didn't seem to be one to get snagged on pride as he took the hand up.

When he was on his feet again, his flat eyes rose to my crown, "You've won over the Shadow King, too?" I nodded and he just turned away from me and started down the path, "Odd."

That wasn't the reaction I was expecting. Oliver and I followed him down the path, not really sure what to say to that. The path wove out of the plants and down by the water. Eyes drifting over the view of paradise, they caught on a large blue circle of water right off of the shore. It was a huge hole, and the water inside just got darker the further it went down.

"It's pretty isn't it?" Nirvana asked, glancing toward the water, "Don't fall in, you'll be eaten by the Lusca."

"The…what?" I looked back to the water, taking a few steps to the side.

Nirvana turned around to face me and continued walking backwards as he lifted up his arms and wriggled his fingers, "It's a gargantuan sea monster that lives at the bottom of that blue hole. It inhales the water around it, eating all who fall in."

I flinched away from him and a little closer to Oliver when he jumped my way, "There's no way that's real."

Nirvana shrugged as he stepped back around to be walking normally again, "Do you want to go hop in and find out?"

He chuckled when I stayed silent. His entire presence was just creepy as hell, I could understand why Oliver was weary of him. As we walked in silence, I couldn't help but let my nerves get to me again. I was going to face a moody Dragon that I really needed to like me but I had no idea if they would. Oliver looked up to me, probably aware that my heart had dropped into my stomach. But there wasn't much he could do to help me, and I'm sure he knew it. This was on me, I'd have to have the bravery to face this and he couldn't give it to me.

"Hey Oli?" I tried to distract myself, "Is there some cool story behind that sword of yours?"

"Do you mean Jaxon?" He looked to me, "Have I never told you about it, Sire?" When I shook my head, he lifted up his hand and I watched in awe as the sword materialized again. "Jaxon is a legendary demon sword. It can only be summoned by those who have survived its slash. When in the hands of a demon, it is very dangerous and possesses the potent ability to blight. But right now it is simply what it appears to be, a sword."

"You survived its cut?" I looked to him from the shining metal.

Oliver nodded, making the sword disappear.

Something cried out and made me jump out of my skin. We all stopped, looking around for what was making the noise. It sounded scared, hurt and small. I was the only one to step off of the path in search for it. Oliver and Nirvana just stood there, watching me.

"We're on a time limit, Sire." Oliver leaned up against a tree.

"It might eat you." Nirvana said as he jumped up, grabbing onto a tree branch with his hands and just hung there.

"Don't you have a job to be doing?" I looked up to the swinging Reaper King as I pawed around through the plants on the ground.

He yawned, "I'm sure it's fine. It would be suicide to pull something on the Dragon's turf. And this is slightly less boring than hanging in a tree alone. I also want to watch you get eaten, so I'll stick around."

I didn't particularly like Nirvana. Oliver didn't appear thrilled with him either as he nonchalantly put more space between them. I shifted around in the plants, able to hear the cries of the little creature louder now. Before I could think, I jumped back when something brushed past my hand but reached back for it immediately after. When I picked the thing up out of the plants and held it up, both Oliver and Nirvana jumped back. I didn't realize why until I got a good look at it. I couldn't drop it, that wasn't nice, but I was also startled by the baby dragon. It took all my willpower to not let go of it as I stood.

My company shuffled away as I got back on the path. Looking at the little, purple baby dragon, I found that it was somewhat cute. You know, if I was able to fully ignore the fact that it could probably kill me on a whim. It squirmed in my hands in order to fully face me. Its little shining black eyes looked as if the stars were trapped in them. It didn't seem angry, if anything, it seemed perky. It purred or something as it squirmed some more. I loosened my grip and it went crawling up my arm, to my shoulder, then jumped into my crown. Once it was comfortable up there, it let out the tiniest roar of sorts.

Oliver and Nirvana stood there, eyes locked on the dragon in my crown as it spun around slowly.

"Well," Nirvana stepped away, "that happened."

Oliver's eyes fell to mine and I just shrugged. After a few more moments, he sighed and shook his head with a smile. "You're something else, Sire."

The dragon purred above me and I could just nervously smile.

"That's so strange, though," Nirvana said as we continued along the path. "I was sure the Great Dragon was the last of them. But that baby isn't even dead."

"Wait," I nearly tripped on an uneven stone, "you mean there could be more alive? That's horrible. The world will have to deal with its own issues *and* dragons." Looking up toward my crown, I went on, "All those apocalypse movies got it wrong. It won't be some virus or zombies or nuclear fallout that brings the end, but dragons."

"I doubt the Great Dragon would allow that." Nirvana kicked a rock and we all watched it bounce down the path.

The dragon mewed, or something, I don't even know.

"Hey, Oli," I started again after the rock we had been watching rolled to a stop, "what should we name it?"

"We are not naming it."

A smile bounced to my face as I looked over to Oliver, "Aw, why not?"

He rolled his eyes over to me, trying to suppress his smile. "Because it is not a Boggle therefor you have no right to name it."

"How about Spencer?"

"Now what about that little dragon has possessed you to think that Spencer is an appropriate name?" Nirvana joined in. "I think it looks like a Ringo."

"Ringo?" I laughed, "Now that's stupid. I think it looks like a Spencer. Fight me."

"Alright." Nirvana lifted up his arm and the wind blew a little as his scythe appeared in his hand.

Oliver jumped between us as Nirvana lifted back his blade.

"It's a figure of speech." He glared over his shoulder at me, "Right, Sire?"

Standing there, frozen in place, hands up, I nodded.

"Oh." Nirvana dropped the scythe and it dissipated. "Okay. Sorry. My bad."

Nirvana was scary.

"You know, Sire, you really should have figured this out by now. But your figures of speech don't translate well with those of us who have been dead for this long."

Suddenly as I looked up and was met with a mountain that had been in the backdrop our whole journey. Staring up at it, I wondered how I had been so occupied with Spencer that I hadn't seen a whole mountain until we were right upon it. It slowly got closer as the path opened up to a patio of stone. Several other paths fed into it, and I could only assume that the other factions had either gotten here already or were on those paths somewhere. I wondered if I could just act like I didn't notice the mountain. Maybe they wouldn't make me go into that ominous cave over there.

"So that cave over there-"

"What cave?" I smiled, cutting Oliver off as I tried to hide the shaking of my hands by shoving them in my pockets.

Oliver smiled as he walked up to me, "Come now Sire, you can do this."

Looking away from him, my eyes locked on the stone path under my shoes, "You have too much faith in me."

He stopped in front of me, lifting his hand up to the top of my head. "Well one of us has to because I surely know you won't."

"You're all bark and no bite," Nirvana said through a yawn.

Oliver turned, taking his hand away from me, "Do not speak of my King in such lowly ways. He is deserving of much higher regard."

"Prove it."

My eyes rose to Nirvana.

He raised a brow to me.

With a groan, I looked back to Oliver. "Do I have to go in there alone?"

It appeared that he hadn't thought about that until then. He suddenly lost all that confidence he had a moment before as he looked between my eyes, visibly troubled. I knew why he'd be concerned. Perhaps the Dragon would recognize him and say something telling in front of me.

"So Knight? Are you going to desert your post," Nirvana started toward the cave entrance, "again?"

Oliver's jaw went tight as he turned to look Nirvana's way. "Is it your goal to speak needlessly, Reaper?"

"Is that any way to speak to your escort to the after life?" Nirvana stepped into the darkness.

Oliver looked back to me. "I will accompany you, but I must stay a few step behind. Is that alright?"

I nodded, a little off set by how stern he got when interacting with Nirvana. I guess the Reaper just really pushed Oliver's buttons. We started to the cave entrance, each step making me doubt myself more. Spencer hummed and made little dragon noises in my crown as I walked further into the darkness.

"You're going to be alright, Sire." Oliver took my hand in the darkness.

My grip was probably tighter than normal, "I hope so."

Suddenly the darkness was chased away by a bright yellow light from the other end of the tunnel. It was followed by a roar that shook the ground and cackling of demons. Oliver let go of my hand as two red glowing figures came sprinting toward us. Emerging from the shadows, Nolan and his Handler laughed, running past us and toward the exit of the cave.

"Good luck, Boggle." Nolan called, "You're going to need it."

Preparing myself to die all over again at the hands of a dragon, I watched as they escaped into the light. Starting again, my pace quickened as to get me ahead of the other two. I was a King Candidate after all, I had to be outwardly brave, at the very least. Reaching the end of the cave, hesitation took hold but I forced myself forward. The cave opened into a vast cavern. Gold, gems, crowns, and more littered the ground in massive heaps. For some reason I was expecting it to not look like I was expecting. Maybe some things that we knew about dragons were actually true after all.

Lit torches lined a clear path through the gold and treasures. Oliver and Nirvana followed several steps behind me as I ventured forth. I expected to see the Great Ghost Dragon already but to my surprise, there was nothing there at the end of the path, just a nest of gold. Spencer made some cute little sounds above my head and distracted me for a moment.

The air in the room went cold.

"Who dares disturb me?" The loudest, roughest, voice I had ever heard boomed out around us, making the piles of gold bounce a little. "I have already met the candidates. Leave."

I cringed under the volume of the voice.

"I believe you missed one." Nirvana called out as if he didn't fear death. Although, he sort of was death, so I guess that made sense.

"What nonsense do you speak?" The voice yelled, causing the air to vibrate.

The ceiling glowed until something came flying through it. A massive transparent dragon came swooping down into the golden nest. Upon impact, the ground shook so much that I nearly fell from my feet. The dragon was just like I was expecting, as classic as it could get. But something about that made it scarier than if it were something more fantastical. It looked at me with its eyes that put the galaxy to shame, making me want to step back but I didn't. It took a deep breath, its exhale blowing my bangs from my eyes. I was paralyzed in its gaze, as if it was prying into my very core.

"A Boggle?" They started quietly as they lifted their head smoothly. Then, as if a switch flipped, they flung their head up, yelling. "A Boggle! How dare a Boggle defile my sacred home?" They stomped, whipping their head around, "You are no candidate in my eyes, you worthless lower faction. How dare you, how dare you. You are sickening, disgusting, worthless."

I wanted to turn and run, but I knew I couldn't. If I wanted to prove to myself that I really was worthy of my Kingdom, I could not run. I couldn't help but wonder as it spewed fire at the ceiling if they acted this way toward Tola, too?

"Do not make a mockery of me by disgracing me with your presence." They started to drop their head down toward me, opening their mouth wide. I only had a moment to see their multitude of teeth before they were surrounding me.

Spencer cried out.

The Great Ghost Dragon froze before it could clamp its jaw closed around me, teeth hovering inches away from me.

Staring at rows of teeth as they surrounded me, strings of saliva falling to the ground, I was suffocated by the dragon's terrible breath.

Slowly lifting up their head and closing their mouth, they backed off. "Is that my little one?"

My undead heart had totally stopped beating. With a harsh breath out, I lifted my hand up to my crown and Spencer jumped out onto it. "You mean Spencer? I found them crying out in the plants off of the path on the way here. I didn't want to just leave them there. Are they yours?"

The Great Dragon sat in pause.

Spencer fidgeted, as if they wanted to be let down. I knelt to the floor and let them go. They went running toward the gold pile but struggled to climb up. I walked up behind them and helped them up the small mountain of coins. They went blundering happily toward the Great Dragon's tail then pranced up it, onto their back, up their neck, then atop their head.

I stepped back to my spot with a smile.

"Did you call my little one, Spencer?" Its tone was a tad sharp.

"Yeah," I said as I looked up at the little dragon. "I didn't know their name and I thought that one would fit."

"Why give so much thought to something so insignificant?"

I looked back down to the terrifying Dragon before me. "I gave a name to every member of my Kingdom that didn't already have one, too. Everything needs a name, and someone to remember it."

A beat passed.

"You are a Boggle, no?" It asked, far softer than before. It was then that I noticed he didn't have to move his mouth to speak, it just sort of happened.

I bowed, "I'm Kasper, King of the Boggle. It's nice to meet you, Great Ghost Dragon."

They walked around in a circle, shaking the ground with every step as they settled back down, resting their head atop a pile of gold so that their eyes would be level with mine. "You are a newly dead, are you not?"

"I am." I tried to keep eye contact but it was hard.

"I am Drake." Their voice was wise, even, nothing like the yells they displayed earlier. "A young, newly dead Boggle dares to stand before me. Curious. I see that you don't only have the support of the Boggle, but of the Angles and the Shadows. You must be something to earn respects as high as those."

"I'm just trying to be the best King for the Boggle, they deserve no less." I tried to speak confidently but I could feel my words falter.

"I shall be the judge of that, child." I was surprised by that tone so I looked back to his eyes. The moment they made contact with me, the air around started scalding my lungs, suffocating and paralyzing me. His eyes tore me open and looked at every part and the way they worked together, I could just feel him doing it. It hurt, the way his gaze pried into me and for a brief moment, I was terrified. I was scared of many things, trapped in his gaze. I was afraid that he'd see something in me that would prove me unworthy, that he'd see a fatal flaw that made me unfit to rule, that he'd see that I really was worthless as the living thought I was. But there was something I feared far more than those things. I was terrified that he'd say that I was fit to be the Almighty Ghost King.

I tore my eyes away from his, unable to bare the contact any longer. The Dragon sat in pensive silence, breathing deeply. I could feel Oliver's eyes on my back and I just knew that he must have been disappointed in me. A good King would have maintained eye contact, a good King wouldn't have backed down, a good King wouldn't be afraid.

"You are very scared, child."

Tensing, the statement stung, but of course they could tell, they were the goddamned Great Ghost Dragon.

"You are full of doubts but you fight on, you are afraid but you stand strong, you are flawed but you can still love."

I managed to look up to them, they didn't speak as if those were bad things.

"You, King Kasper, are unlike any other candidate that has ever passed through my cave. The others stand like fools, so sure of themselves, hiding behind facades and reckless confidence. Yet you are terrified but have the courage to stand before me anyway. They keep intense eye contact, but you looked away, they spoke boldly, but your words faltered. You, child, are truly worthy."

My breath hitched as my blood ran cold.

"And that is your greatest fear, that you are indeed worthy." The Dragon paused, and I could be wrong, but it nearly looked as if their eyes were smiling. "Those who fear power are the only ones to be trusted with it for they are the ones who understand the destruction they hold." They bowed their head lower so that the little dragon was at my level. "You, King Kasper, have not only earned my approval, but also my support."

The little dragon breathed a tiny burst of fire toward my crown, adding another gem. The Dragon lifted their head, looking into my eyes again. I could see my reflection in them, though something was different. Floating atop my head wasn't my crown, but the Almighty one.

"I'm glad I didn't eat you."

Laughing, nervously, I averted my eyes, "Yeah, me too."

The dragon laughed loudly, shaking the island. I looked around and kept my balance as the gold shifted out of its piles, covering the cleared path. My eyes snagged on Oliver as he stood back there, hand up to his mouth, eyes shining as they smiled at me. My heart jumped when I saw that and I nearly tripped when I was distracted.

"Come here child," the Dragon said, "climb upon my back, I shall return you to the shore."

"Are you sure?" I turned back around to look at them, "we can walk back like the others."

"But Kasper, you are not like the others." They lowered his head, "You and your followers may come up this way."

I looked back to Oliver and Nirvana and they just started toward me. Oliver kept his eyes on the ground, obviously trying to not look at the Dragon. Nirvana jumped upon the Dragon's head like it was nothing as I waited for Oliver.

"You." The Dragon's head popped up, knocking Nirvana off of their head and onto their back as they moved closer. "You have been here before."

Oliver stumbled back, eyes wide on the Dragon's as he froze. There was a moment of pause, one where I could just about hear the pounding of Oliver's heart. I watched as his world ended in terror, the Dragon's gaze holding steady. When the Dragon slowly lowered their head again, Oliver stumbled to the side. I ran over to steady him, holding him close. He was trembling.

"How interesting." The Dragon started quietly. "You have changed. You are now a Boggle, too? I saw much horrible power in you before, but through the flames you once commanded, I see something new has been forged. Honorable, brave, kind, you have become all the things I was once sure you never would be capable of. I am pleased, Oliver." The Dragon chuckled as they lowered their head all the way. "Goodness, you're more scared than your King was. There is nothing to fear, if he is your leader. Now both of you, get on."

Oliver stood, staring, his tremor frozen with his tense shoulders. Running to his side, I took his hand and startled him as he jumped, his eyes searching mine. Smiling at him, I gave a nod as I started to pull him along toward the Dragon. Shoving him up in front of me, I helped him climb up onto their lowered head. Following him, I slipped a little but before I could fall, Oliver had my hand in his. Smiling down to me, it appeared he had regained his composure. Pulling me up, we stood atop the Dragon's head, surrounded by riches. As the Dragon began to raise his head, Oliver glanced about. Looking back to me, he leaned forward, closing the space between us.

Taking my hand in his once more, he held it close, "I love you," Kissing my forehead, his smile was brighter than the gold.

Sliding down the dragon's neck, we ended up on their back and there we found Nirvana. He sat there, staring at us with the first obvious display of emotion I had watched paint him, as he stared at Oliver. His gaze then dropped down to our intertwined hands and he opened his mouth, about to say something when the dragon took off, knocking all of us from our balance. Sitting next to each other on the back of the Dragon, hand in hand, Oliver and I smiled at each other as we fazed through the roof of the cave and out into the sky.

Flying over the entire island, I could see all the boats docked around it and the planes landed on a large flat area. The ghosts below looked so small as we went higher. I could see storm clouds surrounding the island, but none over the island. As if it was the paradise at the center of the devil's waters, the treasure in the eye of the storm. It was beautiful.

The dragon flew around, somewhat showing off and making it extremely hard to hang on. Looking over to Oliver, his long hair flying out behind him in the wind, I tightened my grip and smiled. I never thought I'd get to ride on the back of a Dragon. If only all those bullies could see me now, they'd be so envious.

The Dragon started to descend, making me a little sad but I knew that I had to return. When he landed, his gust of wind knocked over the other Candidates as they stood on the beach together. Shaking while standing up, Oliver and I let go of each other as we struggled to regain balance. Sliding off the side of the dragon, landing on the sand sent streaks of pain up my legs. Hissing through my teeth as I straightened, satisfaction took hold as I watched the other candidates fuss about and try to get up. No one said a word as Oliver and I began to approach, but my steps stopped when I heard a thud from behind me. Turning, my eyes landed on Nirvana as he laid, face down, in the sand.

I really tried not to laugh as I walked up to him and knelt down, "Hey, are you alright?"

He sat up and scooted away from me, his dull eyes now alert and locked right on me.

"Sire," The Dragon said, startling me. I stood to look at them as they bowed their head. "call upon us if you are ever in need, we shall protect you in any way we can."

"Thank you, Drake."

The Dragon laughed as they flew off, gusting us with the air from their wings as they flew away.

"What do you think you're going to accomplish?" Nolan's ever bitter voice tainted the tone from behind me, "You're not impressing anybody."

Turning to face him, I pocketed my hands, "Whatever do you mean?"

"I bet you think you're something, gathering the allegiances of others." Nolan approached me, his rotting flesh sagging more with each step, "But you're not."

A clink of metal stole my attention causing me to look back. Oliver stood, sword materializing in hand as he started to move between Nolan and I. Raising my arm up in front of him, I smiled and gave a light nod. After a moment of hesitation, he disarmed.

Nolan stopped in front of me, a little too close for comfort, "It doesn't matter how many weak factions you gather, you will not become strong. It's a weakness in itself, seeking the support of others."

"That's your problem." I smiled, despite the stench of rot overpowering my senses, "If you don't unify the people, what sort of leader are you?"

"You are nothing Boggle," spitting in my face, Nolan puffed up with all the empty bravado in the world, "just accept it."

Wiping his spit that burned like acid off of my face with my sleeve, I took a step his way, making him step back, "I am a Boggle, a proud one. And if you know the first thing about us Boggle, it's that partaking in games is our specialty." I dropped my tone, "Prepared to get played."

When Nolan's hand started toward my throat, I knew what was coming. But I also knew that Oliver had saved me from blights worse than what was about to be inflicted, so I was not afraid.

Time itself felt as if it were split by the scythe that came down between Nolan and I, nearly slicing his arm. We slowly looked to the side to see Nirvana, scythe in hand, death in his eyes.

"Losing your temper when verbally provoked?" the Reaper King used his Scythe to shove Nolan back, "How disgraceful."

Nolan scurried away, hissing things under his breath in his retreat, as Nirvana stood before me. He looked me up and down, a look of annoyed determination on his face.

"If you had seen Oliver the day I met him, if you knew what he once was, you would be shocked to see what he has become. I don't know how you and your Kingdom did it, but you changed a monster to a protector. I had never seen him actually smile until I saw him with you, I had never seen him set his pride aside and laugh, before you. And frankly, I didn't think it was possible, either. If only you had heard the things the Dragon said about him before, maybe you'd understand how truly amazing his transformation is." His eyes drifted to Oliver, "For, of all the humans I have led to the afterlife, Oliver was the only one that scared me." His eyes jolted back to mine, "And if you and your Kingdom are capable of bringing out the best in Oliver, then you surely can bring out the best in the Paranormal."

He bowed and with it, brought the back of his scythe down into my crown. I stood, wide eyed and shocked as he added another gem to my crown. He looked up to me from the bow with a wicked smile I had never seen him wear before.

"It's time to change up this game. Don't let me down, Kasper."

I stood, nodding for that was all I could manage as I stared down at him.

"Now, you better behave yourselves because I swear if I'm called into extra work again to be your babysitter," he swung his scythe, "some heads are gonna roll." Pulling up his reaper hood, he grumbled to himself. "I'm too old for this shit." And with that, Nirvana disappeared into a black puff of smoke.

I stared at where he once stood as silence sat in the air. A laugh took me, Nirvana was actually precious. He looked 15, if not younger, so it was dreadfully funny that he was probably older than all of us and completely done with our shit. The others stared at me, Oliver smiling at my side. The Dragon was right, I was scared as all hell, but at least I wasn't gawking like the rest.

Sky rumbling, I looked up to see the darkness begin to approach. Looking back down to the others, my smile could have perhaps been a bit less challenging but I was on top of the world. Nolan looked away from me as the orbs blocked out the light from above. One after another, the black orbs swooped down and swallowed us up. Falling didn't faze me as we were thrown out the other end a few tumbling moments later. Standing, my smile clung to me, we were before the Almighty King. But this time we were not met with roaring cheers. It was as if we had been thrown from one vacuum to another. This time the air was heavy, this time the tone was dry, this time, the Ghost King was standing on the stage.

This time, I had gotten the message across.

Walking up to the King, I bowed, "I do hope I've lived up to your expectation, Sire." I looked up to him from the bow, my smile unfading as I straightened, "Perhaps exceeded it. What was it that you told me when we first met? That I had a lot to learn. Well, I can assure you Sire, have learned a lot."

He stared at my crown that now had four gems filling its entirety, "You are playing a dangerous game, Boggle."

"Oh I know," turning my back to him, my casual tone was audacious but I didn't care, "but trust me, I don't intend on losing." Stopping, I looked out over the subjects of limbo, "I promise."

I had set just about everyone in that room on edge with my smile, with my confidence, with my promise, it was palpable, the hateful unrest. Though I was no stranger to those looks, they felt reminiscent of an old white lady on a bus who didn't like the way I dressed, rooted in nothing other than the juvenile frustrations of an oppressor losing hold.

My confidence was not unfounded, I had it because I knew that I had five very special Kingdoms behind me. The only way one could be confident standing on their own was if it was fake, but I was confident now because I wasn't alone at all, and it was one of the best feelings ever. Almost as good as turning around to see the other Candidates glaring at me. I was going to kill them with kindness, make them a unified people, and break the system, whether they liked it or not.

As I walked back to Oliver's side where I belonged, he raised a brow, probably wondering where I got the guts to do that.

Whispers roared from the crowd, muttering and wayward glares, all directed right at me and my smile. A low rumble started to build in the air, a pressure so strong it was the white elephant. What a power to have, the ability to unsettle an entire kingdom with my smile.

The tension snapped when the Almighty King did, "Silence," the reverberations of his voice sent shock waves of quiet over the kingdom as he turned toward the candidates, "The final trial nears, but do not become stagnate in the between. Soon I will crown a new king, prepare for your character to be tested beyond its limits." Swinging his arms around, his beady black eyes locked on mine as smog began to obscure him until he vanished, leaving a chill behind.

A shiver took me.

"Until we meet again," his voice choked around us until it faded away, leaving nothing but shrill silence.

Growling, Nolan shoved past me as the black orbs appeared in front of us. Watching as every other candidate and handler disappeared into their orbs, being sucked away into the darkness, I held my head high while they looked down. Once they were all gone, their factions filtered out as well. Approaching my orb, I looked around before my eyes landed on Oliver. Taking his hand, I ran forward, dragging him behind as we crashed into the orb. Sent in a free fall, spinning through nothingness, I pulled him into me, kissing him.

Being thrown out the other side of the orb, Oliver and I were torn away from each other, wiping out in the grass. Laughing as I sat up, suddenly I felt the weight of a million eyes on me. Staring around, I was surrounded. Cheers exploded about, the entire Boggle faction must have been there in the courtyard, looking at me.

Rushing me, a sea of whispers ruled the air as they congratulated me, thanked me, cheered me on. Standing in the crowd, I enjoyed the company of my kingdom. I knew them all by name and spoke with each as personally as I could. There was a lot of them, but I did do my best to remember something about all of them. As I waded my way through the sea of friends, my eyes rose to see a few visitors.

"Hey!" Gaston waved as he tried to not bump into any Boggle.

Favio bowed his head, close at Gaston's side.

Nirvana, despite standing there with us, ignored me.

"You're a force to fuck with," Gaston threw his arm around me, brighter than the sun as usual, "talking to the Almighty that way."

"Well," I ducked out from under his arm, "I was never afraid of ghosts."

Nirvana groaned, pulling up his hood but still refusing to look at me.

There I stood, looking over my Kingdom, friends at my side, all I could do was smile. I had never been invited to a party before, but I had always wondered. Les had tried to throw me birthday parties with just the two of us, but this was different. Like some sort of Happily Ever After, a place where everything felt right. Oliver at my side, my supporters surrounding me, I felt like I was exactly where I was supposed to be.

Oliver pulled me into a dance in the Boggle main hall, the others cheering in their soft whispers and animal sounds. I could hear Favio threatening to disembowel Gaston if he touched him as Gaston tried to pull him to the dance floor, too. Whizzing by my head, Spencer chased Iris around as Nirvana sat on Domino's head, hood pulled up and pretending like he wasn't smiling.

"Sire."

My attention was captured, looking back before me to see Oliver and his smile. I got lost in his eyes, not seeing anyone else anymore. We still couldn't dance, but we still didn't care. Oliver spun me out, making me laugh as he spun me back. I was surprised when he pulled me rather close. No space between us, I had never felt more dear than I did when he held me. Tense, his movements snagged a bit as we stepped around. Eyes locked, anticipation built as he held me captive in his gaze. Pulling me even closer, his smile, his face starting to turn red, it sent a spike of something wonderful through me. Closing the space, his lips met mine, burning like gin as he kissed me. Slowly, my eyes closed as I wrapped my arms around him. Taken away by the moment, I couldn't hear anything except for the beating of my heart, but then I remembered where we were.

Gaston whooped, shattering my world as I stepped back from Oliver. His smirk was shockingly unconcerned with the ramifications of blowing our cover, it was forbidden after all. As he turned me in the dance, my view passed over Favio as he shook his head, over Gaston as he jumped about, over Nirvana as he pulled his hood over his face, over the boggle as they buzzed.

Oliver chuckled, pulling me close again as he slowed the dance down, "They're all your followers, right? I'm sure our secret is safe with them."

After a few moments, the tension drained from me as I leaned my head on his shoulder, I supposed he was right. A smile found its way to my face, it felt amazing to know that he had no reservations about showing me off like that. My parents would have flipped, if I had a bold boyfriend like him in life. As we danced around slowly, nothing else in the world mattering, my mind drifted with that thought. If Oliver and I had been alive at the same time, what sort of story would we have had? Would we have met in class, or maybe when I was out being silly and searching for ghosts? Would he think me unglued, or would he humor me? He'd probably sit behind me in class and hit me with his ruler when he saw that I wasn't paying attention. A light laugh took me as I tightened my hold on him.

Oliver hummed in question.

Shaking my head, my smile so strong it almost hurt, I buried myself in his arms.

Yes, this was it, my Happily Ever After.

Once upon a time, I was never interested in storybooks. Back then, I thought love was unfathomable and that being loved was even more so. I never saw myself as a leader, or in the slight bit personable. I was dirt under the Kloven legacy rug. It wasn't until someone lifted up that rug longer than to just check if I was still there, did I see otherwise.

Gaston joined Iris in the relentless teasing of a more mature kind than I'm comfortable relaying, but they were laughing so much that I didn't have the heart to stop them. Oliver joined in a little, really surprising me. Since when had he had an adult sense of humor? Sure, I had told him to try to come out of his shell some, but that was not what I had meant. Shoving him away from me as he laughed, I buried my face in my hand, smiling.

When he winked at me, it was game over.

Knight Oliver Vestile, The Great was mine forever.

I can't recall a time in my life that I hadn't been just waiting for the next thing, but as I stood at the end of the party, bowing before my kingdom, I wished that it didn't have to end.

"Thank you all for the faith you have placed in me. I will not let you down." I stood from the bow, smiling at them. "I'm going to flip this whole game board off the table."

Gaston floated up to my side, his smile gold like him, "They certainly will rue the day they messed with the Boggle King."

"You had quite the gall earlier," Favio stepped around Gaston, his deathly eyes prying into me, "speaking to the Almighty King like that"

"I thought he was going to banish you right there." Nirvana continued through yawn, "I was so let down when he didn't."

"Yes, well," I laughed, looking away and running my fingers through my hair, "I might have been a little carried away, but I felt like it needed to be said."

"Whatever happens in the final trial, this is history in the making." Gaston grabbed onto Favio, starting toward the gate. "And I'm proud to be a part of it."

"I share the same sentiment, Boggle King." Favio made some attempt at looking professional as he struggled against Gaston's hold, "Just don't get yourself banished."

Nirvana stood there, the only one left, as he looked between Oliver and I, "You even made him fall in love?" His eyes stopped on mine. "What the fuck are you?

I bent over to be eye level with him, voice soft, "Just me."

He groaned, bonking me in the head with the back of his scythe. "Don't make me regret following you."

As he started for the gate, I could just smile at his back, rubbing my head, "I'll try not to."

He waved his scythe as he walked into the gate.

"You have quite a Kingdom, Sire." Oliver stepped up next to me, taking my hand. "You've earned them, and that's more than any other King can say."

We walked back into the castle together, most of the Boggle already going about their own shenanigans somewhere in our endless park. We walked up the winding stairs and down the big empty hall into the much too open room. I sat down on my bed as he closed the door. Concern raced through me, the tone had taken a dive, dead on the floor. But as mind raced over all the possibilities, it landed on one as he walked back to the bed and sat down next to me, not looking at me.

"I said I'd explain, and I feel that it is in order after what the Great Dragon said."

I sat there, looking at the bedspread that was far too fancy for me. Did I make him go through the pain of explaining it all to me? From what I knew, it was nothing pleasant and I'm sure he didn't want to revisit it enough to retell it. But would he be more bothered to know that I already did? I was looking between two options, risking having my person dented in his eyes, or allowing him to do something I know would hurt him.

There wasn't even a choice there, not really.

"When I was alive, I-"

"Oli," I hadn't thought this through, now that I had cut him off, he just looked at me, waiting for me to finish what I was saying but I didn't even know what I was saying, "I uh, I know."

Oliver blinked at me.

I slowly looked up to him. "I didn't want to tell you that I knew because the more time that passed, the more I kicked myself for not saying anything. I didn't know if Favio would want me to tell you that he told me, and he's too scary for me to ask…" the silence I had brought into this world with my words began to choke me, "I'm sorry, this isn't how I wanted this to come out, but I don't want you to have to force yourself to retell it."

Face flushed, my core was muddled into a mangled wad equal parts self-loathing and mortification. I wish that I was better at articulating things in a form more eloquent than word vomit. The pause he placed between us was pensive as his eyes studied mine.

"Then we're even."

My eyes jumped to him, "What?"

He looked back to me, smiling a little. "I didn't tell you anything about the Royal Connection until it was an issue for the same reason, I didn't know how. But I am rather taken aback by that. He told you of my past and it hasn't colored me poorly?"

I shook my head, "No, of course not. Why would I judge you on the past that made you the person I fell in love with? I'm just upset that history got it all wrong." I leaned back against the headboard, a long breath leaving me. "Tola seemed wonderful."

He looked down to the bed, leaning against the headboard next to me, "Yes, she was a rare soul." After a few beats too many, he looked back to me. "So you're aware of my previous Kingship then?"

"Had I not been, you would have had some explaining to do with a sentence like that," A smile found me, despite the darkness, "do you remember when I said that you could have become the Demon King?"

"I do," A breathy chuckle left him, lightning the tone a bit, "it was quite startling."

I leaned over on his shoulder, this room felt far too big. "If anything, it's comforting to know that you understand the weight that this crown holds." I got a little closer to him, "Despite it floating, it gets really heavy sometimes."

He nodded, leaning over onto me, too. "I do understand. And that's why I know you can bare it."

If ghosts could sleep, I was comfortable enough there to doze off. Taking his hand in mine, I laced my fingers through his.

"What will happen if I fail the final trial?"

"Then you just return here and have to bow to whoever else wins. You are a sound ruler so you should still be in power when the next King trials come around to try again."

I groaned with a laugh, sitting up, "Again? Shit, I've barely made it through this one."

He laughed too, "I don't think you're going to have to worry about that, Sire."

Standing as I stretched, the tension left me, "Thank you," bending over, I untied my shoes and placed them under the bed. Oliver followed suit as I jumped back on the bed, a yawn taking me.

Laying down, staring up at the ceiling, I may have breathed too deeply.

Oliver crawled up on the bed, laying down next to me, "Something the matter, Sire?"

"This place is just so big, sometimes it gets to me." I rolled over onto my side, "After the trials are over, can we build a smaller house somewhere in the realm and live there sometimes instead?"

He rolled over to face me, his hair falling over his shoulder, his wispy side bangs obscuring his gaze, the glow of his eyes reflecting off the silk of the sheets, "Whatever you desire, Sire."

Shuttering, the way the undertones of his smooth voice made that rhyme sound hit my every button.

"Oh? Do you not like that?" His smile was a little too evil for my liking as he pushed himself up with his arms, hovering over me, "Is this not something you desire, Sire?"

I rolled away from him and went back to facing the ceiling with a groan.

When he chuckled, I knew I was doomed. Leaning over me, his voice became soft, "What do you desire, Sire?"

"For you to shut up."

He laughed, falling down onto me and leaning his forehead on my shoulder. Wrapping my arms around him, I loved that he was cold to the touch, but so warm beneath that.

He leaned up and continued to smile, "If that is your desire, Sire, then I shall do as I'm told." He paused and I knew in that moment that this wasn't over, "But," the brat was really coming out today, "on the off chance that I don't do what you desire Sire, what are you going to do," he raised a brow, "make me?"

Oh, so he wanted to play this game?

"Shut up and kiss me, Oliver."

His eyes flickered, my order was law.

"Yes, Sire."

Crashing into a kiss, he was so stupid, I couldn't help but smile.

Chapter 9
Fatal Dilemma of the Heart

Boggle Birds chirped outside the window, disturbing the peaceful quiet.

"Can we go Flipside before the last trial?" Leaning my head up from laying on Oliver's chest, I hovered over him.

"Do you have business to attend to there?" He ran his hand down the back of my head, causing my hair to fall over my face.

I nodded, nuzzling back down, "I'd like to see how Hugo is doing. I have a feeling that I'll probably be busy if I win this trial, so I'd like to use this time before it wisely."

"Alright," he leaned his head over on mine, "we can head that way whenever you're ready."

We spent a lot of down time laying like that, nuzzled together on my bed. Just existing, I suppose. It was hard, running constantly with no real way to tell one day from the next. It didn't catch up with us often, but when it did we just had to stop for a while. But I didn't mind, I got to lay there, his arm wrapped around me, his heartbeat under my head. It was a peaceful break from an otherwise vivid world.

I could just lay in his arms forever.

Oliver kissed me atop the head some time later as he sat up, "If you want to go Flipside, we should be safe and go sooner rather than later. Last thing you want is to be forcefully summoned while we're out doing something important."

I groaned, sitting up too. He was right, why was he always right? He smiled at me, ruffling up my hair and I enjoyed the contact. We started out of the castle and I spoke to the passing Boggle as we left. They had surprisingly complex social lives, for little floating creatures and pets. Apparently Susie cheated on Will with Joanne and now Will was getting back at her by sleeping with Roxy and I didn't even know how that worked but I also didn't want to know. So I just wished Susie the best of luck as I walked past the little ghost light.

Oliver quietly laughed as he took my hand, pulling me into the portal with him. Looking back at my Kingdom, a smile took me as I fell into a tumbling stupor. They were my wonderful followers and I deeply cared about each and every one of them. Kneeling on the other side of the portal, hand to my mouth, I hissed through my teeth. I never really did get used to that.

As I stood, I wondered if I even could vomit as a ghost. It surely felt like I could, every time I went through a portal or gate, but it never happened so I still didn't know. The bodily functions that did and didn't work after death were rather odd. Some did, some didn't. Like how we didn't need to eat but could, couldn't sleep or bleed, but then other sensations and pain were still there. My heart obviously still beat, I could feel it often enough, but I only knew of a few other things that worked internally for sure. I tried to not think on it too much, it didn't make sense anyway.

It was early summer Flipside, so time must have slowed down because more time than that had passed in the Ghost realm. It was nice out, the sun sitting low in the sky, suggesting that it was late afternoon. I wondered where Hugo would be. The portal dropped us near the downtown area as always so we took a slight walk and ended up at the Historical Society. Fazing through the door, I looked around, thinking on all the after-school evenings I had spent there.

If only I could thank them, the staff who never judged me.

An idea ran into my mind as I started up the stairs, sending me into a sprint all the way to the third story. Passing by George as he touched a picture on the wall he had no business touching, he called out to me but I didn't stoop. Turning a corner, I nearly ran though the little girl but she jumped back, laughing. Ducking under the employee only rope, I danced around piles of files on the floor all the way to my old desk. Looking over it, it appeared they had gotten a new research assistant volunteer because there were stacks of photos needing to be cataloged left out strew about it. Catching up to me, Oliver and the others ran up to the desk as I looked around. Not a living person in sight, I glanced to Oliver with a look and he just nodded with a slight sigh. I really wasn't supposed to do stuff like this, but he wasn't going to try to stop me.

Taking a pen into my hand, I pulled out a piece of paper. Quickly, I wrote out a note, thanking them for being so kind to a misfit kid like me. It flowed so easily, like I had been holding it in without realizing. I told them that I was okay, that I was going to do great things, that they'd be proud of they could see me now. Signing it, I looked it over and hopes that it would be enough to prove to them that it really was me. Folding up the paper, I slipped into Vanessa's office and sat it on her desk, the pen she knew was my favorite sitting atop it.

"You've made it through the first two trials?" George asked after we caught up some, sitting in one of the exhibits because we were ghosts and we could do whatever we wanted, "That's great."

"Win them all!" The little girl swung her legs as she sat at one of the historic school desks, "You'll be a great king."

"Sire," Oliver said as he pushed himself up from the wall and he didn't have to say any more for me to fill in the blanks.

Standing, I started toward the door, "Thank you, I'll do my best." They followed us as we started down the stairs, "Hey, George, what is the date and time?"

He had to think for a moment, "It's currently Wednesday, quarter to three in the afternoon."

"Perfect," I stopped at the door, "Hugo should be just getting out of school."

Fazing through the door, I steadied myself on the other side.

"Don't forget to come visit us when that crown of yours gets bigger, okay?" George called out as we left and I waved back in response.

Before I could even tell Oliver where we were going, we ended up at the school. Standing there, I stared at the school's sign, feeling utter unprepared. A lot of time had passed Hugo, and I needed to make sure that he was doing alright.

But,

A lot of time had passed Hugo, and I wasn't sure if I was ready to see that. Walking down the sidewalk, I looked around all the kids that were running about the school yard. With every step, my heart beat faster, dropping bits on anxiety into my muscles. Hugo always wanted for Les to pick him up in the same spot every day, but as we approached it, he wasn't there. Trying to suffocate the nerves that discovery fried, I wandered around, Oliver following close behind.

"I have never seen this many children," The unsettled tone his words carried made me laugh.

"This is how we're raised these days, just thrown into the fray with a bunch of people around our age under a tyrant teacher and told to just sort of figure it out. The strong rise, the weak become their steps, and the social pecking order stays in line."

Oliver tried to muffle his laugh and I turned to look at him, "My my Sire, you don't sound the least bit bitter."

"Oh?" I continued on with a huff, "Then maybe I need to try harder because I certainly am."

Eyes searching over each gremlin that ran by, a dark thought began to bud in the back of my mind. What if I wouldn't recognize Hugo?

Eyes scanning, I stopped in my step as relief crashed into me when.

Hugo.

Bolting forward, Oliver took a couple moments to catch up. When I slowed down, all I could do was smile. There he was, surrounded by his peers, smiling. They were talking, laughing, throwing a football around between them. I just stood there, beaming. Yes, this was what I wanted for him. Walking around him, I started to bring my hand to the top of his head but stopped because I knew it would go through.

He had gotten taller and wore his hair a little differently, but he was still my little brother. Oliver nudged me a little, startling me. I looked over to him and he dropped his eyes to my hand frozen above Hugo's head. I raised my brows in question and he just nodded. Looking back to Hugo with a smile, I gently put my hand on his head and ruffled up his hair. It was long enough that he would be able to feel it, but not long enough for me to become totally visible. He jumped and turned around, eyes searching the air and looking right through me.

I brought my hand to my mouth, covering my smile as my eyes watered a little. "I'm so proud of you, Hugo." I knew he couldn't hear me, but I didn't care.

He slowly turned back around when his friends asked if he was alright and teased him a little, making him laugh. He had exactly what I never did, what I always wanted. Les called out to him from the near road side and all of the boys went running toward the limo and past me. I turned around and watched them, gaping.

"What? No." Chasing after them, I couldn't believe it, "He's having friends over?" I watched as they got into the car. "Oh my god, he's having friends over." I looked to Oliver, making him jump. "Oli, *he's having friends over.*"

Oliver just stared at me for a moment, "That's lovely, Sire."

"It is." I looked back to the limo as the last door closed. "It really is."

Les walked around the limo then looked up. When his eyes snagged on me, he waved with a smile. I waved back and he got in, leaving me to watch the limo drive away.

"I never had friends over." I said as we left the school yard, the setting sun behind our backs. "I never had friends in the first place, actually."

"Yes," Oliver wrapped his arm around me as we walked along, "I know, you were lonely. But now you have an entire Kingdom that sees that crown above your head. The living really missed an opportunity there, too blind to see it."

Smiling, I looked to the ground. I didn't know how to respond when he said stuff like that. But I knew that he could feel my appreciation. He was surprisingly bold when it came to love, that was the last place I expected him to shine. It was staggering, that someone could love me and be proud of that fact.

Suddenly a shiver screeched down my spine.

"Are you alright?" Oliver retracted his arm as if he had done something to me.

I stopped walking, looking around as a dot of red faded from my vision. Blinking, my skin crawled, leaving me vaguely unsettled, "Yeah."

Oliver took my hand and we went on. We walked along for a long while, I pointed out buildings and places that I once frequented. I told him small little stories about growing up in that town and some of the stupid things I did for the sake of ghost searching. He laughed along with me, seemingly interested in my little pointless stories. His grip on my hand didn't waver, his eyes stayed engaged with mine, and it made me a little nervous to have that sort of undivided attention. As if he could notice every little thing about me in that moment. But as nervous as that made me, it was affirming to know that even when he noticed everything about me, he still smiled.

"My childhood was bland comparatively." He replied when I asked about his. "I just did work around to help anywhere I could before I could go into formal training to become a knight." He laughed a little, "But my sister and I would sneak around and do stupid things for fun, we're lucky we never got caught."

I wanted to ask about Tola many times, but I didn't want to dig up pain for him. "What was she like?"

He looked to me, swinging our intertwined hands a little. "She was really good with animals and people, everyone loved her. She took care of those who no one else would and had some of the strongest bonds with people that I've ever observed. I really looked up to her, despite being the older one." His smile didn't fade, though his tone softened, "It never mattered how high I went up in rank, she never treated me any differently. Which, while somewhat bothersome, was truly humbling and helpful. She took care of me when I wouldn't take care of myself and made sure I slowed down when I needed to. Our parents were always rather busy so we had to look out for each other."

We stepped around a sprinkler as it watered the grass and Oliver appeared completely derailed as his gaze stayed locked on the sprinkler head.

"What is that?"

Looking back to the sprinkler, I laughed a little, "It waters the grass."

"Where…" his gaze narrowed on it, "Where does it summon the water from?"

Smiling, I got closer to him, "An underground pipe system."

His tone was hushed as he looked ahead, "Witchcraft."

The clicking of the sprinkler the only sound between us, I broke the silence.

"She sounded lovely," I looked to cracks in the sidewalk passing below, "I'm sorry to bring up old wounds."

He shook his head, "Some of the thoughts are unpleasant, sure, but it doesn't hurt; not like it used to. It just reminds me how startling long I've been around." He looked to the world we were walking through. "Everything is so different and magical, views and beliefs have changed, war has evolved, things I couldn't ever dream up are realities today and are simply taken for granted. It's truly something." He paused before tightening his grip on my hand and looking over to me. "But what I think is the best thing of all is us. Because, despite being born in two totally different places, times, worlds, we are able to still connect. No matter how much time has passed, humanity still trumps it."

"Careful there, Oli, if you get any mushier you may turn into a pile of glop."

He laughed, shoving me a little, "Say what you will, Sire, but you're smiling."

"How did you ever kill people?" I shoved him back, "You're like a marshmallow."

"Well I don't know what that is… But times were different and I had a vastly different mindset. It's been nearly a millennium since then, which is beyond me really. I unfortunately spent a lot of that time wishing that I died that day on the battlefield." He looked to me, "But I suppose the fates really did have a plan that I just couldn't see yet."

We came to a stop at the place I was hit by a car and died, I hadn't been back since it happened. The memories were still hazy, but there was one thing I'd never forget. My eyes snagged on where he had been standing as my blood splattered across his little shirt.

There was a small cross and some scattered plastic flowers sitting on the ground by a tree nearby in memorial. I laughed a little at that, someone apparently sort of cared at one point, it was in distress now though. Looking up to the street, I thought back on the moment that car struck me. It didn't hurt as much as I thought it would, I guess that's what happens when you die upon impact. That was where this all started, the place that everything changed. Not only for me, but for Hugo, for my family, for my classmates, and for Oliver. Had I not taken that step, had I not chased after the blue of Oliver's eyes, so much would be different. But as I looked up to Oliver from the road, I didn't wish it any other way.

The wind started to blow but as I looked around, I saw that it didn't disturb the trees. Looking up, the sky began to darken and familiar orbs generated in the clouds.

"This is it, Sire." Oliver looked down to me, bringing his arms up over my shoulders and pulling me close. "Are you ready to become the King we all know you can be?"

I wrapped my arms around his waist. "I was born ready."

He laughed at that a little as I leaned forward and kissed him. Falling in love with Oliver was a lot like being hit by that car. When it happened, I didn't necessarily feel it until suddenly everything changed. The sun set as we lost ourselves to the kiss, standing at the spot that I lost my life. Cars raced past, unaware that the biggest Paranormal event in nearly a millennium was about to take place. And that the outcome of it would have an effect on not only the Paranormal, but the normal, too. It was my responsibility as the representative of that time to protect it, because to me, my world was jaded, but to Oliver, it was magical.

Darkness engulfed us but we didn't take much mind until we were torn apart in the tumble. Falling out the other end of the portal, I landed on my knees. Hands on the ground before me, the first thing I felt were the cold stones. Vision blurring back into place, metal bars pulled into focus. Standing, I swayed and stumbled into the wall. Was I in a holding cell? Glancing around at the stone walls, the damp cold started to seep into my core. Pushing myself up from the wall, each step echoed around me as I approached the bars. There wasn't much I could see from inside, but there appeared to be a circular arena on the other side of them. Stepping back, I crossed my arms over my chest, covering the vulnerability being alone created.

It made sense, that I had to face this alone. In the end, no matter how much support stands behind me, I am the king. This was it, all on me now. When my shaking breath escaped me, a cloud appeared. Somehow this place was cold enough that it made a ghost seem warm.

Bringing my hand up, I took my crown from my head and looked over the gems. One golden and pure, as if the feather of an

Angel created it. The next dark and churning, like the shadows Favio commanded. The following a stone that encased a flame, ever burning inside. And the last motionlessly dark but full of endlessly beautiful stars. I had the Angles, the Shadows, the Dragons, and the Reapers on my crown, but those gems stood for so much more than the factions that gifted them to me. They represented the faith and trust I earned from them, they stood for the promise of victory, the hope for a change.

Letting go of my crown, it floated back above my head.

Those gems were also what made it so heavy.

"Welcome Kings!" The Almighty King's shaking voice boomed through the building. From how it echoed, the building must have been huge. "This is the final trial. After this, I shall select the next Almighty Ghost King." I heard a crowd larger than any before roar into cheering sending acute shocks of anxiety through my bones. The entire Kingdom must have been present. "The order in which the Kings shall compete will be random. The final trial is a simple, yet very telling one. So simple that I am, in fact, not going to tell you what it is you must accomplish."

My breath hitched, cutting the cloud it formed short.

"Being king means you must be intuitive, always doing the right thing. For your mistakes, your misjudgments, hold the safety of many in their shortcomings. Prove within five minutes, to not only me, but all of limbo, that you are worthy of this crown." A beat passed, "Now, the first to face this trail shall be the Earthbound King, Ruth."

I ran up to the gate, watching as a gate on the opposite side of the circular structure slowly rose, shaking the ground with it. Emerging from the dark, the Earthbound King walked out with the grace of a goddess. She nodded me as she approached the center of the area and looked up. Though she appeared composed, I could see it, the underlying tremor in her stiff padded shoulders.

I tried to breathe, to calm down. Maybe this wouldn't be as bad as he made it sound. He was just dramatic, that's all. It was his last big show before retiring to some ghost island somewhere. Straightening as I put my hands on the bars before me, eyes on Ruth, I took a deep breath. I still had this, my confidence, my support, and mostly, the advantage of not going first.

"Are you ready, King?" The Almighty King said from above.

Ruth nodded, her floor length skirt blowing in the draft.

"Let the trial…begin!"

One of the Almighty King's black orbs appeared before Ruth and a moment later, a young girl came falling out from it. Ruth went stumbling back hands flying to her mouth.

"Mother?" The girl asked, obviously confused.

Ruth was speechless but the heartbreak was so evident that I could feel it in the air. Her eyes shot up, and in that moment I witnessed all hell bloom behind them. The Almighty's chuckle shook the air as Ruth took another step back, the click of her heals echoing. Suddenly the girl started yelling and clawing at her head, falling to her knees as her shirks tore the air. Rushing to her side, Ruth tripped on her heels and fell to her knees next to the child, hand on her back. As Ruth consoled her, I watched Ruth's composure start to fracture.

The girl fell silent.

Standing, she took two sharp steps back, her little body rigid and tense. Her arm slowly raised from her side, her hand reaching into the front pocket of her apron. Ruth stood, hands extended in front of her, her cautious posture so unlike her. When the child looked up, her eyes held an eery red glow.

"Kathleen," the quake in her voice, the shaking of her hands, Ruth's display began to chip away at my resolve, "please."

Taking something out of her apron, Kathleen smiled as she brandished an ornate dagger. The entire kingdom burst into whispers but Ruth didn't seem to hear them.

"Darling, please," she stepped forward, "give that to me, let me help you."

Cascading brown hair reminiscent of Ruth's, Kathleen's accent mirrored hers as well, "You want to help me?"

"Yes," Ruth was breathless, taking another step forward, "I always wanted to help you."

Shrill laughter took Kathleen as she stepped back, swinging her arm with the knife about, "You're lying," Bringing the knife up to her own throat, Kathleen's wayward smile tainted her every word, "You did nothing to help me last time, Mother. Did you have to lose me to realize that you loved me?" Taking a step forward, she made Ruth step back, "Or is it your own guilt you wish to assuage?"

As if her mind had stalled, Ruth was rendered motionless.

Kathleen removed the knife from her throat, admiring the way it glistened in the light, "You know Mother," each step grew less steady as she approached, "what if it did go differently this time?" Turing the knife outward, she pointed it toward Ruth, "If you wish to atone, allow me to do the honors." Bringing the knife up to Ruth's neck, Kathleen paused, "What, after all this time, that's all you had to say to me? I'm sure you never stopped thinking about me, after I got the best of you."

Ruth did not move, her eyes locked forward.

"How pathetic," Kathleen swayed forward, ripping Ruth's crown off and threw it to the ground, the clang bringing silence over the crowd's whispers.

"Ruth!"

My yell had left me before I even thought to call out for her.

Snapping from her shock, Ruth looked over my way but it appeared that she couldn't see me as her eyes searched under her furrowing brow. Jumping back, as if she immediately came back to her situation, her attention returned to Kathleen.

A renewed composure about her, Ruth's posture corrected itself, her tremor calmed. "I'm sorry."

Kathleen stood, staring up at the towering woman as humility unlike anything I had ever seen shaded the prideful King.

"I couldn't swallow my pride, I couldn't tell you I was wrong," Ruth stepped forward, hands lowering, no longer on the defensive as she stopped before the child's kneeling down, "No, I wouldn't do it, I could have, and I chose not to." Her hands hovered, not making contact with Kathleen as she went on, "You didn't deserve that, you deserved a better mother. I love you, I'm sorry I made you feel so unloved."

Shoving Ruth's hands away, Kathleen stumbled back, "It's a little late for that now," pulling the knife back up, tears started to glass over her eyes, "why didn't you say that back then? If you had then… then I wouldn't have," bringing the knife to her neck, her hand shook.

"I know, my darling, I know." Ruth's softness dulled the edge on the air as she slowly approached the child as she backed up into the wall, "I cannot undo the past but we have now," kneeling before her, she opened her arms, tears beginning to destabilize Ruth's tone, "everything will be alright. Come here, just for now."

When the knife hit the ground, the clang ruled the air. Crashing into a hug, Ruth held Kathleen close, taking her up into her arms. They exchanged soft words I couldn't hear and as I watched, my blood went stale.

The Almighty said this would be intuitive, so easy to understand that it went without explanation. But as Kathleen started to glow and fade from Ruth's arms, I was no closer to grasping what was expected of me. Bit by bit, Kathleen turned into little blue orbs until the light exploded, causing Ruth's embrace to collapse on the void. As the lights faded into the air around her, Ruth stood strong, tear streaming from her closed eyes, her quivering lip partly hidden by a curtain of her hair that had fallen loose from her tight bun.

"Congratulations, Earthbound King, you have passed the final trail."

A bell chimed and with each revelation of the gong, my core sunk further, my hands grew colder, my grip on the bars loosened. The rearing cheers of her faction turned into white noise in my ears. As the last ring faded, Ruth walking out of my sight, my confidence faded with it. Weakness washing over, taking my will with every wave, I was left, staring forward at nothing but my inevitable demise. We had come so far, fought through two other trials, made statements and enemies, to lose it all here, under the viewership of the entire kingdom.

"Now that we've had an excellent example set by the Earthbound King, it is time for the next candidate to prove their worth." The Almighty's voice echoed into what sounded like oblivion, or maybe it just felt that way now that I was empty too. He paused and I held my breath, feeling it combust in my core, causing a vacuum as that moment lasted an eternity. "How about the Boggle, since you were just so excited to be involved with the last trial."

The grate began to rise before I processed what he had said and the tone he had used. Bars sliding out from my hands, I stayed, frozen as it lifted entirely into the ceiling. If I couldn't pass this, I wasn't worthy of being a King, not to limbo, and not to the Boggle.

I wouldn't deserve the support I had gained, the lower factions were counting on me to represent them, to honor them.

"What's the matter, Boggle, nervous?" The Almighty had broken formality in lieu of mockery, "Where is that charisma now?"

The kingdoms roared into laughter as my feet carried me forward before I had a moment to think. This would have bounced off of me before, but with every step, the dread that was planted when I called out to Ruth grew, flowering in my stomach, thorns and all. I should have known better than to anger the Almighty right before a trial, this was his game and I was merely a pawn, a prisoner marching toward his slaughter.

Looking up, I was crushed by the weight of the eyes. Surrounded by a kingdom sized coliseum, I was the bullfighter walking into the ring without a weapon. Eyes resting on Oliver as he stood, Gaston at his side, the Boggle cheered for me but I couldn't hear them. As if I were underwater, there was a film separating me from them, a delay, an echo. Though his expression was neutral, I could sense Oliver's unease in his posture, but the last straw to my confidence was the look on Gaston's face.

Never before had I seen the Angel's smile fade.

"Now, Boggle," Sitting in a separate grand rafter, strewn over a bisellium decorated in golden metal work and glistening gems, surrounded by his noxious cloud, was the Almighty. "You have a knack for conquering challenges," leaning forward, he brought his hand out, holding something over the arena, "but how will you fare against what you fear most?"

When he dropped a black orb, I only saw it for a moment before it exploded over me, splashing my world with ink. Clouding my view of above, Oliver was obscured by the darkness. Like I was standing in a bowl of water, ink dropped and expanded around me turning into surroundings that were nothing like the arena I knew I was standing in.

An illusion?

Taking a breath as a scene appeared around me, I noted the feeling of the stone beneath my feet. As long as I knew it wasn't real, I could beat it. But, as I looked around at the images forming, I realized that I didn't even know what I feared most.

Lockers came to life on the walls, the discolored speckled ceiling panels fading to life above my head, even the air gained the scent of suffering teenagers as I was dropped right back into the dead end high school. Stepping around, I was impressed, the detail was staggering. Walking up to my locker as it sat, defaced as usual, it was wild that he even knew what names they called me. As I brought my hand up to the locker, the cool metal tingling on my skin, I tried to not wonder about what the others could see.

When I watched Ruth, it appeared she couldn't see out, and I couldn't fully see in. But what did the illusion look like from above? I glanced up to the brown leakage stains on the off-white paneling, could they see the illusion too or was I just walking around touching nothing?

"Hey, Kasper."

Turning, my nerves jumped at the voice. Materializing before my eyes, camo and all, was Russel. Walking down the halls as if he owned it, some big shot in podunk Blazing Star, Russel was backwoods incarnate. Closing in on me, he backed me up into the lockers. His dusty red baseball cap with some political phrase, his muddy boots and dirty jeans, he really did think he was cool. It was really unfortunate, the way he dressed, because under that unkempt mess of brown curls and bad attitude was a smooth pair of eyes.

Grabbing me by the collar, he slammed me into the lockers, the familiar metal thud occupying my ears as the wind was knocked out of me, "You're a joke," the originality was impressive as his signature snarl came out to play, "a Kloven who talks to ghosts."

Shaking my head, a smile finding its way to my face as relief flushed through me, I looked between his eyes, new life to mine, "Russel Taylor, my greatest fear?" Laughing, I knocked Russel's stupid hat from his head, "And here I was concerned."

Russel looked around, "Who are you talking to," shoving me into the lockers harder, the childish rage of a confused farm boy shone through, "fuckin' creep."

Eyes rolling back down to him, I brought my hand to the side of his face, causing him to jerk his head away, the disgust palpable, "As much as I love to play our little game, Russel, you don't scare me anymore." Shoving him back, he let go of me as his clunky shoes thudded on the tile floor, "You see, I've faced demons and dragons, an insecure redneck ain't shit."

Obviously grasping for straws, I watched every confused feeling race over his features, "You're a disgrace, your family should disown you."

"Ah yes, the family name card," I walked toward him, "I agree, they really should. Good thing I'm dead, they don't have to deal with it anymore."

"Dead?" He backed into the opposing lockers.

"Yeah," holding up my hand, I smiled as it turned transparent, "dead."

Shoving it into his core, it fazed through. Staring down at it, his bad boy act crumbled as he blubbered, unable to utter a single coherent word. After one last satisfying look at the terror that painted him, I ripped my arms up through him, disappearing his figure into ink. As the space around me dissolved, the ringing of the bell echoed through me, signaling the completion of my trail. Smiling, my brief moment of doubt had blown over, replaced by confidence high enough to touch the sky. As the barrier above me cleared, my eyes locked on the Almighty.

There were no cheers, the arena silent as all eyes sat on me.

"How does it feel, your Highness, to be bested by a Boggle?"

Rumbling shook the ground as the Almighty stood, his cloud growing, darkening the space. "You believe you've bested me?" The tone he used reminded me of Russel, of an insecure cornered bully lashing out, "Well Boggle, it appears that you still have a lesson to learn," raising his arms up, I watched the kingdom drop into concern as a large orb began to grow in the palms of his ancient, massive hand, "You forgot your place," reeling his arm back as he floated above me, his smile tore across his aged skin, "allow me to remind you."

The bell stopped tolling.

I had no time to run, no time to look for a way out of the arena.

The last thing I saw as the gigantic black orb came hurling toward me was Gaston holding Oliver back. When the orb hit, it crashed through the barrier above and right into me, sending me flying across the arena and into the stone wall. Coughing so hard, I would have tasted blood had I still been able to bleed, my senses were thrown into a panic. Tumbling to the ground, my hearing went out upon impact. Laying there, motionless, my eyes fell shut. In the moment before I blinked, I knew where I was and what I was doing, but as they slowly opened again, I knew none of those things.

Face on the floor, it was cold against my skin as my senses returned to me. Shaking as I pried myself up from the ground, my breath hitched when I realized I was in my high school. Standing, I swayed into the lockers. Looking about, the beige lighting, the off blue lockers, the stained ceiling and grey tiles, something seemed off. This was my school, but since when had it been so worn?

Yelling erupted from down the hall and I knew exactly what it was the moment I heard it. My feet moved before my body knew it was running and as I barreled around the corner, someone gasped for air. Facing the bathrooms, the ruckus echoed out of the men's room.

"I can't believe you'd use his death for attention."

"I'm not-" water hitting the floor filled my ears with unwelcome sensory, "I saw him."

"Yeah right," scuffling, a struggle started as I walked into the bathroom, "You're just saying that because you're washed up and want the clout from his curse."

Running down the line of stalls, I could see shoes under the last one, and a set of knees on the floor. Water hit the floor as the person on their knees was dunked in the toilet again.

"It's been seven years, you need to grow up. It's not his fault that you pissed away your chance to be successful like your family."

Standing outside the bathroom stall, hand raised to open it, I froze.

The guy on the ground coughed, water sounds filling the air, "Ghosts are real."

Yanking the stall open, I stared forward. A young man held another down, head in the toilet as he struggled. Lunging forward, my hands went right through him as I tried to yank him back. Falling forward and into the wall, I hit harder than I had expected to. Whirling around, footsteps came rushing into the bathroom. Relief washed over me, someone was coming to help. The stall door flew open and several more young men came in but as the light fixture above us flickered, I saw they were smiling.

Ripping the young man from the toilet, they threw him to the floor.

"You're a freak, Hugo."

The light flickered again.

"Hugo?" Trying to shove the boys away, I continued to go through them, "Hugo no."

They laughed as he tried to pry himself away, "Why are you fighting?"

Taking a fist full of his hair, one slammed Hugo's face right into the floor.

Red.

"Kasper," Hugo's voice cracked under the attack, "Kasper, help."

I was paralyzed.

"Kasper."

They slammed him again.

"If you're so sure your brother is a ghost," they dragged him across the floor, smearing his blood as it poured down his front, "then why don't you want to join him?"

Following them out of the stall, I kept trying to yank them away and every time I fazed through, my heart started to crack further. Pulling him up from the floor, they held Hugo up there for a moment, four against one. It was then, in the florescent lights, that I saw him well. His blond messy hair, his dark jacket, his teary brown eyes and defined jaw, he looked just like our father.

His eyes landed on me and for a moment, they widened.

Throwing him into the mirror behind him, his back shattered the glass. His yells surrounded me and with every hollow thud, every kick, every punch, every laugh, every splash of blood, my world started to darken. Hugo, how had this happened to Hugo? Hugo wasn't like me, Hugo had promise, Hugo had friends and sports and the looks and the chance to become something.

The lights flickered.

"If your brother was a ghost," one took a shard of the mirror in hand, lording it above Hugo as he laid, unmoving on the floor, dazed hazy eyes staring forward, "he wouldn't let this happen to you."

The lights went out.

Static laced the air, the power outlets on the wall beginning to snap, shocking the world in flashes of green light with every crack. The shattering of a mirror shard ruled the air. Rumbling vibrated the floor, the stalls opening and slamming shut. The hum of my crown above my head grew as it gained speed, my steps accompanied by the crackling of glass under my shoes.

"You're right," looking to the boys as they stood close together, deer in my headlights, a wayward smile ripped me more than it helped. Bringing my hand up to them, light started to glow from it, "I won't let you."

Lightning began to rain around us, painting the world in silhouettes as I took one of the bullies by the collar. Striking us, the young man screamed out as the lightning brought me to life in his eyes. Seeing my reflection in his tears, the terror taking his features, it made me forget the most important thing about ghosts. Throwing him, he flew all the way out of the bathroom and into the hall. The others tried to escape but I blocked off the exit with a wall of lightning, trapping them. As if my powers had taken hold, every moment that passed was one that I slipped more.

Iris had said something once, about what was to be the downfall of a Boggle King.

Our hearts were just too big, so big, that when they broke,

I threw one of the bullies into a few of the others, knocking them all into the ground.

It shattered, the shards turning to shrapnel.

Striking them with lightening, I left them, writhing on the floor.

The pieces hitting everyone who stood too close.

Trying to run away, I yanked them all back.

Like the final stone had been removed.

Slamming them into the floor, I painted the tiles in their blood.

The entire wall came crumbling down.

Picking themselves up as they sobbed, the boys escaped the bathroom, their screams echoing down the hall.

And I was left, smiling in the wreckage, uncaring of who it harmed.

The hum around us subsided, the lights flickering back on, and we were left in silence.

"Kasper?"

Turning, the blood of my victims splashed over my front, my eyes stopped on Hugo. Sitting on the floor, hands supporting him from behind, he must have put distance between us because he was further away, blood smeared in his path. When I took a step toward him, he slid back and away from me.

"Hugo?"

Scrambling, his shaking hand swept across the floor and when it raised, it held a shard of the mirror directly at me. Trembling, his eyes held nothing but echoes of the child I once knew as his grip tightened on the shard causing blood to drip down his wrist. The sound it made when it landed in the puddle we shared made everything stop. His breathing labored, his eyes glassy, posture defensive, back to the opposing wall, Hugo was all grown up.

When I started to step forward again and visible panic crashed into him, I froze mid step.

"It's me Hugo," slowly raising my hands, I couldn't breathe, "your big brother."

"No," Hugo's voice shook as fear started to transmute into something else under the pressure in his eyes, "you can't be. Kasper is a ghost, and ghosts are good."

Standing, surrounded in blood and broken mirrors, in leaking sinks and unhinged stall doors, he was right. "I'm sorry I just," taking a step forward, my eyes fell to the bloody water puddles under my shoes, "I had to save you, they were going to hurt you."

"Hurt me?" As he shakily stood, it became quickly apparent that he was taller than me now. "that was nothing." Stepping forward, his eyes darkened by his furrowed brows, tears fell from them, "Nothing compared to watching my idiot big brother step out in front of a fucking car," his approach turned into a pursuit as he quickened his pace, "nothing compared to years of ridicule because I swore I saw your ghost."

Reaching his trembling hand up as he lunged toward me, I could do nothing as he shoved me back. Stumbling away, any will to fight drained from my muscles, leaving them empty and weak. Pinning me there, one hand full of my shirt, the other holding the shard to my chest, Hugo, bloodied and broken, had all hell burning inside him.

"Nothing compared to watching your favorite person desperately beg for love and attention from something that was never there, unable to see who was standing right in front of him the whole time."

"Hugo... I'm-"

Cutting me off with his tightening grip, my little brother who wasn't all that little anymore looked even more like our father with every passing moment, "I don't want your apologies, I want your guilt." Throwing me to the floor, he stood over me sending out rings in the puddle beneath us, "This is your fault," extending his hands, he looked around, "All of this," bringing his free hand up, he wiped the blood from his face, "everything." Stepping on my chest, he held me to the ground with all of his weight, "If you were sorry, you wouldn't have shown yourself, if you were sorry you wouldn't have done this to me. I'm a freak, Kasper, a freak just like you, and it's your fault," dropping to his knee, he knocked the air out of me. Kneeling over me, his shaking hand held the shard in the air. "I had promise, I loved you, but all of that died along when you did, and now," his tears started to surface through his angry words, "now I hate you."

Laying under his attack, eyes barely focusing, the only thing I could see was him, his defined features, his movie star face warped into a frown, his quivering strong brows, and his clenching jaw. The cold of the water seeped into my clothing, the smell of iron laced my every shuttering breath.

"That makes two of us, kiddo."

Shaking his head as he closed his eyes, they opened with a renewed intent so potent I knew there was no fighting it. Hugo had become a hell of a kid, somehow without my even noticing. How had time passed so fast? Where had I been before? I couldn't bother to explore those thoughts further because they didn't matter, the only thing that mattered was holding me to the ground below him.

Hugo's blood dripped down his jawline and onto my neck as his tears subsided, "You were too busy looking for the unknown ahead of you to see me at your side. You let go of my hand for a ghost," his grip tightened on the shard, cutting his hand further, "This time," he brought the shard up toward himself, "take me with you."

It was a blur of slippery movement, my lunging for his hand, pulling it back and away from his throat. Kneeling in front of him, pulling against his strength, my shaking body started to fail me.

"Hugo don't."

"Why not?" He pulled back on me, trying to bring the mirror shard to his neck.

"Because," my hand got slit on the shard as we struggled, causing me to quickly muffle my pain through grit teeth, "it's not too late for you, you can still be something here."

"I don't want to be," he started to overpower me, "there's nothing here for me to be other than a freak."

"Please," my voice cracked, the tears threatening to obstruct my vision, my shaking straining hands threatening to give out, my little brother threatening to die, everything started to fall apart, "don't do this."

The smile that took him, I'll never forget it, "Maybe when I'm a ghost you'll pay attention to me."

Slitting my hand, Hugo ripped the shard away from me. The tear of flesh, the sound of the shard shattering on the floor, I was blinded by gushing blood, suffocated by the weight of his body crashed into mine.

"Hugo"

"Hugo"

I couldn't see.

"Hugo"

It couldn't be.

Laying there, the heat of his blood burning my skin, I tried to move my arms up to hug him but I couldn't. As my vision cleared with the tears, my body was motionless as it mirrored his. Staring forward at the discolored ceiling, my eyes couldn't move. The light from my crown began to dull as a part of me died, executed by Hugo's hand. Shaking, I tried to move my arm up to touch him but it fell back down, landing in the chilled puddle.

The slowing beating of my heart became the loudest thing in my world as my vision began to blur. Darkness started to creep into the corners of my vision as the cold from the water under me won out, the lights above us flickering until all that was left was darkness.

As my eyes began to close, they felt so heavy that I wondered if they just wouldn't open again.

Searing white, a rush of air, the roar of a crowd yelling, the sensory attempted to stir me but it simply rushed me by. Something protruded through the wall at my side, sliding down as if it were slicing the fabric of space time. The world around me ripped, warping around itself until it imploded into clouds. Hugo's weight disappeared, the wetness of his blood vanished, and the cold under my back became warm. Voices echoed around me but they couldn't string together words, my mind delayed, the images passing above my eyes trailing.

The echoes bounced about enough that finally one word did come through them all, "Sire."

Blue entered my vision, leaving a line of light behind it.

A hand touched my chest and like I had stepped into the vacuum of space, every single thing dawned me in that moment. My hearing sharpened, my senses woke, my eyes cleared, leaving me staring right up at Oliver.

"Sire," his concern snapped into something else as he dropped to his knees at my side, Jaxton in one hand, the other moving to my back, "are you alright?"

Bringing a hand to my head, my world slowly came back to me.

"How disgraceful, Almighty Ghost King," Oliver stood, pulling me up with him as he yelled toward the King's box, "Kasper defeated your trial, this is just senseless cruelty."

A wave of agreement echoed out from the Earthbound, Shadow, Reaper, Angel, and Boggle factions in the stands. Slowly bringing himself to his feet, the Almighty's noxious cloud grew, the light darkening further.

"I will not stand for such insubordination, a Boggle is nothing."

"Obviously not, your Highness," Oliver gestured to the all but rioting factions, "his support is staggering." With every word that left him, his eyes became brighter and his tone, sharper, "Othello, you're slipping. This is not how you want to punctuate your reign."

The ground rumbled, causing to Oliver step in front of me, sword in hand.

"Oliver," the booming of the Almighty's voice shook the entire stadium, "because we were once friends, I was willing to overlook your defiance. But this is a great disrespect." Floating up, flying above us, his throne of clouds formed beneath him, "You may be above factions, but you are not above me, and nor is your king." Extending his arms, he spun slowly, "You will see, you will all see, what is to befall a Boggle who forgets their place." Stopping as he faced us, I was only just starting to gain my wits about me again as the gravity of my predicament hit, "I would banish you both myself but we're here for a show, so," raising his arm up, a black orb began to form in it once more, "make it a good one."

As the orb flew our way, Oliver raised his sword to face it. Though as it approached, it grew smaller, gaining speed. Taking a swing at it, Oliver missed. His back was to me when it hit him, causing him to bring one of his hands flying to his face. Stumbling back, he muffled his yell as he doubled over. The silent anticipation of the crowd was crushing as Oliver agonized.

"Knight!" Gaston's voice was so distressed it was nearly unrecognizable as it echoed around us.

Eyes scanning the seating as I ran to Oliver, they snagged on Gaston as he fought with several uniformed Shadow People Guards.

"Kasper, run!"

Gaston was silenced, shoved down behind the railing of the rafters.

Reaching Oliver, I put my hand on his back as he visibly struggled with something I couldn't see, hand in his hair, teeth grit, yell trying to escape.

"Oli," I bent over at his side, looking up to the Almighty, "What did you do to him?"

The chuckle that left the Ghost King chilled the arena as he floated back to his seat, "I think you need to be more concerned about what he'll do to you."

Oliver's yells subsided.

My hand burned.

Jumping back away from him, shaking my hand as the burn refused to cease, the shock of the coliseum was staggering. What could they see that I couldn't?

"Oli, are you all-"

As Oliver turned around, battery acid shot through me, depositing an overdose of adrenaline in my muscles.

Red.

His eyes locked on mine, the red glow from them so radiant that it shone on the stone walls around us. His charming demeanor was twisted, the smirk on his face contorting the refined features I had come to know better than my own. Swinging his sword up through the air, he slung it over his uneven shoulders as the blade roared into flames. The smoke that rose from the ground beneath his feet took shape and as it reached above his head, it stopped, forming a crown.

This was no longer Oliver, not the one I knew.

This was the Demon King, and I had no idea what I was going to do.

Rushing toward me, he was a crimson blur in my eyes as I was knocked to the ground. Rolling away, I fought to get to my feet but I was knocked from them again. Roars of laughter bellowed from the demons, the Almighty's above the rest, as I stumbled to my feet. Every move I made was defensive as I ran from Oliver, his heavy footsteps never far behind. Mind flatlining, my thoughts shattered before they formed.

His hand seared into my back as he shoved me forward into the wall. Nearly tripping as I turned to face him, the cool stones behind my back not enough to erase the burning of his fingers on my skin. Smirking, sword raised, Oliver stood in pause; as if he relished every moment. Eyes darting up, I could see my faction visibly distressed. When the blade began to fall, I darted forward and under Oliver's swing across the arena, the sound of metal scraping over stone chasing me. Slowly turning, he dragged the tip of the sword on the ground, bringing sparks to life as his eyes rolled up to me.

"Oli," I brought my hands up, "this isn't who you are anymore," stepping back, I was mindful of the wall, "you defeated the Demon King before, you can do it again."

Oliver's chuckle sent poison through my veins, stopping my heart.

"Why would I do that?" Bringing the blade up, he pointed it directly at me as his approach came to a pause, "There's nothing impressive about a Boggle."

Standing there, staring down his sword, I found myself faced with the past. Running wouldn't do me any good, and there was no way I'd win in a fight. The only person who could save me had eyes glowing crimson. Though even then, I could feel it, the King Connection. It was faint, but if I could feel it, perhaps he could too.

There was one thing impressive about us Boggle.

"Hey Oli," I smiled, walking forward.

I was told to not repeat the past.

He raised a brow.

Warned that it would come to this.

"Remember when we first met? You told me something."

I wanted to have the audacity to defy destiny.

He started to lower his sword.

To prove that Boggle were worthy of respect.

I walked past his blade.

Boggle may have not been the mightiest.

Closing the space between us, I wrapped my arms around him.

But we did have something that no other faction did.

Pulling him into a kiss, he relaxed in my grip.

Heart.

"Everything is going to be alright."

If the strongest thing in a Boggle was their heart, then I was going to make his beat so hard it would bring him back.

Mind numbing pain tore through my center.

I flew back, entire body trembling as my vision blurred. Oliver stood there, his red eyes churning with his wicked smile. My heartbeat became the only thing I heard as I slowly looked down. Oliver's sword stuck right through my chest, a massive blight quickly grew from the wound, climbing up my body, burning every inch.

Favio told me I had two options. Have the audacity to try to do everything differently, or have the bravery to follow the same path, but do it right.

Choking, I coughed up black sludge.

I had tried to be audacious, to knock over the board, scatter the pieces and alter the strategy

Ripping the sword out, Oliver threw me to the ground.

But despite my optimism, my confidence, my daring was my demise.

Inky darkness poured from the wound, surrounding me as I laid on the ground, hand clutched over my shirt.

Yelling erupted from the stands.

I too had stumbled into a fatal dilemma of the heart.

Oliver's steps as they grew closer blurred in my ears as my vision began to fail me. A hand latched around my collar, dragging me up into the air with unmatched strength. My world zeroed in on one thing, Oliver's eyes. Tears streamed from them as his smile warped his features. He was in there somewhere, and I wasn't compelling enough to exhume him.

Sword dissipating from his grasp, it turned into a dark red light in his palm. As it began to grow, I found myself another blighted Boggle King. Bringing his hand up, the light encompassed my world, blocking out the light from above. Hands up to Oliver's as he held a fist full of my shirt, I could feel the deep tremble in them. As I watched the red ball of energy form in his hands, I looked back to him. So this was the last thing Tola saw and she still smiled? Perhaps she didn't give up, but saw what I had behind those red eyes.

"Why don't you fight?" Oliver tightened his grip.

I could only smile at him, "Don't underestimate the folly of man, Oliver."

Red turned blue but it was drown out by black when the light crashed into me.

I had broken the spell, but a moment too late.

Sent flying, I didn't feel the ground against my back when I landed. The only thing I could feel were the tendrils of blight as they crawled over my skin, wrapping around my neck, choking me. Echoes of yells muddled in my ears, footsteps bouncing around in my mind. A thump at my side, something faint and warm tried to beckon to me as I quickly lost out to the cold.

Gold, bold unchecked gold, pierced the vail of pain. Light raced through my veins and with every beat of my heart, sensation returned. Bleached out, my eyes struggled to see anything other than white. Shapes started to take form, the first ruling my vision that of a glowing ring.

"Kasper," took over my ears, "hang on, please."

A breath came to me, followed by a cough as I tried to sit up. Shaking violently, coughing up sludge, I held one hand to my mouth and the other up to my chest. A warm hand landed on my back as I fought to breathe. Eyes screaming into focus, I was met with a sight.

Oliver laying on the ground, hair disheveled, a blight crawling up his neck. The King Connection insignia glowed brightly from under his shirt, lighting up through the layers. But with every moment, it began to fade. Reaching out toward him, my breath failed to come to me.

"Sire," Gaston pulled me into his arms, "don't move."

Gold deposited into me once more, his bouncy locks falling over his face. He looked like an entirely different person when he wasn't smiling. Hand on my chest, I could see the glow from it start to chase away the blight, bringing peace to the screaming wound.

"This blight is bad, almost too bad, but I think I can handle it."

"But," I coughed, "Oliver, he's-"

"I know," Gaston's brow furrowed, his eyes unmoving from my wound, "but I can't heal both of you."

"Then don't," pushing myself up from his arms, I swayed as I stood, "I'll be alright."

"But Sire," Gaston stepped forward, reaching out for me.

"I'm okay," smiling at him as I tried to relax my shoulders, I turned toward the Almighty, "I promise."

I couldn't face him, not while lying.

After a hesitant moment, I heard Gaston's muddled footsteps race toward Oliver as he hissed something under his breath. Gold radiated out from behind me, casting my shadow long across the arena. I just had to hold on long enough to look strong, I had to, after my kingdom watched me fall. The pulsing poison in my chest began to crawl away from the wound again, slinking over my skin, as Gaston's light began to fade from my blood.

My eyes locked on the Almighty's, and despite his expression being that of stone, I could see it; the burning hatred in his eyes. Even while cheating, he was bested by a Boggle before his subjects. A smirk found its way to me, despite the pain, standing tall, I was the center of attention.

Hand tightening on the arm rest of his chair, the Almighty struggled to stand. Slowly, he brought up his arm, a dark light beginning to glow from his hand. I fought the instinct to step back, standing my ground. We were witnessing it, a god falling from grace, an Earthbound succumbing to human flaw.

The orb in his grasp grew, festering around itself in a warped muddle. My eyes never left his as the contact grew combative. Oliver coughed from behind me, Gaston sighing in relief so potent it brought a bit of peace to me.

The tension broke in the stands as factions started to yell in protest, begging the Almighty to spare me, but I didn't flinch. I could see the quiver in his frame, the weakness in the light of his crown, I was willing to bet this was a bluff. A cornered King, losing his grip, faced with his demise. Holding the light out toward me, it illuminated his darkened features and for a moment I saw it, the glass in his eyes.

Darkness flashed as the orb shot out from his arm, swinging it to the side.

The ring of the grand bell ruled the world, stunning the crowed as I stood, victorious. With a great huff, the Almighty sat back in his throne. Smiling, I looked up and around to the surrounding beings. Waving to my faction, cheers exploded, bringing a smile to me. A staircase appeared out of the stone, leading to a seating area before my faction. Turning, my eyes met with Oliver as Gaston helped him to his feet. Running, I didn't feel my feet carry me to him. Taking up his other side, I helped walk him toward the stairs.

"Are you alright?"

The way Oliver looked at me, the utter annoyance, it elated me as I laughed.

"Kasper," we started up the stairs, slowly, as Gaston's golden glow continued to pulsate through Oliver, "what the fuck were you thinking?"

My smile distracted me from the pain as we neared the top of the stairs, "Don't underestimate the folly of man, Oli."

"I could have banished you," he hissed as we gently helped him sit down, "even though you broke the spell, the blast still hit you, right? How are you still standing?"

"I'm a king," sitting down next to him, I stretched my arm over his shoulders, pulling him close, "I'm just fine."

Gaston wrapped his arm around Oliver from his other side, his hand finding its way to my back. Gold caught the corner of my vision, causing me to look up to him. The pointed look I got from him was all too telling, the Angel was done with my shit and saw right through me. Smile still on my face, I closed my eyes as I leaned onto Oliver's shoulder, Gaston's healing starting to chase away the blight.

"Red really isn't your color."

He leaned his head onto mine as the Almighty called the crowd to quiet down, "I'm sorry you had to see me like that. I was weak and fell to his spell, by the time I broke it," he took my hand in his, "you were harmed."

Shattered mirror shards flickered through my mind, making me open my eyes to interrupt the flashback, "No, you saved me." Rubbing the back of his hand with my thumb, a deep breath took my core, "It's all going to be okay, we made it out, and showed all the factions just what we're made of."

The last toll of the bell rang out, leaving silence in its echoes.

I had done it, the thing Favio thought impossible.

History had repeated itself, but I beat it.

"Next," the Almighty's voice wavered, "Demon King."

The rumble of a grate raising caught my attention as I watched from the area above. As the grate reached the top of the opening, my eyes were locked on the door. A part of me was a little too excited to watch Nolan suffer.

"Demon King," the Almighty's voice shook the arena.

No one emerged from the door.

Gaston's shadow festered, growing as it ripped away from him. Colors bled into each other, creating nothing but black, white outlining everything in the flat contrast as Favio fell out of the shadows and dropped to his knees. Gaston flew from my side, running to him as color returned to the world, but something about it looked duller than before.

Wounded and blighted, Favio was disheveled, coughing, as he writhed on his knees. Exchanging quiet words with Gaston, Favio's composure shattered.

Standing, the Almighty started to float down toward us, "Favio, what's the meaning of this?"

"The Demon King," Favio didn't look up from the ground, "I couldn't stop him."

The sky tore open above us, the temperature spiking as the world gained a red tint. The Demon faction exploded into whispers, laughing and roars as smog erupted from the rip in the sky. Plummeting from it, a wave of smoke crashed into us, choking me with its toxic burn. Flying to my feet when a metallic clang followed, I couldn't see anything in the smog. Raising my hands, my crown lit up and its spinning quickened as it cracked with electricity. With a wave of my arm, the darkness blew away, clearing out our area of the arena.

On his knees, the Almighty sat, trapped in a cage.

Laughter bellowed out around us as the demon approached from every direction. Oliver and I ran toward the cage, shoving demons away as they tried to swarm it.

"Kasper," Favio struggled to stand as he joined us, "he's taken a human into his realm."

"What?" Oliver fought at my side, nearly falling from his feet before I caught him, "why?"

One dot after another connected in my mind, gaining speed with each one until a terrible picture pulled into focus, "A sacrifice."

Favio nodded, "I tried to rescue them but," he was taken by a cough, the blights barely reacting to Gaston's light, "Nolan has become stronger," the demons began to close in, "my investigation suggests he just needs this last ritual to gain the power he needs to overthrow the Almighty before he chooses a rightful successor."

Favio was burned, blighted, completely ruined and in no state to face the Demon King. Our shadows ripped from around us and out of them rose shadow people of all sizes, warding off the demon waves as they came crashing in. Oliver stepped up into my back, his hand lighting up with his precious blue as he shoved some demons away. Lighting struck from the sky on my command, taking a few demons out as well as I created a wall of electricity surrounding the cage. Coughing, a searing pain stretched through my abdomen. Bringing my hand to my mouth as another cough took me, black tar seeped through my fingers. Wiping it away on my pants, I tried to fight the pang of dizziness that took me as I stood behind my comrades, my lover and friends.

"He's trying to stall," Favio said as he leaned into Gaston, "we need to intervene."

"But how," Oliver turned, the wall of lightening framing his features in sharp white light, "we'd have to make it all the way to a kingdom gate."

"*Boggle*," The Almighty's voice rang out above all else as he sat on his knees in the cage. Turning to see him, no one else did, as if I were the only one who heard him. Slowly, he struggled to look up to me. In those eyes that held galaxies, for a moment, I saw humanity, "*You cannot allow Nolan to take this crown,*" his mouth did not move as he spoke on, his words echoing in my head as the world around me began to slow, "*I sense the blight in you, it is too far gone. You won't last the battle, and Gaston's power is depleting. You require immediate attention that you will not receive, and I cannot give you.*" His trembling hand rose up to the bars, the darkness rapidly infecting him at the touch, "*I forgot what it means, to be a King. Allow me this penance,*" A black orb shot out from his hand, ripping through the lightning and expanding on the other side as it threw a horde of demons away and onto the floor of the arena. "*The choice is yours, but I know you will make the correct one.*" Bringing his finger up through the bars, he touched my crown. Upon the contact, my wall of lightning swelled, my crown's light beamed so brightly it nearly blinded me. In the flash, the man kneeling before me was no longer the aged Almighty Ghost King, but a younger, far less weathered man with the build of a super hero and a smile so bold it instilled a faith in me I had never had in myself. *"You have my blessing."*

His hand dropped from the bars as the light dimmed, falling toward the ground. As he collapsed in a heap, I saw his smile still, unfading on his ancient face. The moment he hit the ground, he didn't make a sound as he eroded away into a cloud of dark dust. The Almighty's crown was all that remained as it spun to a stop, the metallic clanging of its base meeting the stone below ruling my world.

The red tint grew darker, corrupting the colors around me.

Coughing, I felt myself fade with each one.

I had been victorious, defeating the history that yearned to repeat.

Now it was my turn to write the ending.

Turning to face the black orb as it sat in the midst of a paused battle, my eyes drifted to Oliver. He stood, glowing hands out, pushing a demon back into my wall of lightning. They drifted to Gaston as his golden glow kept Favio standing as he fought along side his faction. They passed over the waves of demon, the evacuating Earthbound, the still and unmoving Poltergeist. Lastly they landed on my faction, the Boggle as they helped everyone get out. Bringing my hand to my chest, I could feel the poison grow.

This was what it meant to be a king.

Time snapped back into place as the Almighty's crown fell silent. And explosion of events occurred all at once, as if the momentum of the fight had built and finally released. Running toward my wall of lightning, eyes on the black orb, I knew my time was limited. About to run through my lightning, a hand grabbed mine, yanking me back. I didn't have to turn around to know who it was, despite everything else, the underlying warmth of his cool touch brought me peace.

"Where are you going?"

I couldn't face him, "To stop Nolan."

"What," his grip tightened, "let me come with you."

"I can't," bringing my hand forward into the storm of lightning, it washed over me like water, "you can't pass through here and if I drop it, we'll fall to the demons."

Wavering, his hand started to loosen, "Look at you," letting go, he crashed into me from behind, holding me close, "becoming the king I always knew you'd be."

Turning around in his grasp, I plunged my forehead into his shoulder as I hugged him back. It was no use, he could feel what I felt, he knew how scared I was. Putting up a bold front for the kingdom would fool everyone except him. Pulling back before he could open his eyes, I kissed him.

"I love you Oliver."

He smiled, I could hear it, "I love you too."

As I pulled back, a demon broke through our front, hurling itself at Oliver's back. Before I could even say a thing, Oliver's blue eyes flashed red for a moment as he spun around, slicing the demon in half with his glowing hand, a low rumble on his breath.

"Go," he called out, looking over his shoulder, his eyes glowing purple, "and please," he smiled at me, "come back."

Stepping away from him as quickly as I could, I brought my arm up to my eyes and wiped away the budding tears. Running forward, I passed through the veil of lightening, unable to turn and face my friends. The electricity poured over me like rain pelting against my shoulders and head, bringing a chill to my skin. Each step that took me away from Oliver tugged at my spine, causing something deep inside to cry out at the separation. The gravity of the dark orb swept me up before I could run into it, pulling my feet from the ground and swallowing me.

It felt an awful lot like being hit by a car.

Nothing.

Chapter 10

TO BE A KING

Rolling when I violently hit the ground, the faint screaming of car horns faded from my ears. Coming to a stop, laying unmoving on the rough rock beneath me, my mind entertained a thought.

What if this was all a dream?

What if I opened my eyes to face the asphalt, to sit up and see the car that hit me.

What if Hugo was waiting for me to get up and be okay?

Would I be relieved?

Or devastated?

Heat gnawed through my clothing, biting at my skin. Vision blurring, back to me, the uncertainty of what would be on the other side in clarity stopped my breathing. Molten rock, ambient red glows and the hum of earth shifting, I was met with hell.

Shaking as I picked myself up from the sharp ground, my staggering breathing was taken over by a cough. Clutching at my collar, my coughing fit sent a dizzy pull over me as I sat there, barely able to hold myself to my knees. Closing my eyes as the blood dropped from my head, everything was dark for only a moment before a light pierced it.

Opening my eyes, my surroundings were showered in white gold. My crown began to spin faster, the light closing in on me. When it made contact, it dropped into my blood, bringing ease over my body. With a trembling hand, I took my crown from my head. Turning it around in my grasp, I was met with Gaston's gem as it nearly blinded me with its bold glow.

Despite the pain and heat, despite the reality and blight biting into my core, I smiled as I placed my crown back above my head.

Standing, I made a real attempt to take in my surroundings and gather my mind. Stone structures surrounded me, standing in similar distress and disrepair. Damn near everything was on fire, the air held a tinge of sulfur, and the sky was obstructed by heavy smog. Stepping around, I stopped. So tall it's towers tore the smog, a castle sat in the near distance. Fire belching from the windows, the brimstone wonder called to me. Feeling like the main character of some young adult dystopian novel, I started my approach. The light rushing through me restored my vigor by the moment, putting the pulsating pain in my chest on hold as I barreled over boulders and over streams of lava.

I had learned a lot about being a king.

Jumping away when a bubble of lava popped, I hissed through my teeth when some of it splashed on me.

It was more than a crown.

My hands stung as I pulled myself over a rough volcanic rock, ripping my skin up.

It was the weight.

My shoes made little sound against the dense ground as I raced up the stairs to the castle's doors.

It was more than a war.

Monolithic redwood doors didn't give when I crashed into them, knocking me back a few steps.

It was the promise to win.

Stumbling, my footing betrayed me as I went tumbling down the stairs.

It was the kingdom behind me, a knight at my side.

Shaking, I picked myself up, eyes locked on the door.

It was my undying belief that ghosts are good.

Thunder rumbled in the sky as I brought myself to my feet. Each step up the stairs I took increased the pressure, the anticipation, the build. Stopping at the top of the stairs with my scuffed up formal shoes, I brought my hand up to the doors. Exhaling, a smirk crawled to my face.

It was smiling even if I was scared.

Lightning exploded from the sky, ripping a smoldering streak down the wooden door. When the light faded from my eyes, my ears were met with a chorus of cracking burning wood. Stepping through the crack, the cindering seared door on my either side, I was careful not to trip as I set my other foot inside the castle.

The foyer surrounding me, the onyx marble floor stood in contrast to the sulfur yellow structure. Vaulted cathedral-like ceilings, war-time tapestries decorated the walls, torches lit one after another in a line up the winding stairs as my other foot made contact with the ground. The fire sent shadows dancing over the floor, crisply in time with the dramatic dancing of the flames. Taking a step forward, I stared upward at the endless staircases as they climbed above my head.

Taking a moment to tackle the insurmountable tack before me, I tried to not be overworked by the sheer size of the castle. It was at least seven times larger than Castle Boggle, I had no idea where to start. Jumping when my eyes caught on unsustainably movement in my peripheral vision, my heart leapt into my throat as I stared at the shadows around me. Once moving, they were all suddenly still. Ripping from their objects, the shadows aced in circles around me, closing in before I could run away. In a black flash of light from my crown, the shadows crashed into mine, sculpting a different silhouette than mine from the darknesses.

"Sire," the gravely voice made the ground under my shoes rumble, "King Favio sent me, the demon assault is relentless and our defenses are becoming weary. How may I be of assistance?"

Trying to stuff the panic that invoked back into my core, my smile remained, "Great, thank you. What's your name?"

"Is that…" the shadow ripped from my feet, "necessary information at this juncture, Sire?"

Deep breath taking me as I started forward, I eyed the stairs, "Someone's name is always necessary information."

After a pause, the shadow followed me up the stairs, crawling across the ground, "Rodger,

"Well Rodger, help me search the castle for the captive? It's too big for me to do on my own." As I started to ascend the stairs, a sharp pain ripped through my middle, causing me to nearly fall, grabbing onto the stone hand rail for support as I clenched my teeth, trying to hide the pain.

"Sire," Rodger jumped from the ground, becoming an entire figure before me, hand extended and bent in slight bow, "leave it to me. Rest and I will locate them, you are in poor shape."

Before I could protest, Rodger spilled back into the floor and expanded, covering the entire castle in their shadow, rendering my surrounds into nothing more than white outlines. Dropping to my knees as I struggled to breathe, the shadow cooled the air around. Panting, it didn't matter how much air I took in, it felt like I was losing more with every exhale. Closing my eyes as my world started to spin, I tried to exhume memories from the Earthbound ball and the demon attack. They had whispered about this, but in my pained haze I couldn't pull anything into focus.

Leaning my forehead against the railing, I didn't let my smile fade even as tears budded in the corners of my eyes.

It was the strength it took to carry that crown, no matter how much it hurt.

That's what it meant to be a king.

"Sire," I jumped when Rodger's voice came from in front of me, "the captive has been located. They are on the third story, in the sole company of the Demon King."

This was it, my duty as king.

Standing, a breath that took some of me with it as it escaped me. "Thank you."

Rodger connected to my feet and with every running step I took up the stairs following them, my weight was lifted, as if they were aiding my movements. Standing tall, pushing myself to the brink of my abilities, the stairs flew under me. I had to use Nolan's absence at the trials to my advantage. My wound was an unknown to him, I had to make him believe he was facing me in peak condition. I needed to walk in there like he was about to regret ever existing. He had angered the Boggle King and it was time for him to feel the wrath of a patient faction pushed over the edge.

Rounding a corner on a stair flight landing, I nearly ran into something. Falling back into the opposing wall, Rodger flew up and kept me from falling down the stairs. Standing there, slowly looking my way, was what appeared to be a janitor, but just like everything else in this cursed realm, they were on fire. Fire in hand as they stood in pause, their beady eyes from under the flames sat, unmoving on me. A moment later, their gaze dropped from me as they continued to slowly mop the floor with fire.

Stepping around them, Rodger and I slowly increased the space between us until we rounded another corner. Sprinting down the halls, a beautiful castle passed me by. I was unable to appreciate it in the given situation, but from what I could see, it looked like it had been nice once. Not always this pit of hell we were trapped in. I wondered what caused its descent into distress.

Nearly tripping up the second flight of stairs, I grit my teeth, kept my head up, didn't stop.

Rodger helped me as I started up the third flight, my vision narrowing on the top of the stairs. I just had to get up there, I just had to get the captive back, I just had to get out.

I just had to come home.

With a final push from Rodger, I stumbled over the last stair and to the flight landing in front of two large mahogany doors. Unable to breathe, choking and gasping, I fell to my knees. My ears rung out as my vision fell away from me. For a moment everything was numb, the blight all I could feel as it crawled over my chest and up toward my neck. The light from my crown started to dim, Gaston was wavering. My senses dragged themselves back to me and as I opened my eyes, I saw Rodger on the ground before me. It appeared that they were speaking, but my rung out ears were useless.

"I can't hear you, I'm sorry," my voice felt soft as it left me, "I don't think I'm going to last much longer in this place."

Rodger nodded and slinked up from the ground, helping me stand and steadying me as I swayed to my feet. Electricity cracked in my blood, my drive to do my crown justice infecting me. As my ears dulled back to me, my hearing was fuzzier it had been before. Straightening, I quietly thanked Rodger.

"Alright," my tone quiet, I fought for self possession as I approached the door, "if I can get the captive to you, can you get them out?"

"Yes, but," Rodger floated up behind me, "what about you Sire?"

"What about me indeed," placing my hand on the door, I smiled over at the shadow, "the captive's safety is paramount, but Nolan must be stopped." A beat passed and as I spoke on, I wasn't sure if it was for Rodger's comfort, or my own. "I'll figure it out, I am a king after all."

My hand started to glow and as I took a deep breath, I closed my eyes.

Being a king was promising to return, but accepting it may not happen.

Lightning exploded in front of me, blowing the doors away. Running through the smoke and debris, my smile was unfading. Red painted the surrounding some as it cleared, the air so hot it stung as it blew toward me. I only saw the wall of fire closing in for a moment, but as an orange glow lit to life on my crown, reflecting off of the surrounding smoke, I knew I had nothing to fear. Walking forward, I greeted the flames with a smile as they crashed past me. I had the Great Ghost Dragon at my side, fire didn't scare me.

Hands in my pockets, smile on my face as the smoke cleared, my eyes were set ahead, ready to meet with my foe.

"Hello there, Boggle."

Nolan's voice cut through the smoke as it dissipated, showcasing him as he stood in the center of the ballroom, a large ritualistic circle drawn on the ground around him.

I looked around, my raised brow challenging him as my eyes landed on his, "I like what you've done with the place, the eternal hellfire was a nice touch."

"I envy those who have never met you."

It hurt to laugh but I couldn't help it, "You flatter me."

"I cannot express how satisfying it is to finally put you in your place," Nolan yanked someone out from the smoke and to his side, "Boggle."

If the breaking of a heart had a sound, it wound be a stifling sob of a child.

"Hugo?"

Standing there, fighting against Nolan, was my beloved brother. His hand was black, blighted where Nolan had touched as tears fell from his angry eyes. Electricity started to snap around me, burning the smoke in the air.

"Let him go."

Hugo looked to me and it was then, that moment, that I had wished this was a dream. That I'd wake up on that concrete, being loaded into the back on an ambulance. I'd rather live my entire life paralyzed, permanently damaged, than exist in that moment because the look on his face hurt more than anything else ever would.

"Kasper?"

Running forward, my feet carried me faster than my mind could process because by the time I saw the smile on Nolan's face, it was too late. The ritualistic circle drawn on the ground lit up and sent a wall of black light up into the ceiling, trapping us.

"Do you really think I'd need a kid for a sacrifice?" Nolan threw Hugo to the ground so hard he bounced with a sickening thud, "You Boggle are all thatsame," he dashed toward me in a blur, throwing me into the wall of light, "bleeding hearts."

Knocking the air out of me, he clasped his familiar claws around my neck, digging into my skin with his talons. Smile still on my face, I watched as his expressing warped from satisfaction to frustration when I didn't blight under his touch. His eyes rose to my crown and I could see the light of the Angel's gem reflecting in his soulless orbs.

"What," I said through the choke, "did you really think I came alone?"

Lifting my hand up to his chest, my skin hummed with electricity. His eyes only met with mine for a moment before I smirked. With a roar of thunder so loud it shook the castle, a beam of lightening sent Nolan flying across the circle and into the opposing wall. Dropping to my knees, I fought to breathe. Looking up, my eyes jumped to Hugo as he laid, motionless on the ground. Stumbling with every panicked step, my faced faltered as every breath burned more than the last. Reaching him, I lifted him from the ground. Limp in my arms, my panic flailed until I saw his chest rise and fall.

Running toward the entrance as Nolan picked himself up from the ground, I was met with the black wall. Looking down to the circle, it was drawn in what looked like dried blood, there was no way I could easily break it. Turning around as I shifted Hugo into one arm, I extended my hand. Vision blurring as my arm swayed, I mustered all that I could in that moment and sent another beam of light lightening into Nolan before he could fully stand.

Trembling, I looked back to the wall before me.

Hugo stirred in my grip.

"Kasper..." he smiled, nuzzling into me, "I knew you were a ghost."

Breath hitched, I was left staring forward.

I couldn't think, my mind frazzled, with the haze of smoke clogging it. As panic started to mount, I could hear Nolan scape to his feet. White exploded, creating a hole in the wall before me, stilling my thoughts. A vision of gold overwhelmed my senses, bringing great calm and peace. Standing on the other side of the hole was Rodger, arms extended as the hole quickly began to close. Footsteps raced toward me from behind, my beloved brother in my arms, my strength fading, I knew what I had to do.

The hole wasn't big enough for me to pass through.

"I'm sorry Hugo," Handing him to Rodger, I didn't let my smile fail me again, "Keep him safe, then when it's all over, bring him to Oliver. Show him Hugo's blight."

Rodger enveloped Hugo in their shadow and as they shot away, their voice was left, nothing more than an echo, "Yes Sire."

The hole closed.

Being slammed into the wall, Nolan's claws dug into my back, causing me to yell out. Throwing me to the ground, I rolled as heat exploded out around us.

"Originally this was going to have to be rushed, but," Nolan stepped up to me as I laid on the ground, dazed, "But thanks to your little stunt earlier, the Almighty can't stop me so," lifting me up from the ground by my neck, the demon's wayward smile tore at his rotting flesh, "I think I'll enjoy myself."

Walking with me as I choked and struggled under his grasp, he dangled me over the center of the markings on the floor. A sick satisfaction painted his features as a blight began to grow under his hands, causing me to cry out as the white gem in my crown faded.

"Pathetic, even when you band together you lower factions are powerless against us." Jabbing his other hand into my core, his claws dug into my blighted wound causing me to yell as he twisted them. "Looks like Oliver got a good hit on you, I wish I had been there to witness it all. A little bird told me, it was all very exciting." Ripping his claws out, black blood bellowed out from my core, "What a unworthy king you are."

"I'd say you are the unworthy king," tears streamed from my eyes, but my smile didn't fade, "having to cheat your way to the Almighty crown because you know you're too rotten to earn it."

"We're not all that different," he threw me to the ground, slowly approaching as I struggled to pick myself up, "doing what we must for our kingdoms. But I have the power to provide for them, you don't, so why," he stepped on me, shoving me into the floor as he increased pressure on my wound, "why do you keep smiling?"

Thunder rolled outside, shaking the stone castle walls. "Don't underestimate the folly of man, Nolan."

Lightning struck him, knocking him away from me as I stood. Panting, losing strength with every passing moment, I could barely stay on my feet. Hand to my face as each breath tore my throat, I didn't know a way out. The only way to get rid of a paranormal being was to banish them, but very few possessed the ability. One could be blighted into banishment, but could a demon even get a blight? How would I even inflict one if he could?

He brought himself to his feet, his claws screaming as they scraped against the marble floor, "Do you really think this display will change anything? There will always be evil so tainted it can darken any light. You're foolish to think otherwise, so why fight it?"

My eyes couldn't raise, locked on the ring I was given the day I died. "I always have, and always will, believe that ghosts are good." Looking up to him as I closed my hand, I stood stall, "As long as I believe that, as long as others do, there will always be a light your shit can't put out."

"What a silly sentiment," he walked around, extending his claws as he closed in, "as long as there are Demons, we're going to do everything we can to destroy the peace. You can't stop us," he stopped right in front of me, our eye contact not breaking, "you can't stop it." He dropped a finger to my chest as he backed me up into the black wall of light, "You couldn't even stop your lover."

Breath hitching, my eyes locked on his, my smile grew ever so slightly.

"This is true, but," a tingle started up my arm, "I'm going to stop you."

Jaxon's full weight dropped in my hand.

Swinging the sword, I slashed across Nolan's chest, causing his warped scream to rip the air as he flew away from me.

"If I'm so useless, why am I the one you need to sacrifice?" I dragged the blade behind me, it was far too heavy for me to hoist proudly, "I think it's because I have something you don't," lightning started to strike around us, "something every king needs." Pulling up Jaxon, I pointed it directly at him as he sat on the ground, glowing circle below him, "heart."

His palpable shock only lasted a moment before it was overtaken by a grimace as he flew to his feet. Fire exploded around us, creating a wall that started to close in. The flames turned black, their heat radiating so violently that it caused a whirlwind. In a flash, he had me in his grasp, holding me in the air as he stood, in the center of the circle.

"Your audacity is blinding, Boggle. What do you think you're going to do with that, blight a demon with their own sword?" The markings on the ground started to glow brighter as he laughed, "You almost had me there for a second. But in the end you fell short, just like the Boggle King before."

Hand tightening on Jaxon, my smile didn't leave me as the darkest gem on my crown started to glow, the light reflecting in his eyes. Sending a shock through my body, I made him let go. When I landed on the ground, paralyzing pain shot up through my legs, but my smile didn't leave. Of all my weapons, that had proven to be my most powerful. Looking up to Nolan, I could see it, the unsettled tension born of anticipation, his eyes on my crown.

A breath escaped me.

Being a king was doing the right thing.

Jaxon's blade started to turn black as thunder rolled above us, the electricity in the air snapping around. The shadows that were casted by the approaching fire came to life under our feet, wrapping around his legs. He fought, but it was no use as he was subdued to his knees, the markings underneath us growing even brighter. As fire rained down, it didn't burn me, orange starting to glow from my crown. My strength began to return as white bellowed out from above me, but it was only a burst, one last stand, one final strike.

My king connection pulsed. I could feel him, crying out. Bringing my blighted hand up to my chest, all I could do was beg for forgiveness.

Grip tightening on Jaxon, my eyes snapped to Nolan as the thunder grew louder.

"What a pity," snatching his crown with my other hand, I studied it, "this crown deserved better."

Throwing it to the ground I raised Jaxon in the air as the darkness engulfed its entire blade. The Reaper's dark gem the most potent of them all as my crown gained speed, the pressure in the room growing. For a moment my eyes caught on the shadow I casted, Jaxon held above my head. But as the fire danced behind me, Jaxon's shadow was not that of a sword, but a scythe.

"I'll see you on the other side," tears fell from my eyes despite my smile, "Nolan."

When I accepted the crown, I never expected to be an executioner.

Sending all the power I could through the blade as I plunged it down over the back of Nolan's neck, lightening exploded, raining down like hellfire, erasing both of us in the light. The last sound I heard was his yell as it mixed with the roar of thunder, the crumbling of rock, the warp of power. The world turned soft blue, the light of the circle below us drown out, and all that was left was nothing.

A lot like being hit by a car.

It was a moment where everything mattered but at the same time, nothing did. A sort of paradoxical suspension that was both disorienting and comforting. When the light faded from my eyes, the world around me was a never ending plain of soft blue.

Standing before me was a young man, one who looked far too young to die. Scruffy hair, a boyish charm, his lively eyes and charismatic disposition was magnetic as he stood there, staring at me. Nolan in life must have done awful things, but was no demon compared to what he had become in death. The Nolan I saw before me in that suspended moment was, at his core, good. I just knew it from the tears that streamed down his face as the blade of Jaxon ran through him.

His head severed.

That fractured point in time shook around us then imploded, exploding all around us. In a snap, I was flung from my senses, Jaxon dissipating from my hand. I flew through white nothingness, debris and fire around me. The roar of rubble mixed with a blaring white noise and together they drove my mind into witless absence.

Being a king was everything to me.

My world went dark in the impact and like that, everything I had become was gone. My life spun around my head in echoes and blurred images. It was all so messy, lonely, disconnected. My failures were punctuated with the sharp steps of my mother's stilettos, my shortcomings highlighted in Hugo's smile. Obsession framed my life, a pitiful grasp for control, for drive, direction. It came to a culmination in the headlights of a car, ending right then and there, without fruition.

Though.

Upon death, my world became colorful, laced with meaning and love. The images raced me by so quickly, I could barely catch them. Such is life when you're having fun. It was such a short time, but as I floated there in nothingness, surrounded by my life, I knew it was good. Fading with that feeling into a greater nothing, I had a fleeting wonder.

What awaited me in a death after death?

Chapter 11

GHOST KING

A familiar cool touch slowly brought me back into my senses, a little at a time.

I knew that feeling, it was the purifying power that Oliver possessed. Did that mean I made it? I survived? I couldn't move or open my eyes but as I laid there, I increasingly became more aware. When I could open my eyes, they wouldn't focus. But from the colors I was seeing, I didn't think I was anywhere safe. Dancing reds, endless black, I was still in the Demon realm. But who was healing me? I tried to move but I was trapped under something and unable to. All I could see was the faint blur of long orange hair.

"Oliver?" I managed to ask so quietly I barely even heard myself.

The person shook their head as they gently pushed me back down into a laying position. I couldn't fight, I didn't have the strength. A pang of pain screamed through me, causing me to yell out, barely able to breathe as I lost my wits to agony once again. I don't know how long I laid there, fading in and out of alertness. It must have been a long while, though, because by the time I was able to regain my mind about me again, I was no longer in pain.

Alert, I flew up and immediately hit my head on something, sending myself backwards into the ground again. Ice jolted through me when I heard a laugh. Slowly opening my eyes and looking to the side, I saw a young lady. But not just any young lady, King Tola Vestile herself sat in the rubble next to me.

She smiled at my surprise, pulling her knees up to her chin, "Hello there, you must be Kasper."

I was absolutely captivated, she was otherworldly as light blue orbs floated around her, her hair blowing in a wind I didn't feel, "Yeah."

Carefully this time, I sat up and didn't slam my face into a chunk of wall. Looking around, I saw the Demon castle in absolute ruin, its scattered pieces laying about the entire area. A blue tainted hole in the black sky where we would have been on the third story, it was as if I had ripped the fabric of the Demon realm. My hands flew to my chest but to my surprise, there was no longer a wound there and the blight was entirely gone. My eyes drifted back to Tola.

"You've done a good job as the next Boggle King, Kasper. It eases me to know that they are in such good hands."

Rubbing my face with my hands as I tried to calm the racing of my mind, a devastating deep breath escaped me, "I didn't plan on making it out of that," eyes drifting toward the hole in the sky, I forgot myself, "What sort of king does that to their people."

I choked on my words when my mind caught up and remembered just who I was talking to.

"What sort of King, indeed." She mused, "I've been watching and I know all that you've done." She stood and I shakily followed as she went on, "You've made my brother happy," she looked to me, her eyes making my blood jolt upon contact, "quite happy."

I looked away quickly, her presence was just too intense for me. "He's done the same for me."

An awkward beat passed as I briefly wondered just how much she had been watching.

"Did you heal me?"

She turned from me with a small hop over a rock, "Yes, you're not through with your work. Unlike me, you're not getting out that easily." She laughed as she stepped behind me, putting her hands on my back and shoving me forward, "Now come along, you need to return before my brother kills himself again."

"How are you here?" I asked as I tried to not stumble on the burning rubble.

"Kings never truly move on properly after they fade. We're always apart of our Kingdom."

As we approached the Demon gate, I felt something tugging on my insides. It was my connection with Oliver, leading me back to him. It was only a light tug, as if the connection was weakened. He must have thought I was banished.

She shoved me right up to the gate then turned me around to face her again. Crossing her arms, she smiled brightly as she looked me over, "Take care of the Boggle for me, and make sure Oliver lightens up some," her smile faded a little as her eyes dropped, "And please, don't tell him about this. It's better that he's moved on."

It felt like my time in her company was coming to an end even though it had only started. She was just as much a part of this story, this kingdom, as I was but she was all but a stranger. I wanted to ask her so many things, for Oliver to get to see her again, but as her form began to fade into transparency, I knew there was no time for any of it.

She extended her hand to me, "King Kasper, go forth and conquer."

I reached out to take her hand, "Yes, Sire."

She smiled and when our hands met, she turned into a silhouette of light that flew into the ring I wore, lighting it up a bit before it faded. I clenched my fist, looking at the ring before turning to face the gate with a smile.

Though she was gone, she wasn't really.

Facing the gate, I knew it was the last thing standing between me and Oliver, between me and what was held in a death after death. I promised my return, but as I stood there, I was reluctant. The Almighty was gone, the Demons were without a king and I? I had blood on my hands.

The image of Nolan's head bouncing as it hit the ground caused my stomach to flop.

The world waiting for me on the other side of this gate was entirely different than the one I left.

It felt a lot like being hit by a car.

Stepping into the churning light, I fell into the portal. As everything spun around in my mind, the pieces that had been fragmented in the fall started to reconnect and every dot led to one thing.

Hugo.

Being thrown out the other side, I couldn't keep my balance. Stumbling from my feet to my knees in front of Castle Boggle, my hand flew to my eyes as my world stopped spinning. The grass felt nice on my knees, the fresh air clearing my lungs of sulfur with every breath. Looking up from the ground, I was met with the presences of every Boggle as they stared back at me, frozen mid-float. As they rushed me, exploding in cheers, I was relieved to know they had all evacuated safely. Iris flew up to me and I smiled, expecting a warm welcome but was met with,

"Run."

"What?"

Whispers broke out around me and suddenly the crowd parted. In a flash of blue, my world was knocked out of focus for a moment as my back slammed into the Boggle Gate. When everything veered back, I was met with a flash of red.

"You said you'd come back," Standing there, hand full of my shirt Oliver pinned me to the Boggle Gate. Eyes glowing violently, they flickered red with every sharp syllable, "not sacrifice yourself."

"I did come back," extending my arms, I smiled under the attack, "see? I'm here."

Tightening his grip, he increased the pressure, "No, I felt it," he brought his other hand up to his chest, grasping at his shirt, "you were gone."

Looking between those eyes, I could see the barely tamed red undertones, the vivacious bite that rested just inside. Oliver was like a fine drink, the first sip hurt, but with every one after that, he just tasted better, the burn warming, the complexity apparent.

"I like your feisty side."

Sighing, his anger visibly disarming, he closed his eyes for a moment. When they opened, they had cooled back to their normal blues, "Please, don't do something like that ever again."

Beaming as he loosened his grip, I ruffled up his hair, "Yes, Sire."

The tension broke when his eyes glassed over and his anger turned to sadness. He yanked me into a kiss and wrapped his arms around me so tight I could barely breathe. As he buried his head in my shoulder, and cursed me under his breath as he fell apart in the hug. Looking forward, holding Oliver close, I saw Hugo. Relief dripped into my blood as I watched him and Iris play. But then reality veered back, reminding me that he wasn't supposed to be here.

Running my hand over Oliver's back, stopping at his head, I kissed his cheek, "I'm sorry I scared you."

Starting to gather himself, Oliver tightened this grip on the hug for a moment longer before letting go and stepping back, "I just can't lose you."

Inspecting him, it appeared his blight had been healed, "What happened after I left?"

We started to walk through the crowd and toward Hugo, the Boggle parting to make a path for us as they quietly whispered support and thanks, "The demon forces had almost broken through your defense when a godly lightning storm chased them away. When it ended, only a few moments later, your wall fell and everything stilled. We evacuated the rest of the factions and Gaston called on his faction to assist in the recovery efforts. Just as we had healed the injured and returned to Castle Boggle, Favio's assistant brought us Hugo, and not you."

My nerves started to fray further with every step I took closer to my brother, "Did you take a look at his hand?"

Nodding, his tone grew quieter, "He had direct contact for so long that I couldn't entirely purify it. However, it shouldn't cause him much issue, same as your blight from childhood. I'm sorry Sire, I did truly do my best."

"No, I understand," I looked back to Hugo who still hadn't noticed me approaching. "Thank you for helping him."

A beat passed.

"What became of Nolan? I no longer sense-"

"Sire."

Oliver and I tripped over ourselves, nearly running into a bunch of Boggle, when Favio spoke at my other side out of nowhere. Looking to my right, Favio walked in perfect step with me, brows raised.

Favio blinked at us, "My apologies, I didn't mean to startle you."

We regained our composure and nonchalantly acted like that hadn't just happened. After my heart rate fell back to normal, I stopped, stepping off to the side of some of the tall bushes and a tree so that Hugo wouldn't turn around and see us, "We don't have to worry about Nolan any longer."

The way Oliver and Favio studied me, the quiet wave of realization crashing over them, I wished I hadn't been looking to see it.

Favio nodded, "I see," he bowed his head, "We played right into his hand. Their attempt to capture you at Castle Earthbound when you were disarmed failed, and after that the Almighty put travel restrictions which further crippled their plot. The only way to lure you into Castle Demon was with Hugo, and if I had realized sooner none of this would have happened." He looked up to me from the bow, "You wouldn't have had to do something so unpleasant. My deepest apologies, Sire."

I messed up his hair with a grin, "You do your best, that's all I can ask. Thank you."

"With that said."

Favio, Oliver, and I, all flew from our skin when a voice came from the tree.

Nirvana stared down at us from one of the branches, not amused in the slightest. He cleared his throat, "With that said, others may try to do the same in the future to get to you, Kasper."

"You are the hopeless hero type, Sire." Gaston added, swinging down from another tree branch, hanging upside down by his legs. "All they'd have to do is follow you again and snatch someone else important."

"And having that in mind," Favio was hardly able to maintain eye contact with me, "we feel that it is in the best interest of all parties for you to cut all contact with those Flipside."

My heart slowed to a stop.

"The entire Kingdom has now seen that you will go rushing to help in this situation, if anyone ever wanted to get to you ever again, they'd know exactly what to do." Gaston said as he swayed from the tree, getting closer to Favio.

"But I doubt they could track him down again without you leading them to him." Favio took a step away.

I looked around the tree to see Hugo laughing, and as much as I didn't want to admit it, they were right.

"And it won't be a problem, that he's been through all this." Nirvana said as he swung his leg. "I can scatter the memories and make then resemble a dream, so his normal life won't be hindered."

Staring at Hugo and how tall he had become, I pondered what it would mean, to become simply a dream. Broken mirror shards, the wet cold tile of a bathroom floor, the sensory sent a shock through my chest. My greatest fear, it was in my hands to prevent it.

"Sire," Oliver took my hand in his, "I know this must be hard but-"

"No, I understand." I tried so hard to smile it hurt, "I wouldn't want him put in danger like this again. And like you said, they can't find him if I don't show them where he is. I'll go take him home and that will be it, it's alright. It's better this way."

There was a moment of pause, a space in time where my friends could see right through me.

To be a king was to do the right thing.

If Hugo saw me upset, he'd be sad too. I just had to lock it up, ignore it, until he couldn't see me falter. I had smiled at a Demon King in the depths of hell, but this was so much harder. My friends looked like they wanted to stop me but knew they shouldn't as I walked around the tree and up to Hugo. I savored the last moments before he saw me, each step taking me closer to taking the first away. His eyes drifted past Iris and the moment they landed on me, I stopped.

His smile was brighter than anything I had ever seen.

Running to me with reckless abandon, Hugo crashed into my legs. Kneeling down, I pulled him into a hug, making sure to not hold him too tightly because soon, I was going to have to let go.

"Are you alright?"

"Yeah," his smile was evident in every word, "I finally got to go on a ghost adventure with you," he stepped back from the hug, his little eyes glassy, "our last one got cut short."

Needles shot through my body, "I'm sorry."

"I know," his smile looked so effortless, like he had no idea what was to come, "but it's okay, I can see you again now!" Turning, he looked up to Castle Boggle, "You were right, ghosts are good, and you're the king of them."

"Well," I stood, placing my hand on his head as I desperately fought to maintain my composure, "king of some of them."

My shoulders trembled as my jaw clenched.

An arm laced around my side as Oliver pulled me close. My heart began to slow as calmness deposited in me. His eyes glowing a little brighter, I could see his king connection through his shirt. I perhaps got lost in the moment because it lasted a bit too long.

"He's the one, isn't he?" Hugo asked, startling me from my thoughts as he looked up to us from the ground, arms crossed in smiling challenge, "The person you were always drawing?"

I was stunned into silence as I stared at him.

"I knew it," Hugo's Cheshire grin grew, "when I'd go through your notebooks he was all over them."

"Oh?" Oliver tightened his grip on me.

"Yeah," Hugo bounced, "what's your name?"

Every letter was tainted in his mischievous smile, "Oliver."

Hugo took off running around us, a trail of boggle following him, "Kasper and Oliver sitting in a tree, K-I-S-"

One thundering step from Oliver's side later, I scooped Hugo up off of the ground and held him in the air by the back of his shirt.

"What do I tell you about going into my study and touching my stuff?"

He giggled as he hung in my grasp, "To not to."

I wanted to stay in that moment forever.

I wished I had appreciated moments like these when I was alive to have them.

"Alright well," I tossed him up to sit on my shoulders, "It's time to get you home, Les is probably worried."

He whined as I started toward the gate, "I like it here, can't I stay?"

"You have school in the morning."

Flopping around, he hung upside down over my back, "But-"

"School is very important," Gaston's voice came from behind me as several sets of footsteps came racing up.

"You are the keeper of the Kloven legacy," Favio's voice held an unusual light to it, "It's your responsibility to carry that now."

Hugo's groan threatened to make me laugh, "Yeah whatever."

When I started to approach the gate, I turned to see Oliver, Gaston, Favio, and Nirvana all following a few steps behind.

"You guys can stay here if you'd like, I'll only be a bit."

I received no reply and was simply met with a wall of concerned eyes. It was foolish of me to think they'd buy it, the smile I was so desperately trying to maintain. Boggle floated up to us, whispering goodbyes as Hugo sat back up, waving while we passed. Every step that brought me closer to the gate increased my heart rate. Domino floated by above us in the sky and Hugo called out to them, his excitement filling the silence.

A deep breath took me as I reached the gate, the others stopping a few steps behind. Hoisting Hugo off of my shoulders, I placed him on the ground.

"Hugo," I knelt down in front of him, "will you promise me something?"

His determined eyes reflected the glow of my crown as he nodded.

"Keep your friends close, they'll become the most important thing in your world. Work hard in school, try to not anger mom and dad, and please," I messed up his hair some, "don't give Les a hard time." A pause took me as my core began to crumble, as my front started to fall, as it all came crashing into me. My voice wavered, "Enjoy growing up, you're going to be great things."

He laughed, trying to fight my hand away from his hair, "You make it sound like I'm never going to see you again."

"And most of all," my voice was barely above a whisper as I fought to keep my smile, "what will you always remember?"

He stared at me, obviously confused, "Stay out of your study?"

"No," the laugh that took me nearly broke the tears that threatened to bud in my eyes loose, "like yes, but no."

"Oh," he laughed, "ghosts are good."

Nirvana's shadow started to approach.

"Hey, Hugo?"

He looked at me, and despite his wide curious eyes having bore witness to such horrible things, they held such light.

"I'm proud of you," my voice cracked, "please don't forget that."

Nirvana stood behind Hugo, his hand hovering above my bother's head. With a small nod from me, before Hugo could say another word, Nirvana placed his hand on Hugo's head and he went out like a light. Falling limp into my arms, I caught him, holding him close. A shuttering breath hissed through my clenched teeth as I stood, my smile returning with me. Turning to face my friends, I was adamant to be alright.

I couldn't break yet, there was still work to be done.

Though it appeared by the looks they wore that I was only fooling myself.

Stepping into the portal, I didn't struggle in the fall. The darkness swirled around me, like galaxies crashing into one another. As I stepped out the other side, my center was still. Standing there as the rest came through, I realized the secret to traveling in the portals. Fighting only made it worse. Standing in front of my family's home, I heard Gaston's gasp as we approached it.

"You lived here?"

"Unfortunately," I started up the marble steps.

Stopping at the top, my friends behind me, a dull ache threatening to rip me apart took root in my stomach. Holding Hugo close, I fazed through the door.

"Whoa," Gaston gawked about as I started toward the stairs, my shoes making no sound on the floor, "this place is gorgeous."

"They are of an esteemed line," Favio said, staying close behind me.

"I suppose," I started up the stairs and Gaston raced toward us as to not be left behind, "we are simply actors, nothing particularly esteemed about that." Rounding a corner, Hugo's room at the end of the hall came into sight, "I didn't ever fit into their ranks, I was never skilled at acting."

"I wouldn't say that," Oliver's quiet voice made the world grow darker.

Reaching his room, I carefully pushed open the door as to not make too much sound. It hadn't changed too much from before, but now there were posters of football players lining the walls, gear strung over the floor, trophies in place of books on his shelves, and homework left unfinished on the desk. Laying Hugo on his bed, I will never forget the last moment we made contact. He was so warm, so small, so kind. Pulling the disheveled blankets over him, I straightened them. Brushing is hair out of his face, I took one last look at him.

This was it.

This was goodbye.

It felt irrevocably real, but wholly fictitious at the same time.

Stepping back, I bumped into his dresser, knocking something over. Before it could hit the ground, my shadow jumped to catch it. Glancing out the door where the others stood, I saw Favio nod. The shadow reached up and handed me the picture frame I had nearly destroyed. Turning it over, I was met with two smiling faces. I didn't know he had this picture of us. Carefully, I placed it back on the dresser, pretending I didn't notice how much my hand was shaking.

Starting toward the door, I hoped that Hugo would remember how much I loved him, even if it is only in a dream.

The glow of my crown dimmed.

Stepping out the door, my eyes caught on him briefly before I closed it.

Being a king was taking the implication of my crown seriously.

Being near me would only prove as a threat to him. He was going places, and I couldn't allow myself to stand in his way.

"Master Kasper?"

I jumped a bit more than I'd ever like to admit when Les started running down the hall toward us.

"What are you doing here?" He stopped, looking over my entire group.

Staring at him as I took my hand back from the door handle, I shifted my weight, "Did you… not notice?"

Les stood there in pause, "Notice?"

"A demon kidnapped Hugo and you didn't notice?"

"A what did what?" He rushed toward Hugo's door but I stopped him, "Is he alright?"

"He's safe now, but," I stepped away, keeping some distance, "he'll think it was a dream. Because of all this, I've decided it's best I don't return here, I wouldn't want to make you or him an attractive target again." Starting away, I couldn't look at him, the kind older gentlemen that cared for me when no one else did, "Thank you for everything, Les. Please take good care of him."

I didn't have to see him to be able to tell he was bowing, "But of course, Master Kasper. It has always been my pleasure."

That tugged at my heartstrings a little more than I expected. Walking past him, trying to keep my smile up, I laughed, "Maybe I'll see you again someday if you ever actually keel over."

The others followed, each nodding to Les as they passed and started toward front with me.

"I'll look forward to it," Les called, laughing as I fazed through the door.

Standing on the porch, I didn't turn around as the others followed me.

One by one I heard their shoes meet the ground outside.

Walking forward, a bounce in my step as I descended the stairs, I started toward the front gate. Passing my car, I heard the group follow me, but silence ensued. Shoulders stiff in an attempt to keep them still, hands in my pockets to hide the quiver, my eyes rested on the sky.

"You are no longer injured," Favio broke the silence, "who healed you?"

"It's a king's secret."

"Sire," Oliver's steps quickened, "if there is someone powerful enough to reverse the damage done to you, we should utilize them."

"I'm sure they'll be around when we need them." My ring flickered, a little blue star in the twilight.

As we started toward the park, I couldn't take my eyes from the moon.

"We are going to have a lot to deal with when we return. The demon faction is without a king, their castle is destroyed. The Almighty is gone, we are socially destabilized, don't know who to trust. I'll have my work cut out for me," My laugh stung, but that didn't stop it.

I was running.

Stopping at a street side, my eyes rolled over to the distressed memorial.

Just like back then, I didn't know what to do, so I ran.

But this time, my run was slow. It was calculated steps, a stroll even. Rooted in the still before a storm, the mounting pressures in the atmosphere became an eye I didn't want to step out of. When I died, I was given a goal, handed a crown and told to win a bigger one. But now we stood in the wreckage of that adventure, ashes raining from the sky, aimless.

My shoulders trembled, "What is one to do once they put out the fire?"

"Rebuild."

Turning, the light of the moon revealed what I had tried to hide, "But how?"

Oliver's sweet smile brought warmth to the night as he walked up to me, bringing his hand to my face as he wiped away my tears, "Together."

"You did what you set out to do," Favio approached, though kept his usual professional distance, "now that the pieces are scattered, the board on the floor, it's your turn to write the rules."

As Gaston and Nirvana joined my side, Oliver summoned a portal before us, "You don't have to shoulder this alone," he reached up and tapped my crown, quickening its rotation a bit, "we know that it's heavy."

In a series of flashes, crowns appeared over everyone's heads. Looking around, I was surrounded by friends, and for the first time, I felt apart of something. Nirvana's made of silver smoke, Gaston's of golden light, Favio's of silky ink, and Oliver's of tamed cinder, they had all been where I was standing right now. Smiling as I wiped the tears that refused to leave, it didn't hurt.

"Favio," my voice hitched with my shuddering breath as I devolved, "will you please watch over Hugo, I don't, I don't want him to be alone."

A rare smile took him as his eyes lost their usual edge, "It would be an honor, Sire." Breaking the distance he had placed between us, he wrapped his arm around me, his touch shockingly human, "You're too sweet."

"Is it hug time?" Gaston crashed into us, destroying any personal space as he laughed.

A dejected sigh later, Nirvana joined us and pulled Oliver along with him. Laughing through my tears, face hot with embarrassment, I stood in the middle of everyone. Their crowns dissipated, just leaving mine as its glow grew brighter again, its rotation speeding up. As everyone stepped back, Oliver stayed, holding me.

Forehead pressed up against mine his long orange hair framed by the moonlight, nothing existed but him in that moment, "Are you ready to face your kingdom, Sire?"

Nodding, a happy shaking breath caused me to shudder as I gathered myself.

Taking me by the hand, Oliver's smile was unfading. Favio stepped through the portal first, quickly followed by Gaston. As he started for it, Nirvana stopped.

Turning to me, he barely maintained eye contact, "You did the right thing," looking off into the starry sky, he turned back toward the portal, "I didn't cut ties and I regretted it."

He disappeared with his next step, nothing but glitter left behind as the swirl of the portal took him away.

Staring at the churning magic before me, I thought it was silly that Oliver could conjure this but my cellphone was witchcraft.

Taking me forward with him, Oliver yanked me into his arms. Kissing me as he stepped back, taking me into the portal too, we fell into the glittery suspension. Losing myself to him, his skin feeling like home against mine, my heart started to level. Pulling back, his glowing eyes were the brightest thing in the darkness as we were thrown out the other side.

Tumbling over the grass, neither of us had thought that through. Laying at my side, Oliver laughed through the groan as he picked himself up. Extending a hand to me, I stared up at him. The churning night sky behind him, decorated in clouds and treetops, his hair blowing in the pleasant breeze, Knight Oliver Vestile the Great was perfect.

Taking his hand, I was thrust back into rotation in the wake of disaster.

"Boggle," turning, I saw Ruth approaching, the Poltergeist King at her side, their factions in mass behind them. "You are unharmed?"

Nodding, I met them in their approach, Oliver not even a step behind me, "Are you?"

"Fortunately, it appears the serious blighting was kept to a minimum, well," she brought her hands up from her side, the crown of the Almighty in them, "with an exception."

Staring down at it, the crown had dulled without a mighty head to hover above.

"Where is Nolan?" She handed me the crown when I reached for it.

Inspecting it, it must have weathered countless battles, nicks in it despite its mastery metal work. "I banished him."

Shock infected the crowds surrounding us as Ruth took a step back, even the Poltergeist appeared unnerved.

"But, how?"

Looking up to Ruth, I slowly brought my free hand up. But a calling thought later, Jaxon's weight materialized in my hand, dropping it down a bit as it fully landed. Upon my deep breath, it started to turn black as the Reaper gem on my crown glowed brighter. "Luckily, Oliver tried to disembowel me with this."

His sigh from behind made me laugh.

Tossing the sword back, Oliver jumped to catch it as the black tint snapped away. "So, what are we to do with this?" I held up the crown and looked at it in the light, the Almighty castle in the backdrop.

"Well, it is intended to be worn," Favio said as he approached. "Regardless of Nolan's actions, Limbo is in need of a ruler."

The Poltergeist stepped back, joining their faction as they just stood there, staring with their pinhole light eyes. Ruth's gaze rolled to me as mine met hers as well. Eyes dropping to the crown, I knew what the right thing to do was. A smile taking me with a deflating breath, my eyes jumped to Ruth.

"You should take it," I approached, "you are a steady hand, it's what a kingdom needs in a time of turmoil."

"But you too wished for the crown," her towering stature became more apparent the closer I got, "why would you give it up now?"

Smiling up at her, I held the crown out, "Being a king is doing what's right, not just for me, but everybody." Looking back to my friends, I saw their approving nods, "I look forward to working under you."

When I bowed, she just stared at me, I could feel it in my back.

The Earthbound began to cheer from behind her.

Taking a knee before me, she bowed her head, "If you insist, I will do my best to lead us through these trying times."

Almighty crown in hand, Ruth on her knee before me, my kingdom behind me and hers watching, the weight of the crown became notable as I started to bring it above her head. Her crown turned to smoke as it was replaced with the Almighty's. Carefully, I let go. It bobbed for a second, dropping into rotation, hovering above her hand.

A smile took me as her kingdom roared.

The crown dropped from the air and came crashing into her head.

A muffled groan later, she glared up to me, hand on the back of her head.

We stared at each other as silence crushed the crowd then slowly, our eyes dropped to the crown as it sat in the grass at our shoes. Picking it up, she straightened as she tried to place it above her head but it refused to float.

"Kasper," Oliver said as he stepped to my side, eyes above my head, his concerned urgency bringing unease to me, "where did that gem come from?"

Brow raised, I took my crown from my head. Turning it around in my hands I was met with a new gem I hadn't noticed before. It was light blue, clouds trapped inside like a summer's day.

"I'm not sure…" thought back through the pain, through the fight and panic and sorrow, and as my mind raced, it snagged on one moment. "Right before he disappeared, the Almighty touched my crown. But I thought it was just to open the portal to the Demon Realm."

"That appears to be a blessing, Your Highness." Favio said as he knelt down to pick up the crown, "Othello was a dear friend, though he was never good with words."

"What," I took a step away from them, suddenly very aware of every set of eyes on me.

Favio's laugh, his smile, it was all the answer I needed.

Tossing the Almighty's crown into the air, it floated above us, spinning.

Falling slowly, as it got closer I stepped back again but it followed. My crown turned to smoke in my hands and for a moment my eyes met with Ruth's before the crown made contact. She was smiling. The sky clouded, wind ripping around as the crown stopped, floating a few inches above my head. The building pressure snapped as bolt of lightning struck from the sky, going straight through me and to the ground. The grass at my feet burned as I was lifted into the air. As another bolt struck me, power so strong it was dizzying deposited into my blood as my yell was drown out by the thunder. The wind spun around me, the clouds warping into shapes, visions in my eyes. The rolling thunder turned into words too blurry to understand as fuzzy scenes played out before me. As it all came to a culmination, one final thing pierced the storm.

The glowing pinhole eyes of a poltergeist.

I dropped from the sky, landing on my knees. The world around was bleached white as I struggled to stand. Stepping back, the person kneeling before me sent shock waves through my body. Looking up, the Almighty Ghost King smiled at me.

"Kasper," he stood, a younger, livelier version of the man I had ruled under, "Was I unclear before?" laughing, he stopped a few steps in front of me, "I know this feels like the end, like your fight has concluded, but this is only the beginning. That crown atop your head holds many secrets, and I'm sorry to leave them to you." He turned and looked around as the white surrounding us began to fade, "Please be a better king than me, they deserve it."

As he turned back to smile at me, he exploded into a cloud of little lights. Spinning around each other, they collided and turned into one light. Taking a step back as it raced toward me, I brought up my hands to stop it. Crashing into me, the light was absorbed into my ring and in a flash, the crown atop my head began to glow with a blue tint.

When everything snapped back, my eyes opened to see a sea of bowing bodies. Stepping around, I was surrounded. Every Earthbound, every Poltergeist, Boggle and being, had their head down. Dumbfounded, I stood in the center of it all.

I… I won?

Gaston and Favio leapt to my sides, each taking one of my arms as they smiled at each other. Kneeling for a moment, they both sprung into the air, me their unwilling hostage. Lights exploded around us, wings came to life on Gaston's back as shadows spun around Favio, growing into dark wings on his. Flying me up and above it all, cheers roared from below. Looking down at the kingdom, my kingdom, I still couldn't believe it.

Looking up to the crown floating above my head, I could see the gems of my subordinate factions, the metal around them holding my blue wispy glow.

I was the Almighty Ghost King?

Taking me back to the ground, I was swarmed by the Boggle.

Fireworks exploded above us, dotting the night sky in sparkling particles. Shooting stars rained down around us, a meteor shower lighting up the world. Oliver wrapped his arm around me, pulling me in close. My subordinate kings at my side, my kingdom before me, the wreckage behind, all I could do was smile.

"This crown isn't as heavy as I had expected."

Oliver leaned his head on my shoulder, "It is undoubtedly heavier than your last, you're just stronger."

Was this the end, or only the beginning?

Sometimes it is hard to tell.

Book 2

PHANTASMAL

Coming Soon

484 Valentyne

"We all fight our demons, Hugo, but yours may just be real."

Find my other novels and audiobooks

Algernon's Anomaly

&

Watch Me

And others, on Amazon, Audible & iTunes

Thank you for reading, and please leave a review on Amazon or Goodreads to help others finds my work!

Forever yours,

Valentyne

& Follow me on TikTok @mralarming for more book content!

Made in the USA
Columbia, SC
03 December 2024